IN THE FAR P. MOUNTAINS

BY

JANET MACLEOD TROTTER

ii

Text copyright © 2018 by Janet MacLeod Trotter
All rights reserved.

Published by MacLeod Trotter Books Ltd

www.janetmacleodtrotter.com

Cover design by Michael Star

ISBN-978-1-908359-76-6

Dedication

For my gorgeous and lively granddaughter, Connie – you bring joy into our lives. A heroine in the making!

MAP

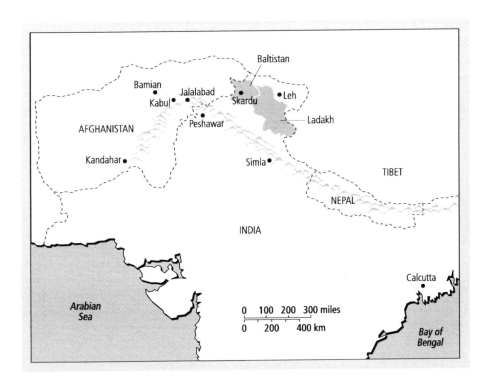

Chapter 1

Northumberland, 1810

Alice Fairchild was born on a rock in the North Sea during a storm. Giving birth, her mother, Charlotte, writhed on the lumpy bed high up in the lighthouse while the roaring wind shook the tower and drowned out her screams.

'Hush, madam,' Effie, the keeper's wife, fussed. 'You'll frighten my boys with your noise.'

'I don't care!' Charlotte snarled. 'Just get this *thing* out of me.'

Effie was offended but bit back a retort; it was the fear and pain of childbirth that made this strange gentlewoman say such things.

'It's coming – just push a wee bit harder,' she encouraged.

'I'm dying!' Charlotte wailed. 'I'm going to die in this horrible place, and he'll never know, and it's all because of this – this—' She screamed as another agonising contraction paralysed her body.

Effie had never seen such unseemly behaviour at a birth; this woman bucked and shrieked like someone possessed. As the shutters rattled and sea spray hissed through cracks in the brick walls of the lighthouse, Effie tried to calm the uninvited guest, who had stepped alone off a small boat just hours before the storm began. Effie worried about her husband, marooned in the lamp-room above, trying to keep the guttering candles lit. Through the hatch to the kitchen below, she could hear her two young sons squabbling over cards and disobeying her order to stay in bed. But who could sleep through such a storm or this caterwauling from Mrs Fairchild?

An hour later – an hour of cajoling, shrieking, blaspheming and sweating – a long-legged baby with a crinkled red face emerged with a querulous wail of indignation.

'A lass!' Effie cried, eyes smarting with tears. 'You have a bonny daughter, Mrs Fairchild.'

Charlotte recoiled. 'I don't want to see it.'

'After all that hard work?' Effie exclaimed in disbelief. 'Just a wee cuddle—'

'Not now.' Charlotte sank back, utterly exhausted. 'Please take it away.'

Effie was shocked more by this rejection than by the hours of invectives and swearing. She and Arnold had lost three babies – all of them girls – between ten-year-old Danny and five-year-old Sam. Effie kissed the bleating infant.

How could a mother not want to hold a living baby in her arms?

* * *

Hours later, Charlotte woke, numb and sore and wondering where she was. The claustrophobic room reeked of tallow, sweat and blood – *her* blood. In the flickering and dancing of the weak lamplight, the curved walls seemed to be moving towards her. She lay on a four-poster bed that had no room for a canopy; the bed posts scraped the ceiling as if they held it in place.

Was it still night-time? Low down in the wall, the shuttered window let in no crack of light. The wind continued to howl. The baby. Had it just been a

1

nightmare? Charlotte winced at the pain of sitting up. No, the ordeal had been only too real. Someone – perhaps that lowly lighthouse-keeper's wife – had tried to clean her up but there was no sign of the thing that had been pulled out of her. The horror of it swept over her anew. How had she not known it was a baby growing inside her? There had been cravings for sweet foods and the strange twistings in her belly that she had worried were the manifestations of some parasite; women in pregnancy billowed like full sails but her small hard bump had hardly shown.

She struggled out of bed. She must leave. Her lover, Captain Nielsen, would arrive at any moment to rescue her; they had agreed a rendezvous at the island's secluded harbour. Charlotte lost her footing on the rag mat and fell hard on the rough wooden floor.

Effie's head appeared through the hatch in the floor at the sound of her cry. 'Madam, what are you doing? Is it the chamber pot you need?'

'I need to dress. I must go.'

Effie chided, 'It's back to bed you must go, Mrs Fairchild.'

Charlotte tried to resist. 'I have to leave. He's coming for me.'

Effie gave her a reassuring pat. 'No one could launch a boat in this storm. You'll just have to be patient, madam. We'll get word to your husband that you are safe as soon as we can.' She coaxed a trembling Charlotte back under the covers.

'How long will it last – the storm?' Charlotte panicked.

'Could be days.'

'*Days?* I simply can't stay here that long.'

'I'll bring the baby up for a feed.'

'I don't want it,' Charlotte said, tears of frustration springing to her blue eyes. 'I can't—'

'There's nothing to it. I'll help her latch on.' Effie ignored her protest. 'You'll soon get into the way of it.'

'No, I won't – I refuse to!'

As soon as Effie disappeared down the ladder, Charlotte pulled the covers over her head and yelled in fury. By now she should be safely away with her Danish sea captain, Eric Nielsen. Where was Eric now? Was he safe in harbour or tossed in the storm? The thought of shipwreck – or, worse, that he might never come at all – plagued her. But he loved her – adored her – so of course he would come. It was he who had chosen the lighthouse island so as to attract as little attention as possible; Eric said that George Gillveray at Black Harbour House was always spying through his telescope at shipping. She just had to be patient. But Charlotte knew she wouldn't be; never in her life had she understood why patience was considered a virtue.

* * *

The storm lasted three days, but the swell of the sea was so violent for the following three that Arnold Brown, the lighthouse-keeper, said no boats could land safely at the island no matter how experienced this Captain Nielsen was.

2

'Don't know which is worse,' Effie complained, 'the foul weather or that madam's moods.'

Charlotte was bad-tempered and tearful but Effie was insistent that Charlotte put the baby to her breast.

'No one else here can feed the lassie.'

Effie plagued Charlotte with questions: what was she doing travelling alone in her condition without even a maid? Where was her husband? Why had she come to the island? To stem Effie's curiosity, Charlotte swallowed her irritation and played the grieving widow.

'Colonel Fairchild died of his battle wounds,' she wept. 'He's buried abroad. I'm going on pilgrimage. Captain Nielsen has kindly agreed to take me. My maid suffers terrible sea sickness. Another one will be provided for me on board.'

Charlotte was unsure if Effie believed her – the lighthouse-keeper's wife sighed and muttered under her breath in some heathen language – but she treated her with robust kindness if not with the deference that Charlotte expected from a woman of such low degree.

Charlotte tried not to order Effie about like her servant; she hated the stuffy bedchamber but was even more loath to descend to the cramped kitchen with the cooped-up boys, their scolding mother and taciturn father who was trying to sleep. And the querulous baby. She did not think of the infant as hers and dreaded the times the creature was brought to her for milk. It would latch onto her like a leech and suck until her breasts were sore and she could bear it no more. She prayed for deliverance and for Eric to come. Long hours of boredom stretched between feeds. Only to dark-eyed boisterous Daniel – who brought her indigestible meals of porridge or pease pudding – did Charlotte take a liking.

'Stay and talk to me, Danny; stop me dying of boredom,' she pleaded, and then spent an age telling him about her life in a grand house outside Newcastle. At times, Charlotte wondered what had possessed her to run away, paying off her maid and pretending to her husband's family that she was going to London for a month. Then she thought of Eric Nielsen – handsome, jovial and reckless – who was offering her a new life of adventure.

A week after Charlotte gave birth, she demanded to be taken up to the lamp-room. On shaky legs she climbed the ladder to the top of the lighthouse and, with Danny holding her arm, gazed about. She hoped each speck on the horizon would be Eric's ship come to rescue her; each time her hopes were dashed as yet another ship sailed on. A week of incarceration turned into two and then three – every day she stood on the wooden gantry for hours at a time – but Eric did not come.

One day, Arnold told her bluntly that they were running low on supplies and that he could row her and the baby across to Black Harbour on the mainland.

'Would you like me to carry a message to your own people,' he asked, 'to fetch you home?'

'No!' Charlotte cried in panic. 'I must wait for Captain Nielsen as arranged.'

Arnold sighed. 'And if he does not come?'

'He must be delayed by the storm. Give me another week, then I promise I will go.'

3

Arnold took Danny to help him carry supplies. When they had gone, Effie coaxed Charlotte down to the kitchen and poured her a drink from a dusty bottle kept in a linen chest.

'Sherry,' said Effie. 'Drink it, madam, and then we can have a wee chat.'

While Charlotte swigged gratefully at the sweet, warming liquor, Sam sat eyeing her from his stool, where he kept watch over the baby in her makeshift cradle. Effie sensed her discomfort and packed the boy off to pick shellfish from the rocks.

'I'll keep an eye on Baby,' said Effie, shooing him down the ladder. When he'd gone, she smiled. 'Wee Sam's appointed himself her guardian angel, so he has.' Then her look turned serious. 'It's none of my concern – this business with Captain Nielsen – but would it not be better to delay this – er – pilgrimage until the babe is weaned?' When Charlotte said nothing, Effie went on. 'My husband could get a message to Captain Nielsen's ship; tell him all is well but now that there is a baby—'

'He mustn't know about the baby,' Charlotte blurted out. She reddened. 'I mean I don't want him burdened with having to accommodate it – the pilgrimage mustn't be delayed.'

'That can hardly be avoided,' said Effie. 'If he comes he will find you here with your child.'

'Not if you say it's yours! Keep the child,' Charlotte pleaded. 'I beg you.'

Effie was shocked. 'The child is not ours to keep.'

'I can give you money.'

'We don't want your money,' Effie bristled.

Charlotte burst into tears and sank to the floor. 'I didn't know I was with child! I am ruined!' she wailed. 'Why won't you help me?'

Effie, alarmed, put her arms about the distraught woman.

'Tell me the truth, Mrs Fairchild,' Effie urged, pushing the tangle of red hair out of Charlotte's eyes.

'Colonel Fairchild isn't dead of his wounds,' Charlotte sobbed. 'He's been away fighting the French for four years – we've only been married for five. I've hardly seen my husband and can barely remember what he looks like.'

'So is the baby the captain's?'

'Yes, but he doesn't know about it. How could he, when I didn't even know myself?'

Effie was gentle but firm. 'You should go back and face your husband.'

'I can never do that.' Charlotte was adamant. 'Colonel Fairchild is a stranger to me. I am going to my captain and no one will stop me.'

'Then the child is his responsibility.'

'It would be too much of a shock,' said Charlotte.

'But if he cares for you, madam, he will accept the girl,' Effie encouraged, 'and she's a bonny wee thing.'

'Maybe in time he will. But not now. Please, would you keep it? I know nothing of babies – you are a born mother, and Danny has told me how you long for a daughter and of the three who are buried on the island.'

Effie gasped. 'He shouldn't have told—'

4

'Now is your chance,' Charlotte interrupted. 'Take mine and bring it up as your own. Please, Mrs Brown!'

Charlotte scrambled to her feet and, reaching to grab the baby, thrust her into Effie's arms. Effie's heart melted anew as the infant fixed her with trusting, inquisitive blue eyes.

'Perhaps we could keep her for a while.' Effie's resolve weakened.

'I'll come back for it, I promise,' said Charlotte.

* * *

No one was more surprised than Effie when, later that day, a ship appeared off the Black Needle – the most easterly of the treacherous reefs – and sent out a rowing boat to the island to fetch Charlotte Fairchild.

The young woman could not flee the lighthouse fast enough, ordering the silent stocky Sam to struggle down the ladder with her baggage. Effie had sudden qualms about the baby; what on earth would her Arnold say about her foolhardy gesture?

'You will come back for her, won't you?' Effie asked, gripping Charlotte as she stood at the top of the ladder.

'Of course,' Charlotte said, impatiently pulling away. As she reached the storeroom below, she hesitated and glanced back up. 'Thank you for all you've done for me, Mrs Brown. I've left money in your bedchamber to compensate you for your trouble.'

'There was no need,' Effie protested. Just as Charlotte hurried out of view, Effie called, 'Wait! What shall we call the child?'

There was a pause, then Charlotte called back. 'My mother's name was Alice. So I suppose Alice will do.'

Effie hurried up to the lamp-room to watch the contrary gentlewoman escape in the open boat to the waiting ship. Her heart drummed to think how she had taken an active part in the plot; her husband would be furious. Well, the deed was done and fate had dropped a baby girl into her empty lap. Effie hastily descended and went outside to milk their goat.

By the time Arnold and Danny returned, Effie was sitting in her chair, spooning milk between the baby's pink lips. The infant was making soft smacking sounds while Sam crouched beside her holding the baby's tiny fist and humming tunelessly.

'Come here, Danny,' Effie said to her eldest son, putting on a brave smile, 'and say hello to your wee sister Alice.'

Chapter 2

Isle of Skye, Scotland

Four hundred miles north-west of Black Harbour Island, in the same storm that caused Alice to be born in a lighthouse, an uprooted beech tree changed the course of young John Sinclair's life.

'Can you take the boy with you today?' Mairi Sinclair asked her husband that blustery morning. She was exhausted from the early stages of her second pregnancy and could hardly move from the box-bed without being sick.

'Aye,' John's father said, ducking out of the door of the neat gardener's cottage with John at his heels.

Grateful, Mairi Sinclair waved them away with a wan smile. Some folk had questioned her insistence on marrying the tall Lowlander – he was a man of few words and fewer still were Gaelic – but he was strong and dependable and Mairi loved everything about him, from his dextrous hands to his bashful pride in their handsome son. Five-year-old John had her dark looks and green eyes but his father's energy and good humour. The boy followed like his father's shadow, struggling to match his broad strides. The two of them were inseparable around the Foxton estate, where Sinclair was tasked with growing food for the gentry and laying out the formal gardens.

'We'll bring you apples,' young John called back, grinning.

Father and son spent the morning in the walled garden, digging up cabbages and beetroot and picking the last of the fat, juicy raspberries among the yellowing bushes. Autumn was on its way but it was only when they emerged from the sheltered garden that Sinclair realised how the wind had strengthened. As they climbed the hill behind the modern mansion house, John was nearly knocked off his feet. He clutched at his over-sized bonnet while his father studied the clouds amassing over the mountains.

'Run home, Johnny,' his father ordered. 'Storm's coming.'

'We haven't picked the apples for Mammy,' John said, his look stubborn. He liked nothing better than being out in a gale with the clouds racing overhead making him dizzy while his father anchored him with a large, warm hand.

His father hesitated and then nodded. Heads bent into the wind, they carried on over the hill to a small wood that had been planted a century ago by the MacIans when they had ruled the glen. Little had they guessed how two generations later their lands would be sold to a new landlord from the south and their fortress demolished along with its old Gaelic name. Foxton was an ambitious, brash piece of the Lowlands exported into the heathery, wind-blasted hills of southern Skye. Jeremiah Fox had made his money importing rich fabrics from India – colourful calicoes and silks – and his mansion was embellished with exotic white-and-gold cupolas to remind him of his days in the East India Company. Sinclair, his broad-shouldered gardener, had been brought from the south to tame the bracken and plant trees to shelter Foxton from Atlantic gales.

'Look at all the apples!' John slipped his father's hand and rushed into the wood. The ground was sprinkled with the small, hard fruit shaken out of the trees. He picked one up and took a bite, his face puckering at its bitterness. John spat it out.

His father laughed. 'Good for pies, Johnny.'

They set about filling a sack, John trying to imitate his father's whistling. All the local people sang songs as they worked, including his mother, but his father whistled like a bird, and John knew it was a sign that the big man was happy. Above them the wind roared and the treetops swayed and John laughed as he dodged a falling apple.

'Enough.' Sinclair swung the small sack over his shoulder as the first spatters of rain carried on the wind.

'Just a few more,' John protested, not wanting this time with his father to end.

Sinclair strode ahead. 'Come on, Johnny, or we'll get a soaking.'

'Just this one,' John said, diving for a large apple with a rusty tinge that caught his eye. Maybe this one would taste sweet for his mother.

As he crouched down, a noise like a musket shot cracked overhead. John fell back in fright. His father had stopped and turned to wait for him. Sinclair didn't even see the tree crashing towards him, unleashed like a wild thing, tearing up its roots in its hurry to fall.

John screamed, 'The apples!'

His father barely had time to glance backwards when the tree felled him. He spun round as if he were trying to fight it off with a swing of the apple sack. Then he lay beneath it like a beetle trapped under a stick, legs twitching, face half-buried in the moss, one eye staring in bewilderment. Apples spilled out of the sack. The rain came sweeping in.

John crept forward. His father was scaring him. 'Get up, Father.' He prodded his shoulder. Why didn't he just stand up? The tree didn't look that big. His father could lift anything he wanted. But he was making strange grunting noises and his eye was rolling.

John sat back on his haunches and began to wail. His father was hurt and the apples were ruined and he didn't know what to do. He wanted his mother. Suddenly his need for her was overwhelming. John scrambled to his feet and started to run. Brambles tore at his jacket and scratched his face as he blundered out of the wood into the full violence of the storm. Long before he reached home he was soaked to the skin, clothes nearly torn from his trembling body.

His mother was standing at the cottage door watching anxiously for husband and son. John could barely stammer out what had happened. Neighbours heard her screams and braved the storm to search for Sinclair. By the time they found him, crushed under the beech tree, his breath had stopped and the life had gone from his eyes.

* * *

Jeremiah Fox was sorry about the death of his very capable gardener but felt none of a Highland chief's sense of obligation to his staff. He was already regretting his wife's romantic notions of a summer residence in the Highlands where she could come and paint and he could shoot game, and they had already left for Edinburgh and civilisation when the accident happened. He had no wish

7

to deal with the local population, and a man of his social position shouldn't have to. He paid a factor – an estate manager called Brewis – to handle the unfortunate affair.

'*See that the widow is provided for,*' Fox wrote to Brewis, '*by which I mean that she is conveyed back to her own people without delay with some victuals for the journey. We shall need to find another head gardener as soon as possible. In the meantime, try to get rent for the cottage as best you can.*'

Even Brewis, a hardened former sea captain, thought his employer's attitude callous. He had liked Sinclair, a fellow Lowlander, and felt pity for the pretty young widow, Mairi, and her affectionate son, John. The poor boy hadn't spoken a word since his father's death nor cried a tear at the funeral – a foolishly lavish affair for people of their lowly class – and Brewis feared young John had gone mad from witnessing Sinclair's grisly death.

He went to Mairi Sinclair with a proposition.

Mairi had been waiting tensely for a formal visit from the factor. She knew it was only a matter of time before she was evicted from the cottage where until two weeks ago she had been so happy. How she dreaded the day they would have to leave! Yet, looking around the kitchen-parlour now empty of its fire-irons, china, copper pots and chairs, which had all been sold to pay for the funeral, Mairi thought how the soul of the house had died along with her husband.

She offered the factor a cup of water – their milk cow had also been sold – and watched him look around in vain for somewhere to sit.

'Mr Brewis,' Mairi said, wanting to get the painful moment over, 'I have made arrangements to return home to my father and sister at Ramanish – me and the boy. If you could just give me another week to settle my affairs. I know the landlord wants me out.'

Brewis flinched at her directness. He had expected her to whine and plead with him to stay on, beg for a job in the dairy or kitchen. He had planned to be magnanimous but her quiet dignity unnerved him; she had not even called him sir.

'Do you not wish to stay, Mistress Sinclair?'

'What is there to stay for?'

'You could be my housekeeper,' he blurted out.

Her eyes widened. 'You already have a housekeeper, Mr Brewis.'

'My wife, then.'

They stared at each other, Brewis just as startled by his sudden impulsive proposal as she was. What had possessed him? He stuttered in explanation.

'I-I would welcome the company. Mine is a lonely position in this place. You are an outsider like me. I would give you a comfortable home and—'

'Mr Brewis,' she trembled, 'I have just buried my husband. How can you suggest such a thing?'

'Not immediately perhaps, but in time. A woman in your position can hardly be choosy. And I would take on the boy.' Brewis gestured at John squatting by the fire. 'Give him work in a year or two.'

Mairi gaped at him; the man was serious. She looked at his craggy weather-beaten face with the grey hair sprouting from his nose and felt leaden inside. Older than her own father, Brewis was a hard taskmaster around the estate but

8

as fair in his dealings as his master allowed. He might be kind – he seemed genuinely fond of John – but she could never love him or bear to have him touch her in intimacy.

'It's not just the boy you would be taking on,' Mairi said, dropping her voice and glancing at John. But the boy was sitting hunched and lost in his own thoughts. 'I am carrying Sinclair's baby.'

Brewis flushed. She saw his discomfort and waited for him to retract his offer. John was a strong, robust boy who could be put to work even at his tender age, but a pregnant woman and then a mewling baby were a different matter. He frowned with indecision, then cleared his throat.

'My offer still stands, Mairi. But I am not a patient man and neither is my master – he wants a new tenant here as soon as possible. I will give you the week you ask for, then you will either come and live with me at the factor's house or you can go to Ramanish. Either way, you will have to leave this cottage.' He looked around for somewhere to put the cup and, seeing no table, handed it to Mairi. 'I very much hope you will agree to be the future Mrs Brewis.' He tipped his hat – a battered old-fashioned naval one – and strode to the door. 'Good day to you.'

Mairi nodded. 'Good day, Mr Brewis.'

She sank down beside her son, pulling him into her arms and lapsing back into Gaelic. 'Oh, Johnny, what shall we do?'

He gazed at her mutely, his vivid green eyes troubled. She squeezed him tightly. Where would her grieving son best be healed: Foxton or Ramanish? Foxton would give him security but be a constant reminder of his father's accident; Ramanish would mean hardship in a cramped cottage shared with cattle but surrounded by their own people.

That night they bedded down in the box-bed but Mairi didn't sleep for the anxious thoughts that spun in her head. For the hundredth time she cursed the storm, the tree and the wretched apples that had led to Sinclair's death. Her beloved husband! The pain was suffocating. John moaned and cried in his sleep.

She'd be a fool to turn her back on Brewis's marriage offer, yet she could not bear to be his wife. Some neighbours would call her haughty and headstrong if she refused him; others would distrust her and say she grew above herself if she accepted him. She fell asleep just before dawn and dreamt of the sea at Ramanish crashing onto a grey beach, and her great-grandfather – the old Spaniard – swinging her up and carrying her over rocks to the sandy meadow beyond.

When Mairi woke, she had made up her mind.

* * *

Will there be apples at Ramanish? Will we sleep in a box-bed like at home? Why do they call us the Spanish MacAskills? Are we really going to climb over that mountain?

All these questions buzzed around in John's head but he could not find words in his mouth to say them aloud. His father's death had put a seal on his lips like wax to paper. Instead, he clutched his mother's hand and walked through the village in the early morning light. Neighbours came to their doors wrapped in woollen plaids to watch them go. The wife of the shoemaker scurried forward and thrust a cloth parcel at his mother.

'An oatcake for your journey. You've a long way to go.' The woman glanced anxiously at the Cuillin Mountains behind.

John saw his mother's eyes water at the woman's kindness. 'Aye, but it's a clear day and I want to be gone before the weather sets in again.'

The wild, wet weather that had lasted most of October had given way to clear, cold air and bright blue skies, morning frosts and a dusting of snow on the peaks to the north.

'Thank you for this.' His mother stowed the round of oatmeal in her basket and squeezed the woman's hand before moving on.

Why aren't we going to say goodbye to Mr Brewis? It had been three days since the man with the funny hat and the hairy nose had been to visit. Ever since then his mother had seemed in a hurry to cross the mountains and stay with his Grandfather MacAskill and Aunt Morag.

'You'll be happy there,' his mother had promised.

John was doubtful; the stern grey-haired man who had come to his father's funeral and reeked of whisky did not seem the type to grab his hand and run with him through the wind like John's father used to do.

They hurried past the path to the factor's house, his mother yanking on his hand. She muttered, 'Better this way, Johnny. Don't want to embarrass the man with an outright refusal. And today is perfect for travelling – not a cloud in the sky. Tomorrow the mist could be down. He'll understand.'

Who will? John was baffled.

They walked all morning. John had never been this far from home before. When they stopped on the mountain path for his mother to catch her breath, they turned and looked back and saw a tiny Foxton House surrounded by miniature gardens, trees and newly walled-off fields like in a painting. Behind towered the jagged, forbidding range of the Cuillins, thrusting black peaks in an intense blue sky. A massive bird wheeled overhead in lazy circles.

What is that? His mother saw him squinting into the dazzling autumn sun.

'It's a sea eagle. See the white patches under its wing tips? That's how you know. Grandpa Carlos told me how to spot birds when I was a girl. No doubt he'll tell you too.'

John wondered if this was the stern grandfather or whether he had another. His mother talked more about their family as they continued on.

'Grandpa Carlos was a soldier. He came from Spain to fight for the Jacobites when he was no more than twelve or thirteen – he's not sure exactly. Over a hundred now but he can still catch a fish and gut it. He's my great-grandfather, so he's your great-great-grandfather. Outlived his own sons.'

John wanted to know who were the Jacobites and where was Spain and how old was a hundred; it sounded as old as could be. But he kept his questions tucked away and ran to keep up with his mother, enjoying her stories. The further they got from Foxton, the more she told him about his family at Ramanish.

'Your Aunt Morag is older than me and looks after the home for your grandfather. Got a hump on her back so no one will marry her but she's the kindest person I know.'

John imagined his aunt, whom he had never seen, as looking like his mother but carrying a sack of apples on her back. As the climb steepened, his mother grew breathless and her words dried up. They stopped for a bite of oatcake and a swig of water, sitting in a pool of sunshine and leaning against a large, warm rock. His mother closed her eyes and dozed. John clambered over the rock and scrambled up the loose scree, sending a shower of tiny stones down the slope. The eagle – or perhaps another bird – soared high above. The silence of the mountains filled his ears until they hummed and he swallowed to clear his hearing. He banged two stones together and listened to the echo bounce around, just to check he had not turned deaf. This world of rock and sky and silent birds was thrilling.

He must have climbed further than he realised. The hillside went into shadow and he could hear his mother calling from below like a frantic crow.

'John? John! Come down now!'

When he skidded to a halt by her side, she shook him. 'Never run away like that again. I thought you were lost. It's dangerous in the hills. Come on, we've wasted too much time.'

John fell into step behind his mother, the magic of his scramble vanishing. The sun faded behind hazy cloud. As they wound higher, the deer path they followed grew stonier and the wind picked up. Finally, they came down the other side, grabbing onto tufts of heather, and John craned for a view of the sea and the grey beach and the MacAskill castle that his mother had told him about during the walk. But all he could see were more mountains in front, hemming them in and blotting out the sky like stone giants.

They wound along a path – a drover's road where cattle were taken to market, his mother said – until the track split in two and once more they followed the one climbing upwards.

'It's shorter this way,' his mother said. 'We'll be there by nightfall.'

She didn't speak again until they were high up in the mountain and scrambling along the stony pass. John's leather shoes rubbed and pinched and he began to flag. All day he had been hot, toiling in the sunshine. Now the air was suddenly icy and his cooling skin made him shiver. He was tired and hungry but his mother didn't seem to notice; she kept looking up at the sky and pulling him along as if they were late for something. The heavens turned from pearly blue to dark grey in minutes. Flecks of sleety rain whipped at his bare knees and face.

'Come on, John,' his mother urged, pulling her plaid over her hair. 'Don't slow down.'

But she was labouring too in the rising wind and thickening sleet. Mist descended and hid the path ahead. Sleet turned to hail, stinging his cheeks and making him cry.

'Stop your bleating!' she ordered.

They pressed on, his mother dragging him behind her. They stumbled and slipped over rocks. Abruptly, she came to a standstill, chest heaving, face frowning. She peered ahead and then behind. Her indecision frightened him more than her cross words.

The hail eased into soft, wet snow. It descended on them like a cold blanket, sticking to their clothes and hair. He thought his mother was going to burst into

11

tears, her face puckering and bottom lip trembling like it had when his father's body was brought to the house for her to wash.

'Over there,' she said, pushing him towards a black shadow in the falling snow. 'You can squeeze in there.'

Tripping over numb feet, John was propelled forward by his mother. The black shape turned into a crevice like a shelf in the overhanging rock.

'Climb in,' his mother ordered, heaving him up.

John's feet slithered on the icy rock and his hands stung with the cold as he hauled himself up. He lay panting, his mother's face staring from below, pale as the moon.

Now you get up, Mother! He willed her to follow, yet he couldn't see how there would be room for them both. It was no bigger than the kitchen shelf where the crockery used to be stacked.

She hesitated and then pulled off her plaid and raised her voice to be heard over the wind. 'Wrap this round you, Johnny.' She stuffed it around him. 'Bundle yourself up like a parcel.' She smiled at him as if they were playing a game.

But you'll get cold, Mother. He gazed back at her. With one last effort she stood on tiptoes and pushed him as far into the crevice as he would go. For a moment she gripped his arm – a hard, possessive squeeze – then, with a sigh, she let go.

'I'll be right here just below you,' she called, 'so don't be afraid.'

All John could see was whiteness but he burrowed into his mother's plaid and felt warmth creep into his limbs, knowing that she kept watch just out of sight. The light drained away. John slept.

* * *

Drovers returning from the south found the boy two days later, wrapped in his mother's plaid, stiff with cold and heart barely beating. The woman was long dead, frozen and half standing up as if keeping watch; they wouldn't have noticed the boy if she hadn't been there. They met a search party from Ramanish led by the strong boatman Norman MacAskill, worried that his widowed daughter and grandson had not arrived from Foxton. The first and last time the drovers ever saw the hard-faced Norman fall to his knees and weep like a child was over the corpse of his favourite daughter.

He carried his grandson through the melting snow of the mountain pass, willing him to live, refusing attempts by the men to take their turn in carrying the boy.

John felt his limbs coming back to life; they burnt with pain. His first sight of Ramanish was from a great height – an eagle's view – as he descended with his grandfather to the coast. The mountain gave way to cultivated strips like ripples in a patchwork bedcover. Beyond, sheep and cattle grazed on open pasture that ended abruptly in a huge crescent of grey sand and rock. Thatched houses dotted the hillside, but it was the black fortress that stirred his interest. It clung to a long finger of land that jutted out to sea. Around it on the rocky shore, fires smouldered and smoke rose and drifted over the castle as if an enemy were laying siege.

'Ramanish Castle.' His grandfather pointed it out. 'The home of our chief – though he's far from home just now.'

John puzzled over this wandering chief and who he might be and why nobody seemed concerned that their enemies were setting fire all around his castle. He wanted to ask his mother but she didn't seem to be with them. Where had she gone? She had promised to stay with him but now she had vanished.

John was taken to a low thatched cottage that he thought was a cattle byre – there were stocky black and tawny cows tramping in and out of a muddy entrance at one end – but at a far door a woman flew out to meet them, flapping her arms like a hen.

'You poor wee lamb!' she cried, and wrested him from his grandfather's tired arms. She was strong but ungainly, with a huge lump on her back. She hugged him tight. Her eyes were like his mother's, though she smelt of peat smoke and not lavender. 'I'm your Aunt Morag and I'll look after you now, don't you worry.'

Once inside, he struggled to see in the smoky dark. An old man, skinny as a bird, was squatting by the fire. As John's eyes adapted to the gloom, he saw the man give him a gappy smile like a baby's, his skin as wrinkled and brown as a walnut.

'I'm Grandpa Carlos,' he said in a reedy, high-pitched voice, rising stiffly and hobbling over. He touched John's face with bony fingers. 'You are my first great-great-grandson. You will be a soldier like me.'

John was not sure if this was an order. He stared and stared at this man that his mother had said was over a hundred but just couldn't imagine him as a sword-wielding soldier. A puff of wind could carry him off.

'Enough talk about soldiers,' Aunt Morag declared. 'John needs something to eat.'

Mother will need to eat too. He squatted next to the old man but would not touch the porridge his aunt gave him. *I'll wait for Mother.* John sat, his stomach aching with hunger, while his anxious aunt chivvied him to eat. But he wouldn't eat without his mother. He sat till his bottom was numb and the porridge cold, yet his mother did not come. Eventually his aunt pulled him into her arms and began to sing softly just like his mother did. Suddenly he was crying. And as he sobbed and she sang, John felt her tears in his hair too.

13

Chapter 3

Northumberland, 1818

'Sit still, Alice,' Effie cried in exasperation, 'or I'll tie your legs to the chair!'

Alice squirmed and wriggled; she hated having her hair combed and pulled into plaits. What was the point? Her flyaway red-gold hair always came loose the minute she went out in the wind. She was restless to join her brothers outside; Danny and Sam were on the cliffs hunting for birds' eggs. They wouldn't wait for her; they never did. Danny said girls shouldn't climb cliffs and Sam always knew she'd catch up with them anyway. They had been cooped up in the lighthouse for days by spring gales and lashing rain and she was almost bursting to be out.

'You'll help me with the washing, so don't think you can go running off,' said her mother, reading her mind.

'Oh please, Mammy,' Alice cried. 'Just for an hour and then I'll do whatever you want.' She did her best to sit still and sweeten her mother's mood. 'I'll milk Sandy, then we can make cheese.'

'Washing first.' Effie was firm. 'It's perfect drying weather. I'm sick of fighting through wet washing hanging in the kitchen.'

Alice appealed to her father, who had just descended from the bedroom, where he'd been catching up on sleep after the night's watch.

'Da, can I go and milk the goat?'

Arnold looked warily between wife and daughter. 'You must be a help to your mother, Alice.'

'I will, I promise. But I want to see that Sandy is all right and milking *is* helping, isn't it?'

He retreated to the horsehair sofa and picked up last week's newspaper, studying it as if he hadn't already read it from cover to cover.

'Well, Arnold?' Effie said, pulling the hair ribbon tight. 'Tell Alice her duty is here with me. I can't manage all that washing on my own.'

'It's a day for being outdoors,' he said without looking up. 'Let her get some fresh air first.'

Effie rolled her eyes but Alice seized her chance and jumped up. 'Thanks, Da.' She was through the hatch and swinging nimbly down the ladder as an argument broke out between her parents.

'You're too soft on the lass,' Effie complained.

'She's still young,' Arnold said.

'At eight years old I was out mending fishing nets with the women and carrying creels of fish from the shore.'

'We want something better for Alice, don't we?'

'Nothing wrong with hard work.'

'And nothing wrong with a bit of play too.'

'Play?' Effie retorted. 'She runs around the island like a wild thing . . .'

Alice hurried out of earshot down through the boys' bedroom with its spartan beds. Clothes and detritus collected off the shore spilled out of wall cupboards. She stopped long enough to pull on a pair of Danny's breeches – he was the older but smaller and slighter of the two brothers – and discard her skirt and petticoat. Down again she descended to the windowless storeroom below. With light from the open door through which her brothers had already escaped, she sidestepped sacks of flour and sugar, crates of potatoes, milk churns, water barrels and coal buckets, coils of rope and boxes of candles. She loved the smell of this cavernous room, a mix of tallow and dusty sacks, wooden oars seasoned with linseed and the sourness of maturing cheese.

Taking a huge breath, she filled her nostrils with the heady smell, and then she was out of the door and scampering down the iron ladder to freedom.

* * *

Alice loved Black Harbour Island; she pitied children who had to go to the mainland school and sit in rows and have the teacher whip them with a birch cane when they got something wrong. That's what Danny said happened in the parish school where he had gone until he turned fifteen; where Sam aged thirteen still went when weather and tides allowed. Gillveray, the eccentric owner of Black Harbour House – a horse breeder, botanist, traveller and amateur inventor – had set up the school, appalled at the lack of learning among the sons of the local fishermen and labourers.

It never crossed her parents' minds to send her to school. Arnold taught Alice after a fashion and answered her incessant questions about plants and birds, the stars and the sea. From him she learnt how to tell the time by the sun, to predict when a storm was coming by observing the fish disappearing into deep water, to trim the wicks on the candles in the lighthouse lamp-room and mend the wing of an injured swan. He had taught her not only to swim but also to read and write – a waste of time declared her mother, but it had opened up a fantastical world of books.

Arnold would read to her during stormy winter days; stories of Ancient Greeks, Egyptian pharaohs, medieval knights and French kings; heroic men called Hannibal, Roland, Ossian, Richard the Lionheart and Alexander the Great; heroic women called Cleopatra, Helen of Troy, Boadicea and Saint Hilda; Bible stories, fairy tales, Arabian Nights and poetry. Her father bought books whenever he went to the mainland and salvaged them from chests brought on the tide from shipwrecks. Her mother complained they were a fire hazard and confined half of them to the lower storeroom. Alice loved their musty mildewed aroma and the sepia stains like age spots on their creamy pages.

But better than all the stories was her island playground; a treasure trove of rock pools and swaying grasses, sheer cliffs and sheltered harbour, home to colonies of raucous birds, tiny shrews, migrating geese and glistening jellyfish that vanished as mysteriously as they appeared. Above all of this towered the lime-washed lighthouse, like a guardian angel with its all-seeing fiery eye that winked and glowed through the dark to warn away ships and keep everyone safe.

Sandy the goat had got loose from her tether; Alice found her grazing on the eastern cliff alongside her brothers. Danny had lowered himself over the edge and was reaching out with a long pole, his legs planted astride a thin chasm that

15

dropped to foaming sea below. Cautious Sam was up above, lying on his stomach, holding out a basket for Danny to fill.

Alice's stomach curdled to see the risk Danny took, yet part of her yearned to be beside him. Heights thrilled her.

'Can I come down?' she called.

'Be quiet!' Danny hissed.

'You'll disturb the nest,' Sam whispered, patting the grass beside him. Alice crouched down at his side.

They watched as Danny eased the pole with the makeshift net into the nest. With a sudden shriek, the gull lifted and flew at Danny. He recoiled, dropping the pole. It clattered down the rock face. Danny wobbled and grabbed at thin air. Alice screamed. He was going to fall. Sam scrambled forward and flung out an arm, grabbing at Danny's jacket. It was just enough to stop his brother toppling forward. Danny regained his balance and a sure footing on the ledge below.

He stood heaving for breath while Alice sobbed with relief.

'Come back up, Danny,' she pleaded. 'Forget about the eggs.'

His thin, handsome face puckered into stubborn lines. 'I'm not going to be beaten by a stupid bird.'

He inched back along the ledge and leapt across the narrow chasm. Alice clamped a hand over her mouth to stifle a scream. Sam looked on, his body tense but round face expressionless. His older brother would do whatever he wanted and the opposite of what anyone else suggested.

Danny plucked the nest from its cleft in the rock and, clamping it against his chest, he jumped back across. He threw the nest and eggs onto the cliff top. One of the eggs toppled and smashed. Alice quickly gathered the two undamaged ones and placed them gently in the collapsing nest; she looked around guiltily for the mother gull.

'Give us a pull up, Sam,' Danny ordered.

His stocky younger brother hauled him back up top. Danny collapsed in the grass, panting and laughing. In relief, Alice giggled and threw her arms round him.

'Get off!' Danny pushed her away, but he was still grinning, pleased with his daring.

'I wish I was as brave as you,' Alice said with an adoring look.

'You can't be – you're only a girl.'

Alice didn't like to be reminded of this. She sat up and pointed. 'Look, I saved the other eggs from rolling over the edge.'

Danny stood up and thrust his hands in his pockets, staring out to sea. He had lost interest in the eggs.

'Ship went on the rocks out on the Farnes last week. Reckon there was silver plate from Holland for the taking.'

Alice always wondered how Danny knew so much about life off the island when he spent most of his time taking it in turns with their father to man the light.

'One day I'm going to captain a ship – bring gold and spices back from the east, and make a fortune.' Danny's face shone with excitement.

16

Alice felt dismay; she didn't want Danny to leave or for anything on the island to change. 'But who will work the light with Da if you go?'

'Sam will – or you can. I don't care.'

'I don't want you to ever go away,' Alice said, seizing his hand.

He shook her off and laughed. He was just teasing her, as usual; she could tell. Abruptly, he swung his foot and kicked the nest and the eggs over the cliff. Alice gasped in shock. It made Danny laugh louder.

'Just a stupid gull's nest.'

He turned away so he didn't see Sam launch himself at him. Sam knocked him to the ground. Winded, Danny looked up in surprise as Sam stood over him.

'What did you do that for?'

Sam shook with anger. 'I helped you get them eggs too.' Then he strode away.

'No, you didn't,' Danny shouted after him. 'You didn't dare. I did it all myself!'

Alice was torn between running after Sam and staying with Danny. She hated it when her brothers argued.

'Soft in the head,' Danny muttered once Sam was out of earshot. Alice could tell he was working himself up into a bad mood.

'I have to milk Sandy,' she piped up. 'Will you help me take her home, Danny?'

He sighed, picked himself up and held out a hand. 'Come on then. I'll help you catch her.'

Alice grabbed his hand in relief. When Danny smiled at her it was like the sun coming out.

* * *

As Alice grew older, her brothers had less patience with her tagging along in their wake.

'Stay and help Mam,' was their constant refrain when she tried to follow. She hated being confined to doing chores in the lighthouse even though Effie nagged her to stay and keep her company.

'We lassies need to stick together – and you'll never make anyone a good wife if you can't cook and sew and keep a tidy home.'

'I won't need to,' Alice would reply with a toss of her plaits. 'I'm going to be an explorer and travel the world on Danny's ship when he's a captain.'

'Danny's going nowhere,' retorted Effie, 'and neither are you, lassie.'

At fifteen, Sam left school and joined his father in manning the lighthouse, relishing the lonely hours in the lamp-room tending the temperamental candles and filling in the logbook with times and observations. Danny, a man now at twenty – though he looked no older than his brother – spent all his spare time off the island, rowing himself ashore to Black Harbour and disappearing on spurious errands.

'Gillveray wants help on his boat,' or 'Gillveray has offered me a day lifting carrots.'

Arnold was unhappy at the increasing time his eldest son spent away but he could hardly protest at him helping out their landlord; Gillveray was an enthusiastic supporter of the lighthouse and gave money for its upkeep.

But sometimes Danny would come home smelling of drink or not at all. He was vague about the company he kept or where he went and his parents' worry mounted.

'Where do you get the money to drink?' Arnold confronted him. 'Not from me.'

'Gillveray pays me for the odd jobs I do. A man's entitled to quench his thirst at the end of a day's graft.'

One day, Arnold had made a rare trip off the island to buy books and tobacco. That evening, when Sam had gone up to the lamp-room, a terrible argument broke out with Danny.

'You've lied to me and your mother,' Arnold accused. 'Gillveray has hardly set eyes on you these past months. You haven't been working for him at all.'

'I have,' Danny protested, his slim face reddening. 'I brought back carrots, didn't I?'

'Not from his farm,' Arnold snapped. 'You bought them, didn't you?'

'What if I did?'

'Where are you getting the money?'

'Earned it.'

'Where? In the Black Harbour Inn? 'Cause that's where I hear you spend most of your time. You're the talk of the village – swaggering about with the riff-raff of the county, giving us a bad name.'

'That's lies!' Danny cried, squaring up to his father.

'Gillveray doesn't lie! He says you've been seen out with *wreckers*.' Arnold hissed the name in disgust, grabbing his son by his jacket. 'Tell me the truth or by God I'll take the rod to you!'

Alice sprang forward. 'Please, Da, don't hurt our Danny.'

Arnold released his grip and Danny shook him off, his bullishness returning.

'So what if my friends are wreckers? I'm proud of 'em.'

'Oh, Danny,' Effie gasped.

Alice slipped to her mother's side and squeezed her hand.

Arnold exploded. 'That a son of mine – a lighthouse lad – should sink so low. You're a thief as well as a drunk—'

'I'm no thief!' Danny shouted. 'There's nothing wrong with salvaging what comes in from the sea. It's God-given; that's what the priest says. Are you calling the priest a thief too? Wreckers are helping their families by saving what the sea would take.'

'At the expense of the lives on board?' Arnold said in disdain. 'Men like that stop others from going to rescue the drowning so they can watch them die and steal their possessions. Gillveray said they once started a fire to confuse ships into thinking it was our lighthouse, hoping some boat would end up on the rocks.'

'Well, he's told you wrong,' Danny said hotly. 'It's God decides who lives and dies, and He causes the storms that wreck the ships, not the wreckers or any fires. Who are we to interfere? We're doing nothing wrong saving the cargo where we can. This place is full of bits of metal and wood off old ships.'

18

'That's different,' Arnold snapped. 'That's flotsam picked up on the shore.'

'Well, we pick up stuff before it reaches shore. What's the difference?'

Alice had never seen her father so angry or Danny so insolent. Her heart hammered painfully; this was the worst argument she could remember.

'You can't be both,' Arnold said, his voice trembling.

'Both what?'

'A lighthouse-keeper and a wrecker.'

The men glared at each other. Alice held her breath. Effie stood up and moved between them.

'Please, Daniel,' Effie urged, 'don't leave the lighthouse. We need you, son. This is where you belong. One day you'll be first keeper like your father – a man who folk respect.'

Daniel looked at his mother. Alice could see the tension in his face; the indecision. He relaxed his fists. 'I'll stay – for now.'

Alice jumped up and threw her arms around her brother, squeezing him tight.

Arnold nodded but his voice was still angry. 'I'll take the next watch; you'll take the last.' Then he retreated up the ladder.

* * *

Alice was unsure what woke her. Pink dawn light already glowed at the low window in the chamber that she shared with her parents. She could see the shapes of her parents under the bedcovers and hear her father's gentle snoring. His watch was over; Danny must be up top now. Perhaps it was her brother's moving around upstairs that had disturbed her. How awful the shouting had been, with poor Danny being accused of being a thief and a drunk. Her father was wrong to be so angry; Danny was just helping his friends.

Unable to sleep, she slipped out of her camp bed and padded softly up the ladder into the lamp-room. The place smelt smoky; the candles in the lamp were guttering. Danny was slumped in the corner, asleep.

Shocked, Alice rushed over and shook him. 'Danny, wake up! Da will kill you.'

Danny opened bloodshot eyes. 'Leave me alone.' His breath smelt sour the way it did when he came home after drinking at the inn. There was an empty bottle on the floor.

'You have to get up,' Alice pleaded. 'The candles are spilling wax – they need a trim.'

'In a minute,' he slurred, and closed his eyes.

'Now, Danny!' Alice said, shaking him again.

This time her brother rallied, rubbing his eyes with the heels of his palms and shaking himself awake. He stood, stretching and yawning.

'Get yourself back to bed,' he ordered. 'It's nearly time to put out the candles anyway.'

'Only if you promise to stay awake. You will, won't you?' Alice asked, hesitating.

'Aye, of course I will. Just closed my eyes – I wasn't asleep.'

19

Alice knew he had been but said nothing. As she put her feet on the ladder he said, 'You won't tell Da though, will you?'

She shook her head. 'You'd better get rid of the bottle though.'

Danny gave a sheepish grin and nodded. Alice experienced a strange twisting inside. She felt special that Danny and she now shared a secret, yet her adoration of him had diminished a fraction. Sam would never have drunk liquor and fallen asleep on duty; Da had drummed into them that sleeping on the job was the biggest crime a keeper could commit. Men had lost their livelihoods and gone to prison for doing so; no one should ever risk the light going out.

She watched Danny pick up the bottle and open one of the casement windows to hurl it out. A sudden gust of air whipped the latch out of his hand. As he struggled to pull it closed again, one of the candles flared in the draught and toppled. Alice gasped as pools of whale oil from the melted candles instantly went alight.

'Danny!' she squealed.

He turned and gaped, unable to believe his eyes. The whole lamp was ablaze, the glass cracking in the heat. He picked up a bucket of sand and hurled it wildly. He flapped at the flames with the logbook.

'You're making it worse!' Alice cried.

Danny dropped the book as it went alight. The fire took hold of the tinder-dry floorboards.

'Get out!' Danny yelled, scrambling for the hatch and almost toppling Alice off the ladder.

'Da!' Alice screamed, as they tumbled together into the room below.

Her parents were roused by the commotion. They had hardly had time to leap from their bed when the room filled with choking smoke.

'Go below!' Arnold ordered. 'All of you.' He started up the ladder, attempting to close off the hatch, but the heat beat him back.

Effie wailed. 'The Lord save us!'

They retreated below to the kitchen. 'Take Alice outside,' Arnold ordered his wife. 'Danny, wake Sam and bring up the water flagons.'

The last Alice saw as her mother bundled her downstairs was her father flinging pails of water at the ladder and the hatch above in an attempt to stem the fire.

But it raged through the old building like a hurricane, devouring its timber floors and stairs, its ancient cupboards and furniture, scorching the brick in its race downwards. At the foot of the lighthouse, Alice screamed for her father and brothers to escape too. They came just as the storeroom exploded in a conflagration of oil and tallow and coal.

Arnold dragged his stunned wife and daughter by the hands as far away upwind from the burning tower as they could go.

By the time Gillveray spotted the fire and sent a boat to rescue them, the lighthouse was a reeking, smoky wreck and their island home was no more.

Chapter 4

Northumberland, 1820

George Gillveray took pity on the distraught lighthouse-keeper and his traumatised family – he liked and respected Arnold Brown – and housed them in an attic wing of Black Harbour House, his rambling semi-fortress with battlements and a gun-court from where he fired an ancient cannon to warn ships in the fog.

'We'll build another lighthouse,' he declared, 'bigger and better with the newest lamp and lenses that money can buy.'

George set about negotiations with Trinity House, who commissioned the lights around England's coastline, for a modern light on Black Harbour Island. He invited the Scottish engineer Robert Stevenson to visit and give advice on the latest innovations and took it upon himself to lead the project.

'We'll have a temporary ship's light at sea while the lighthouse is being built,' George said with enthusiasm, trying to rally Arnold out of his depression.

But Arnold's spirit had been broken by the loss of his home, his books and his work tending the light. He had lived by the rhythm of the seasons and the days; he'd been king of his isolated domain. Now he spent his time standing on the gun-court gazing gloomily out to sea at the blackened skeleton of his former haven. Worse still, all his brooding led to the suspicion that Danny had deliberately started the fire.

'You wanted it gone, didn't you?' he accused his eldest son. 'You and your wreckers! You put your own family's life at risk for greed.'

'That's a lie!' Danny was outraged.

'Then how did it start?' Arnold challenged.

'I told you, a gust of wind blew the candle over.'

'How did that happen?'

'It just did.' Danny reddened.

'You have guilt written all over your face!'

'I didn't start the fire—'

'It was me,' Alice intervened. She couldn't bear the bitter arguments; they had lost everything they possessed but this tearing apart of the family was far worse.

The men stopped to stare at her.

'I opened the window. I couldn't sleep and went upstairs to keep Danny company. It was an accident. I didn't realise how strong the wind was – the latch flew out my hand.'

Arnold looked at his daughter in disbelief. 'You're just saying that to save your brother.'

'No, I'm not.'

'Then why did you open it?'

Alice hesitated. She couldn't mention the liquor bottle or blame it on the smoky atmosphere for either would condemn her brother as negligent.

'There was a bird tapping – it looked injured. I wanted to let it in.'

Her father's face crumpled. 'You foolish child.'

'I'm sorry, Da.'

Danny shot her a look of gratitude. But Arnold's expression was so bleak as he stalked from the room that her heart turned leaden.

After that, Alice escaped outdoors daily beyond the fortified house and grounds to the fields and hills beyond. George was struck by the lively ten-year-old and her open, enquiring nature; she was an enchanting child. Often he found her taking refuge down at his home farm, helping to tend the animals.

Alice was in awe of the tall, energetic landowner who reminded her of pictures of the Duke of Wellington – his nose long and his look imperious – but he spoke to her kindly and shared her passion for nature. He gave her a present of a brown-coated sheep with horns and nimble feet.

'It's from the Highlands in Scotland,' said George, chuckling at her look of curiosity. 'I breed them on the estate – up in the hills – and they produce the sweetest milk and mutton. Remind me of the sheep in the Indian mountains.'

'You've been to India?' Alice was round-eyed.

'Worked at the Botanic Garden in Calcutta,' George said. 'Fascinating place, India. A botanist's paradise.'

'I've never been further than Black Harbour,' Alice admitted, 'but I've read about faraway places in Da's books.'

'You can read then?'

'Aye, but all his books got burnt in the fire. Da's very sad about that and so am I.'

'Then you and your father must help yourself to the books in my library,' George declared. 'Any time you want.'

Alice beamed. 'Thank you, sir.'

'The boys too.'

Alice giggled. 'They wouldn't be so thankful – they hated school.' Then she clamped a hand over her mouth, remembering the school was Gillveray's.

He laughed. 'Then we'll not force them into the library.'

'Sir,' Alice ventured, 'they might not like books but Mam says they should be earning their keep here. Danny's good with boats and Sam can mend anything – though he lives for lighthouse-keeping.'

George touched her shoulder. 'Of course they must have something to do. And what about you, Alice?'

'I could help with the sheep, sir. And I can grow vegetables.'

He gave her a considering look. 'I'll have a word with Miss Lambert.'

'Is she the shepherd's wife?'

'No.' George smiled. 'She's the school teacher.'

Alice's face fell. She had heard nothing good about school and didn't want to be cooped up indoors like her brothers had been. But Gillveray looked determined, and Alice soon found herself attending his charity school. Miss Lambert, whose chins wobbled as she spoke, took an interest in the lighthouse girl who thirsted for stories and gazed at the maps on the wall, memorising the names of countries and capitals. Very soon Alice became her keenest pupil, escaping from the tension in the Brown household to the schoolroom.

* * *

22

As the new lighthouse began to be built, the strained family relationships slowly repaired; Danny got a job ferrying supplies for Gillveray while Arnold and Sam took it in turns to work on the lighthouse ship. Effie helped out in the kitchens.

'I can gut fish better than any,' she said, rolling up her sleeves to the task. 'We island lassies followed the herring fleet every season – that's what brought me to the east coast – and how I met my husband. I was Gaelic-speaking but for a word or two: he taught me to speak the English.'

'A good catch for a herring girl!' Cook teased.

'Lucky for him, more like,' Effie declared. 'Not many lassies would put up with living in a leaky lighthouse on a rock all their married lives.'

'Well, you've two strong sons to show for it,' said Cook, 'and a beautiful daughter. She's like Rapunzel with her long reddish-gold hair. That's your Alice – Rapunzel in her tower!'

Effie liked Cook and the company of the kitchen women but felt uneasy at the attention Alice attracted. It was unlikely after ten years that the selfish Charlotte Fairchild would return to claim her daughter, yet Effie still lived in dread that she might. Though Alice could try her patience a dozen times a day, Effie loved her as fiercely as her own. The girl lit up the room with her sunny nature and constant singing. The sooner the new lighthouse was built and they could retreat back to the island, the better.

* * *

Alice was fascinated by the building of the new tower. She often skipped down to the harbour to watch the massive blocks of granite, hewn to fit together, being shipped out along with tools, crates of food and barrels of beer for the thirsty workers. The men who came and went were tough and wiry and brought tales about working on slippery rocks thigh deep in water; they would put up with any conditions as long as there was tobacco, ale and playing cards at the end of the day.

'Where do the men live?' she asked George Gillveray. 'And how do they get the right bits of stone to fit together and will the sea not knock over the stones if there's no lime to bind them? How do they stick to the rock in the first place?'

Delighted at her interest, George took Alice to his lookout tower, high above the gun-court, and let her look through his telescope.

'See how they are hammering in iron bolts? That's how they fix the foundations to the rock. That wooden tower next to it is a temporary barracks where they live.'

Alice gazed at the men working away with pickaxes and chisels like an army of ants, the fire from a makeshift forge belching out smoke. She saw how the sea spray soaked them but they carried on regardless. Pulleys and cranes swung to and fro, lifting the giant slabs of cut stone from the bobbing supply ship while the men lowered them in place like precious jewels.

George showed her the plans for the new lighthouse laid out on his desk.

'See how each circle of stone slots on top of the one below? The stones are all numbered and checked on the drawings. They fit together like a giant puzzle.'

23

'Will there really be seven storeys below the lamp-room?' Alice gasped, tracing her finger over the diagram. 'We only had four in the old one.'

'This tower will be nearly twice as tall, Alice,' George said eagerly, 'and seen for many more miles around. Besides, with your growing family, there will be need for more rooms. Your brothers may choose to marry and bring wives to live there who will want more comfort than you had in the old one. Your mother told me how the sea sometimes came through the walls and you had to take shelter in the top two rooms. Well, there'll be no need for that in the new building. Solid as a rock it will be, I promise.'

Despite Gillveray's optimism, there were frequent setbacks to the lighthouse building. Once the autumn gales came, the men were taken off the island and employed in the quarry yard until the following spring when the work could start again. Arnold and Sam left the lighthouse ship for the winter months too and made do with keeping a fire alight on a derelict tower built to alert against French invasion during the recent Napoleonic wars but now obsolete. That first winter, a ferocious storm tore away the barracks and swept the forge out to sea. As soon as the weather allowed, Gillveray and his engineers went out to inspect.

'Not as bad as we thought,' he reported to Alice. 'The stone foundations have held and the barracks can be rebuilt. It's only put us back about a month or two.'

Alice often watched the progress of the building that following summer from the lookout tower, George allowing her to come and go as she pleased and view it through the telescope. She made friends with Molly, the dairyman's daughter, who went to the same school but much preferred being outdoors with Alice, playing hide-and-seek around the farm or collecting shells along the shore and pretending they were treasure. Fair-haired Alice and dark-haired Molly became inseparable companions, giggling over secrets and staying in each other's homes. Alice took her once to the lookout tower to show her the lighthouse but Molly was scared of the old house and George's booming laugh ringing through the corridors and never came again.

'Your Danny's a handsome lad,' pronounced Molly, a year older and wiser about the world than Alice. 'Thomasina Johnson has got her eye on him.'

'The plump lass whose mam runs the post office?' Alice asked.

Molly nodded. 'Saw them walking out together on market day – arm in arm!'

'Never!' Alice was disbelieving.

'They were.'

Alice didn't like the thought of Danny spending time with a girl. She wanted their family to stay as it was forever, even though her eldest brother rarely spent time at home since they had come to the mainland.

'He doesn't have time for girls.' Alice was dismissive. 'Danny likes being with his friends, drinking and playing cards when he's not working hard.'

'Well, I know what I saw.' Molly was adamant. 'Mark my words; Thomasina will have a ring on her finger by this time next year. She always gets what she wants. Ever since her dad died, her mam can't say no to her – and neither will your Danny.'

Molly was right about Danny courting Thomasina but wrong about the speed of their courtship. Three years after the old lighthouse was burnt down, the new one was ready to move into, but it was the same five Browns who returned to live there. On a blustery September day in 1823, a boatload of local dignitaries and the Browns went out to the island to inspect it for the first time. An excited George Gillveray dispensed free rum, ale and roasted meat to the labourers and gave a speech praising their immense courage and hard work. The chief engineer led the men in three cheers for Gillveray and his persistence in getting a modern lighthouse built.

Alice gazed up at the tower, a huge white finger stabbing the sky, but it was the inside that really took her breath away. An iron staircase wound its way upwards instead of rickety ladders between trap doors. The bedchambers had windows on the landward side shaped like flower petals and the kitchen had a cast-iron range with a boiler for hot water.

Stepping into the lamp-room, she gasped. 'But it's beautiful.'

A huge hexagonal iron lantern housed a myriad of mirrors and lenses spread out like a crystal fan around the lamp – a proper oil lamp with no need for hazardous candles, and it caught and refracted light even before it was lit. The outer gantry was equipped with brass handles to grip onto that were shaped into dolphins and fish. Alice ran her hands over the polished metal.

She grinned at George. 'Not even a palace would have such fancy door handles.'

He laughed. 'Fit for a princess.'

Alice blushed. At thirteen she had a girlish crush on the handsome landowner, even though he was so much older. She often imagined him riding a stallion over the mountains of northern India, with his unruly brown hair and glowing hazel eyes, leading men into battle. For once she was tongue-tied. She pretended to find something of interest to gaze at on the horizon while listening to George and her father talk animatedly about the French-designed Fresnel lenses and the merits of an Argand lamp and parabolic reflectors. Alice was silently grateful to their kind benefactor for pulling her father out of his long depression and giving him a new purpose in life. Her heart gave a dull ache to think that, once they moved back to the island, she would not be seeing George every day as she had the past three years.

* * *

But before the week was out, a startling proposal was made.

'Alice has a sharp mind and an aptitude for learning,' George said, having summoned Arnold to his study. 'Let her stay on in school till she is fifteen like her brothers did. Miss Lambert thinks she has the makings of a teacher.'

Arnold was undecided but Alice seized on the idea.

'Please let me, Da!'

Her father soon gave in to her pleading, as much out of gratitude to Gillveray for all he had done for their family as conviction that Alice had twice the brains of her brothers. He accepted the landowner's offer despite Effie's protests.

'The lassie's head is already stuffed full of learning – there's no room left for common sense,' her mother cried.

'She can stay for another year or so,' Arnold bargained, 'then come and take her share of keeping watch, like you did before the lads grew up.'

25

So Alice and her pet sheep Wellington stayed on the mainland during term time and lived with Molly's family at the dairyman's cottage. Alice spent her free time helping in Gillveray's garden or borrowing books from his library. She went home in the holidays. She had never been so happy. At fifteen, she was as tall as Danny, with strong limbs and a full figure, long burnished-blonde hair tied carelessly at the nape of her neck, and a slim oval face with wide blue eyes framed in dark lashes and a generous mouth that was constantly twitching into a smile.

She was quick-witted yet dreamy by nature, practical yet given to flights of fancy that made Molly laugh and shake her head.

'You want to fly through the air like a bird! Where do you get such notions?'

Alice dreamt of being a teacher like Miss Lambert – and might have done so despite her mother's objections – but the florid-faced teacher was found dead in the schoolroom one winter's morning.

'Heart failed,' George told a distraught Alice.

Effie lost no time in summoning Alice back to the lighthouse to help the family. She went with a heavy heart, finding the island cramped and its life restricting after the years at Black Harbour House. She'd brought Wellington with her, and whispered to the sheep about her sadness and pined for George Gillveray. By the following spring, news came that the school had closed and Gillveray had gone travelling again, perhaps in search of a wife.

This rumour caused Alice pain but spurred on Danny to propose to Thomasina. They married that summer and the post mistress's spoilt daughter came to live with them at the lighthouse.

'Sam doesn't need a large bedchamber all to himself,' their new sister-in-law declared within a week of arriving, 'and I need somewhere to put all my trunks of clothes.'

Alice retorted that a lighthouse-keeper's wife had no need of so many outfits but Thomasina burst into tears and Effie chided her daughter for making the girl cry. Sam meekly agreed and moved into one of the empty storerooms. Thomasina didn't try to hide her look of triumph and was soon ingratiating herself with her mother-in-law. Alice swallowed her annoyance. Effie was happy to have a woman in the house who was content to cook and sew and keep her company.

But soon Thomasina was pregnant and gave up doing any chores, declaring herself too delicate. She ordered Alice around like a servant. Alice's one escape was helping her father with the night watch, keeping the brilliant flame of the new lamp alight. She would stare out at the sea and wonder if her life would always be confined to this tower. Thomasina had swept in to their lives like an autumn bluster; Alice had a gnawing sense of unease that the girl was going to cause further storms – especially for her.

Chapter 5

Skye, 1813

The day that the laird, Hercules MacAskill, returned to Ramanish was one that young John Sinclair would never forget.

'Are you coming up the hill to wait for the chief?' his friend Donald from next door ran over to ask.

John turned to his grandfather, who was sharpening a sickle on a stone in the doorway. *Please can I go!* The eight-year-old gave his grandfather a pleading look.

Norman shook his head and raised his voice as if John was stupid, not merely mute. 'He'll come soon enough and I need you to keep the cow from trampling the barley.'

'We could take Fula the cow with us, sir,' Donald suggested.

'Don't be daft.'

'Let them go, Father,' Aunt Morag intervened. She was standing in the doorway hunched over her knitting. 'All the other children are going. I'll keep an eye on the cow.'

'You?' Norman was dismissive. 'A cripple can't run after beasts – and it's other people's cattle need watching too. I'll not have my barley ruined – we need to eat this winter.'

'You mean drink,' Morag muttered. 'Most of it goes into that whisky-still out the back.'

'Watch your tongue, woman!'

Morag rolled her eyes at John but said no more. They both knew that once Norman had set his mind against something, then nothing would change it. So John had to watch Donald run off without him and join the other children of the village as scouts on the mountain path, ready to alert the people of their landlord's arrival after thirteen years away in India.

John spent a frustrating morning in the fields, flapping at the crows to keep them off the corn, and using his grandfather's birch stick to prod any cattle that strayed too close to the open strips of barley, oats and potato patches. He often did menial tasks around the village – lifting peats for the homestead fire and carrying basket-loads of seaweed for the kelp workers because he was bigger and stronger than most boys his age. That's why none of the other boys picked on him for not speaking and just accepted him as he was. But on a day like today, John wished with all his heart that he could find the words to beg his grandfather to let him be the first to see their returning chief. (He hardly remembered a time when he could talk – like a chattering herring gull his mother had once said – but since he had caused his father to die and his mother to disappear, their loss weighed on his tongue like stones.)

So when Donald ran back, whooping through the village that a band of riders on horseback with baggage ponies were on their way, John abandoned his duty among the field rigs.

'He's got a savage with him,' Donald said in excitement, 'in funny clothes. Must be his slave.'

27

Villagers poured out of their houses and came up from the shore where they had been gathering seaweed to throng the path leading to Ramanish Castle. John and Donald pushed forward to the front. Long before he set eyes on his chief and his entourage, John heard Willie the Piper leading them down the mountain to a skirl of bagpipes.

All of a sudden it started: the singing. As the riders came into view, John felt a deep primitive joy inside as the spontaneous chanting rose into the air – half war cry, half love song – welcoming home their longed-for leader. It was an ancient song and one that his mother had sung to him; his eyes stung with tears as he listened.

Hercules, dressed in trews and a faded red army jacket under a tartan plaid, rode in front on a sturdy brown mare. His large, weather-beaten face was cracked by tiny lines and his red hair under the army bonnet was unfashionably long and tied back. To John he looked like some Jacobite hero from the last century. But it was the man who rode behind on a black horse without stirrups or saddle who made his jaw drop. He had nut-brown skin (like John's Spanish great-great-grandfather who had died two summers ago) and a full black beard. He wore a voluminous green cloak that only half hid a sword, and his head was swathed in white cloth like a giant bandage with the end hanging down over his broad shoulder. He had the beaked nose and dark flashing eyes of a hawk.

'There's the slave,' Donald said, nudging John.

Looks more like a bodyguard, thought John, noticing the long slender musket strapped to the foreigner's horse.

Behind rode a band of clan gentry, dressed in their finest clothes and bonnets for the occasion. The village boys ran alongside, waving and cheering. A beaming Hercules called out to people he recognised, shouting greetings. As the procession neared the rocky rise that led to the castle, he pulled his horse around and, facing the crowds, took out a silver pistol and fired into the air. The foreigner whipped out a gun, cocked it and did the same.

Women screamed and the horses behind whinnied in fright. As children and dogs scattered, Hercules and his companion roared with laughter.

'Tonight,' their chief bellowed above the noise, 'you will all dine with me on the shore. You boys,' he said, pointing at Donald and John still wide-eyed in alarm at the shooting, 'what are your names?'

'I'm Donald, son of James, son of Donald the blacksmith, sir,' John's friend answered at once. 'And this is John, grandson of Norman, son of Iain, son of Carlos.'

'One of the Spanish MacAskills?' Hercules raised an eyebrow. John nodded. 'Show me that you have the strength of your forefathers and gather up wood for a fire for our feast. Can you do that, my young warriors?'

'Aye sir,' Donald gasped, and John nodded vigorously, overwhelmed by the honour of being singled out in the crowd.

They didn't wait to see the chief and his bodyguard of men ride on to the castle but took to their heels to scavenge for driftwood along the shore, followed by a horde of children eager to help.

That night, as the stars came out, the people of Ramanish and the surrounding villages feasted on roast mutton and goose cooked over open fires, the first meat that most of them had tasted all year. Dusty barrels of claret and casks of brandy were brought up from the castle cellar and Hercules went among them, sharing bowls of claret and brandy punch with the men. His laughter and deep voice rang out across the still loch as he regaled his people with stories of far-off lands and military campaigns.

'Went with Elphinstone to visit the King of Afghanistan – he owns a diamond as big as my fist,' Hercules said, punching the air, 'the Koh-i-noor. But I brought back a greater treasure – my friend Azlan. He is a true Highlander and a warrior just like our people.' He clapped a hand on the Afghan's shoulder. 'The only difference is he prays to the east and doesn't speak Gaelic – yet.' Hercules chuckled.

John hovered close to the circle of men grouped around his chief, staring in fascination at the bearded fighter with the long dagger in his belt. The foreigner squatted on his haunches while he ate but did not touch a drop of the free-flowing liquor. The Afghan caught his eye and winked. John was so astonished his mouth fell open. The man grinned, revealing a gap in his upper teeth and carried on slicing meat from a bone with a small, sharp knife and popping the morsels in his mouth.

Later, Donald's father fetched his fiddle and struck up a tune and the villagers danced on the widening beach as the tide ebbed. The celebration went on all night, the men (including John's grandfather) bringing out jugs of illicit homemade whisky to share around while age-old clan stories were told. As dawn broke, Willie the Piper played a slow haunting salute to his patron and master; it was the signal for families to drift home to snatch sleep before the new day.

A drunken Norman roused John and pulled him out of the bed-closet that was wedged between the byre and the living space, where John had just fallen asleep.

His grandfather was slurring and almost incoherent. 'Disobeyed me! Fula in field. You ran off.'

She was tethered, John wanted to cry out.

'Don't give me that look!' He reached for the birch stick and swung it at his grandson. John dodged out of the way. 'Stand still!'

'Father' – Morag scrambled up from her bed by the fire – 'leave him be. Don't spoil such a grand day.'

'You're the one who spoils him,' Norman growled. 'Needs teaching a lesson.'

As he raised the stick again, Morag hurled herself between her father and nephew. 'Stop!' she cried, grabbing the stick as he brought it down. A glancing blow scraped her cheek but she wrested it from him and it clattered to the ground. John dashed forward, picked up the stick and ran off with it out of the house. He hurled it like a javelin over the yard wall; it disappeared into the mossy bank where his grandfather's illegal still nestled under a rocky outcrop by the stream.

Returning to face his grandfather's wrath, John found him on his knees by the fire, weeping into his hands.

'Help me get him to bed,' Morag said.

They pulled and cajoled Norman to his feet; he was not a big man but had a wiry strength.

'Sorry, Morag, sorry,' he mumbled. 'Didn't mean to hit you.'

'I know you didn't. Come on, Father, it's your sore head you'll be sorry about in the morning.'

They heaved him into the old box-bed in the corner of the kitchen, its sides and curtains blackened from years of peat smoke. Soon he was snoring but John was reluctant to return to his bed in the closet. As usual Morag understood. She put a gentle hand on his head.

'You can sleep by the fire for a wee bit. It'll soon be time to be up.'

They bedded down together on the truckle bed that got folded away during the day. John lay staring at the fire, his aunt's comforting arm encircling him. He found it hard to remember his old home at Foxton – a white-painted dresser for crockery, a hearth with a chimney and curtains at a window that opened – but little else. This windowless room around a central fire with his aunt's spinning wheel and grandfather's tools was much more familiar now. Its smells calmed him; fish strung overhead curing in the smoke, the pungent fleece of a sheep nailed to the wall to dry out and the all-pervading peat smoke that seeped into hair and clothes.

'Your grandfather wasn't always this bad-tempered,' Morag murmured. 'He was a great cattle drover as a young man and brought ribbons and buckles back from the markets in the south – but those days are long past. He's had a hard time making a living since. Still, you're not to blame for any of it, so he shouldn't take it out on you. It's just when the drink's in him . . .' She gave a long sigh.

He loved his Aunt Morag almost as much as he'd loved his mother, though he still felt hollow inside when he thought of his tall father and his gentle mother. Nightmares of falling trees still plagued his sleep and his mother would appear in his dreams but he had no memory of how she had vanished; no one had ever told him. Where had she gone and why had she left him? John had an unhappy feeling that his grandfather blamed him for not bringing his mother safely over the mountain from Foxton and that was why the old man didn't like him and spoke of him as simple in the head to the neighbours.

* * *

A summons from the laird for help with harvesting the hay went round the following week. Hercules expected everyone to drop what they were doing and come to his fields while the weather was fine. When Norman grumbled that it was more important to get on with the kelp, which brought them in money, Morag reminded him, 'The chief doesn't ask a penny piece in rent for our land and house – the least we can do is help out at the harvest.'

John was delighted to escape from the chore of humping huge creels of seaweed to the kelp fires on the shore; those sinister reeking piles that he had seen on first arrival at Ramanish and had thought were the work of enemies laying waste to the land.

With Donald beside him, he set about scything the tall lush grass that grew on the lower slopes down to the sandy bay, moving to the rhythm of the men and women singing as they worked. Everyone able-bodied was there – even the factor Falkner and his giggling daughter Katrine, who spent more time chucking hay seeds in the air, and Hercules and Azlan, who rolled up their sleeves and helped alongside.

John kept glancing at the muscular Afghan in his baggy trousers, boots and a multicoloured jerkin over his shirt, a long knife strapped to his belt. When they stopped to eat the oatcakes and cheese that the women had brought, Azlan went a little way off, removed his boots and washed in the stream. Then he unfolded a small piece of cloth and began to murmur before bending, kneeling and bowing down on the ground.

The boys gawped. 'Do you think he's doing magic?' Donald whispered.

'He's praying,' Hercules told them. 'No need to stare, boys.'

John flushed, gazing up at his chief in awe.

'I was sorry to hear about your mother going,' said the laird. 'She was a fine girl and pretty too – I see you have the same deep complexion. But no doubt Morag *crotach* looks after you well, eh?'

John nodded.

'That's good. And the old Spaniard Carlos – is he still living?'

John shook his head.

'Hardly surprising,' Hercules grunted. 'He was ancient when I was a boy but he seemed destined to live on forever. A great old man. But perhaps you never met him. You don't have much to say for yourself, do you? The Spanish MacAskills usually say twenty words when two would do.'

John wanted to tell him how he did remember old Carlos – had listened to his stories about soldiering as a boy for the exiled Stuart kings. His great-great-grandfather had been growing a third set of teeth and had started to speak again in Spanish – a language that hadn't passed his lips for nearly a century – before he died.

'John can't speak,' Donald piped up, 'but he understands a lot.'

Hercules raised an eyebrow. He turned his attention to Donald and began to ask after his family, chuckling at the boy's lively replies. John felt frustration well up inside him but his throat was tight as a cork in a bottle. Azlan joined them, squatting down to eat the simple fare. He passed comment in a language John had never heard before. The words sounded like the chuckling of a fast stream. Hercules laughed and made some riposte.

Morag came ambling over to check on John, glancing warily at the fierce-looking foreigner in rapid-fire conversation with their chief. She curtseyed in greeting to Hercules and he raised his bonnet in return.

'I hope the food's to your liking, sir?' she asked. 'You must have missed our good oatmeal and sheep's cheese this long while.'

'Indeed I have.' He smiled. 'Though my friend is finding the oatcake a little indigestible.'

Morag bristled. 'And why is that?'

Hercules chuckled. 'He says it is the food of mules in his country.'

John saw the flush of indignation on his aunt's face and hoped she wouldn't say anything rash.

Hands on hips, Morag retorted, 'Tell him that this food has been eaten by Scottish kings and clan chiefs for centuries; if it's good enough for them, then it's good enough for our chief's servant.'

As an amused Hercules relayed her words, John saw the frown deepen on the Afghan's brow. They had a rapid exchange. People all around were stopping their conversations to stare. John moved nearer his aunt in case the man should lash out at her.

Azlan spoke to Hercules, his voice angry. The laird turned to Morag.

'He says we should lock you up in the castle dungeon for your insolence to a man.'

Morag retorted, 'He'll have to get used to women's plain speaking or the dungeon will be full by nightfall.'

John tugged at his aunt to stop but by the gleam in her eye he feared she was enjoying baiting the stranger. Hercules translated her reply. Azlan got to his feet, his face stormy. Suddenly the Afghan threw back his head and bellowed in laughter. Then he put his hand on his heart and gave a slight nod in Morag's direction without making eye contact.

With a snort of amusement, Morag bobbed an awkward curtsy in return.

Later, John's grandfather took her to task for her forwardness.

'I'll not have a daughter of mine make a fool of herself with that heathen foreigner.'

'Not so heathen,' Morag quipped. 'He says more prayers in one day than folk round here say in a year.'

'To some foreign god,' Norman snapped.

'His prayers go up to Heaven the same as ours,' said Morag, 'and if our chief has no objection to them, then neither should you.'

John, fearing his grandfather would explode with rage at his aunt, grabbed the birch stick that had replaced the last one and ran out of the hut, flinging it into the heather. Norman came striding after him, cursing and shaking his fists.

'When I find it, I'll thrash your hide!'

John ran off and didn't come home till after nightfall by which time his grandfather was half-comatose with whisky and had forgotten to be angry with the boy.

* * *

John's fascination with Azlan grew daily. He crept close to watch him pray and listen to his language, which spilled like music into the clear air. When Hercules and Azlan rode out, John would pull Donald away from his chores to clamber the hillside and spy on the hunting party. One day Azlan caught a hawk but did not kill it; he trained it to fly high and return to sit on his wrist.

One evening he came to the village and greeted the blacksmith with one of his strange bows and began to speak in his musical tongue, pointing at the forge dog. James, Donald's father, was baffled. Others quickly came crowding around, curious about the visitor who had come without his master, their chief, and was making wild gestures and gabbling unintelligibly. The words were just as strange to John, yet somehow he understood the gist of them. John stepped forward, picked up one of the puppies nestling half-hidden beneath the dog – a lean wolf-like male with white flecks on its grey muzzle – and held it out to Azlan.

Azlan beamed and nodded. Then swiftly he drew out a small knife with a brass handle and grabbed at the puppy.

'No, don't,' Donald's father shouted in alarm, lunging at the Afghan. 'Keep your hands off it!'

Startled, Azlan waved the knife at his attacker. James grabbed a hammer. Norman and two other men muscled forward, ready to fight.

John, still gripping the puppy, flung himself forward to protect Azlan.

'Out of the way, boy!' his grandfather barked. 'Our dogs are not for eating.'

John shook his head. Turning, he took the knife from Azlan and handed him the puppy. Then he handed the knife to Donald's father. James hesitated.

Donald piped up. 'It's a gift, Father, for the puppy. Isn't that right, John?'

John nodded. Azlan was stroking and nuzzling the puppy, grinning with delight. James took the knife, admiring its elaborate brass handle studded with green stones. He was soon showing it off to the other men. Norman continued to scowl, still suspecting some trickery, when Morag came over with a bowl of cream.

'That's a fine way to greet a guest, with fists and hammers,' she chided.

At once, James gestured for Azlan to sit with them outside the forge. Morag handed the Afghan the bowl first. 'Not for that greedy pup though,' she warned.

He gave a puzzled frown. In explanation, John reached and took the puppy while nodding for him to take the bowl. Azlan did so, slurping at the cream. He licked his lips and grinned, giving Morag a shy glance as he passed the bowl to James. It made her smile that dimpled smile that reminded John of his mother.

In the weeks and months that followed, John saw a lot more of his chief's bodyguard, as Azlan often came by the forge to have his hunting knives sharpened, lingering at John's door to show him new tricks that he had taught the puppy, now called Wolf. Man and hound were never apart and Morag complained about the exuberant dog rushing in and knocking over her pots, but she always had a cup of water or bowl of milk ready to offer Wolf's master.

Sometimes Hercules and Azlan would stop by the burning kelp pits where John and Donald were unloading the creels of seaweed and beckon the boys to go with them to the hunting grounds in the mountains. They would run along and flush out the birds for the men to shoot. If they brought down a deer, the boys would carry it back, strung from a pole, and take home a share of it to their families. Often Hercules would chatter to his friend in his own language; the chief told the boys it was Pashto. Donald understood not a word but John found himself picking up meaning, drinking up the words thirstily and mouthing them soundlessly.

One day when Azlan asked Hercules what was the meaning of the Gaelic word *crotach*, John croaked in Pashto 'hump on back'.

The men stared at him as if he had grown wings. Donald gaped.

'My mother's sister; Morag hump on back.' The words came out weak and husky.

'Are you speaking Afghan?' Donald asked in amazement.

Hercules slapped his thigh. 'Well, I'll be damned! Spanish John has a tongue after all, Azlan. You were right all along.'

Azlan gave John a penetrating look with his dark eyes. 'You understand all that we say?'

John shrugged.

'Tell me in words, my brother,' Azlan ordered.

John swallowed hard and cleared his throat. 'A bit. A big bit.'

Azlan clapped a hand on his shoulder and looked in triumph at Hercules. 'Didn't I say this one was a young Afridi? He has the heart of a lion and speaks the language of kings.'

Hercules chuckled. 'You were right, my friend.'

Donald pulled on John's arm. 'What are you all saying? Tell me in Gaelic.'

John began to shake. He wanted to explain but felt too overcome. Something momentous was happening yet he wasn't sure what. Azlan threw an arm around his shoulder and hugged him.

'Are you crying, John?' Donald asked. 'Why are you crying?'

'Donald, *Og*,' Hercules said gently, 'I think your friend has found a way back to us.'

* * *

After that, John was inseparable from Azlan, becoming his most devoted gillie on hunting trips, learning to ride and manage the horses as well as look after the dogs in the kennels, Wolf being his favourite. He became fluent in Pashto, which amused his aunt but infuriated his grandfather. Sometimes, when drunk, old Norman would take the stick to his grandson.

'Speak Gaelic, you little heathen!'

But John could easily dodge his wild blows and defied him with an oath in Pashto. The villagers thought him even more eccentric for speaking in a foreign tongue than when he was mute but Donald stood up for his friend and accepted this new development like the change in the seasons.

* * *

The following summer, a sailing ship moored off the peninsula and visitors were ferried ashore to the castle. Word went round that they were eminent men from the Lowlands. To his grandfather's consternation, Hercules summoned John to the castle.

'What have you done, boy?' Norman fretted.

John hid his nerves as he went. He had only ever been into the kitchens and outhouses around the old keep and never into its living quarters. He was ushered up stone steps into a cavernous sitting room with casement windows set in walls six feet thick, musty-smelling hangings and a faded multicoloured carpet under his bare feet. Guests, sitting on chairs of sprouting horsehair, were bent over a table covered in charts and drawings. Someone was bashing the keys of an out-of-tune piano and Hercules was standing in front of a large fireplace smoking a pipe.

To John's relief he caught sight of Azlan, who beckoned him forward with a wink of encouragement.

'These are friends from the south,' Hercules explained to John in Gaelic. 'They are from the Northern Lighthouse Board and are doing an inspection of the Western Isles.' Then he switched to English as he introduced them. John found his hand being vigorously shaken by a Mr Stevenson from Edinburgh.

'One of Scotland's best engineers,' Hercules praised him to the man's obvious delight.

There were three other men, the last being a tall man with a beaky nose and wild, curly hair.

'I'm George Gillveray, a friend of your chief's from our India days. Do you understand Hindustani too?'

John had never heard of Hindustani.

Hercules declared. 'Not yet, but give me a year with the boy and he will.'

'But you understand English?' George asked.

John nodded.

'His father spoke it,' Hercules explained.

'Ah, yes, such a sad business. And to lose your mother too, poor boy.'

John flushed; they had been talking about him.

The men gathered around and quizzed him as if he were some strange creature from a faraway land. John, at Hercules's bidding, answered in Pashto, which his chief then translated for his guests. They wanted to know why he would not speak Gaelic.

'Do you choose not to?' asked Stevenson.

John shook his head. He could not explain it. He threw Azlan a pleading look. To John's surprise, Azlan answered in halting English.

'The words – they will not come. English, it died with the father; Gaelic, with mother.'

'That's a most surprising suggestion,' said Stevenson.

'But an interesting one – and plausible,' George said. 'The boy had two terrible shocks one after the other; first his father's death and then his mother's. It's no wonder he stopped speaking.'

John went cold. What were they saying? He turned to Azlan, appalled.

'M-my m-mother? She's dead?'

Hercules frowned. 'Surely you knew that?'

John shook his head.

'Oh, my poor boy! She died of the cold in the mountains,' his chief explained. 'She lies in the burial ground on the hill. Your grandfather must have told you?'

John's heart began to hammer. No one had told him! His chest tightened so that he could hardly breathe. He saw the looks of shocked amazement on the faces of the visitors, but it was the pity in his chief's eyes that he could not bear.

John turned and tore from the room, knocking over a side table that held a tray of delicate glasses. As he fled, he heard glass smash. He knew that he should go back and apologise but all he wanted to do was get out of the castle and as far away as possible.

Escaping outside, John sped past the kelp fires, the settlement of turf houses and the field rigs. People called out to him but he did not answer and did not stop until he reached the tumbled-down stone church and its sloping burial ground, his lungs bursting with the effort. The church had long fallen into disuse for lack

35

of a minister and because a long-absent chief cared little for religion. John and his friends never played here as it was said to be haunted and under the spell of 'the little people' – malevolent fairies who could cause sickness in cattle and death to those who cursed them. But if his mother was here, he must find her. Chest heaving for breath, John searched the mossy graveyard overgrown with thistles and ferns.

There were a few ancient gravestones of MacAskill chiefs lying prone among the lush grass, their images of medieval knights and galley ships worn down by centuries of weather. A handful of upright stones bore the names and dates of tacksmen, the tenant farmers who held land from the chief. But most of the graves were unmarked or bore simple undressed stones, the curved grassy mounds the only testament to family ancestors. Even if his mother were buried here, he would never find her.

Then he remembered where his great-great-grandfather Carlos had been laid to rest three years ago, in a far corner of the burial ground under a rowan tree. To his surprise, he found the thistles had been cut back and yellow primroses studded the grass. Someone came here to tend it; Aunt Morag perhaps? John crouched down and put his hand on the stone marker. Was his mother here too, sleeping with the ancestors? The leaves of the rowan fluttered above, sighing in the wind. Grief choked him. All this time he had blamed himself for her disappearance, thinking she had hated him so much for the death of his father that she could not bear to be with him. Yet for years he had lived in hope – a childish hope – that she would return. How stupid he had been! She had been dead all along, perished in the snow. John bowed his head and let out a sob.

Why had no one told him? They should have. He had a right to know! Suddenly John was filled with hot rage. It coursed through his blood like a poison. They had lied to him – his grandfather, his aunt, his neighbours and friends. All of them had kept the truth from him and let him believe that one day she might return.

Seething with anger and misery, John strode down the hill. He barged into his grandfather's house. Norman and Morag looked up in surprise – he smoking a pipe, she stirring the pot.

'Back so soon?' Morag smiled.

John was shaking uncontrollably.

'What is it?' Morag reached to put her arms about him but he shook her off. He felt the words rising up inside him from the core of his being; Gaelic words that hadn't passed his lips for half his life.

'Why didn't you say my mother was dead?'

They both gaped at him, astonished.

'Are you speaking the Gaelic?' Norman demanded.

'My mother,' John cried. 'Tell me about my mother.'

His aunt looked confused. 'John, I don't understand . . .'

He glared at his grandfather; now that he had found his tongue he couldn't stop. 'You told me she was lost – gone – but never *dead*! I had to hear it from a stranger at the castle. Everyone else knew apart from me!'

Norman laid down his pipe. 'What foolishness you talk. Of course she's dead. Why else would you be living here?'

'I thought she had left me because it was my fault my father died – if I hadn't made him stay to pick apples that tree would never have killed him. She was so sad she couldn't bear to have me near her—'

'No, you're wrong,' Morag interrupted. 'She loved you more than her own life. Tell him, Father,' she urged Norman. 'Tell him what happened.'

'I don't want to hear any more lies,' John shouted.

'Don't raise your voice to your grandfather,' Morag chided. 'Sit you beside him and listen.' She pushed him gently onto a stool.

'Nobody's lied to you.' Norman looked stricken. John saw tears in his grandfather's eyes as he struggled to speak.

'Your mother saved your life that day on the mountain when the snow came so quickly. She wrapped you in her plaid and pushed you into a crevice in the rock. She knew it would mean certain death for her – unless help came quickly – but we didn't know she had set out that day. If only we had searched for her sooner. I will go to my grave with that guilt in my heart . . .'

'I remember her telling me to hide in the rock,' John whispered, 'but I thought she had left me there.'

'No,' Norman said, his voice shaking with emotion. 'She stayed right beside you until the cold took her life. No mother could have done more for her son.'

John felt suddenly weightless, as if a great burden had been taken from his shoulders. His mother had loved him after all. A memory came back unbidden of standing under a dazzling sky watching an eagle hover overhead and his mother telling him what it was as he stood in her warm hold. John bowed his head, fighting back hot tears.

'I'm sorry if you thought your mother was still alive,' said Norman, his face scored with anguish. 'I never thought it needed explaining.' The old man stood up and walked out of the house so that the boy would not see his tears.

Morag crouched down beside John. 'You were too young to go to the funeral and we thought talking about her would upset you even more. Your grandfather finds it difficult to speak about your mother – she was very special to him. To both of us.'

John leant towards her and buried his face in her hold. Then he let the tears come; great wracking sobs that came up from his belly.

Morag stroked his hair and crooned. 'She would be very proud of you, John.' She kissed him on his head. 'And glad in her heart that you've found your voice again.'

Chapter 6

Skye, 1820

At fifteen, John was a robust and popular figure around Ramanish, riding out bareback to hunt with Azlan, as expert at falconry now as the Afghan was. When his grandfather had died three years previously, Hercules had fostered John, taking the boy under his roof and treating him like the son he had never had. John was tutored at the castle alongside sons of local tacksmen, proving a quick learner in the classics, mathematics and languages. He had a passion for maps and was fascinated by Hercules's ones of India. He loved to point out to his friends the kingdom of the Afghans and the Khyber area from where Azlan came. Yet it was the vague unmapped areas to the east and north that intrigued him the most.

'But what about there, sir?' John had once asked of Hercules, tracing his fingers across the large blank areas where only tentative brushstrokes denoted mountains. 'Before you get to Russia or Tibet.'

'The Himalayas,' his foster father had said.

'Yes, but who lives there?'

'Mongol tribes – Himalayan kings,' Hercules would answer with a shrug.

'One day,' John had declared with a passionate look, 'I'm going to be an explorer and find out.'

He was a restless youth and often escaped to his friends in the village for sport and to help in the fields as he had always done. He had an unruly streak; he was a daredevil who would climb pinnacles in the mountains for wagers. Aged twelve, he had disappeared with a party of drovers, driving cattle to the mainland markets, curious to see the world that lay beyond the island. He had got as far as the southern Highlands before men from Ramanish had caught up with him and fetched him home, where his furious and ailing grandfather had given him the biggest thrashing of his life.

They had sparred right up until Norman's death, yet John missed him more than he would have imagined. His grandfather had been cantankerous and bullying in drink but occasionally, in tranquil moments, had shown John a grudging affection. But to John his grandfather could never take the place of his beloved father, and he had kicked against the old man's petty strictures. If it hadn't been for his Aunt Morag's constant intervention, there would have been no peace in the home of the Spanish MacAskills. More and more, John had looked to Hercules as a father figure, and once Norman had been laid to rest with his forebears in the simple family grave under the rowan tree, John was happy to go and live at the castle.

To the surprise of all but John, Morag – after her father's death – had swiftly married Azlan, who chose to move into the village house with her.

'I am more at home here among the animals with my woman,' the Afghan declared, 'than in that cold and draughty fortress. Morag keeps me warm.' He chuckled.

John knew how happy the foreigner made his aunt and she turned a deaf ear to gossip about her marrying a heathen. At harvest dances and village weddings, she went proudly on his arm, exultant that the pitying looks she had endured for years on account of her crooked back had turned into envy and admiration.

Azlan was not the only man who caught the interest of the womenfolk. Tall and broad like his Lowland father, John's handsome, dark looks and vivid green eyes brought him attention from the village girls and the sisters of his friends among the gentry. By seventeen, young Sinclair was in demand as a dancing partner at Highland balls held in neighbouring country houses, and he even returned to Foxton Hall for the twenty-first birthday party of Jeremiah Fox's youngest daughter. Overcome by painful memories at the sight of his former home and its apple orchards, John got very drunk and was seduced by Miss Fox's lady's maid.

Discovering a new enthusiasm for the opposite sex, John was constantly falling in and out of love. Azlan grumbled that this distraction was blunting John's concentration for hunting and shooting game but Hercules was indulgent.

'It's in his Highland nature,' the chief declared. 'John has the courage of a tiger and the heart of a poet.'

Of all the local girls, it was the factor's spirited daughter, Katrine, whom John pined for the most. Ever since he had first seen her dancing in the torchlight on the beach at Hercules's return feast, ten years ago, John had admired her. But Katrine was three years his senior and seemed merely amused by his adoration. She treated him with casual indifference – teasing him for the poems he wrote for her and pushed into her hand when he called with gifts of venison for her father.

'What a funny boy you are!' Katrine would giggle and give him a playful shove. 'You'll have to improve your spelling if you are to become a proper romantic poet.'

John redoubled his efforts in the classroom, struggling to rid his thoughts of Katrine's brown eyes and her red lips that he longed to kiss. Then, when John turned eighteen, Hercules threw a party for his young ward and Katrine attended with her father. John danced with her more than any other girl and while supper was served in the interval he took her hand and led her onto the gun-court to look at the stars.

With heart thumping, he kissed her hand and said, 'You must know I'm in love with you?' She arched her eyebrows. He ploughed on before his courage failed him. 'Will you marry me, Katrine?'

She stifled a laugh. 'No, certainly not!' He looked so crestfallen that she put a hand to his burning cheek and added, 'But seeing as it's your birthday, you can give me a proper kiss.'

John grinned back, pulled her into his strong arms and kissed her vigorously on the lips. If her father had not come looking for her, John was sure Katrine would have kissed him a lot longer – perhaps agreed to meet him later to continue their courtship uninterrupted.

But her father led her swiftly back to the dance and shortly afterwards they left. To his frustration, Katrine was sent to Edinburgh for the social season and did not come back till the following year. John was sent half mad with longing, baffled that his passionate letters and poems were answered with brief, infrequent notes that told him of a life of balls and outings but nothing of her feelings.

'They must be going astray,' he complained to his foster father. 'I know she cares for me.'

Then news filtered back that Katrine was engaged to be married to an Edinburgh lawyer. John refused to believe it until he saw with his own eyes that his beloved wore another man's ring. Her father brought her to visit Hercules, who gave her a wedding gift of a gold filigree box that had once belonged to a maharajah. John sat through the ordeal mute with fury and misery – angered at himself for being so wrong about her feelings for him. It struck him that Katrine smiled at everyone with the same warmth – and had probably only let herself be kissed by him because it was his birthday and she had felt sorry for him.

Hercules, together with Azlan, took the lovesick John away on an extended hunting trip.

'Best remedy for a broken heart,' his chief declared. 'The only woman I ever loved was the wife of my commanding officer. Doesn't do to dwell on what might have been.'

After that, John courted Donald's giggling, red-cheeked sister Peigi, who was as enthusiastic as John was to kiss and cuddle in the heather on short summer nights. He imagined himself in love and might even have proposed and settled down in marriage with the affectionate girl had things not changed dramatically the following spring.

* * *

The year 1825 came in with ferocious storms and great hardship for the people of Ramanish and far beyond. Cattle froze to death, children sickened and empty-bellied people turned grey and gaunt with hunger and worry. Hercules sold off paintings and silver to buy in grain to keep his half-starved tenants alive. John went with Azlan into the mountains to hunt what they could, but the snowdrifts were deep and treacherous and John was haunted by memories of his ordeal as a child.

When the spring finally came, people were thankful yet weakened by the ordeal. A lethargy seized them and a spirit of gloom hung over the village. Hercules encouraged them back to the kelp burning but it was harder now to make any money from it.

'Since peace came to the Continent,' Hercules confided in John, 'the chemical factories can get an abundance of cheap potash from Spain instead of our kelp ash. Falkner says the kelp trade is dead – and we can't even fetch good prices at the cattle markets anymore. He's telling me to invest in sheep like they've been doing on the mainland.'

'But sheep farming needs a lot of land and only employs a handful of men,' John said. 'What can the others do?'

Hercules sighed. 'Precisely.'

The castle roof leaked and the ancient structure needed repairs but the MacAskill chief would not entertain giving up the old ways of farming or generous entertaining. Yet others of the impoverished gentry were selling up or renting out their land to incomers – men with money to invest. It grieved John to see his foster father's spirits droop as one family after another moved south to the cities or emigrated to Australia.

'I'll join the army or the navy,' John suggested, 'and make my fortune abroad. Then we'll have money for the estate.'

'Certainly not.' Hercules dismissed the idea. 'You will continue with your studies and go to university like a gentleman.'

'But you went soldiering, Father.'

'That was different. We were at war with the French.'

Morag consoled a frustrated John when he visited. She was now the mother of a lively dark-eyed five-year-old son, Iskandar, on whom Azlan doted. Iskandar followed his cousin John around like an eager puppy.

'The chief has your best interests at heart and he doesn't want to lose you to the army,' said his aunt, giving him one of her wistful smiles that reminded him of his long-dead mother. 'And Iskandar and I don't want you going to foreign places where we won't see you again for years either.'

So John agreed to go to Aberdeen University to study classics and law, setting off in the spring on horseback with a bag of meal to help pay for his lodgings. At first he was overawed by the granite-grey city with its prestigious buildings and bustling commerce as well as a noisy harbour full of trading ships and fishing boats. The raw east winds brought the shriek of gulls and the people spoke a dialect of English that was alien to his ear. But he soon found fellow Gaelic speakers among the students and, to please his patron, he knuckled down to his studies. If he became a well-paid lawyer, he could help reverse the fortunes at Ramanish and in time take on the role of running the estate when Falkner retired.

Yet, as the summer came, John's restlessness returned and his desire to be out in the fresh air rather than labouring over books was overwhelming. He longed for the mountains of Skye and to go hunting with Azlan. The fertile farmlands of the east were monotonous to his eye, and he gazed out of his lodgings at the sea and thought how it stretched away to Norway and beyond it to the Baltic and Russia, as he had seen on his foster father's maps. He hankered to be anywhere but where he was.

* * *

Returning home for the summer only added to John's impatience with his studies. That autumn, back in Aberdeen, he fell in with a wilder group of students who spent the shortening days drinking in the city's inns and discussing politics and adventure rather than attending lectures. That year, John failed his examinations and was sent home to face a dismayed and angry Hercules.

'What am I to do with you?' his chief despaired. 'I have put myself in debt to further your education and this is how you repay me!'

'I'm sorry, sir, but it's not what I wanted,' John protested. 'The life of a lawyer is too dry and tedious.'

'Your life in Aberdeen has been anything but dry from what I am told! Drinking and carousing with the sons of Whigs and ne'er-do-wells.'

41

John beat a retreat to his aunt's house and the uncomplicated adoration of his cousin Iskandar. To add to John's unhappiness, while he'd been absent, Peigi had given her heart to Duncan, son of Willie the Piper, and a piper-in-training himself. They had been joined in a hand-fast marriage – one that bound the two lovers for a year to see if they were compatible. Rumour had it that Peigi was pregnant. Azlan swiftly took John into the mountains to hunt. Tracking deer by day with Wolf at their heels and camping under the stars at night, John unburdened himself to the wise Afridi.

'I want to go abroad and seek my fortune – make my chief proud of me as a man and not as someone who amasses money. I want to help him save the estate but I can't do it confined to books and ledgers – and there is nothing for me here.'

'I understand the hunger in you, my friend,' Azlan replied, 'and so does Hercules. He knows that he will have to let you go sooner or later.'

'Then help me persuade him to find me a commission,' John urged. 'Please, Azlan! I want to join the East India Company army and go east just like he did.'

'It is not an easy life,' Azlan cautioned, 'but one full of dangers. Many young men have died violent deaths or perished to disease before the age of thirty pursuing it.'

'My chief survived.'

Azlan gave a flash of a smile. 'He had me to watch his back.'

'Then I will find a comrade-in-arms as good as you, Azlan – one of your Afridi tribe.'

The Afghan clapped him on the back. 'If I was your age again I would go with you.'

'Do you miss your homeland?' John asked.

Azlan stared up at the stars while he stroked the back of Wolf's ears. 'This is my home now and will be till I die – *inshallah*.'

John felt a stab of envy for his chief's closest friend and companion; Azlan had proved himself a great warrior and huntsman but had now found happiness and love with Morag and Iskandar. John could not imagine being that content anywhere. Ever since he had been uprooted from Foxton as a small boy he had never felt completely settled – he would always be an outsider yearning for something just over the horizon.

* * *

It took many months of letter-writing and petitioning from Hercules to his contacts in the south – old comrades and former East India Company merchants who had grown rich on eastern trade – before the chief found a sponsor for John. It was halfway through 1827 when abruptly patronage came from a surprising source: Jeremiah Fox of Foxton Hall, who had once employed John's father as his head gardener. Perhaps Hercules had impressed on him his obligation to the orphaned John or maybe the chief had offered him some adjoining land; no one would say. But John was overjoyed at the news.

'Come September, you'll be going to the south of England to train for the Company,' Hercules told him.

John threw his arms around his foster father. 'Thank you, sir! I'll make you proud, I promise.'

'Just return to me one day,' said Hercules fondly. 'That's the only promise I ask.'

The whole village turned out to wave John off. Hercules and Azlan were to ride with him to Kyleakin where he would cross to the mainland and make his way on by coach to Inverness and then Edinburgh. From there he would sail to London.

Morag held back her tears with difficulty but Iskandar howled to see his father and beloved cousin preparing to leave. John caught sight of Peigi standing in the doorway of her house, rocking her newborn baby in her arms, and gave her a nod. She returned an embarrassed smile. It struck him how he was glad for Peigi and yet relieved not to be tied down in marriage or burdened with a child. At twenty-two he rejoiced at being without romantic ties – he had not proved himself good at judging women or keeping them happy – and perhaps he was destined to be one of those men who lived a bachelor life unwilling to commit wholeheartedly to any other.

As the three men set off along the track that skirted the lower slopes of the Cuillins, John heard a voice – his beloved Aunt Morag's – begin a tremulous chant. It was taken up by those around her, spreading among the people like flames along corn stubble until the air was ringing with their song of farewell. John's eyes stung with emotion at the tender tribute from his mother's people, who had taken him to their hearts when he had been so young and bereft. He turned at the corner, just before Ramanish disappeared from view, and raised his bonnet in a salute.

Their singing rang in his ears until he was far away – even following the tearful embraces with Hercules and Azlan – and the memory stayed with him long after the sight of his beloved Skye hills had vanished into the distance.

Chapter 7

Black Harbour Lighthouse, 1827

'You've ruined the lace on my dress!' Thomasina wailed. 'It's in shreds. Have you been bashing the washing on stones again?'

Alice looked up from her book. She had sought refuge with Sam in the lamp-room, but her sister-in-law's voice was echoing up the iron staircase. Any moment now, Thomasina's flushed and indignant face would appear from below and she would harangue her further. Alice could hear her mother trying to placate a whining William – Danny and Thomasina's demanding and spoilt son – and stop him climbing after his mother. Alice knew that Effie was worn out with running up and down stairs after the boy while Thomasina rested, heavily pregnant with her second baby. Not so immobile though, thought Alice, that Thomasina couldn't stir herself to berate her over the washing.

Sam threw Alice a look of sympathy but she knew her quiet brother was not going to intervene on her behalf. He steered well clear of domestic wrangling, preferring to keep watch over a volatile and unpredictable sea rather than try to calm the emotional storms in the lighthouse.

'I'm not your lady's maid,' Alice called out. 'If the dress is so precious you should wash it yourself.'

'You know I can't manage while I'm so heavy with child – and I've William to look after. Why can't you be more helpful to your mam? I bet you're up there readin' again.'

Alice sighed and stood up, tossing her long hair over her shoulder. 'Wish me luck going into battle,' she muttered, rolling her eyes at Sam. 'I'll try to repulse the enemy before she reaches the lamp-room.'

'What are you saying?' Thomasina demanded. 'Are you talking about me to Sam? You're always plotting against me, the two of you. What have I ever done to deserve your name-calling?'

Alice could tell by her querulous voice that Thomasina was working herself up into a state. It would end with Effie siding with the highly strung girl, chiding Alice and giving in to William's demands. It had been like this all winter, cooped up in the lighthouse all getting on each other's nerves. Her father and Danny had argued endlessly over lighthouse duties and Thomasina's spendthrift ways. Now spring had come, her father and Danny had taken the opportunity to go ashore and stock up on supplies. Arnold had wanted to take Sam but Danny had insisted on going and Sam didn't mind.

Alice had longed to go with them – she had re-read all of George Gillveray's books that she'd borrowed over the winter at least three times and was desperate for his company and conversation. She had been overjoyed when her benefactor had returned the previous year from a botany trip to the Continent without having procured a wife as had been rumoured.

But Thomasina had caused a fuss at the suggestion; why should Alice be given special treatment? Why was Mr Gillveray so interested in Alice? It wasn't seemly now she was nearly seventeen. And if anyone went ashore it should be her, Thomasina, because she missed her mother more than anything.

'Nobody's name-calling,' Alice said, meeting the other girl on the stair. 'I'm sorry if I've spoilt your dress. I'm sure Mother can mend it. Come back in the kitchen and I'll make a pot of tea.'

'I hate that foreign stuff,' Thomasina complained as Alice guided her down. 'The smell makes me sick. I don't know how you can drink it.'

'Well, I'll warm you some milk,' Alice said, trying to placate her. She could hear her mother doing the same to a fretful William on the stairs below, chivvying him outdoors.

'I don't want milk.'

Alice was about to lose patience when abruptly Thomasina crumpled into a chair.

'I hate it here! I wish Danny wasn't a lighthouse-keeper. I wish we could live onshore like normal folk. The thought of being stuck here another winter and with two bairns . . .' She hid her face in her hands and broke down sobbing.

Alice went to comfort her. 'It's been a long winter for all of us. But summer's coming now and you'll get out more – Danny can take you over to see your mother and perhaps you could spend a week or two with her?'

Thomasina looked up, her face puffy with crying. 'Do you think so?'

'Of course. Danny thinks the world of you – he'll take you if you ask him.'

'You'd like that, wouldn't you?' Thomasina was instantly suspicious. 'You'd like nothing better than to get me out the way. Then you'd have Danny to yourself. I know you've always been jealous of me.'

Alice gave up trying to please her. She went in search of her mother and William, who had gone outside to watch for the return of the lighthouse boat. Alice was determined that she would be on the next trip to the mainland; she would row herself over if she had to.

* * *

'Show me where India is,' Alice said, spinning the globe with her long fingers, her face flushed with wonder.

George Gillveray grinned as he stood beside her at the table in the library window. He knew Alice would be enchanted with the globe and had been looking forward all year to showing it off. He'd had to wait impatiently till June before she had visited; bringing back his books, she gabbled out stories as if she had had no conversation since they'd last met. He had been struck anew by her blossoming beauty, her red-blonde hair pinned loosely back from her slim face, with its high cheekbones, dimpled cheeks and large blue eyes full of merriment.

'Here,' he said, stilling the moving globe, 'this is India – and this is where we are.'

'Halfway round the world!' Alice gasped. 'And how do you get there?'

'When I first went to India it took five months to sail around the Cape,' said George, pointing out the Atlantic route, 'and then across the Arabian Sea and round into the Bay of Bengal to Calcutta.'

Alice traced her finger along the route, her lips parted in wonder. 'And now?'

'Two years ago, a ship went under steam and did the voyage in under four months.'

45

'Steam?'

'Yes, with coal-fired engines. But the quickest way to the Orient is via the Mediterranean and then travel overland through Egypt to the Red Sea. It's rough going but it's half the journey time compared to sailing around Africa.'

'We are such a small country in comparison with the rest of the world, aren't we?' Alice marvelled. 'Black Harbour Rock isn't even a dot in the sea.'

'It may not be important to the map-makers' – George smiled – 'but its lighthouse and inhabitants are very important to me.'

Alice glanced away, awkward under his scrutiny. For the first time she noticed how his hair was going grey and sparse at the temples and his once firm jaw was softening into jowls. Middle-age was robbing him of his good looks yet he was the same kind and interesting man. She knew he was fond of her and her family and it was partly for this reason that she had come seeking him out. Relationships at the lighthouse were strained to breaking point.

'Mr Gillveray,' she began and then hesitated.

'Yes, Alice?'

'I know I have no right to ask any more favours of you – you have done so much for us Browns – but I wouldn't ask just for myself.'

'You're worried about Daniel? I can tell from the things you've said.'

'Aye, I am, sir. He's not happy in his work – and his wife isn't happy living at the lighthouse – and my poor parents are worn out with all the arguing.'

'But what can I do to help?' asked George ruefully. 'I can hardly conjure up another lighthouse just to keep Daniel and Thomasina happy.'

'Not that,' Alice said with a flash of a smile. 'But what Daniel has always wanted is to have his own boat; he wants to be on the sea, not looking out at it day after day. He's an active lad. And I was thinking – well – Black Harbour doesn't have a lifeboat and it would be a good thing, given the number of ships that get into difficulty even with the lighthouse being here.' Alice gave him a direct look. 'Wouldn't it be better to have lads like Danny on hand to rescue the drowning – and get paid for their efforts – than to leave the shipwrecked to their fate and the wreckers?'

George frowned, turning to the window and gazing out to sea.

'So you are suggesting that I buy Daniel a boat?'

'It would be your boat, sir, but Danny could be employed to steer it and he could live off the bounty money from any rescues; folk will pay generously if their lives are saved. And when the boat's not needed for that, Danny can use it for fishing and the like – supply your kitchens.'

George turned and met her look. 'Where do you get your wisdom from, Alice, for one so young?'

She blushed. 'Not wisdom, just common sense – and a lot of reading, thanks to you, Mr Gillveray.'

'You're right, we should have our own rescue boat here, and not have to rely on waiting for the one from North Sunderland.' He nodded. 'Leave it with me, Alice.'

She gave him a broad smile, hardly believing that her bold request had been taken seriously. But desperation had made her forthright; she did not think her family could endure another winter incarcerated with a mulish Danny and a bickering Thomasina.

'Now,' said George, 'I want to show you this new plant I've been growing. It has the most spectacular red blooms – it's a rhododendron tree from the Himalayas.'

Alice grinned, giving the globe a triumphant spin on her way out.

* * *

Danny leapt at the chance to run Gillveray's lifeboat and was soon offering jobs to his friends as rowers. Alice did not tell him that it had been her suggestion but he guessed she had something to do with it and gave her a grateful pinch of the cheek.

'Gillveray won't be disappointed in me.' He grinned. 'Give me a couple of years and I'll be buying the boat off him.'

Thomasina lost no time in moving out of the lighthouse and back to her mother's in Black Harbour. 'She'll be glad of my help in the post office and she can give me a hand with the bairns.'

'Would you like me to come and look after William at your lying in?' Effie asked. 'Your mother will have her hands full.'

'I'm sure we can manage,' said Thomasina, 'but I'll send Danny to fetch you if you're needed.'

The days that followed their departure were eerily quiet, except for Sam's soft whistling and Effie's brisk spring-cleaning from top to bottom of their quarters.

'I miss wee William.' Alice's mother sighed, once her burst of energy had subsided. 'It'll be silent as snow this winter.'

'It'll be bliss,' Arnold said, and winked at Alice. They grinned at each other as they retreated behind their books to read.

* * *

At the end of summer, Thomasina's baby daughter arrived early and Danny came rushing out to the island to summon his mother to help out. Effie returned two weeks later, exhausted and with an infection that lay on her chest and wouldn't shift. Her coughing kept Alice awake at night yet Effie refused to send for a doctor. Slowly she recovered but as she did so, Arnold sickened. He wheezed like fire-bellows and his chest rattled and the energy drained out of him. Alarmed, Effie ordered him to bed and she and Alice took it in turns with Sam to watch the light through the night.

A week later – after a spell of calm, clear late September weather – Sam came down from the lamp-room, his fair face frowning.

'Storm's on its way. Rowing boat needs lashing.'

'I'll help you,' Arnold wheezed, struggling to sit up in the truckle bed Effie had set up next to the range for warmth.

'No, you won't,' his wife ordered. 'You're still weak as a kitten.'

'I'll go,' Alice said, quickly following Sam down the spiral staircase.

Outside, she thought Sam was being over-cautious. Only a light breeze was blowing. But within minutes the wind had completely changed direction and was lifting her hair and skirts like sails. Quickly, she helped Sam secure their open boat more tightly to the iron rings along the man-made jetty. She rushed to make sure her pet sheep, Wellington the Second, and the family's two goats were securely shut in the stone hut in the lee of the lighthouse and then retreated inside.

All evening the gales whistled and moaned around the tower. Although they felt much safer than they would have in the old rickety lighthouse – which would have bucked and groaned in such a force – their anxiety increased when the rain began. It hit the stone like gunfire.

'Let's pray that all the ships get safely to harbour this night,' whispered Effie.

'Let's hope they didn't set out,' said Arnold, spitting phlegm into a basin and lying back exhausted from the effort.

Alice watched tensely. She had never seen her father ill like this or so despondent. She went over and kissed his glistening forehead.

'Don't worry; Sam and I will keep good watch tonight and make sure the lamp burns brightly.'

* * *

Alice took the first watch. To her, there was something exhilarating about being up in the lamp-room in a storm with the wind and rain battering on the glass and the brilliant light reflecting out into the black night, illuminating the tempest. Nothing was as destructive or magnificent as a storm at sea, and she and Sam were pitted against it, tending the lamp and defying its power. She marvelled at how engineers like Stevenson and enthusiasts like Gillveray had the imagination and knowledge to create such indestructible towers – and at the courage, muscle and sweat of the builders who had hewn it out of rock.

At midnight, Sam came to relieve her. She handed him the logbook, exchanged smiles and went below to snatch some sleep before the last watch.

Something woke her. An animal shriek. Alice sat up. Was it Wellington? But that was ridiculous; she would never hear a sheep bleating in this storm. It must have been a dream. Then she heard it again; a tearing, screeching noise.

'Alice!' Sam shouted down the hatch. 'Alice, come quickly!'

She didn't even bother to pull on her dress but scrambled up the steps in her undergarments. Sam was gripping the telescope, staring out into the dark.

'What is it?' Alice asked, but even as she did so, dread clawed at her belly.

'Oh God!' Sam moaned. 'They've hit the Black Needle.'

Alice peered out at the hellish night.

'I don't see—'

Suddenly the light swung around and lit up the reef like a flash of lightning. A ship was impaled on the rocks, its bows pointing up to the sky as if in supplication. Its main mast was gone. Seconds later it was plunged into darkness again. But the noise – the terrible grinding shriek of splintering timber – could be heard above the gales.

'It's breaking up,' said Sam.

48

Alice held her breath as they waited for the light to flash again. Waves the size of cliffs crashed over the reef and tossed the stricken vessel about as if it were as light as a toy.

'Perhaps it will hold together,' Alice whispered. But she knew in her heart that it wouldn't. The storm was as ferocious as any she had witnessed. 'Oh please God, save the people!' she gasped, taking the telescope and searching the ship.

Minutes later, Alice and Sam watched in horror as faraway figures leapt from the sinking ship into the foaming, raging sea.

'What can we do?' Alice demanded.

'Nothing,' said Sam. 'You know we can't.'

She covered her face in her hands, unable to bear the sight of the passengers drowning and being helpless to prevent it.

Sam handed her the log. 'Fill it in. That's something you can do.'

Alice wanted to throw it at her brother. How could he be so callous? But as he set about tending the lamp she sat and recorded their work with shaking hands and found it calmed her nerves. What use were her tears or cries to the shipwrecked? She too had to weather the storm and pray there might be survivors to be rescued in the dawn.

'Danny will go out and fetch them in, won't he?' said Alice. 'Any who last the night?'

Sam gave her a sorrowful look and then nodded. 'Aye, likely he'll be out there as soon as he can.'

* * *

Weak grey light came with the dawn yet the sea still boiled like an overfilled pot and the rain continued to splatter at the windows. The ship had sunk below the waves. Alice's heart ached at the sight. Sam went below to report the night's tragedy to his parents. Alice heard their anxious voices and her mother's cry of anguish. But she couldn't go below – not while there was a chance of spotting survivors. Sam had been fatalistic.

'They've gone. All we can do is report the wreck and pray for their souls.'

Stubbornly, Alice kept watch, her tired eyes straining at the telescope for any sign of life. Even if one passenger or crew member survived it would be worth Danny's boat being launched to save them. As the sky lightened to a pewter grey, she circled the lamp-room and looked anxiously to shore. She wondered if George too had watched the shipwreck in misery from his mansion. But there was nothing stirring on the shore and no sign of Danny's boat. Gillveray must think it too dangerous to send his men out to sea when the storm was still so severe.

Alice sighed. She would take one last look and then go below and try to sleep – if she could ever rid her mind of those desperate people jumping to their deaths.

Through the spray, something caught her eye. She raised the telescope and trained it on the low jagged rocks west of the Black Needle. Something was caught there; the mast that had sheared off before the ship had sunk.

Alice tried to steady her shaking hands. She gasped and nearly dropped the spy glass. 'Sam!' she yelled. 'Sam, there are folk on the rocks. Quickly, come look!'

49

An incredulous Sam confirmed what Alice had spotted. 'There're six or seven of them,' he gasped. 'How in God's name have they—'

'They must've hung onto the mast and been carried onto the rocks,' Alice cried. 'We have to help them.'

'We can't.'

'Aye, we can! In the rowing boat.'

'Father's not well enough and I can't manage the boat on my own and pull people out of the water.'

'I'll help you.'

Sam's look was doubtful.

'The lifeboat is still nowhere to be seen,' Alice said urgently, 'and those people can't hang on much longer. We must at least try.' She took him by the arm. 'Can you stand by and watch them drown like those poor souls last night, Sam? 'Cause I can't!'

Sam nodded and without further argument they clattered downstairs to report the sighting to their parents. Effie shrieked at the idea of them putting their lives at risk so recklessly but Arnold supported them.

'If there's no sign of the lifeboat then you must go. It should be me doing it,' he said, 'but Alice will just have to take my place. We can't stand by and let these people drown. It's our Christian duty as lighthouse-keepers.'

Pulling on oilskins and boots, Alice and Sam hurried below. The wind nearly knocked them off the outer steps. Alice clung to her brother as they slithered across the rocks to the rowing boat. Thankfully, Sam's tightening of the rope the previous day had kept it secure.

Alice almost fell into the boat as Sam unlashed it from its moorings. She grabbed at the oars to stop them flying overboard. Sam took them from her and rowed away from the jetty. As soon as they were out of the meagre shelter of the natural harbour, the sea tossed them about like flotsam. In minutes they were soaked through as waves crashed over the sides. Sam gritted his teeth and made for the outer rocks, his bulky arms straining against the force of the sea. Strong though he was, Alice could see him quickly tiring. Crawling forward in the boat, she squeezed onto the bench beside him and took over the starboard oar.

They pulled in unison. Spray stung her face and hair whipped into her eyes but Alice clenched her teeth and thought of nothing but keeping a rhythm – and of the desperate people stranded on the deathly reef.

As they drew nearer the rocks, the survivors began to cry out. Through the spray, Alice could make out a couple of men and, astonishingly, a woman and a girl huddled on the rock just above them with one of the crew, a cabin boy wearing a sailor's neckerchief, who hardly looked older than the terrified child.

'Oh, thank the Lord!' the woman sobbed.

Alice and Sam tried to manoeuvre the rowing boat near enough for them to scramble aboard but the swell was too great. They risked either being dashed against the rocks or sucked under by the pull of the waves. They bobbed helplessly. The men – one young, one older – looked grey-faced with cold and exhaustion. Perhaps they had used up all their energy pulling the others to safety. The child and cabin boy were whimpering in fear while the mother exhorted their rescuers not to give up.

'You must save us! God has sent you. Please help – I beg you! At least take my girl! I care not for myself but don't let Mary die!'

Alice was in awe of the woman's fierce determination to save her daughter even if the rest were to perish.

'Give me both oars,' she shouted to Sam. 'I'll try to keep the boat steady while you reach out for them.'

Sam did not argue. Alice took his oar as he scrambled towards the bows. She clamped her jaw at the pain in her shoulders as the sea tried to wrench the oars away. She held on and pulled hard. The boat lurched back towards the rock. Sam braced himself against the bow and stretched out his arms.

'Work your way towards me!' he bellowed.

The younger man, strongly built, roused himself from his comatose state. 'Come on; don't be afraid,' he encouraged the woman and child. 'Give me your hand.'

'Take Mary first,' the woman urged.

The young man took the girl onto his right shoulder – his left arm was hanging useless and bloodied where his jacket had torn away – and struggled down the rock. Sam reached out and grabbed her.

He placed the shocked girl behind him in the boat and leant out to take the woman next. She was hanging on tightly to the injured man who was helping her down the rock, his face a grimace.

One by one, Sam hauled the survivors into the rocking boat, while Alice wrestled with the oars to keep the craft as close to the rocks as she could. Her arms burnt with pain and exertion. The cabin boy and the older man were pulled aboard. Just the younger man was left on the rock. As Sam reached to help him, a wave crashed over the bows and knocked him back. The boat seesawed dangerously and spun around. The stern was now facing the rock and Alice could see the man clearly for the first time. He was half-submerged in the water where he had scrambled towards Sam. His dark hair was plastered to his face – a handsome young face scored with exhaustion – and his eyes held her look. She knew that if she glanced away he might give up, the effort too much.

Alice half stood, wrested an oar from its rowlock and thrust it towards him.

'Grab it!' she yelled.

He gave a low roar and, with the last of his strength, struck out for the oar. He held on with his right arm. Alice almost lost her balance. Then Sam was beside her, pulling on the oar too. Just as the man reached the stern, the boat bucked again and struck his head. He lost his grip on the oar.

'No!' Alice screamed as she lost sight of him.

Sam pushed past her and leant overboard. He grabbed at the torn jacket before it sank from view and pulled hard. The man reappeared. They locked arms and Sam fought to haul him from the treacherous waves. Alice leant out and grabbed his other arm. Pain was seared across his face but she heaved at his wounded limb.

Moments later, they dragged him aboard and all three lay panting in the stern.

'We're heading for the rocks again!' the woman shrieked.

The cabin boy had moved forward to hang onto the oars.

'Good lad,' Sam panted, steadying himself and taking the oars from him.

'I c-can help,' the youth said through chattering teeth.

Together they rowed away from the rocks. But very quickly Alice could see that the young sailor was completely spent and no match for Sam's strength. She clambered back and told the boy to look after the injured man who was lying unconscious at their feet. She took up the other oar. With all the strength left to them, Alice and Sam rowed as hard as they could back towards the island.

As they made it to the island jetty, Alice's heart swelled to see both her parents waiting in the wind and rain to help them all ashore. The cabin boy and Sam shouldered the injured man and then Effie was taking Mary from the exhausted arms of her mother and hurrying up the lighthouse steps.

Twenty minutes later, the five survivors and their rescuers were safely in the lighthouse kitchen, wrapped in blankets and being served hot broth and tea, while a fussing Effie hung up their sodden garments to dry and rubbed numb hands and feet back to life. Only the young man appeared badly injured by their ordeal; Effie had bandaged his left arm and the gash to his forehead and put him into the truckle bed in which Arnold had been recuperating. He lay with his eyes closed, his breathing shallow, too weak to eat more than a mouthful of broth.

'That brave young man saved my Mary's life,' the woman, called Martha Scott, told them, her voice full of emotion. 'Slipped from my grasp, she did. But he held onto her even while the mast was crushing him against the rocks – that's how his arm got injured. He did it for my Mary.'

The woman could not hold back her tears of relief. They came flooding down her cheeks as she rocked her daughter in her arms.

From the older man, a merchant called Hobson, they learnt that the ship *Berwickshire* had set out from Leith with a cargo of whisky and beef cattle bound for London. There had been more than twenty passengers on board. It was the cabin boy Peter's first voyage. Mrs Scott was going to visit her sister, who was about to set sail for a new life in Canada.

'I think our young friend over there was on his way to join a regiment – he's from the Highlands,' said Mr Hobson. 'You can tell from his clothes he's a gentleman.'

'He's called Sinclair,' said Peter.

'His name's John,' Mary spoke up suddenly. They were the first words the girl had uttered since being rescued. 'He said we weren't going to drown 'cause he wears a lucky Spanish penny round his neck that would keep us safe. And it has, hasn't it?'

'Yes, my sweet pea' – her mother kissed her head and smiled – 'it has indeed.'

52

Chapter 8

Alice woke after a dreamless sleep to hear the chatter of voices in the kitchen above and for a moment wondered who their visitors could be. Then the ordeal of the previous hours came rushing back. It was growing dark again already. She dragged herself out of bed and put on clean, dry clothes; it would soon be time to light the lamp. She could hear her father's wheezing breath coming from beyond the partition; the effort to help had put him back in bed.

Upstairs, Mrs Scott and Effie were cooking potatoes to go with slices of ham, hunks of bread and churned goat's butter. Mr Hobson was reading one of Arnold's out-of-date newspapers and Peter was playing cards with Mary. John Sinclair was still asleep, his pallor grey and glistening.

'He hasn't stirred for hours,' Martha Scott said worriedly.

'Rest's what he needs,' said Effie.

After they had all eaten, Effie and Alice organised beds for their stranded guests. Martha and Mary bedded down in Danny's old room, while Hobson and Peter shared Sam's.

'We could give Mr Sinclair my room to himself,' Alice suggested, 'so he wouldn't be disturbed.'

'I don't think we should move him yet,' said Effie. 'He's still cold to the touch, poor laddie.'

Alice knew that her mother, on hearing John was a fellow Highlander, was feeling protective towards him.

'I'll keep an eye on him between watches,' Alice offered.

* * *

While Sam took the middle watch, Alice sat dozing in the candlelight beside John. At times he moaned in his sleep and cried out. She bathed his brow with a cloth – he was alternately shivering and sweating, his forehead burning hot yet his fingers icy cold. A worn coin depicting a helmeted head lay on a chain around his neck. His lucky Spanish coin. After a moment's hesitation, Alice loosened his shirt, blushing at the touch of his chest hairs, and gently wiped away the sweat from his upper body.

She whispered soothing words though she doubted he could hear her. 'Don't fret, Mr Sinclair, you are safe now. We'll make you better again. And we'll send word to your family as soon as we can.'

She wondered who his family might be. Would word already have spread about the sinking of *Berwickshire*? Did he have a wife or a sweetheart who would be out of their minds with worry? For a while he would settle into a calmer sleep but it wouldn't last. By morning he was babbling incoherently.

'It's not the Gaelic he's speaking,' Effie said, baffled.

'Maybe it's Spanish,' said Mary. 'He said his Grandpa Carlos was Spanish.'

'Do you think he needs a doctor?' asked Martha in concern.

'No one can get out here safely in this swell,' said Effie. 'We'll just have to do our best and pray he pulls through.'

53

'He will,' said Alice stoutly, 'I know he will.' She could not say that she had seen it in his eyes, that moment of destiny out on the reef, when she had known his determination to live.

* * *

He was swimming up from a deep pool – like the one below the waterfall at Ramanish where he would plunge in naked after a day in the saddle – holding his breath. Then, just as his lungs were about to burst, he broke the surface of the water.

John woke with a start, gulping for air. A cool hand touched his cheek, pushed back his hair. He opened his eyes and saw her.

It was the face in his dreams – that of a Viking princess with high-boned cheeks, vivid blue eyes and a riot of copper hair falling over her shoulders. She watched him intently with those large blue eyes. He had seen her before; he was quite sure of it.

Her lips parted and let go a small gasp. 'You're awake.'

He gave a weak smile, his breath ragged as he answered. 'I'm not sure I am. Unless my dream has become reality.'

She laughed softly, her cheeks dimpling and turning pink. 'Is that the famous Highland charm?'

He licked his dry lips. 'How do you know where I come from?' His head pounded as he tried to remember where he was.

'Your fellow passengers told us what they know of you, Mr Sinclair.'

It came back to him with a jolt. The storm and the pitching ship. The shrieking as the lamps smashed and plunged them into darkness. The scramble to get out on deck. He had managed to grab a screaming Mrs Scott and her daughter and hang onto some rigging – they'd been thrown clear of the sinking ship and others had come too.

He gulped. 'Did they . . . Who managed . . . ? Is the wee lass . . . ?'

'Aye, Mrs Scott and Mary are safe, thanks to you. And Mr Hobson and one of the crew – Peter from Leith. They're all fine. Eating us out of house and home but in good health and spirits.' She hesitated and then added, 'I'm afraid that no one else has survived. Were you travelling with friends or family?'

He shook his head, feeling his eyes sting, and for a moment was too overwhelmed to speak. In what unimaginable terror had the others drowned? She appeared to understand and kept talking. He liked her strong voice with its sing-song accent.

'You've been here four days – had a touch of fever. We moved you into this room to have a bit of quiet. The others are longing to get off the island now and on with their lives.'

He looked around, feeling dazed. The tiny room had curved walls with an inset cupboard and a flower-shaped window. He was lying on a narrow bed with a simple table supporting a tower of books beside it.

'Where am I?'

'In Black Harbour lighthouse.'

It sparked a memory; his eyes widened. 'You were the one rowing the boat!'

54

She nodded.

'You saved my life. Or else you are an angel and I've gone to my maker?'

She smiled. 'Not an angel; just the lighthouse-keeper's daughter.'

'An angel of mercy then.' He smiled back. 'A very brave and beautiful one.' He was pleased to see the compliment brought another flush to her cheeks.

'They say you are joining a regiment in London?'

'Not exactly,' said John. 'I'm going to train at Addiscombe for the East India Company army.' He shifted and tried to sit up but a pain shot down his left arm and his head began to pound again. Only the pretty young woman had distracted him temporarily from how weak and ill he felt.

'Don't move.' She put out a hand to stop him. 'You need to rest.' She stood up. 'Do you think you could manage some soup now and a mug of beer?'

'Only if you are the one serving it,' John answered.

She rolled her eyes and stepped towards the door.

'Wait,' he said. 'Does my angel of mercy have a name?'

He saw her lips twitch in amusement or impatience. 'Miss Alice Brown. But you may call me Alice.'

'Thank you, Alice,' he replied. 'Thank you for helping me.'

She gave a quick nod, as if his gratitude embarrassed her. Then, with a swish of skirt and a flick of burnished hair over her shoulder, she disappeared from the room.

* * *

Alice hummed as she prepared a bowl of vegetable soup, mashing the lumps of potato and carrot to make them easier to swallow. She was so relieved that the young Highlander had survived the fever and appeared to be over the worst. After two days, they had carried him down to Alice's room; Mr Hobson and Peter had contracted heavy colds and they did not want John's condition to be made worse by any contagion.

The women had managed to keep his wounds clean and free of infection and they believed he should recover fully given time. He was weak but well enough to tease her, she thought wryly. As Alice stirred the pot, she couldn't prevent a smile at the memory of his calling her an angel. She knew it was a young man's attempt at flattery, yet she had done more for him than anyone had asked, spending long hours tending him and willing him to live.

To him, she was a stranger. But to her, John had become dearly familiar. She had bathed him and brought down his temperature, changed his dressings and sung to him when he cried out in a strange language. Her mother and Martha had taken turns wetting his lips and wiping his brow but it was she, Alice, who had sat with him the most. She could not tell anyone how much she liked to gaze at John's strong-jawed face, with its straight nose and firm, generous mouth; how she delighted in his dark lashes and the way his black hair licked around his temples. When she pressed a cool cloth to his forehead, she saw how pale her fingers were against his nut-brown skin, skin that told of a man who relished the outdoor life.

55

She could have dismissed her desire to be with him as the dedication of one human trying to save the life of another. But when he had opened his eyes – those startling green eyes – and focused on her, Alice had felt her stomach twist and her heart lurch in a way it had never done before. Then the way he had spoken her name in his Highland lilt had made her heart melt further.

'Can I come and see John too?' Mary asked.

Alice smiled at the girl. 'Aye, you can help me feed him. He's been asking after you.'

'Has he?'

'Yes. Can you carry the mug of beer with two hands?'

* * *

It was noon on the fifth day before the sea had calmed enough for a boat to finally make it out to the lighthouse. Danny and his crewmen arrived with much needed supplies for the Browns.

'Gillveray has sent these – and us to fetch the shipwrecked,' he told his parents. 'He's been watching out since the storm.'

'Thank the Lord,' cried Martha. 'We've been such a burden to your kind family.'

'No burden,' said Effie, though Alice could see the relief on her mother's face. Martha hugged Effie.

But Danny was surly. 'You could have been on the mainland days ago if we'd been allowed to do our job – but Gillveray wouldn't risk the lifeboat even though me and the lads pleaded with him.'

Sam looked up from trimming the wick of a kitchen lamp. 'You mean you didn't have the stomach for it.'

Danny was immediately riled. 'It was our job to fetch them off the rocks – you've stolen our bounty. Me and my crew need it more than you.'

'That's enough, lads,' Arnold said, his voice still croaky though he had insisted on taking his turn in the lamp-room since the shipwreck.

But Sam squared up to his brother. 'If they'd waited for you, these people would've been drowned. Me and Alice couldn't have left them.'

'Alice?' Danny was incredulous.

'Aye, she helped row the boat. Father was too poorly.'

'Yes,' Hobson spoke up, 'your sister has been a true heroine. We will always be indebted to her and your family.'

Danny seemed nonplussed by this. He gave Alice a resentful look but said no more, curtly instructing two of his men to help the survivors down to the boat.

'One of the passengers, John Sinclair, is not well enough to go yet,' said Alice firmly. 'He was injured in the storm. Perhaps you could get word to his family that he is alive?'

Danny noticed the way a blush came to his sister's cheeks. 'I can post a note,' he agreed.

Alice hurried below to take a message from John, which she wrote down swiftly and gave to her brother. Danny's interest was piqued.

56

'Hercules MacAskill of Ramanish? Is he one of the gentry then, this young lad?'

'MacAskill is his foster father. John was orphaned very young.'

'Rich then, is he?'

'I don't think so. That's why he's going to join the army and seek his fortune.'

'How do you know so much about him?'

Alice felt herself go hot. Since John had gained consciousness they had talked much to each other about their lives. 'I've been nursing him.'

Her brother gave her a teasing wink, like the Danny of old. 'I'll come back for him in the next week or two if you signal he's well enough to travel,' he offered.

She smiled. 'Thanks, Danny.'

There were hasty goodbyes and promises to send money to recompense the family for their hospitality, which Effie and Arnold protested were not necessary.

The Browns waved their new friends away, standing in the autumnal sunshine. Effie gave a sigh of relief as they turned back to the lighthouse. 'They were good folk,' she said, 'but I'm glad it'll be just us again.'

Arnold gave Alice a quizzical look. 'Not quite just us – there's the young soldier still under our roof.'

'Alice is looking after him so well,' Effie said, 'that the laddie will soon be back on his feet.'

Alice turned swiftly, so that they would not see the smile on her lips, and dashed eagerly up the steps ahead of her parents.

* * *

'Trumped!' Alice cried, slamming down her nine of hearts on John's king of spades.

'You win again.' John grinned. 'It's just as well we're not playing for money.'

He sat back at the kitchen table, his arm in a sling. Over it, he wore a rough woollen shirt of Sam's – the only one that would fit his broad frame.

Alice laughed. 'So how will you repay me?'

John glanced across the kitchen to where Effie was churning butter. The Brown father and son were out fishing. He lowered his voice.

'With a poem to your beauty and cleverness at cards.'

Alice smothered a giggle.

'Will you be writing it in English or the Gaelic?' the watchful Effie asked him in Gaelic.

John threw back his head in laughter, answering her in their native tongue. 'The Gaelic, of course. It's the language of love, is it not? I will tell how Alice got her beauty and bravery from her mother.'

Effie turned back vigorously to her task without answering.

'What are you saying?' Alice demanded. 'It isn't fair that you talk about me in secret.'

'Like the bards of old, I shall write about the beauty and generosity of my patrons here on Black Harbour Island. You shall be remembered in verse long after I am gone.'

57

Alice smiled but it pained her to hear him talk of when he would be gone. Although she longed for his recovery, she dreaded the day he would have to leave. Each day with John seemed to fly too quickly. She felt no desire to be anywhere else but in his company; she no longer thought of trying to get over to see Gillveray or stock up on books from his library. Her keenness to visit Black Harbour House had dwindled since the rescue in the storm.

One day, ten days after the shipwreck, John emerged from his bedchamber with his arm out of its sling. He pulled on his own jacket, the torn sleeve of which Alice had mended. Alice looked at him in dismay.

'Walk with me outside, Alice,' he bade her with a defiant look at Effie. Arnold was sleeping after his shift and Sam was out digging up potatoes.

Effie let them go with a nod. Alice knew her mother had a soft spot for the young Highlander.

Outside, the sea was calm and the sky cloudless. He took her hand and slipped her arm through his as they walked across the narrow island, out of sight of the lighthouse windows. She thrilled at his touch. They could see for miles; from Gillveray's grazing land in the west to the rim of sparkling sea beyond the Black Needle. It was impossible to imagine how deadly the sea had been the night of the storm that had thrown Alice and John together. He stared out to sea, his green eyes narrowed in thought, and Alice braced herself for what he was going to say, for she knew their time together was almost done.

Turning to face her, John said, 'Dearest Alice, it's time that I was going. If I delay much longer I will miss my chance of a commission in the East India Company. And I cannot let down my chief after all he has done for me.'

Alice gulped and nodded, her heart leaden.

'Besides, your parents have been more than generous to me and I must not be a burden to them any longer.'

'Not a burden,' Alice insisted.

'But I want you to know that I go with a heavy heart,' he continued. 'I have grown to care for you greatly. You must know that, Alice?'

She looked into his eyes and saw the same mixture of passion and sorrow that she felt. Her tears brimmed. John cupped her face in his strong hands and brushed away the spilling tears with his thumbs.

'I care for you too, very much,' she whispered. 'I don't want you to go.'

'My darling girl, I hoped as much,' he murmured and then bent to kiss her lips.

Alice felt a jolt go through her like a lightning bolt. She pressed her lips back against his. She had dreamt about kissing them so often, she could hardly believe it was happening. His good arm went about her waist and pulled her to him. She was heady at the contact, his mouth covering her face with hungry, tender kisses.

He winced when she put her arms about him.

'Sorry! Your arm . . .'

'Don't be sorry.' He smiled. 'I would endure twice as much pain just to have you embrace me, my sweet Alice.'

They kissed again, Alice's heart thudding at her daring. She knew they were being reckless and that he was about to disappear out of her life but she couldn't stop herself. She had never felt so in love or alive as she did at that moment. Who cared about the future?

58

'Alice,' John murmured in her ear. 'Oh, Alice.'

Just then they heard Sam holler. Alice sprang away from John. Her brother appeared on the far side of the island, waving at them.

'Boat's coming! Danny's boat!'

'But we didn't signal for him,' Alice said in dismay.

John grasped her hands in his. 'There's something I wish to say.' His eyes gleamed; there was an urgency to his words.

'What is it?' Alice could hardly breathe for the panic that gripped her. They might never have the chance to be alone again, ever.

'Marry me, Alice!'

She stared at him, open-mouthed. She must have misheard him.

'I want no other lass but you,' John insisted, his look penetrating. 'I know it must seem sudden to you but I've known since that moment I saw you in the boat – my angel of mercy – that you were the girl I wanted as my wife.' His grip on her hands was warm and encouraging, willing her to agree. 'If you say no, I will go with a sore heart but at least I will have no regret that I asked. Regrets are for things left unsaid.'

Sam shouted for them to come and something about visitors.

Alice swallowed. 'Yes,' she said, her voice hoarse with emotion. 'Yes, John, I will marry you!'

He let out an exultant roar, crushed her to him and gave her a long passionate kiss on the lips, not caring that they were now in Sam's view.

'Come away with me then,' John said rashly. 'Let us go south together and be married. We'll start a life of adventure. You'll come with me to India.'

'India?' Alice gasped. She thought of that faraway land of heat and wild beasts, of strange customs, exotic blooms and snow-capped mountains that Gillveray had told her about. Then she thought of the distance on Gillveray's globe and the long hazardous voyage that would take her so very far away from her family and the only place she knew as home.

Alice felt doubt creep in. For all she loved John with a passion that shook her to the core, she had only known him for such a short while – less than two weeks. She couldn't run away with him. What a scandal that would cause her parents! She couldn't be so cruel.

'You look unsure,' said John. 'I promise you I would never leave you. I am not one of those men who woo a woman for his own gratification only to abandon her when he has no more need of her. I swear on the grave of my beloved mother I will treat you well all your life, Alice.'

'I believe you,' Alice said, her pulse racing at his earnest words. 'But my parents might not. If we are to be married we must do it properly.'

'Then we shall go to the mainland at once and find a priest,' John declared.

'No.' Alice was firm. 'When you get to Addiscombe, you must write to my father and ask his permission. Then I will have time to plant the idea in his mind by telling him about your good qualities and what a grand match we would make.'

Frustration crossed his handsome face and then John smiled. 'If that is what it takes to make you happy, then that is what I shall do, sweet Alice.'

'Thank you, John.' She leant up and kissed him again.

'But I will have a hard job not snatching you away with me.' He grinned and lead her back towards the gesticulating Sam.

* * *

Danny had not come for John. He had brought strangers from the mainland who wanted to meet Alice. One was a writer from a newspaper in Newcastle; the other was an artist who wished to paint her portrait. Alice looked in frustration at John. With these men around there would be no chance of any final private words or kisses.

'There is very great interest in you, Miss Brown,' said Moxon, the journalist. 'There is a penny sheet circulating about your heroic deeds.'

Alice looked baffled. 'What penny sheet?'

'Look at this,' Danny said, thrusting a creased piece of paper at her. 'Says you're a heroine and no other lass has ever been as brave. It's selling like hot cakes in the village and beyond.'

'Let me see.' Arnold frowned, taking it and reading. 'Who wrote it?'

'Someone without the gift for journalism,' Moxon said with disdain. 'No doubt he paid one of the survivors for their story.' He smiled at Alice. 'But I would like to hear the story from you. Your brother Daniel says no one has been out here yet. Would you do me the honour of allowing me to be the first to interview you?'

Alice felt embarrassed. 'Why don't you ask Sam? He did more than me to save those poor folk.' She looked around but Sam had not followed them inside.

John spoke up. 'Sam couldn't have done it without you. I saw your bravery with my own eyes.'

Moxon pulled out a small notebook and began to write. 'And you must be John Sinclair, the injured one?'

'Our Alice has been nursing him,' Danny said. 'He owes his life to my sister.'

'I do indeed,' said John, giving Alice a tender look.

Flustered, Alice asked, 'What do you say, Father?'

'I don't see the harm in giving your version of the story,' Arnold said. 'Better to have the truth told than fanciful claims.'

'Exactly,' Danny agreed. 'And Mr Collins would like to sketch you for the newspaper too.'

Alice wondered why Danny was now enthusiastic about her rescue in the storm. Perhaps these men were paying him well for bringing them out to the island? But he needed to provide for a young family so she wouldn't begrudge him. Reluctantly, she agreed to be interviewed.

At the end, Alice insisted, 'You will make it plain that I was only there helping Sam and that he did the lion's share of rescuing the shipwrecked?'

'Of course,' said Moxon. 'Sam will get his due. But I can't deny that it is your story that our readers want to hear. You are a remarkable young woman.'

Effie looked worried. 'I hope this isn't going to bring more people to our door bothering my daughter? We live quietly and don't want fuss.'

'A week or two of interest is all you will have to endure,' predicted Moxon.

They left shortly afterwards – having eaten half a ham and a loaf of bread – with Danny rowing them back to shore and taking John with him. Alice hardly noticed the looks of unease on her parents' faces; she was too heartbroken at John's departure. They had exchanged longing looks as John had raised her hand to his lips in courteous farewell. But he had been unable to say more than general pleasantries and thanks.

Over the next few days, she imagined him travelling on south by stagecoach or on horseback. Or had he taken another ship from Newcastle? She had not had time to ask. And where exactly was Addiscombe? All she knew was that it was south of London. She would ask Gillveray.

It struck Alice how she had hardly given her benefactor a thought over the past weeks. She felt restless on the island, unable to settle to the everyday tasks that normally brought her satisfaction: tending the animals, trimming the lamps and keeping the log. Even reading books could not distract her from thoughts of John and their rash plans to marry. Would it really happen? One day soon, a letter would come from John to her father asking permission – only then would the fantastical idea become a reality.

Chapter 9

Alice was aghast at the feverish interest of complete strangers in her and the lighthouse. She was quite unprepared for the sudden unwanted attention from others – people who she had never met or heard of – that she attracted. Danny brought out boatloads of inquisitive trippers to Black Harbour Island to show them around and meet his sister. The article in *The Newcastle Messenger* had been taken up and repeated in other regional broadsheets and then national newspapers.

The public could not get enough of Alice's heroic story. Pamphlets began to appear about her. These, along with artists' impressions of Alice rowing through the terrible storm, were sold in Thomasina's mother's post office.

'That wretched journalist!' cried Effie. 'He knew we wanted to be left alone. And why are you bringing all these folk here to poke their noses into our home, Daniel?'

'You should be pleased that Alice is so famous now,' said Danny. 'They're raising money for her and Sam.'

'Money,' Sam said scathingly. 'That's all you care about, isn't it? You and Thomasina.'

'It's only fair that we all benefit from a piece of good fortune,' Danny retorted.

'Good fortune?' Alice exclaimed. 'That shipwreck was a terrible thing.'

'Not for you! Look at all these letters I've brought from your new admirers.'

Alice was embarrassed by them. Men were writing to her from far and wide wanting to correspond with her, asking to meet her, to paint her portrait or offering her marriage and riches. Many of the letters looked as if they had already been opened. Alice suspected Thomasina was reading them before sending them on with Danny.

The one letter that she looked out for – the only one she wanted with all her heart – was from John. But none came, either for her or for her father. She was beset with worry that some other ill luck had befallen him. As Danny left on one occasion, having argued hotly with his parents and Sam over the continuing boat trips of sightseers, Alice gave him a letter to post.

Danny eyed the name and address of Addiscombe College with interest. 'I bet Father doesn't know you're writing to that soldier?'

'I just wish to know he got safely to his new quarters,' Alice said, blushing but defiant.

'I don't think you should encourage him. You can make a better match than that Scotch lad.' Danny was reluctant to take it. 'You can have your pick of rich men now, from what I hear.'

'That is my business,' Alice said. 'If you won't post this letter, I'll take it myself.'

'Give it here.' Danny relented.

* * *

Winter storms brought relief from the constant intrusion of boat trippers to the island. For once, Effie and Arnold were thankful for the bad weather. Alice could tell that having to entertain these strangers in her home and feeling obliged to give them refreshments had taken its toll on her mother. She looked ill and anxious.

Sometimes, through the partition wall that divided their bedchambers, Alice overheard urgent whisperings between her parents but the only words she could make out clearly were when they spoke her name. She felt wretched for bringing this unwanted attention to their door. Many were the times she wished it had not been her who had gone out in the boat in the storm that fateful night. Yet, if she had not, she would never have met or saved John.

Oh, John! What was he doing and why didn't he write? Had he changed his mind about marriage? Had his feelings shrivelled like the last autumn leaves? As the winter dragged on, Alice's longing for him strengthened rather than weakened. Yet she would not send another letter begging for him to write to her until he answered the first.

* * *

The spring of 1828 arrived and Alice took a rare trip over to the mainland with her father to collect provisions and visit Gillveray. Perhaps a letter from John would be waiting at the post office? She would go straight there to visit her nephew and niece. As soon as she arrived in the village, Alice attracted a crowd all eager to speak to her.

'What was it like in that storm?'

'Were you frightened, Alice?'

'How much money have they given you for saving them?'

'Is it true you're going to meet the king?'

'Can I have a lock of your hair for good luck?'

Alice was overwhelmed. 'I-I did nothing,' she stammered, 'nothing that you wouldn't have done if put in the same position.'

Arnold steered her away but at the post office more people gathered to gape at her.

Thomasina bustled around with an air of importance. 'Give us some peace.' She shooed people out. 'She's come to visit me and my family.'

Alice noticed how there were pin cushions and hair ribbons on sale claiming to be made from 'bits of the heroine's frock'. She recognised the material from Thomasina's dress with the lace collar that had caused such friction between them the previous year.

Alice and her father made a fuss over the children, Arnold giving William a toy boat that Sam had made him while Alice picked up baby Lucy.

She smiled and tickled the baby's chin. 'You're a bonny one.' Lucy gurgled and grabbed Alice's cheek.

'Have you brought anything for her?' Thomasina asked.

'Sorry, no,' said Alice. 'But Mother sends her love.'

Thomasina looked annoyed. 'I hear you're getting a fortune from that subscription they're raising for you and Sam. Going to be a ceremony with the Duke of Northumberland handing it over. Mr Gillveray's inviting all the posh folk.'

63

'I don't know anything about it,' Alice said, embarrassed. 'I haven't been to see Mr Gillveray yet.'

'Hundreds of pounds, we've heard,' Thomasina said, her eyes gleaming. 'I hope you'll be sharing it with your family.'

'It's up to Alice how she chooses to spend her money,' Arnold said in irritation. 'But I know she will be wise with it.'

'Danny deserves that money as much as her or Sam,' Thomasina said, bristling. 'For all them years working the light.'

Arnold snorted. 'Sam and Alice work twice as hard as Daniel ever did.'

Alice intervened. 'Of course I'll share whatever I get. I'd like to give the bairns something.'

'It's only fair that you do,' Thomasina said. 'You took what was rightfully Danny's. He runs the lifeboat and should have had the chance to pick up the shipwrecked, not you and Sam. I think it was selfish of you, Alice—'

'How dare you!' Arnold stood up. 'The only selfish woman round here is you. Selfish and greedy. Alice doesn't have to give you anything.'

'Father . . .'

'We have business to attend to,' he snapped, 'and can't stay.' He marched to the door.

'Can I go with you, Grandpa?' said William.

'No, you can't.' Thomasina grabbed him and held him back. He squealed in protest.

In dismay, Alice put Lucy back in her crib. 'I'll call again soon.' She hesitated. 'Are there any letters for me?'

Thomasina gave her a resentful look. 'I gave them to Danny. He'll bring them out to the island – not that he'll get any thanks for all his efforts.'

'Thank you.' Alice's hopes rose to think there might be one from John among the other unwanted correspondence.

Outside, hurrying down a back lane, Alice remonstrated with her father. 'Weren't you a bit hard on the lass? She's just sticking up for Danny and her bairns.'

'Mark my words,' said Arnold, 'she's the one behind all this money-making of Danny's – we haven't had a minute's peace since he brought that journalist to the lighthouse, and we won't hear the end of it till she's got every last penny out of you.'

Alice was shocked by her father's bitterness.

'She can have it,' Alice said, dispirited. 'I didn't look for any of this.'

Arnold stopped. Suddenly his anger collapsed. He looked inexpressibly sad as he touched her cheek. 'Dear daughter; I know you didn't.'

* * *

Things were strained between Danny and his parents when he next came to the island, bringing the first of the spring visitors to gaze at the lighthouse and its heroine. While they roamed the island, a row broke out in the lighthouse kitchen.

'Don't you bring any more boatloads!' Arnold barked. 'Your mother can't cope with it. She's bad with her nerves. I won't have you hounding her to an early grave just so you can line your pockets.'

Effie said nothing as she huddled by the black range. She had hardly been outdoors since the previous autumn.

'I'm helping with the family's prosperity,' Danny defended. 'Thanks to me, William and Lucy have new clothes and toys and good food. You should be praising me for that, not telling me off like a bairn.'

'You can make a decent living as Gillveray's boatman not exploiting people's curiosity at your sister's expense.' Arnold was contemptuous.

'Alice doesn't mind,' said Danny. 'Do you, Alice?'

'Aye, I do,' Alice said, sick of the wrangling and downcast that there had been no letter from John in the pile of post. 'I hate all this.'

'You've done very nicely out of it, thanks to me.'

'I don't want it,' Alice cried. 'I just want things to go back to how they were before – when we were just an ordinary family, not a freak show.'

Danny gave her a strange look, his mouth twisting in a mocking smile. 'There's nothing ordinary about you, Alice,' he said. 'Is there, Father? Mother? We all know how Alice is different from the rest of us.'

Abruptly the room went quiet. Alice felt the tension in the air and saw the look of fear on her mother's face. She was baffled by her brother's words – not only what he said but also the menacing tone. Her father's face was rigid with fury – or was it alarm?

Before anyone spoke, a cry came up from below. 'Hello, Mr Brown? Can we come up now? It's beginning to rain and we really would like to meet your sister before we go.'

Danny threw Alice a look of appeal. She hesitated, still unnerved by the strained atmosphere.

'I'll come down and meet them,' she relented. 'But you are never to bring folk into the lighthouse again or cause any bother to our parents. Do you agree?'

Annoyance flashed across his face and then he smiled. 'Agreed. Come on then and act the heroine for your adoring public.'

* * *

It was mid-summer when an invitation came from George Gillveray for Alice and her parents to visit Black Harbour House. There had been weeks of blissful peace on the island since Danny's trips had stopped. Sam would go ashore for supplies but Alice and her parents had kept to the island and out of the public eye. Amorous letters still arrived from Alice's admirers but they were dwindling in number. Finally, the fever of interest in her appeared to be on the wane.

Yet how she still pined for John! Why had he raised her hopes so high to then dash them to the ground so callously? The least he could have done would have been to write and thank her parents. But he had not even done that. What was it about John Sinclair that had so captured her heart? She thought again with yearning of his dark good looks and laughing green eyes, his muscular body and the vitality for life that had helped him recover from being gravely ill. But it was more than physical attraction. She had found everything about him fascinating, from his tragic childhood and life as a chief's son to his friendly enthusiasm and dreams of adventure.

Yet she was forced to admit that he had most probably forgotten her, caught up in his new life and perhaps a new love. She had never been more to him than a pleasant diversion during his forced stay on the island. He might have meant his proposal in the intensity of the moment – in his relief at still being alive – but the feeling had not lasted once he had re-joined the world beyond Black Harbour.

'What does Mr Gillveray want with us?' Effie asked in alarm.

'Most likely to arrange for the subscription to be handed over,' said Arnold.

'Then why is Sam not invited?'

'Mr Gillveray will know that someone has to stay and man the light in case we don't get back in the day.'

This seemed to settle her mother's agitation but Alice worried that the trip would be too much for Effie. It took so little to make her fearful these days. She felt a familiar pang of guilt that she had brought such strain on her poor mother.

'Once this money is handed over,' Alice reassured, 'then we need not talk of the shipwreck or the publicity ever again.'

* * *

Alice had not seen George since the previous year. With her father so riled by Thomasina's behaviour on their spring trip, he had hurried her home having loaded up with provisions, giving her no time to visit Black Harbour House. Her admirers had sent her books and periodicals so she had not missed Gillveray's library so much. She was embarrassed that she had not made more of an effort to see him and thank him for his kindness for starting the subscription in honour of her and Sam.

George greeted them cordially but she detected a reserve in his manner. They were dressed in their best, though Alice's frock was frayed at the cuffs and the bodice was too tight; it had fitted her at fifteen but her figure had filled out and was now that of a woman's. She had knotted a shawl over her chest in modesty.

'You look very well, my dear,' said George distractedly. 'I had hoped to offer my congratulations at your brave deeds sooner than this, but you have been much in demand.'

Alice felt rebuked. 'I'm sorry, I meant to call – was on my way—'

'No need to apologise,' he said with a wave of his hand.

'Are there many folk here, sir?' Effie asked. 'I'm not used to a crowd – would rather sit quietly out of the way.'

George gave her a puzzled look. 'No crowds at all, Mrs Brown. There is just one gentleman here who wishes a private word. He was most insistent on coming to see you but wanted to do so without drawing attention.'

For a wild hopeful moment, Alice wondered if it might be John returned to recompense her parents and to ask permission to marry in person. George led them into the library. A thickset, craggy-faced man of middle age with a shock of grey hair and bushy sideburns stood up. Disappointment gripped her.

He strode towards Alice, fixing her with a sharp-eyed look.

'Alice?'

'Yes, sir.' She bobbed a curtsy. If this was another wretched suitor she would tell him to his face to go home, no matter how grand or rich he was.

'I knew it! You look the image of your mother.'

Alice was bemused. She was nothing like Effie in looks.

'This is Colonel Fairchild,' George introduced him, 'from Tolland Park near Newcastle.'

Beside her, Effie gave a stifled cry. 'Please, no—' Effie clamped a hand to her mouth.

Arnold gripped his wife's arm to steady her.

'Would you like to sit down?' George asked, alarmed at Effie's shocked, pale face. He ushered her into a chair.

'I'm very sorry, dear lady,' the colonel said. 'I know how this must be a shock to you – as it was for me when I learnt of the existence of Alice from a newspaper reporter called Moxon. He came with information about my wife, Charlotte.' He turned to Alice. 'I wasn't sure I believed him and was in two minds about whether to seek you out. But the desire to meet you was too strong.' His eyes glistened with emotion. 'And now I can see such a marked resemblance to my Charlotte. Alice, you are the child I thought I would never have.'

'Colonel Fairchild, how can that be?' Alice gasped. 'I'm not your child.'

And yet seeing her mother so upset, a new dread was clawing at her stomach. This man was no suitor. He was claiming to be her father!

George seemed just as perplexed. 'I think you should explain yourself, Colonel. I did not know you were going to make such a claim. I thought you wished to reward the Browns in some way.'

'I will give them anything they want for looking after Alice all these years,' replied the Colonel. 'It was heartless of Charlotte to abandon her – as she abandoned me – but I want nothing more than to be a good father and offer Alice the home that is rightfully hers.'

Effie let out a wail of distress. Alice looked between them, dumbstruck.

'We do not want your money,' Arnold said, a hand gripping his wife's shaking shoulder. 'We have brought Alice up as our own and love her like our own daughter.'

'But I am your daughter,' Alice said, panic rising in her throat.

'Please,' George intervened, 'someone must explain. You are frightening Alice.' He took her by the elbow and sat her down next to him on the sofa.

'My dear, you are the daughter of Charlotte Fairchild,' said the colonel. 'My wife gave birth to you at the lighthouse and then left you in the care of these good people. No doubt she intended to return for you—'

'She did not!' Effie cried. 'She was a selfish woman who couldn't wait to be free of her baby and run off with that Danish sea captain who fathered Alice.'

'Don't, Effie,' Arnold pleaded.

'Alice is ours – you've no right to take her from us. You must know that she isn't your flesh and blood – any more than she's ours. You were away at the war while your wife was having a dalliance with the captain.'

The colonel's face coloured but he kept his temper. 'I am quite aware of that,' he said. 'Yet Alice is Charlotte's daughter and I would have brought her up as

67

mine. I loved Charlotte and would have taken her back. I believe she would have come back in time – and claimed baby Alice – but she died abroad and never had the chance.'

'I'm sorry,' said Arnold. 'We never knew.'

'Captain Nielsen wrote and told me; I must at least give him credit for that. Later, I read about his ship going down in the North Sea with no survivors,' said the colonel.

Alice was stunned. Her heart thudded painfully. She could make no sense of what they were telling her. How could she be the daughter of some stranger of whom she had never heard? She looked at her parents – dearly familiar – and yet it would seem they were not her mother and father at all.

'So,' Alice said in a shaky voice, 'you were forced to care for me because my own mother – this Charlotte woman – didn't want me?'

'Not forced,' Effie insisted. 'I wanted a wee lass with all my heart. I'd lost three before Sam. Mrs Fairchild knew I was desperate for a daughter – Danny had told her – and that's why she left you. She knew I would love you like my own – the way she couldn't.' Her look was pleading. 'I helped you come into the world, lassie. You must believe that I loved you from the day you were born.'

Alice felt a new stab of pain in her heart at her mother's tender words. Effie was never one to speak of love or her feelings.

'It's Danny who has done this, isn't it?' Arnold was suddenly riled. 'I bet Moxon has paid him a pretty penny for this story about Alice and her high-born mother.'

'Why should Danny do such a thing?' George asked. 'He was just a boy when it all happened.'

'He was ten years old,' said Arnold.

'He used to talk about the lady with the baby,' Effie said in distress. 'Mrs Fairchild made such a fuss of him. I used to tell him not to speak of her and thought he'd forgotten about it long ago till . . .'

'Till what?' George pressed.

'He started making wee comments about Alice being different – ever since all the attention over the shipwreck – letting us know that he hadn't forgotten.'

'He's jealous of her,' said Arnold, 'and has been doing his best to make money out of her since the—'

'Stop it!' Alice cried. 'Don't go blaming Danny for telling the truth – no matter that he's been paid for it. It's you who have lied to me all these years! Why couldn't you have told me?'

'Oh, lassie,' said Effie, on the brink of tears, 'perhaps we should have but when Mrs Fairchild didn't return we didn't think we needed to. To us, you were always one of the family.'

'Didn't you think I should have been told too?' the colonel reproved gently.

George cleared his throat. 'That might have been exceedingly awkward, Colonel Fairchild. You can't have expected the Browns to run the risk of your rejecting Alice; it would have caused Alice unnecessary distress.'

Alice looked at George and saw the compassion and pity in his eyes. She knew he was being kind but it just compounded her humiliation. She was a bastard daughter, rejected by her own mother. What must he think of her?

'That is a fair point,' the colonel conceded. 'I can see how very difficult this is for everyone. But I cannot but rejoice that I have gained a daughter. Mr Brown, you and your wife are good people – that is very obvious to me – but you were only ever foster parents to Alice. You must accept that it is her birthright to come and live at Tolland Park.'

'I see that,' Arnold said, looking wretched.

Effie stifled a sob as tears ran down her cheeks.

'I can give Alice the life of a gentlewoman,' the colonel enthused. 'I hear you are an avid reader, my dear.' He smiled at Alice. 'I have over a thousand books in my library. Possibly more than in Gillveray's impressive collection.' He waved his hand at the bookcases around them. 'And you can have music lessons and learn to ride and have as many dresses as you could wish for. I have lived alone at Tolland for too many years without anyone to spoil. I can give you anything you want.'

'No, you can't,' Alice answered. 'If you think all I care about are possessions and living an idle life, then you don't know me.' She looked at him fiercely. 'You sweep in here like a whirlwind and turn our lives upside down. We all know what you want, Colonel Fairchild, but not once have you asked what *I* want.'

'Alice,' George chided, 'don't be ungrateful.'

'Why should I be grateful?' she protested. 'I don't know this man from Adam and, from what I hear, I don't care for this Charlotte Fairchild either.'

She saw Arnold and Effie staring at her, aghast at her outspokenness. But she couldn't stop. 'You gentry always think we common folk should be forever grateful for the titbits you throw us from your table. Well, sometimes we just want to be left to make our own way in the world and not to be beholden to anyone.'

She stood up and went to stand by Effie and Arnold. 'These are my parents – my people – not you, Colonel. I'm plain Alice Brown, the lighthouse-keeper's daughter.'

Alice took her mother's hand and squeezed it. Effie was trembling; afraid of the Colonel's reaction. But Fairchild surprised them all. He let out a bark of amusement.

'Well said, young lady. Your loyalty to the Browns does you credit. And your defiance . . .' He gave her a wistful smile. 'How like your beautiful mother you are.'

Alice felt wrong-footed by his remark. She had nothing in common with this Charlotte – a callous pleasure-seeker – and didn't want to be likened to her. Yet, she felt a stab of guilt at her impetuous rejection of his offer. He was obviously a lonely man whose wealth meant nothing to him if he couldn't share it with someone. He seemed a good person.

The colonel said, 'Your wishes must of course be paramount, Alice. I hope I may be allowed to correspond with you – and maybe you would write back on occasion and tell me how you are?'

She nodded, squirming with embarrassment at his gallant response to her rudeness.

69

'Then I shall take my leave.' The colonel bowed at the women. 'Mrs Brown, please forgive me for causing you upset. I should have realised how attached you would have become to my— to Alice.'

George summoned the footman to show his guest out. At the door, the colonel turned and said, 'Alice, my offer to come and live at Tolland Park will always remain open.'

'Thank you, sir,' Alice said, her cheeks aflame. She felt wretched at his hurt look and yet angry at him for upsetting her family and putting her in such an impossible position. She just wanted to escape back to the island and hide away. The shipwreck had brought nothing but discord. She wanted none of the bounty or attention that had come in its wake. She was not like Danny. Danny! Why had he done this to their parents? She refused to believe he would have come up with the idea of selling her birth story to that journalist. Thomasina must have wheedled the truth out of him and put him up to it.

Alice and the Browns left swiftly after the colonel. George offered them refreshment but Alice could sense his awkwardness and her parents were keen to be gone. She felt that somehow, by rejecting the colonel's offer, she had offended George too. But her feelings were all at sea and she couldn't work out quite why there was this new reticence between them.

* * *

Back at the lighthouse, Alice tried to settle into the everyday tasks again as if the traumatic meeting at Black Harbour House had never been. But she caught her parents watching her and trying too hard to please her, as if they now thought of her differently – as belonging to Colonel Fairchild – and it upset the equilibrium of family life.

Sam was told. Arnold did not want to risk him going ashore and hearing the gossip second-hand. It was not long before the story was out. Sam came back from the village the following week with a copy of *The Newcastle Messenger*. The main headline was 'Lighthouse Heroine, Alice Brown, is the Long-lost Daughter of Colonel David Fairchild, Veteran of the French Wars'.

There was mention of Alice's mother, Charlotte, giving birth in the lighthouse and then abandoning her baby. The article speculated on whether the shameless mother had run off with a sea captain.

Arnold shook with rage. 'That a son of mine could have stooped so low – making us the butt of gossip from here to Newcastle – for thirty pieces of silver! Never let him set foot on this island again!'

Soon the story was spreading far beyond the north east of England. The letters from would-be suitors multiplied. Now that Alice was an heiress, she attracted the attention of fortune-seekers across the country. Women sent requests to be her confidante; clairvoyants wrote predicting her future and the debt-ridden begged for money. Journalists attempted to land on the island and seek interviews but Sam and Arnold chased them away. They wrote stories about Alice anyway; lurid tales of a pretty young daughter of the gentry being forcibly kept in a remote tower by wicked step-parents who refused to let her leave the island and claim her birthright.

By the autumn, Effie could stand it no more.

'We're being punished for what I've done,' she fretted. 'It's God's retribution. I should never have kept you. This is all my fault.'

Alice was distressed by her words. 'No, it's not,' she replied. 'It's just Thomasina's mischief and Danny's greed. It'll all blow over soon.'

But Effie would not be consoled. Alice found it easier to avoid her mother and find jobs to do outside or in the lamp-room rather than listen to her constant litany of woe.

Standing in the room at the top of the high tower, alone on watch, Alice would be plagued by mutinous thoughts. Effie and Arnold had let her down by hiding the truth from her all these years. Things would never be the same again; the trust between them was gone. What would it be like to live at Tolland Park? What sort of person had her birth mother really been? The Colonel had loved her dearly so perhaps Charlotte had not been all bad. Perhaps she had been young and headstrong and desperately lonely, with a husband far away at war for years on end. How tempting it would have been to fall for a handsome sea captain who paid her loving attention . . .

Alice winced to think how quickly she had fallen for handsome John and his flattery – how easily she had let him kiss her with passion. Was she so very different from her foolhardy mother? It struck her suddenly that she was beginning to think of Charlotte as her mother, rather than the unhappy, guilt-ridden woman in the room below. Gazing out at the pink dawn creeping up over the horizon, Alice had a fresh pang of longing for John. Would she ever hear from him again? If not, would she ever be able to think of him without her insides twisting with regret at what might have been?

As the new day dawned, Alice was overwhelmed by a desire to change things for the better. She must stop hankering after John. She would redouble her efforts to make life bearable again for her family. In the quiet of the lamp-room with the sea lapping gently far beneath, Alice made up her mind what to do next.

* * *

'Are you quite sure it's what you want?' Arnold asked again.

'I think it would be best for us all,' Alice said, trying to be resolute. 'My being here is making life impossible for everyone.'

'And you will be doing right by Colonel Fairchild,' Effie said. Her mother had not wept when Alice had suggested she write to the colonel and accept his offer of a home. If anything, the woman had looked relieved.

'And I can always come back when things have settled down,' said Alice, 'and I'm no longer a story for the broadsheets.'

'Of course you can,' Arnold agreed.

Alice turned away from his sad look; her father would miss her the most. From him she had learnt a thirst for knowledge and a love of books; he had ignited her interest in plants and animals and her passion for lighthouse-keeping and the sea.

She wondered how far Tolland Park was from the sea. Would it be too far for her to ride to the coast? Already she was imagining what her new life would be like – as long as the colonel still wanted her.

71

His reply to her letter came back the same week. One of Danny's boatmen brought it out.

'No doubt Danny already knows its contents,' Sam grunted. 'That's why he's sent it on so quickly. Thinks there'll be something in it for him now you're going to be a lady.'

Alice opened it with trembling hands.

My dearest Alice,

Your letter has made me the happiest man on Tyneside. Of course I still want you to come and live as my daughter at Tolland. Nothing would make me prouder. I want to know everything about you: what your favourite dishes are and who are your favourite poets and whether you would like your chamber decorated in wallpaper or hung with tapestries – and what colours should the curtains be? But we can talk of all that when you are here.

I shall come for you in the carriage a week today.

Your loving father,

David Fairchild

* * *

On the day before Alice was due to leave, she went for a walk to the top of the island with Sam.

'Remember when we used to scramble down for birds' eggs with Danny?' she asked.

'I remember him kickin' them over the cliff,' Sam said. 'Always spoilin' things.'

'Poor Danny.' Alice sighed. 'He's never happy with what he's got – always wanting something more.'

'Don't feel sorry for him,' Sam replied. 'He's boasting round the village about how much money he's making. Got himself a boat of his own, so he doesn't have to rely on Gillveray for charity. And Thomasina's going about in a fancy blue silk dress. And we all know where Danny's got his new wealth from, don't we? Selling gossip about his own sister.'

Abruptly, Sam stopped and gave her an awkward glance.

'I am still your sister, Sam,' Alice insisted. 'I can't think of us in any other way.'

'Me neither,' Sam said bashfully.

They sat near the edge of the cliff watching the birds scream and wheel overhead. Would she miss the sounds of the island? Alice wondered.

'I remember her a bit,' Sam said quietly. 'Your mam.'

Alice's heart thumped at the unexpected mention. 'Really?'

'Aye. I remember her screaming upstairs – in the old lighthouse – 'cause it frightened me. Must have been – you know – when she was . . .'

'Giving birth to me?'

'Aye.' Sam blushed.

So it really had happened; even Sam recalled the momentous night. Somehow it made Charlotte all the more real to her.

'Do you remember anything about her?' Alice held her breath.

'She was pretty. Had pretty hair – red hair that shone in the firelight.' Sam shrugged. 'But that's all.'

Alice wished it was more but it gave her an image to savour and keep.

'I used to sit by your crib though,' Sam said. 'It was a drawer and I thought it was funny putting you into a drawer like the linen. I loved our baby – I loved keeping watch. That's what mam used to say; "Good Sam; you're keeping watch over our wee lassie."' Sam turned to Alice with a sad smile. 'I'll miss you. You won't forget us, will you?'

Alice felt her throat choke with tears. 'Of course not.' She squeezed his arm and smiled. 'I'll come back soon, I promise.'

Chapter 10

Addiscombe Military Seminary, south of England, 1829

'Here comes the gardener's boy!' Vernon Buckley mocked as John crossed the parade ground. 'Been measuring the potato patch again?'

Vernon's friends sniggered. John bitterly regretted ever telling Vernon about his upbringing but when they had been new cadets eighteen months ago, the tall young general's son had been charming and friendly. John had soon realised that it was only a veneer.

'We've been building a pontoon,' John replied, 'so that your dainty feet won't get wet. That's if you ever pluck up the courage to venture beyond the parade ground, Buckley.'

This brought laughter from John's fellow engineer cadets. They were exhausted and mud-spattered after a long day digging defences and constructing bridges. With satisfaction, John saw the fair-faced Vernon flush to the roots of his curly blond hair.

'He blushes like a girl,' Colin MacRae said in Gaelic.

John answered his friend in their native tongue. 'And smells as fragrant as one too. He bathes in more potions and oils than a queen.'

This provoked laughter from the Highlanders among them.

'Listen to the savages talking in their coarse language,' Vernon drawled. 'Not wearing your skirts today, I see.'

John had got used to ridicule from the southerners about the Scottish cadets and he put up with it good-naturedly. Most had soon tired of baiting the northerners – except for Vernon. John was baffled as to why he was singled out the most. Colin said it was because John wouldn't fawn and flatter him as others did, or take part in Vernon's drunken revelries and horseplay with the serving girls. Vernon appeared to have limitless amounts of money to indulge his appetites for drinking and wenching. His room was notorious for breakfast parties with tankards of claret and late-night debauchery where drunken singing kept others awake until the early hours of the morning. John despised the privileged Vernon's self-indulgence and callous treatment of women.

'Wouldn't want you and your wee boys clinging onto our skirts,' John quipped back.

Vernon and his friend Symonds blocked John's way. 'We're going into town tonight, Sinclair,' Vernon said. 'The peasants need teaching some manners. Are you Scotchmen brave enough to come with us,' he challenged, 'or are you too frightened of getting into trouble?'

'We don't all have uncles who are Company directors and can pay off our fines.' John elbowed his way past. 'And we don't fight skinny underfed town lads – that's a coward's sport.'

'You're the coward,' Vernon taunted. 'I've never seen you fight anyone. You'll never make a proper soldier!'

John ignored him and walked away. All he wanted was a soak in a tub of hot water and a hearty meal to keep him going through an evening of study. He wanted to excel in his final examinations in June and make Hercules proud of him. Vernon could afford to fritter away his time at military school – he could pay his way into the cavalry if he failed the engineering or artillery exams – but John could not.

John had relished his time at Addiscombe. He had made firm friendships and learnt much, both in the classroom and out on military exercises. He was one of the top students in mathematics and languages; his tutors were astonished by how quickly he had become fluent in Hindustani and Persian – the courtly language in parts of the East – as well as French and Latin. But for a boy who had grown up speaking Gaelic, Pashto and English, John found other tongues easy to learn and often helped his fellow students too.

It was now hard to remember how he had once been startled by the lushness of the green countryside around the college – so flat and far from the sea – and how grand the mansion and grounds were. The buildings were severely regular in design, with long elegant windows that let the light flood in. The parkland to which the cadets were restricted was thick with tall, broad trees that grew unstooped by westerly gales. With permission, the students were allowed to venture outside the confines of Addiscombe's walls and John and his friends had relished riding about the countryside and exploring this land of abundant farms.

John had proved himself an able military cadet too. He was an expert rider who could handle the most nervous of horses, a talented swordsman and accurate with a rifle. Perhaps this more than anything was what riled Vernon; that the upstart Highlander, who was comfortable running barefoot and riding bareback, was a better huntsman than one brought up on a rich estate with a stable of thoroughbreds and kennels of pedigree hounds.

Only one thing had marred John's time in the south; his estrangement from Alice Brown. His anxiety at her lack of response to his letters turned from bafflement to hurt pride. He had thought of her every day for months after his journey south, images of her fresh-faced beauty and lustrous red-gold hair filling his daydreams. He had craved news of her like a hungry man for scraps of bread but none had come. John had been so sure that Alice had fallen for him as much as he had for her. Why else would she have agreed so readily to be his wife?

But perhaps she hadn't been as eager; she had forestalled his rash proposal by telling him he must first write to her father for permission. He would have rushed to Arnold Brown there and then and begged for her hand if she had given him an ounce of encouragement. Yet she had not. Worse still, her father had not even bothered to reply to his proposal request and he feared that Alice had told him to ignore it as she had all of John's messages to her.

Once news spread in the newspapers about Alice's brave deeds, she became a national heroine. The broadsheets carried dozens of interviews of people who knew her or had corresponded with her – even a few articles that quoted her directly – and there were endless illustrations of Alice, none of which, John thought, did justice to her beauty. It was reported that Alice received proposals of marriage daily. No doubt her new suitors could offer her far more riches than a soldier's pay and a loyal heart. He could hardly blame her for having second thoughts about marrying him.

Yet it hurt him that Alice had not even written to release him from their understanding, let alone thank him for the gifts he had sent. It mattered little to him that she had not acknowledged the blue silk dress to match her eyes or the cask of port for Arnold and woollen shawl for Effie. But to leave him high and dry not knowing if he could still hope to be her husband one day was agonising.

Annoyingly, Vernon had spotted John's name in the newspapers as one of those saved by Alice and had teased him mercilessly.

'My, my, Sinclair,' he had crowed, 'how humiliating to be pulled from the sea by a mere girl. Must have been a blow to your Scotch pride.'

'She has more bravery in her wee finger than you'll ever have, Buckley. She put to sea in an open boat in twenty-foot waves. There was nothing humiliating in being rescued by such a lass.'

John had regretted his outburst; Vernon had needled him constantly about being lovesick for Alice. It was his rival who had delighted in waving the newspaper under his nose with the shock revelation that Alice was not the daughter of a lighthouse-keeper, but of a gentleman and hero of Waterloo. A few weeks later it was reported that the famous Alice had gone to live with Colonel Fairchild at his mansion, Tolland Park.

'Well, well, Sinclair; not much chance of your sturdy boatwoman looking twice at you now,' Vernon had baited John. 'I must say, seeing as little Alice has become one of the gentry, I might try my hand at wooing her myself. Looks a pretty little filly from this picture.'

John had wanted to punch Vernon's lascivious face. Instead he had gone into town and got roaring drunk. Colin had rescued him from being locked up in the local gaol for disorderly behaviour. But for going into Croydon without permission, the college authorities had thrown him into the punishment cellar – the black hole as it was nicknamed – and put him on bread and water rations for a week. There, he had plenty of time to dwell on his foolishness. Alice no longer thought of him so why waste his time on a woman who would never give her heart to him? Perhaps she had already agreed to marry another. Now that she was mixing with the gentry, she would have her pick of eager suitors.

He must learn to harden his feelings in future, John determined. Never again would he give his heart so completely or so recklessly.

* * *

June and their final examinations came. In a stuffy classroom with a hot sun blazing in at the windows, the senior cadets sweated over papers in mathematics, natural philosophy, chemistry and languages. They assembled models of gun carriages and drawings of fortifications for a grand exhibition to which directors of the East India Company would be invited. For three weeks they drilled and practised military manoeuvres in readiness for the day-long public examination, which would be judged by a visiting general.

'General Horton is a friend of my father's,' Vernon boasted. 'I expect to pass with flying colours.'

'Pass out with a flagon of brandy more likely,' joked Colin in Gaelic.

Vernon pushed Colin against the wall. 'Speak bloody English, you heathen!'

John was swift to pull Vernon off his friend. Buckley already reeked of liquor and it was barely noon. His eyes were bloodshot and unfocused. His friend Symonds seemed reluctant to get involved.

'Well, you can hardly speak *your* native tongue,' John mocked. 'But I suppose you won't need to in the cavalry – just have to neigh like a horse.'

Vernon took a swing at John, which the Highlander sidestepped easily. Vernon lost his balance and staggered against the wall. Snorting with derision, Colin and John walked away.

'I hope we get sent to the opposite ends of India,' Colin said. 'Why is he such a drunken oaf?'

'Have you ever met General Buckley?' John replied. 'He's a hard bastard with a hot temper. Even Symonds says so. He still beats Vernon like a schoolboy.'

'How do you know that?' asked Colin in surprise.

'Vernon told me when we first started here – before he took against me. Got drunk and started blubbering like a baby about how he could never please his father.'

Colin gave him a baffled look. 'Were you never tempted to tell his hangers-on what a weakling he is? You could have made a laughing stock out of him – the way he's always trying to do to you.'

John shook his head. 'It would be like teasing a pup that's had a kicking from its master. I pity Vernon more than I dislike him.'

* * *

The day of the public examination and inspection went off as planned, with General Horton and the Company directors pleased with the displays and drills. Prizes were awarded. John received a medal for his language skills – top in his class for Hindustani and Persian – and was one of twenty elite cadets selected to join the corps of engineers.

Colin was chosen for the artillery – the next most valued branch of the Company army. The rest – and those who failed in languages – passed out into the infantry. Vernon was among them.

'I'll be recommended for the cavalry,' he said bullishly. 'That's what I want anyway. Nothing better. We're the cream of the Company army.'

'If you say so,' John said with a dry smile.

'Where as you, Sinclair, will be spending your army career designing latrines for the backsides of the infantry.'

'A noble cause,' John replied, sauntering off.

That night, Colin held a party to celebrate John's medal and their success in passing out. A dozen of the northern men were crammed into his room, drinking brandy punch and singing. Two serving girls brought bread and cheese and were persuaded to stay. Colin played his fiddle and John and his friends taught the girls steps to the Scottish dances.

Abruptly, the door flew open. Vernon, Symonds and a dozen others barged in.

'Having a party without us,' Vernon cried, lurching forward. 'Not very gentlemanly.'

77

Loudly, the group pushed their way in, swigging from half-drunk bottles of claret and port. Vernon seized the punch bowl and drained it off, spilling half of the liquor down his front.

'Carry on, Sinclair,' he slurred, 'with your funny dancing.'

Colin had stopped playing. There was palpable tension between the two groups of young men as they squared up to each other.

'Nancy here will dance with me, won't you, girl?' Vernon grabbed at the waitress.

She resisted. 'Please, sir, I don't want—'

'Course you do,' Vernon drawled. 'It'll hardly be the first time.'

There was jostling and laughing as the new arrivals crowded around.

'Leave her be,' John ordered, 'and get out.'

Vernon sneered. 'Or what? The Scotchie who doesn't fight will try to stop me?'

'Go on, Vernon,' Symonds drunkenly encouraged, 'show the Scotch how it's done. Give her a kiss and I'll have her next.'

The other intruders guffawed and egged him on. Nancy looked scared but it was her air of resignation that made John furious. This had obviously happened before; Vernon and his ilk thought the serving girls were theirs for the taking.

Sickened, John leapt forward and seized Vernon by his jacket.

'Out now, you stinking drunkard!'

Symonds threw a punch at John's head, which made his vision blur, but John kept his grip on Vernon. At once Colin set on Symonds. In an instant the room was in uproar as the two sides traded blows. Fists flew and bottles smashed. Vernon, for all his inebriation, was a strong adversary. He threw off John's hold and swung at him, catching him on the left cheek. John punched him on the jaw. Vernon staggered back. John went after him. They fell into the passageway, battling it out. All John's pent-up anger at Vernon's relentless slurs against him and his friends – all the wounding comments about Alice – found release in the fight.

The two strong men fought on until Vernon put up his hands and gasped, 'Enough.'

John stood back panting, his knuckles raw and his mouth tasting of blood.

Symonds was hauled from the room by his friends, half-conscious. Colin's room looked as if a hurricane had whipped through it; the furniture up-ended and glass everywhere. The girls, John was thankful to see, had fled unscathed.

Colin, shirt ripped and nose bloodied, held up his fiddle and bow in triumph.

He grinned. 'All in one piece.' A cheer went up.

John could feel his eye closing up. Through cut and swelling lips he grimaced. 'Give us a victory tune, MacRae – loud enough for Buckley and his sycophants to hear.'

Colin struck up a march. John and his comrades stamped their feet and bellowed. The noise spilled out into the June night.

* * *

John left Addiscombe in July and headed north with Colin, their wounds almost healed. Vernon and his clique had avoided them since the fight.

'Good luck,' John had wished his rival.

After a moment of indecision, Vernon had replied, 'And to you too, Sinclair. You'll need it more than me.'

They had shaken hands but Vernon's smile had been forced, his blue eyes cold.

John stayed a week with Colin at his home near Inverness and then rode for Skye and Ramanish. Come September, they would be sailing for India. Riding back through the mountains, John's heart burst with longing at the first sight of his island home. He had sent word ahead and Hercules had prepared a feast for him at the castle. His foster father and Azlan rode out to meet him, the Afghan firing off his *jezail* in the air as a salute. John's young cousin Iskandar – now a slim, handsome nine-year-old with his father's dark eyes – rode with them.

The men and the boy cantered down the final slope with whoops of joy. The sea was calm and glinting gold in the evening sun. Beyond, the isle of Rùm lay like a slumbering beast. People waved and called out a welcome as they rode by. John insisted on stopping at Morag's cottage.

'You won't find her there, my friend,' said Azlan.

John frowned in concern.

'There is no need to worry,' Hercules assured him. 'Your aunt awaits you at the castle – along with your new cousin.'

John's mouth fell open. A broad grin spread across Azlan's face.

'You have another child?' John gasped.

'A princess,' said the Afghan proudly. 'Ariana – the pure and noble.'

John leant out of his saddle and clasped his friend. 'Congratulations, Uncle!'

That night there was much feasting and celebration – both for John's homecoming and in honour of his month-old baby cousin. Ariana was pink-cheeked and had a shock of black hair. She looked content in her mother's arms, her large, dark eyes already focusing about her in interest.

John had an emotional reunion with his aunt – the woman who had been like a mother to him when he had lost his own – and she held out her precious bundle.

'Hold her,' Morag encouraged. 'We would like you to be her godfather.'

John's eyes smarted as he took Ariana cautiously in his arms. She gazed up at him and he felt a tug on his heart – a surge of protective love – that took him by surprise. He gripped her with more confidence and she stopped her soft mewling, her rosebud mouth opening a fraction as she continued her solemn stare.

'She knows you already.' Morag smiled. 'See how content she is in your arms.'

Hercules laughed. 'She empties her lungs when I pick her up. But she knows a good man when she sees one.'

John laughed, kissed Ariana gently on the head and handed her back.

* * *

John filled his days with helping out in the fields with the late haymaking – cold, wet weather in the spring had delayed growth – and in cutting peats from the marshy bog for the fire. He went up into the high pastures with his old friend Donald to visit the shieling where Peigi and other young people from the village were tending the cattle. To the dismay of Peigi's family, Duncan, the piper, had not renewed his year-long hand-fast marriage to Peigi and had disappeared to the mainland. If Peigi had any regrets about Duncan, she hid them well by flirting with John.

'You were always my first choice, Spanish John.' She winked and gave him a lingering kiss on his cheek.

John laughed it off and did not encourage her attentions. He was not going to risk being bruised in love again. Besides, Peigi's kiss just made him ache all the more for Alice. No other woman came close to stealing his heart.

After that, he spent his remaining days out hunting with his chief and Azlan. They talked to him nostalgically about India and the lands of the Afridis close to the Khyber Pass from where Azlan hailed. Hercules had once told John that Azlan's closest family had been wiped out in an epidemic of typhoid fever while he was away on a trading trip. Hercules had come across the heartbroken Afghan in Peshawar and offered him a job as his guide in the lawless tribal hills beyond British-held territory.

'If you ever have cause to travel to Peshawar or beyond, my friend,' said Azlan, 'you must say that I am your Afridi brother. You will be welcome in my home.'

John was touched, though he doubted after all these years away from his people whether Azlan's name would give him protection. From what he had heard at Addiscombe, the only defence from the warlike tribes in the Khyber and beyond was strong artillery or a fat purse to buy their co-operation. But he knew the proud Afridi would be insulted by such talk.

On the eve of his going, John went to visit Morag, Iskandar and baby Ariana one last time at the cottage. He felt sad at leaving them – he had quickly grown as fond of Ariana as he was of Iskandar – yet he was excited by the adventure ahead.

As they chatted, John became aware of Azlan watching them quietly from the doorway.

His uncle stepped forward. 'I would like you to have my hunting knife,' he said, holding out the brass-handled, bejewelled blade with two hands.

'I couldn't possibly take it,' John said, overcome by the gesture. He knew how special it was to the Afridi. He carried it everywhere.

'It belonged to my father and my father's father,' Azlan continued. 'You are like a son to me and I wish you to take it.'

John swallowed hard. He took the knife. 'Thank you.' John put his right hand to his heart in a gesture of respect. 'I shall carry it always and think of you, my uncle.'

Slipping the knife into his belt, he stepped forward and embraced the Afghan. Behind them, Morag let out a sob, which set Ariana wailing.

'Look how my women cry for you,' Azlan exclaimed in mock annoyance.

Turning, John embraced his aunt and kissed the yelling baby. When he held out his arms to Iskandar, the boy responded with a bashful hug.

'Come back to us safely,' Morag cried. 'Promise me.'

'My wife,' said Azlan, 'that is for Allah to decide.'

The next day, as morning broke and sun spilled over the craggy mountain tops, John left Ramanish. Hercules stood on the battlements, his piper playing a salute beside him, and watched John ride away. At the top of the pass, John turned one final time to look at his home and the dearly familiar cluster of houses and fields sheltering behind the ancient fortress. Fishing boats were putting out to sea and cattle bellowed at being herded across the hill. He filled his mind with the view; even if he was lucky and survived army life, it would still be many years before he would return home.

He sat erect in the saddle and saluted Ramanish and his chief, the strains of the pipes still carrying to him through the still air. Then he swung his horse around, kicked it into a brisk trot and turned his thoughts southwards.

* * *

John had not intended to detour on his way to London. Colin had already sent word that he was in the English capital and awaiting passage east. But as John made his way by stages across the Highlands, then by coach down through Perthshire and to Edinburgh, he was plagued by thoughts of Alice. The nearer he drew to Northumberland, the greater grew his desire to see her.

He had said goodbye to all those most dear to him and could hardly contain his excitement at travelling to India, but only one thing disturbed his peace of mind – a final chance of seeing Alice to make sure that there was no spark of love left between them to ignite. Perhaps there was a reason that she had not written back to him. Her father might have forbidden it, horrified at the idea of her going so far away to India with a man she hardly knew. Yet Alice might still harbour feelings for him.

Even as he delayed in Newcastle for an extra night at The Turk's Head, John ridiculed himself for his weakness. Alice – if she remembered him at all – would probably be embarrassed by his turning up at Tolland Park. It was nearly two years since the storm that had thrown them together. At nineteen she was probably already married to some rich member of the Northumberland gentry.

He wrote her a note asking to see her, then in an agony of indecision, tore it up and booked himself on the late-afternoon stagecoach to London via York.

Restless, he went out to speak to the hostler. 'How far is it to Tolland Park?' John asked.

'Half an hour's ride,' the man said.

Impulsively, John paid him to saddle up a horse and give him directions. It was five hours till his coach left; he would seek out Alice and declare how he felt one last time. If she rebuffed him again, then he would sail to India without a backward glance.

* * *

The rain was already heavy as he left the city and by the time he reached the muddy lanes leading away from the River Tyne, John was drenched through to the skin. It fell from the sky in torrents. He rode on, tucking his chin into his collar and gritting his teeth.

Tolland Park was secluded behind high stone walls and mature trees; through the heavy rain he could see nothing of the house except ranks of distant rooftops

81

and chimney pots set well back in rolling parkland. John felt a stab of misgiving. He had not expected it to be quite so grand. The high iron gates were firmly shut.

John dismounted and led his horse under an overhanging tree. He would wait for the worst of the rain to ease off and then knock at the lodge house and ask for admittance. Doubts beset him. She might be away. What if she was entertaining and he arrived like a half-drowned dog at her door? He imagined a drawing room full of men like Vernon looking down their long aristocratic noses at him, and the women tittering behind their hands. He would be a laughing stock.

Then he chided himself for his lack of courage. Alice, the brave lass who had put to sea to save the lives of ordinary people, could not have changed so much. Whatever she thought of him, she would not allow him to be humiliated by her rich new friends.

As he strengthened his resolve, he heard the clatter of horses' hooves on the carriageway beyond the gates, and then the call of a coachman. He watched as an elderly man emerged from the lodge house and set about heaving the gates open. A moment later, a pair of chestnut horses emerged from the far side pulling a well-polished carriage behind. The coachman sat above, large hat dripping, and whipped the pair into a trot.

Heart hammering, John stepped forward to see who sat inside the coach. He thought he saw two figures. He ran at the carriage, waving at the coachman to slow down. But the man didn't see him, his head bent against the pouring rain.

For an instant, he saw a face at the window. An elegant woman with hair piled on top of her head in elegant coils, glanced out. He could see her pale swanlike neck and the velvet of her cloak. John gaped. The carriage was past him before it sunk in that the sophisticated woman was Alice. His heart pounded in shock. She had looked right through him without a flicker of recognition. She was even more beautiful than he had remembered. But her vivid eyes had shown no warmth.

John stood by the roadside, mud-spattered from the hasty carriage, and regained his breath. Alice was no longer the girl he had fallen in love with; she was a rich heiress speeding off to some social engagement and completely unattainable for the likes of him.

'Can I help you, lad?' the old gatekeeper called out. He was panting from the exertion of closing the gates.

John went across. 'Let me help you.'

'Ta, lad, that's canny of you. I'm gettin' on in age and not half as fit as I was. I'll let you out the side gate.'

When they had finished, the gatekeeper said, 'You can shelter in the lodge till the rain stops.'

'That's kind of you but I should be getting back to Newcastle – I'm making for London.'

'What's that you say, Durham? I hear that's a canny place.'

'No,' John said loudly, 'London.'

The man looked at him with rheumy eyes, confusion on his face. 'Is there summat you wanted?'

'I'd hoped to see Alice Brown – I mean, Fairchild. But I saw her leave in the carriage.'

The old man grunted. 'Aye, she still gets a lot o' men coming to gaze on her, does Miss Alice.'

'That's not why I came.' John bristled. 'I was one of those she rescued from the *Berwickshire* and I wanted to see her before I go abroad – thank her in person.'

'The *Berwickshire*? Well, you were a lucky lad.'

'Do you think she'll be back soon?'

The man shrugged and stared off down the muddy lane. He lifted his sodden cap and scratched his head of sparse white hair. 'Aye, a lucky lad.' After a long moment he fixed on his cap, hunched into his jacket and turned back to the lodge.

'If you could unlock the side gate for me, sir . . . ?' John reminded him.

He looked round at John as if surprised to see him still there. 'Oh aye.' He fumbled for a key on the ring he was carrying. 'Follow me.'

As John stepped through the opened gate, the man said, 'What was it you wanted, lad?'

Impulsively, John asked, 'Would you give Miss Fairchild a message from me, please? Tell her that John Sinclair from Ramanish came to see her and wish her well.'

The old man gave a rueful look. 'Me memory's not what it was, lad. Best you come back and see her another time.'

'I'm sailing for India in a few days,' John said. 'Please can you try to remember to tell her that John Sinclair called?'

'I'll try, lad.'

On the spur of the moment, John pulled the chain over his head that held his lucky coin and pressed it into the gatekeeper's gnarled hand.

'Give Miss Alice this Spanish coin,' he urged. 'It belonged to my great-great-grandfather Carlos – it fascinated her so I'd like her to have it.'

'Spanish?' the old man said, peering at it in suspicion.

'It's a lucky coin from Spain and it's very old,' John explained. 'Please just give it to Miss Alice and she'll know who it's from.'

'Very well,' he agreed. 'Spanish, eh?'

John nodded. 'Thank you, sir.'

John rode away from Tolland Park, wondering at his foolishness in giving away his special coin, which was a link to his beloved home and family. What did he mean by the gesture and what would Alice make of it?

He gave up trying to fathom his hankering after the girl. He hoped the coin would bring her luck in life; for all his disappointment he still wished Alice to be happy. Now he must turn his mind to a new life abroad – without Alice in it. India beckoned. John urged his horse forward and cantered back to Newcastle.

Chapter 11

Tolland Park, 1833

'Papa,' Alice exclaimed, 'Mr Gillveray is sending me a goat from Bengal!'

David Fairchild raised a bushy grey eyebrow and asked, 'Does he not recall that we have such things in England already?'

Alice laughed. 'This is a special kind – a Himalayan goat. He wants to replace Wellington the Second.'

Her father shook his head in incomprehension. 'Is Tolland Park to become a zoo as well as a botanical garden, my dear?'

'And why not?' Alice smiled.

She dropped George's latest letter on a side table and wandered over to the large drawing room windows. On the sweep of pasture beyond the terrace she could see her sheep grazing – a mix of breeds – alongside some Highland cows, an ancient breed of white cattle and a long-legged llama that had been rescued from a ship.

Her father had not protested at his ornamental lawns being put to such a use; neither had he minded her enthusiasm for turning the hot houses and kitchen gardens into a laboratory for the strange plants that she grew from seeds and cuttings sent from India by Gillveray. Alice knew her father would indulge her in anything she wanted and took delight in her filling the house with the exotic blooms that she managed to grow.

She had been surprised by George's abrupt departure for India after the Colonel's startling appearance five years ago. He had left without saying goodbye in person, only later explaining by letter his wish to return to India. '. . . *perhaps it is vanity but I wish to prove that I still have the vigour of my younger self – and also to make a contribution to the advancement of botany.*'

They had begun an affectionate exchange of letters.

'What else does he say?' asked Fairchild.

She returned to the letter and read through the pages of neat handwriting.

'Oh, listen to this! He's promising to send me some of those *Camellia* seeds I've been begging him for, so I can try to grow our own tea. Isn't that wonderful?' She read on. Her brow furrowed. 'Oh dear, but then he will be away for a while. He's going on a mission further east – to Java – to discover how the Dutch are growing tea. Do you think that will be very hazardous?'

'He's a sensible fellow,' said her father. 'But these long sea journeys are not without risk.'

Frowning, Alice stood up and re-crossed the room to the globe she kept on the table in the window. Her friends thought her eccentric for her obsession with geography and for displaying George's old spinning atlas rather than a bowl of flowers or a china ornament. When word had reached George in Calcutta of her move to Tolland Park, he had sent instructions for it to be sent across from Black Harbour House as a gift for her new home.

'Where is Java, Papa?'

Fairchild pulled himself stiffly from his chair and joined her. They studied the globe together.

'There it is.' He pointed. 'Halfway to China from India.'

'He's hopeful of bringing back more seeds – and some expertise in tea-growing. He sounds very excited about it. He's been experimenting with growing tea at the Company gardens but the conditions aren't right in Bengal by all accounts. George – Mr Gillveray – says that moist conditions are good but elevation is also needed – hilly places where it gets cold for a month or two.' She glanced at her father. 'Am I boring you with all this? I just find it all so fascinating.'

'You never bore me, dear Alice.' He smiled. 'You are the prettiest, most intelligent and loveable girl in the world. And I could listen all day to you talking about tea.'

She laughed. 'Oh, Papa, you are terrible the way you spoil me.' She took his hand and squeezed it. 'You do realise that you have ruined my interest in marriage. No other man would listen to me chatter on like you do or let me pursue my outlandish interests.'

He gave a chuckle of amusement. 'Good,' he declared. 'I selfishly want you to live here till the day I die.'

'And so I will,' Alice promised.

His merriment evaporated. 'My dear, you know I am jesting. I would never stand in the way of you marrying if that's what you desired. It's just you haven't shown any interest in any of the eligible men of the county who come calling.'

'I'm not interested,' Alice said quickly. 'Why would I give up my freedom here at Tolland and put myself under the rule of a husband?'

'So you are truly happy here?' her father pressed her.

'You know I am,' she assured him.

He grew reflective. In recent months her papa had been dwelling more and more on the past, reminiscing about her mother, Charlotte, and blaming himself for leaving his wife alone for years on end.

'I still worry after all these years whether I did the right thing in rushing to Black Harbour to claim you as my own. The Browns' – he hesitated – 'they lost a daughter because of me.'

Alice felt a twisting inside, as she did whenever she thought of her former home.

'Papa,' she reassured him, 'you are the kindest man I know. They would not have stood in the way of my good fortune in being acknowledged by you. Besides, my pare— the Browns had kept the truth from me. Things could never be the same again between us.'

Her father gave her a grateful smile. He would always need her reassurance that he had taken the right course of action.

'Will you go and visit them soon?' he asked. 'Now that summer will allow an easy crossing.'

'Perhaps,' Alice said. She kissed his leathery cheek. 'We'll discuss it later. I want to check on the mangoes in the hothouse.'

* * *

As she stood in the artificial heat of the greenhouse, surrounded by orchids, bamboos and palms, Alice pondered her failure with her estranged parents. For the first two years at Tolland Park she had returned regularly to visit the lighthouse, taking her family gifts of lace, tobacco, books and clothing. Their joy at seeing her again quickly turned to awkwardness. Effie would not hear of her helping out in the kitchen.

'Look at your lady's hands,' she would marvel. 'What would the colonel say if we sent you back with them red and raw from kitchen work?'

Sam was always bashful, disappearing off after an exchange of greetings. Arnold was the easiest to talk to, and the most precious moments were when they sat down together by the black range with one of her new books.

'Read to me, lass,' he would instruct. 'My eyes can't focus as they used to.'

So Alice would read while he smoked his pipe and for a short while she could believe that they were still father and daughter. In her mind he was still her father – that was why she chose to call Colonel Fairchild her papa – and she missed their former closeness. To Arnold she was able to chat about her experiments in the garden with plants from the East and talk about Gillveray's work at the East India Company's botanic garden in Calcutta.

But Effie was baffled by Alice's interests and seemed to resent Arnold and Alice's ability to settle back into their old familiarity. She would never let Arnold sit for long.

'There's work to be done in the lamp-room,' Effie would chide. She would question Alice on her life in society, wanting details of her new friends and suitors.

'So when are you going to wed, lassie?' she always asked. 'Surely the Colonel wants you to make a good match? Are you putting off the young men with all this strange talk of Indian bamboo trees?'

On her first visit back, Alice had stayed a few days, sleeping in her old bed and rising to help in the lamp-room. But already she found it confining in the tiny, dark rooms. The lamp-room was the only place where she felt at home, relishing the wide vista of sea and sky. She had gazed out to the Black Needle and the reef and wondered how she had ever had the bravery to row across with Sam and pull those people to safety. But Effie had chased her back to bed.

'We can't have you getting a chill sitting up all night,' she had fussed. 'And it's no good us getting used to you helping out when you'll be gone back to Tolland in a day or two.'

So her trips to the Browns had dwindled until last year she had only visited once. Alice had been shocked to discover that Sam had met and married Liza, a quiet fisher-girl from Berwick, who was now living at the lighthouse and was expecting a baby.

'Why was I not invited to the wedding?' Alice had remonstrated.

They had all looked away in embarrassment, Sam muttering that it had just been a quiet affair.

Alone later, Effie told her, 'We thought it might be difficult for Liza's parents having members of the gentry being invited. They're just simple fisher folk.'

'Member of the gentry?' Alice laughed in disbelief. 'I'm still the same girl who used to live under your roof for eighteen years! I just wear different clothes.'

Effie had fixed her with a look. 'No, lassie, you're not. You don't even sound like our Alice anymore with your high-born accent. We like to have you visit but you've chosen to live with the colonel and that's the way it is. You're a Fairchild, not a Brown.'

Alice had been deeply hurt and yet she could not blame her parents entirely. She did feel like a different woman from the girl who had lived at the lighthouse, and thanks to her papa she had been able to develop her enthusiasms. She had chosen to go and Alice supposed she must also have modified her accent to fit in with her papa's world.

She had sought out her father in the lamp-room. 'Do you feel I'm no longer one of the family too?' she had asked.

Arnold had given her a long sorrowful look. 'If I could change one thing in my life,' he had said quietly, 'it would be the night of the storm. That shipwreck took away more than those poor folk who drowned. They robbed us of you.'

Alice had felt the tears well in her eyes. She couldn't argue because she had felt the same. If the *Berwickshire* had missed the rocks and got safely to harbour she would never have become famous and the colonel would never have known of her existence. She would never have met John or lost her heart to the Highlander who had vanished from her life as swiftly as he had entered it.

'But it's a selfish thought,' Arnold had said, 'for fate has brought you a new life. You must go and live it to the full, Alice.'

* * *

Standing in the hothouse, her brow damp from the warmth, Alice sighed. She had not been back to the island since that visit. She knew Arnold was right; she should not squander the new chances in life that she had been given.

Fingering the hard, shiny mango, Alice let her mind wander to India and John Sinclair. For the umpteenth time she wondered if that was where John now lived. Had he completed his training for the Company army and gone east? If so, it must have been about four years ago. Had he found a wife there? She preferred to think of him as a bachelor soldier living a spartan life. She had an image of him riding into battle on a mighty horse, wielding a sabre over his head and charging across a dusty sun-baked plain at ranks of turbaned warriors. But perhaps that was fanciful. From what George told her, soldiering out east these days was mostly tedious guard duty at barracks and forts, or skirmishes with hill tribes. George had written wryly about it.

The government is more interested in subduing the natives with missionaries these days. They have recently curbed the Company's powers. We no longer have the monopoly on trade out east and our soldiers kick their heels confined to barracks. But why do you ask about our army, my dear?

Alice had never answered his question. She wished she could put John from her mind for good. Hankering after what she could never have was a fruitless waste of time. Better to live for the moment and enjoy the life she had been gifted.

Her spirits rose once more. She would suggest a ride with her papa through the woods and upriver. He liked nothing better than being out in the saddle and was still an expert rider, whereas his arthritic legs no longer allowed him to walk as far as she could.

Alice left the hothouse and stepped into the welcoming breeze. She saw Stephens the footman rushing down the path towards her, waving frantically.

'What is it?' she called. Perhaps one of the sheep had got into the vegetable garden again.

Stephens arrived out of breath and agitated. 'Come quickly, mistress.'

'Whatever's the matter?'

'It's the colonel,' Stephens said in distress. 'We found him lying on the library floor.'

By the time Alice reached the library, panting and heart pounding, the servants had laid the colonel on a chaise longue. Their stricken faces told her the worst but she rushed and threw her arms around him.

'Don't leave me, Papa!' she cried.

But he was already lifeless and cooling to the touch. Alice buried her face in his chest and sobbed in disbelief.

Later, when the doctor arrived, he confirmed that Fairchild's heart had given out.

* * *

For days, Alice was in shock at the brutal swiftness of her papa's death. She went into mourning and dealt with her grief by keeping busy. She organised his funeral at the local parish church and sat up late replying to all the many black-edged cards of condolence that came from neighbours and friends. Arnold came to the funeral and Alice insisted that he sat with her at the front. There was not enough family to fill a pew; two cousins of the colonel's and their spouses, who had travelled from Country Durham. Alice clung to her father, grateful that he had made the journey.

'Effie wanted to come,' he said, 'was dressed and ready. But she couldn't face it. She doesn't leave the island these days.'

'I know,' Alice said, and squeezed his arm in reassurance. 'Tell her that I'm touched that she tried.'

It was when the funeral and courtesy visits were all over that Alice was struck by how alone she was at Tolland Park. She wandered the house, feeling her papa's presence, yet every room was lacking it. She sat for long hours in the library – that room where he had spent so much time reading newspapers and playing cards with friends – and pretended that he had just popped out for a moment. But as the days and weeks went by, Alice was overwhelmed by the mansion's emptiness.

She lost her appetite for riding, for it had been something they had enjoyed doing together and it made her ache for her kind papa. The only activity that brought her comfort was feeding and tending her animals. Afterwards, Alice would hide away in the hothouses and cry for her dead parents; even for the selfish Charlotte whom the colonel had adored.

Autumn came and with it arrived the *Camellia* seeds from George. She had written to Calcutta to tell him of the colonel's death but knew he would still be away on his tea mission to Java and might not receive the news for months.

As Alice planted the handful of precious seeds in pots in the hothouse, she was engulfed with sadness. The day she had read about the seeds with such excitement was the day of her beloved papa's death. Should she dig them up? To her, the seeds were tainted by the memory. If she hadn't rushed off to the hothouse would she have been able to save the colonel? At the very least, she should have been with him in his final hour so she could have held his hand and told him how much she loved him. But instead she had delayed her return to the house with daydreaming about John and his life in India . . .

Alice blinked away fresh tears. Her papa would not want her to be so maudlin; he would want her to plant the seeds and watch in excitement as they grew. Alice would keep a daily journal of the progress of the plants. It would give her a new purpose.

* * *

The year 1834 came and Alice began to bear life without the colonel. After a year of mourning, she resumed social visits to neighbouring friends and took to daily rides around the estate. She continued to take an interest in the animals though increasingly left their daily care to her farmhands. The Himalayan goat, promised by George, had died en route – George suspected it might have been eaten by the hungry crew of a ship delayed by storms but Alice hated to think of such a thing.

She was thankful to hear of George's safe return from Java and wrote him frequent progress reports of the *Camellia* plants – or rather their lack of progress. Of the half a dozen seedlings, only two had survived. Of those, one was looking sickly and drooping while the other had so far remained healthy and had produced fresh buds that spring.

I feel such a failure and am beset with guilt at your having entrusted precious seeds into my inexpert hands.

George had written back.

You mustn't feel the least bit guilty, my dear. We struggle to grow them here in Calcutta. I am trying with seeds brought over from Java but with little success. However, I have very exciting news that I wish to share with you – you are one of the first to be entrusted with this knowledge so you mustn't breathe a word yet! A Scotsman named Bruce has discovered the Camellia sinensis *growing wild in Assam, to the north of here. We are having the seeds he has sent tested here in Calcutta. Previous samples he sent were rejected as not being the real thing – but I'm convinced by his descriptions that Bruce is right. If so, this could change everything for the Company. We could grow our own supply of tea here in India instead of having to pay a king's ransom for Chinese leaf. Of course we would need to be sure that the quality is as good. Other samples, sent from Burma recently, provided a bitter-tasting tea. I wish you could be whisked out here on a magic carpet to give me the benefit of your superior tea-tasting skills!*

Alice lived in anticipation of George's friendly letters, which now arrived more frequently owing to a pioneering overland mail service via Egypt. Waghorn's service boasted of deliveries from India to Britain in ninety days. She was flattered that George chose to confide in her about his work but it was the allusion to her going out to India that made her insides flutter with nerves. Did he seriously entertain the idea of her joining him out there? She couldn't possibly make such a journey, could she? Not as an unmarried young woman. Yet, thanks to her papa, she was now a wealthy heiress who could do as she pleased. Why should that not include travel? How exhilarating it would be to visit places on her spinning globe that had fired her curiosity for years.

Alice had refused half a dozen marriage proposals in the past year and a half. She had just celebrated her twenty-fourth birthday with a small gathering of friends. One of her papa's Durham cousins and his wife had paid a visit.

'We think it is high time that you were married off,' the Fairchild cousin had said bluntly. 'My cousin David would have wished it. I can act as your guardian in the matter and I have a suitable husband in mind – a man of business and a friend of mine.'

Alice had smothered a laugh of derision. 'That's kind of you, sir,' she had replied, 'but there is no need to trouble yourself. Papa never wanted me to marry. We agreed that I would dedicate my life to the advancement of natural philosophy – and sheep rearing, of course.'

She had hardly been able contain her amusement as the Durham Fairchilds had left with bad grace.

'As headstrong as your wayward mother,' the cousin had spluttered.

'Yes,' Alice had agreed. 'That's what Papa loved about me.'

Alice wrote to George regaling him with the encounter. Impulsively, she ended the letter with a postscript.

I have never ridden a magic carpet, though it sounds the greatest of fun. I wish I too could see India. I envy you your time there.

* * *

Alice was dumbfounded by George's reply, which arrived in the spring of 1835. She sat down in a chair, quite winded.

I have admired you for a long time but during these past few years of our corresponding as friends my admiration and fondness for you has bloomed into something more. Dear Alice, I know that in your eyes I must seem an old man, but I still have the feelings of one much younger. With each letter you send, I have waited in dread of you informing me of your marriage to some young suitor, but you never have. Could it possibly be that your reference to wanting to come to India might mean that you would consider a future with me? What I am trying to say, dear Alice, in my diffident way is: would you consider becoming my wife and making me the happiest man on earth?

Alice spent a restless week pacing the elegant echoing rooms of Tolland Park and roaming the estate in an agony of indecision. Marriage to George? She had never entertained such a notion. As a girl she had been a little smitten with his patrician good looks and had basked in his attention. As she grew older, she had experienced a quickening of her pulse in anticipation of seeing him after long winter months of being stormbound on the island. But this was as much from the excitement of getting off the island for a day and having the pick of the books in his library as from the thought of being with George. Perhaps she had imagined herself in love with him. But the day she had set eyes on John Sinclair, she knew what real love felt like.

She closed her eyes and felt a fresh ache of longing for Highland John. She could still conjure up his handsome face and green eyes shining with desire as if he were there beside her.

Alice let go a pent-up sigh. John wasn't there and never would be. Whereas George offered love and companionship and she knew he would keep his promise.

'I don't love him but I'm very fond of him,' she said, resolution beginning to form in her mind.

That afternoon, she sat down and wrote a reply to George accepting his proposal of marriage and telling him of her intention to sail out to India in the autumn.

* * *

While awaiting his response, Alice went ahead and booked her passage to India with Waghorn's – which was now taking passengers as well as mail – knowing that would shorten the sea voyage considerably. She would travel via the Mediterranean and overland through Egypt to Suez and then on to India by steamer. Her neighbours spoke with alarm about her decision but Alice was thrilled by the thought of seeing Egypt and experiencing a modern steamship – far more preferable than five months sailing around the hazardous Cape. She would leave from London in September. What point was there in delaying her future, now that she had made up her mind?

That summer, Alice kept herself busy sorting out her affairs with the help of her papa's land agent and his solicitor. She sold the mansion and part of its grounds to a shipping merchant. The dower house she kept for herself in case she should want to return to England in later life, and rented out the rest of the estate and farmhouses to her tenants. Letters kept arriving from George telling how ecstatic he was at her agreeing to be his wife and his plans for their future together. He was procuring a house for them in Calcutta – more suitable for married life – and giving up his bachelor quarters. He did not rebuke her for booking her passage via Egypt but sounded as excited as she was.

Alice's mind was only troubled by one thing, saying farewell to her foster family at Black Harbour Island. It was as she was contemplating how she could help the Browns at the lighthouse that Stephens interrupted her musings.

'Sarah, Josiah's widow, would like a word with you, ma'am.'

The old gatekeeper – doddery, forgetful and with a mind that had regressed to early childhood – had died a month previously.

'You mustn't worry about my leaving,' Alice assured the elderly woman, who was peering like an anxious bird from under her cap of black ribbons. 'The lodge house is yours for as long as you live. My lawyer has arranged it.'

'I'm that grateful, ma'am, but it's not that,' said Sarah. 'It's this.'

With shaking hands, she held out a piece of calico tied into a tiny purse with a length of twine.

'I wrapped it in this for safe-keeping. Would have come sooner but you've been that busy, they wouldn't let me see you.'

'What is it?' Alice asked gently.

Sarah shook her head, perplexed. 'Just an old coin on a chain, ma'am. A week or two before my Josiah went to his maker, I found it in a waistcoat pocket – one that me husband hadn't worn for years. When he saw it, he got in a right state about it. In his last days when he took to his bed, Josiah wouldn't settle – me finding the coin seemed to upset him.'

'I'm sorry to hear that, Sarah,' Alice sympathised.

'Kept going on about a Spaniard and how I had to give this to you.'

'A Spaniard?' Alice was baffled. She was on the point of telling the agitated widow to hang onto it as a keepsake when a memory resurfaced.

Several years ago, she had had a garbled conversation with the gatekeeper. Josiah had started to tell her about someone who had come from Spain to see her, then he had lost the thread of his thoughts and trailed off. Alice had dismissed it as yet another stranger trying to intrude into her life and ask for money or marriage. There had been many such men in the first months of her living at Tolland Park. But if this was the Spanish man Josiah had been talking about, then this stranger had come bearing a gift. Her interest pricked, she would look at it before letting Sarah keep it.

Untying the cloth parcel, Alice opened it out to reveal a worn coin and chain, dulled and discoloured from neglect. She rubbed the coin in the calico and held it up to the light.

Alice gasped in shock. Her heart thumped. The coin bore a helmeted head.

'Do you recognise it, ma'am?' Sarah asked fearfully. 'Josiah didn't take what wasn't his, did he?'

'No,' Alice said, breathless. 'I'm sure he didn't mean to keep it. He must just have forgotten.' She gulped. 'And yes, I've seen it before – or one like it.'

Alice's fingers trembled as she stared at the coin. Could it possibly be the same one as she had seen – and touched – lying on John's broad chest? If so, then John had come here to see her.

'Tell me more about what Josiah said,' Alice urged.

Sarah shook her head. 'He wasn't makin' much sense, ma'am. Just kept going on about this lad from Spain and how I had to give you this.'

'From Spain . . . ?'

Then it struck Alice that it was the coin that was Spanish; perhaps Josiah in his growing confusion had remembered that the visitor had something to do with Spain.

'He never said the Spanish man's name?' Alice willed the old woman to remember more. If only she had questioned Josiah more closely at the time instead of dismissing his attempts to deliver a message.

'No, ma'am,' Sarah said with a sorrowful shake of the head. 'He was talking little sense by the end.'

Alice's heart went out to the bereft woman; she had lost her partner of over fifty years.

'Thank you very much for coming to tell me,' Alice said, 'and for giving me this.'

Sarah bobbed an arthritic curtsy and left. Alice instructed Stephens to send round a basket of food from the kitchens for the old widow.

She was left with her feelings in turmoil. Could it have been John? If it had, what had he wanted? Had he, like so many other men, come seeking her out once he knew that she was the wealthy daughter of Colonel Fairchild? Yet Alice did not want to believe John could have been so calculating. The man she had grown to love so quickly had thought nothing of riches and status. He had not been embarrassed to talk of running around barefoot with the other local boys in his village or of his humble origins.

So if he had not been motivated by self-gain, why had he taken so long to attempt to see her, when he had neglected to write to her for nearly two years? Perhaps, on the eve of departing for India, John had had a change of heart and had regretted breaking his promise to her. Leaving the coin was his way of showing that he still thought of her. Or was it just a token of good luck? After all, he had left no note with it nor followed up with a letter.

Alice had a string of sleepless nights as she tried to fathom what it all meant. After a week, exhausted and with her emotions wrung out, she determined to banish such upsetting thoughts. His visit – if it had indeed been John – had taken place six years ago. Even if he had wished to see her then, his feelings for her could have died long since.

As the summer waned, Alice convinced herself that the stranger with the coin had not been John at all.

* * *

On her final visit to the lighthouse before embarking for India, Alice took Sam aside. They went and stood on the bluff where they had played as children. He was now the father of a sturdy boy, also called Samuel, and Alice was touched to see how her brother delighted in his young son. He took him everywhere, riding high on his shoulders.

'I've arranged with George that Beekeeper's Cottage on the estate is to be given to your parents,' Alice explained. 'The time may come when Father won't be able to work the light or Mother manage the stairs.'

Alice had been shocked by the deterioration in Effie. She seemed to have shrunk, her back bent and her once plump figure diminished.

'I want them to have somewhere to go to – it's a pleasant place with a grand view of the sea – and I've made sure it's all fixed up. But you can tell them in time. I know how proud they are, so I'll leave that to you.'

Sam gave her a bashful smile. 'That's kind of you, Alice.'

'And I've left provision for you and Liza and Samuel—'

'No, lass,' Sam protested, 'I don't want your money. We manage fine on what the board pay us.'

Alice kept to herself that it was George's supplementing what Trinity House paid that helped them make ends meet. She reached up and tickled Samuel.

'It's for this special boy.' She smiled. 'Not his daddy and mammy.'

Samuel wriggled and giggled. Alice kissed the boy's soft, plump hand.

'Well, in that case' – Sam grinned – 'I accept your help. Thank you.'

She took her goodbyes, not lingering. A restless Danny was waiting to ferry her back to the mainland. He was still barely on speaking terms with his family.

In the lighthouse kitchen, Effie gave her a fierce hug. 'I wish you luck and a safe journey – though I can't imagine why you want to travel to such a dangerous land.'

'She's getting wed to a good man, that's why,' Sam said with a wink.

'Aye, you'll be a wife at last,' Effie said, consoled by the thought. 'And I hope the Lord blesses you with bairns.'

Arnold pulled gently at his wife. 'Let her go now. The boat's waiting.'

Abruptly, Alice threw her arms around him. 'I'll miss you, Father!'

She felt him stiffen and then his arms were pressing her to him. 'I too,' he croaked, and kissed her brow as he used to do when she was a child. Her eyes welled with tears. Her throat was so tight with emotion she could not speak. She merely nodded as Arnold broke away. The smile he gave her was filled with sadness and love. They knew that this might be the last time they ever met but were unable to say so.

'God go with you, my daughter,' Arnold said as she walked shakily towards the stairs.

Sam went with her to see her into the boat, exchanging curt nods with Danny. Samuel squealed to go with them, but his father held him firmly back. They waved Alice away. It was to be her abiding image of Black Harbour Island; the sight of her brother and nephew – for that is who they were in her heart – standing waving on the rocky shore with the gleaming tower of the lighthouse glinting in the sunlight behind. Her former home, that symbol of a life she had once lived but lost long ago.

Danny grew more talkative the nearer they drew to land; boasting about how well his boat business was doing and Thomasina's expansion of the post office into a dressmaker's and fancy goods shop.

'So it's worked out well for us all, hasn't it?' Danny declared. 'You've got riches beyond any lass's dreams. Who would have thought you'd end up weddin' the landlord, eh?' But when she didn't reply, an anxious look crossed Danny's face. 'You are happy about marryin' Gillveray, aren't you? 'Cause it preys on me mind a bit . . .'

'What does?' Alice asked.

He shrugged it off. 'Nothin'.'

On shore, Alice could sense that he didn't want her to linger. She had hoped to see William and Lucy but Danny did not invite her to visit his home. Instead she gave him some money for his children. He took it quickly.

'Good luck, lass.' Danny grinned and, turning his back, sauntered away up the street, whistling.

She climbed into her waiting carriage and set off for Tolland Park. Suddenly Alice couldn't wait to be gone and for her new life with George to begin.

Chapter 12

En route to India, 1835

As the cart rattled over the stony ground, Alice's teeth shook so violently that she thought she would arrive at the port of Suez toothless. Whatever had possessed her to take this route to India? The voyage through the Mediterranean had been stormy at times but she had a sturdy stomach used to the motions of the sea and she had not minded.

But since landing in Alexandria nearly two weeks ago, agog with excitement to see Egypt, Alice longed once more to be at sea. She and her fellow passengers – mainly East India Company men and a few plucky wives – had been crammed onto barges for a canal journey to Enfe. There they had transferred to feluccas – primitive open sailboats – which had taken them up the Nile River to Bulac, the port at Cairo. They had entered the ancient city on donkeys. Alice had laughed out loud at the sight of Emily Ayton, a captain's young wife she had befriended, shrieking in alarm as her animal took off at a trot.

The old citadel, with its domes and labyrinth of narrow lanes busy with people and trade, fascinated Alice but her fellow travellers complained at being pestered by crowds of curious children and bitten by bed lice.

Yet the hardships of the journey so far were nothing to the bone-jarring discomfort they now endured atop the crude sand carts that bumped their way east across the desert to the Red Sea port.

Dust enveloped and choked them, so that they could hardly see the desolate land over which they travelled.

'Nothing to see anyway,' declared Captain Ayton. 'Just rock and sand.'

Behind them stretched an army of camels loaded up with their belongings. Alice was astonished at what people had thought essential to bring: bath tubs, writing desks, dining furniture, beds and trunkfuls of bedding and clothes.

'Where is all your linen?' Emily had exclaimed, scandalised by Alice's lack of home comforts. 'Sandy told me I must have three sets of sheets for the first sea voyage and another trunk's worth after Suez.'

Alice had only thought to bring two sets for the whole journey, hoping to have them laundered on the way. In Egypt she travelled with a few essentials in a simple basket with a lid. Emily had three bulky carpet bags – their driver was perched on one – and five large trunks swaying along behind in the camel train. Her husband had just as many again.

Emily and Sandy were from Edinburgh and had recently married while Sandy had been on leave from India. To Alice's delight, their destination was also Calcutta. Emily was chatty and friendly, with a riot of frizzy fair hair that she tried to keep in order with ineffectual headbands. Her husband Sandy, perhaps older by ten years, was a genial man whose hair and side-whiskers matched his name.

When they finally transferred to a ship once more, the friends stood watching the mountains of possessions being hauled on board, along with an unidentifiable cargo of chests, sacks and barrels. The sun was setting in a pink dusty haze over low barren hills. An evening star sparkled in the darkening sky. From somewhere a voice gave a haunting, persistent cry above the noise of the dockside.

'He's calling them to pray at the mosque,' Sandy said, pointing at a white-domed building beyond the harbourside.

'Isn't it beautiful?' Alice gasped.

'What is?' Emily asked in bemusement.

'Everything.' Alice spread her hand at the scene.

'You are eccentric in your tastes, Alice.' Emily laughed. 'I can't see anything of beauty anywhere.'

'I can,' said Sandy, seizing his wife's hand and kissing it. 'My bonny wife!'

Emily giggled. Alice felt a pang of envy at their transparent adoration of each other. Hearing Sandy's Scottish accent kept reminding her of John, for all that she strove to banish him from her mind.

'Don't look so sad,' Emily said with a squeeze on her arm. 'You'll be Mrs Gillveray before Christmas.'

* * *

After weeks at sea, the passengers were growing tired of one another's company, the endless games of cards to while away the long days and the dullness of meals where the previous night's dinner was served up cold for breakfast. While sailing down the Red Sea there had been the diversion of frequent stops to take on coal but since then, for days on end, there had been an endless blue horizon and heat that brought on a strange lethargy. Some of the crew were suffering from dysentery and several passengers took ill with heatstroke and liver complaints. Yet Alice marvelled at the creatures that leapt from this southern sea – flying fish and dolphins – and followed their progress.

* * *

They sailed onwards, first to Ceylon and then to Madras. Small boats braved the barrier of creamy surf to ferry passengers to the shore. Alice gazed enviously at the shoreline of golden beaches and swaying palms with Fort St George solid and imposing beyond the sprawling town.

After that, as they headed north to Calcutta through the Bay of Bengal, they hit stormy weather. Emily retired ill to her cabin. Alice spent mealtimes grabbing at tureens of food to stop them flying off the tables. Finally, the sea calmed and two days later they entered the river mouth of the wide Hooghly and journeyed inland towards Calcutta.

Expectantly, Alice and Emily joined others on deck as they eased upriver past thick vegetation.

'Mangroves!' Alice exclaimed.

'Yes; however do you know that?' asked Sandy.

'Mr Gillveray has told me about them. Over the years, he's also sent me seeds for exotic plants and fruit. I tried to grow mangoes in my hothouse but I think they were half the size they should have been. Tasty in relish though.'

96

'You never cease to surprise me.' Emily nudged her. 'I bet you know more about India already than Sandy does.'

Alice could hardly contain her nervous excitement as a series of Palladian mansions came into view, their long gardens sweeping down to the riverside. They looked more impressive than Tolland Park – and just as English.

'This must be Garden Reach,' said Alice. 'Mr Gillveray has written about the merchants' homes with wonderful gardens.'

Then the wharves of the city could be seen ahead.

'That's Fort William,' said Sandy, pointing out a bastion with defensive walls.

'It looks too elegant to be a fort,' Alice said.

'Calcutta is elegant,' he replied. 'Far more so than London. And almost as handsome as Edinburgh.' He gave a deep chuckle.

The ship dropped anchor and a flotilla of slender boats, their rowers standing up and pulling on long oars, came out to meet them. Alice gazed in fascination at the docks beyond – *ghats*, as Sandy called them – which were teeming with life. Alongside the usual warehouses, ship repairs and customs house were flights of wide steps where people were gathered, fishing, smoking, praying and washing clothes. Some of the men wore little more than a loincloth.

Emily had to drag her away. 'Come on, Alice. Don't keep Mr Gillveray waiting.'

Alice's insides lurched at the thought of coming face-to-face with George after seven years. The last time they had seen each other was at Black Harbour House and the awkward first meeting with her papa. She was a different person now and he might be too. Her chest felt tight with nervousness. She tried to control her thumping heartbeat, telling herself that they knew each other better than ever through their long newsy letters. She gave a wry smile. Too late to have second thoughts now.

'Look at you grinning,' Emily teased. 'I can't wait to meet your Mr Gillveray either.'

* * *

'I was watching through the eyeglass,' George said, greeting her in the bustle of the customs house. 'You look very well, my dear.'

He held Alice's hands in his. She flushed from more than just the heat. He had aged; his sparse hair was quite grey and receding from his high forehead and his face was craggy and weathered by the sun. But his smile and concerned brown eyes were familiar.

'I am well' – she smiled – 'and thankful to be here. It's been quite an adventure. I've seen my first camels – and flying fish – but I don't want to go on another ship or sand cart for at least a year. I can't wait to see my first elephant – I think I might have glimpsed one from the ship. Let me introduce you to my new friends, the Aytons.'

She slipped her hands free and looked around anxiously in the mêlée for Emily and Sandy, waving them over when she spotted them.

'They've been such good companions and Captain Ayton is based here in Calcutta so Emily and I will be able to see each other often, won't we?'

Nerves made Alice garrulous but George did not seem to mind. He gave her new friends a cordial welcome.

'I hope you will call on us once you are settled in at Fort William,' he said to Emily.

'I'd like them to come to our wedding,' Alice said. 'May we invite them?'

'Of course, my dear.' George smiled. 'Anything you wish for you shall have. I just long for us to be married as soon as possible.'

Emily smothered a giggle and Alice felt her blush deepen.

* * *

The wedding happened with dizzying speed; George had arranged everything. Within days of setting foot in Calcutta, Alice was married to George in a quiet ceremony at the gleaming new garrison church of St Peter's within the walls of Fort William. The Gothic-style church was grand as a cathedral with its flying buttresses and long tapered windows. Alice emerged on George's arm squinting into the late-afternoon December sunshine, lightheaded at the thought she was now his wife and by tonight would be living in his house in Chowringhee.

Gun carriages and cannon were lined up in neat rows between the severe rectangular brick buildings of the fort. It was almost possible to imagine she was in England, except for the glimpse of exotic trees beyond and the screech of tropical birds.

In a small anteroom, a supper of soup, fish, fowl, potatoes and raisin pudding was laid on with copious bottles of champagne and claret. Alice, unused to alcohol, drank too quickly. She hardly touched her supper except to devour the sickly sweetmeats that were served with glasses of Madeira wine at the end of the meal. By the time they came to leave, her head was spinning and she was slurring her words.

'G'bye, Memily!' Alice clung to her friend, hiccupping and suddenly tearful. 'You're the best f-riend I've ever ha-had.'

Emily burst into tears too and Sandy had to help prise the women apart.

There were ribald remarks about the wedding bed as George's army friends bundled the bridal couple into a waiting *doolie*.

'Is zis a box?' Alice asked in confusion, flopping onto a cushioned bench inside the conveyance.

George laughed and climbed in next to her. A moment later, they were raised into the air as the four runners heaved the poles onto their shoulders and set off at a jog. Within minutes of being jiggled up and down, Alice felt queasy. As soon as the runners set down the carriage, Alice leant over and was violently sick.

She remembered little after that; a vague memory of being carried into a ghostly white house, through musty-smelling rooms. Then she was lying down, her head still reeling as if she were on board a lurching ship. Moments later came oblivion.

* * *

98

The next morning, Alice woke to screaming. She opened her eyes in alarm but it made her head hurt so much she quickly shut them again. It took her a minute to work out that it was the screeching and squawking of birds that had woken her. It was so loud, she thought they must be in the room, but when she opened her eyes a fraction, shading them from the dawn light, she realised the birds were flitting among the trees beyond the open shutters of the window.

George was standing in a nightshirt shaving by the open window, humming to himself.

Alice sank back with a groan; her stomach felt sore and empty.

He turned and asked, 'Is my merry bride awake now?'

Alice struggled to remember the previous evening. Fragments of memory surfaced, the dinner party and some singing. She thought she might have cried and asked Emily to come and live with her. A wave of embarrassment swept through her as more memories surfaced.

'Was I sick last night?' she asked.

George wiped his chin with a linen towel and came over to peer at her. 'It was the *doolie* ride which did it, I'm afraid. It was thoughtless of me. I should have hired a proper carriage.'

'It was my fault,' Alice murmured, 'for drinking too much champagne. Did I make a fool of myself?'

'Not at all,' George said, sitting down beside her. 'You were charming. Emotional but charming.'

Alice squinted at him. She wanted to know if they had consummated the marriage last night. Was she a wife in every sense now? All she remembered was passing out on the bed. She couldn't find the words to ask if they had.

'Today, if you are feeling well enough,' said George, 'I thought I would show you around the botanic gardens. Then tonight we can have a quiet meal alone and an early bed.'

Alice coloured. Was he telling her that they hadn't yet been intimate? She rather thought he was.

'I'd like that,' she answered with a weak smile.

* * *

The trip to the Company gardens on the west bank of the River Hooghly was just what Alice's sore head and jaded nerves needed. She was enchanted by the vast lush gardens, laid out nearly fifty years ago by a Colonel Kyd for scientific research.

'Of course the Company agreed to it so that they could make money,' George told her with a wry smile. 'They brought cinnamon plants from Assam and set up in competition with the Dutch.'

Alice linked arms with her husband as he showed her around, a servant following them with a large fringed parasol to keep the low sun off her pale face. She could see how proud George was of the trees and shrubs growing in profusion around a tranquil lake. There were thousands of specimens.

'Those are Bussora date trees from Mesopotamia,' he said, stopping under tall palms. 'And over there are Persian tobacco plants.' They strolled on. 'These here produce gum for varnish.'

'What's that?' Alice asked, gazing in amazement at a vast tree spreading like an umbrella. It appeared to have sprouted new trunks around its parent one like a mythical creature with many legs.

'That's a *Ficus benghalensis*,' George replied, 'a native to India. Every village has one. The natives call it the banyan.'

'It's like something from a fairy tale,' said Alice, entranced.

Next George showed her around the glass houses until she lost count of the number of spices and fruit trees he had named. His knowledge of their medicinal properties was vast and his enthusiasm infectious. Alice was reminded of what had drawn her to George in the first place; his passion for learning and the natural world. They stepped back outside into the pleasant December warmth.

'What are you smiling about?' he asked her quizzically.

'I'm thinking how lucky I am to be married to a knowledgeable man like you – and to be here in this beautiful eastern garden. I can hardly believe it.' She gazed up at the trees, enjoying the sight of bright green and red parrots darting between them.

When she looked back at George she saw his eyes glinting with emotion.

'Shall we go home, Mrs Gillveray,' he asked, 'and start our married life together?'

Alice's insides jolted. 'Yes,' she answered, 'let's.'

* * *

Their first attempt at lovemaking was not a great success, at least as far as Alice was concerned. Her knowledge of such things was based on what she had observed among her animals and pets. Effie had never talked about such matters and she had had no other close relatives to ask. Alice had thought about asking Emily what would be expected but the opportunity never arose; Sandy was almost always at her side.

Alice had been surprised by the mechanics of human intercourse, holding her breath while George fumbled with buttons and laces and wondering if she should be helping more. He didn't strike her as particularly expert and Alice wondered if he had lived all this time in India without taking a mistress. She had heard gossip on the ship about the lax morals of Company men who gave in too readily to the temptations of native women when left in India for long years of service. The government now frowned on marriage with Indian women but the gossips whispered that many men still 'kept a woman' and even sired children by them.

Alice knew that George's passions were more cerebral but as the days passed she grew to realise that his love for her was more than a meeting of minds. Once they had got over their awkwardness towards each other in the marriage bed, they relaxed and began to enjoy their intimacy. Alice would help shed her clothes and guide George to where his touch gave her pleasure. She explored his body with interest. His limbs were still lean and firm, even though he carried a paunch and the skin on his chest sagged. She closed her eyes and imagined it was a much younger George who made love to her, enjoying the sensations that he provoked.

He was tender and his kisses were full of affection. Perhaps she surprised him with her enthusiasm to get into bed quickly each night.

'You make me so happy, my love,' he declared often and would gaze at her in wonderment.

One morning after they had woken and reached eagerly for each other, George said, 'I still can't believe you agreed to be my wife.'

Alice laughed. 'I still can't believe you asked me.'

'I never thought you could ever think of me in that way,' he said. 'I confess I was filled with jealousy at all those young men who came to worship you and offer you marriage after your brave deeds became well known.'

'I wasn't interested in any of them,' declared Alice.

'Not one?'

Alice hesitated. Her stomach tightened in a pang of regret for John. But she had loved him before all the fame.

'No, none of them. They were just fortune-seekers.'

'Can it be possible that I'm the only man you've ever cared for?' George marvelled.

Alice smothered her sudden yearning for John. She felt guilty for even thinking about him while lying in George's arms. What would she do if she ever came across him in Calcutta? Yet she had never heard his name mentioned by the Aytons or George or any of their military friends. There was no point torturing herself with dilemmas that might never happen.

Alice leant up and kissed his lips. 'No more questions,' she whispered, guiding his hand through the opening in her nightgown.

* * *

As 1836 dawned, Alice relished her new life in Calcutta. Every day brought her new sights and experiences. She loved the grand stuccoed buildings along Esplanade Row and Chowringhee Road; three-storied villas with verandas and porticos gleaming like white marble in the winter sun. She went for carriage rides with Emily across the Maidan, the vast sweep of open ground between the fort and the town.

'That's the Ochterlony Monument,' Emily said, pointing out an elaborate column. 'Sandy says Ochterlony was a brave Company soldier who defeated some fearsome Himalayan tribes – the Gurkhas or some such. Anyway, that's why the British have control of the hills around Simla.'

'George says that Simla is like being in Scotland,' said Alice.

'Has he been there?' Emily asked.

Alice nodded. 'He loved it for all the plant life and the bracing air – but it's not the most comfortable of places. All the cottages are perched on mountainsides and it's often foggy and cold and the social life seems to revolve around drinking.'

Emily patted her arm and laughed. 'Thank goodness we are in civilised Calcutta then. I haven't come all this way for Scottish weather.'

101

Her friend told Alice of the speculation in the fort about who the new Governor General might be now that the Whigs were back in power in London.

'Sandy thinks it will be William Eden – Lord Auckland. He has a wager on it in the mess.'

While their husbands worked, the two friends spent much time together going to plays, music recitals and afternoon tea at the genteel houses in Chowringhee. They would accompany each other to the dressmakers and milliners, ordering up lightweight clothing for the hot season.

Alice would always insist that they detour up Chitpore Road and into Lal Bazaar to watch the artisans at work in their open stalls; potters squatting over their wheels, brassware-makers hammering out jugs and pots and blacksmiths forging curved blades and matchlocks, their assistants working primitive bellows of hide and bamboo. Emily disliked the din and smell of the place but Alice would stop and barter for brass trays and brightly painted fruit bowls to adorn her new home in Chowringhee.

She was mesmerised by the multicoloured piles of spices and the heaps of fresh fruit and vegetables, many of which she had never seen before. The bazaar reeked of a heady mix of frying oil, curry spices, drying animal skins, steaming cow dung and scented tobacco smoke.

George had explained early on that she wouldn't be expected to do any of the housekeeping, which was left up to their bearer, cook and a host of other servants. Once she had agreed the menus for the day and handed over money, her household duties were done. Alice had grown used to a leisured existence at Tolland Park but it was still a novelty to find that in India all the chores – from housekeeper to emptying the privies – were done by male servants.

She began to take a sketch book out with her to record her impressions of this new and exciting land. She drew the people of the bazaar; the stallholders and merchants in their brightly coloured robes and turbans, and skinny holy men with matted beards dressed in nothing but a piece of homespun cloth. Alice sketched women in vivid pink, green and gold saris leaning over high balconies, chatting and observing the bustle below.

Once she witnessed a wedding procession; an elephant bedecked in rich cloth and carrying the bridegroom and his party, followed by men on horseback, dancers, musicians and supporters on foot bearing huge flat sunshades. Alice was so mesmerised by the noisy, joyous scene that she forgot to sketch any of it.

Sometimes she would persuade George to rise early and go to the Maidan as the morning mist lifted off the river and observe the *bhistis* – the water-carriers – at the city's main reservoir, the Great Tank. In a few quick strokes of her pencil, Alice would depict the *bhistis* pushing through the turnstiles that kept out the roving cows and then sketch the men slinging their goat-skins into the tranquil water of the tank. She drew the watchman at his sentry box, ever vigilant to stop any bathing. Behind, emerging in the dawn, would be the increasingly familiar skyline of mansion rooftops, temples, church spires, mosques and government buildings that Alice was growing to love.

Back at their house in Russel Street, Alice would spend the morning sitting under a bamboo shade in the tree-lined garden and turn her sketches into watercolours. She had had a few lessons in painting at Tolland Park but had always preferred being outdoors riding or feeding her pets. Here, in the warmth of the eastern sun, she was surprised to find how content she was to sit for long hours painting in the garden or reading on the veranda.

One time, George returned to find her gazing out across the garden as dusk was falling amid a cacophony of birds.

'Look,' she whispered, 'at that monkey feeding its young one. The mother swings through the branches with the baby clinging on underneath. Aren't they delightful creatures?'

'If you don't mind them stealing food from the breakfast table or the soap from the washstand,' George said with a wry look.

'I'm happy to share my breakfast biscuits with them.' Alice smiled.

'I bet you've been downright encouraging the pests.' He chuckled, laying a hand on her shoulder. 'It's the motherly instinct in you.'

Alice felt her insides flutter at the thought. She was in her twenty-sixth year – old to be starting motherhood – and wondered how soon she would fall pregnant. She knew George longed to be a father and she too wanted a child but nothing had happened yet. Still, there was more than enough to occupy her in Calcutta.

It was George who introduced her to Miss Cook, a lively middle-aged benefactor who ran the Ladies Society for Native Female Education and had helped set up a series of missionary schools in the town.

'I find the Mohammedan girls particularly enthusiastic about learning,' Miss Cook told her over afternoon tea. 'They have a thirst for knowledge that must be encouraged.'

Alice asked to be shown around one of her schools. The eager, cheerful girls sitting at rough wooden tables in a sparse schoolroom reminded her of herself at a similar age. It was thanks to George encouraging her education, and the enthusiasm of her kind teacher, Miss Lambert, that she had been given entry to a whole new world of books and knowledge.

'I'd like to help out too,' Alice said in excitement.

'I'd be so pleased if you would,' said a delighted Miss Cook.

After that, with George's blessing, Alice went twice a week to help out at a school near Chandpal Ghat, close to the river. She was under the supervision of Mrs Meadows, a jovial American missionary of middle-age who had a good rapport with the children. The widowed Mrs Meadows had been in Calcutta for twenty years. Alice read aloud to the girls and helped them learn English.

Emily was admiring. 'It's very worthy of you – and so brave.'

'There's nothing brave about it – it's fun. Why don't you come and help?' Alice suggested.

'Goodness me, Sandy wouldn't hear of it.' Emily laughed. 'He'd worry about me going down to the docks. George is different. He's more – well – friendly with the Indians, isn't he?'

* * *

March came and the temperature rose. The city's gardens bloomed with spring flowers and blossom. Soon the British community was a ferment of excitement about the arrival of the new Governor General. Emily came round bursting with the news.

'It's Lord Auckland, as Sandy predicted,' Emily enthused, 'and Sandy is to be on his staff. What do you think of that? My Sandy an aide-de-camp to the Governor General!'

Alice was pleased for her friend. 'I hope you won't be too grand to socialise with us lower ranks,' she teased.

'Of course not,' Emily cried. 'I'll have you invited to all the best parties in town!'

On Lord Auckland's arrival, there was a ball held in Government House in his honour. It was the most glittering occasion Alice had ever attended and she was grateful that her papa had insisted on dancing lessons when she had first gone to live with him. Dressed in a new silk gown of peacock blue, Alice rode beside George in a two-wheeled gig, joining the stream of carriages and *doolies* making along the Esplanade and across the Maidan. Torchbearers ran alongside. The Gillverays passed under one of the ceremonial gateways and alighted in front of the imposing Palladian mansion.

The ballroom shone with lamps suspended from the ceiling and resounded to the sound of chattering crowds. Everyone was dressed up in their finery. The Company officers in their scarlet tunics and highly polished boots competed enthusiastically to dance with the women, who were markedly fewer in number.

After two dances, George was out of breath and sweating under the heat of the lamps in the crowded room.

'We can sit the next one out,' said Alice. 'Let's go and find some refreshment.'

'My dear, I don't want you to miss out on a single quadrille,' George said, mopping his brow.

'Sandy will dance with you,' said Emily, looking flushed. 'I'd like to sit down for a bit too.'

'Are you all right?' Alice asked in concern.

She noticed a glance pass between the Aytons.

'Perfectly fine,' Emily assured her. 'I just need a cool drink.'

Sandy Ayton stepped in gallantly and bowed at Alice. 'Allow me to have the pleasure of the next dance.'

Alice took to the floor again with enthusiasm, while George went with Emily in search of a glass of punch.

After a few dances, they were joined once more by their spouses. The ebullient Sandy introduced Alice and George to some of his fellow officers, young bachelors who were growing rowdy on champagne.

A tall captain with wavy blond hair and a handsome boyish face stepped forward and bowed with a click of his heels.

'This is Captain Vernon Buckley,' said Sandy. 'Cavalry. But soon to join me as ADC to Lord Auckland.'

The captain smiled at Alice. 'May I have the honour?' he murmured.

She glanced at George, who smiled in encouragement, so she held out her hand and Buckley led her onto the dance floor.

He was an accomplished dancer, his timing perfect and his manner attentive. She learnt that he had been on campaign in Burma and Assam.

'Savage country,' Buckley pronounced, 'but excellent hunting. The Company seems to think the land of value for growing opium or possibly tea. Not for me to judge. I just get on with soldiering.'

'Being in Calcutta will be dull after all that action,' Alice said dryly.

He gave her an assessing look. 'I disagree. It would appear Calcutta is full of attractions.'

Alice blushed under his blue-eyed scrutiny. She knew he was being mischievous. 'As a *married* woman I find there is plenty to do here.'

'Quite so,' he said, 'and marriage would appear to suit you very well. Gillveray is a lucky man. If only I had arrived back from Burma a few months sooner and pressed my suit first. We would have made the most handsome couple in Calcutta.'

Alice was annoyed at his arrogance; the drink was obviously making him bold. 'Now I know you are teasing me, Captain Buckley. I have no interest in boastful cavalrymen so you would have never been in contention.'

He laughed. 'Touché!' Before she could escape the dance floor, he seized her hand and pressed it to his lips. 'Thank you, Mrs Gillveray. I look forward to becoming better acquainted.'

Alice snatched her hand away and hurried back to George.

Chapter 13

Nothing had prepared Alice for the stifling heat of May. The temperature soared, sucking the air from her lungs and bathing her in perpetual sweat. The sun scorched everything, turning the Maidan brown and causing the trees to wilt. It beat down relentlessly. The sky was ochre with dust and the white Georgian buildings dazzled so fiercely that she thought her eyes would burn just by looking at them.

George continued to ride out to the Company gardens. Sometimes Alice would go with him, hoping for relief among the myriad of trees. But even here in the shade, the air was soupy.

Alice was in awe of the servants, who went about their work without complaint, bearing the heat as just another chore. Like the other Europeans, she learnt to keep the house darkened during the day, shutting out the brutal daylight with wet matting hung from verandas and windows to cool any wisp of breeze. One of the servants was employed to circle the house spraying the matting to keep it moist. Wine bottles were kept chilled by wrapping them in wet cloths and suspending them in baskets between trees.

Alice sat in the gloom of the veranda, half comatose in a rattan chair, too sapped of energy to read or paint. It took all her energy to stir herself and sit at the table at mealtimes. For relief, she would ask the bearer to have a basin filled with ice for her to rub on her sweating body. By the time she had stripped off, the ice would have melted and the water begun to warm. But any brief relief was welcome.

'Remember to order some frozen water from the ship, *Tuscany*,' Emily had advised before she had departed for Simla with Sandy and Auckland's entourage. 'Sandy says the quality is far better than the dirty slush that comes from the ice pits at Chinsurah.'

George had confirmed that an enterprising American from Boston had begun shipping frozen water regularly from Massachusetts and was storing it in a specially built ice house near the river. Seeing how his young wife was suffering so badly from the hot weather, George spent a small fortune buying in ice to cool her down.

Alice missed Emily's lively company. She still sometimes caught herself looking out for the Aytons' *chaprassy* running over with a message inviting her to some social engagement. But in April, Lord Auckland and his administration had packed up and left for the cool of the hills – a trek that would take their ponderous caravan of officials and luggage over a month to get to Simla in the north-west Himalayas.

Before she had left, Emily had confided in Alice that she was expecting her first baby.

'That's wonderful!' Alice had cried, overcome with emotion for her friend. They had hugged tearfully.

'I know, isn't it?' Emily had smiled. 'Sandy is happy as a lark.'

Alice had recently received a letter from Emily saying they had arrived safely in Simla and were settling into Daisy Cottage, which was to be their small, temporary home for the summer.

'If only Emily were still here,' she sighed to George. 'I've no one to talk to. Even the parrot's not speaking in this awful heat.'

When he suggested a carriage ride in the moonlight, a lacklustre Alice dismissed the idea.

'It's just as hot out there as in here,' she complained. 'And we women always have to wear so much ridiculous clothing. Why can't we go bare-armed like Hindu ladies and just have a thin veil to cover us?'

Whatever George said seemed to irritate her. Alice hated the short-tempered, dissatisfied person she had become in a few short weeks but seemed helpless to throw off her new moodiness.

'I wish I could have gone to Simla with Emily,' she said. 'Why do you have to work in such a furnace of a place?'

'If that's what you want,' said George, 'then I'll arrange it. I'll take some leave and we'll go next month or perhaps July.'

'Why can't we go now?'

'I have responsibilities—'

'You don't need to work,' Alice protested. 'We have enough money for you to do as you please – the fortune you acquired by marrying me!'

She saw George flinch but couldn't stop her resentful words.

'I'll go myself if you can't be bothered to take me. I can't stand it here a minute longer. I hate this place!' Alice put her face in her hands and burst into tears.

George was horrified. 'My dearest, please don't upset yourself,' he said, rushing to put his arms around her.

She threw him off. 'Don't touch me – you just make the heat rash worse.'

For several days afterwards, George slept on the flat roof over the veranda. Unable to sleep, Alice tossed alone on their bed, tormented by prickly heat and dark thoughts. What had ever possessed her to marry George and leave Tolland Park for this hellish place? She craved the soft sunshine of Northumberland, the dewy mornings and cooling winds. She yearned for salty sea spray and cold rain that would bring relief to her burning, itching body. Alice thought she would go mad thinking about such things.

'That Captain Buckley keeps asking about you,' Emily had said in the days following the ball. 'Sandy has told him firmly to leave you alone – you're a happily married wife.'

Happily married wife! Alice bit down on her hand to stop a scream of panic waking the household. She wished she wasn't anybody's wife.

* * *

George was so concerned at her plummeting spirits that he insisted on calling out one of the Company doctors, Major Jenkins.

'It's not in her nature to be so cross or have such black moods,' Alice heard her husband confiding in the doctor.

A few weeks ago, Alice would have been embarrassed at George making such a fuss over her or being examined by a doctor, but she no longer cared. The major was elderly with a drinker's bulbous red nose, and his hands shook badly as he prodded her with moist fingers. He asked questions about her eating and effluence while George looked on in concern.

'Mrs Gillveray is suffering from melancholia brought on by the hot season,' he announced. 'I recommend a course of bloodletting to cleanse her body and revitalise her spirits. Leeches are the best remedy.'

'Leeches?' Alice was aghast. 'I don't want those horrible creatures anywhere near me.'

George ushered the major quickly from the bedchamber and onto the veranda. 'Some refreshment before you go?' George offered.

Alice lay in annoyance, listening to the major talking about horse riding and gulping down lukewarm hock.

A week later, worn down by George's pleas to try the remedy, Alice submitted to the treatment of the bloodsucking leeches. She was left feeling nauseous and weaker and more dispirited than ever. She began to be plagued by thoughts of walking out into the hot night and never coming back.

Her sanity was saved by a visit from Miss Cook and her plump American missionary friend, Mrs Meadows. They brought a box of sweetmeats and clucked in concern at Alice's listless state.

Plain-speaking Mrs Meadows surveyed her keenly. 'Feeling sick all the time, are you?'

'Yes,' said Alice. 'I can't bear the smell of anything. Even the cooking from the kitchen makes me retch. I've lost the taste for everything except sweets.'

Mrs Meadows summoned the bearer and ordered a hot infusion of tea and ginger.

Alice sighed. 'I don't want anything hot.'

'This will do wonders, my dear,' said the missionary, 'if you're suffering from what I think you are.'

'Major Jenkins says I have melancholia.'

'Complete nonsense!' cried Mrs Meadows. 'I can tell just by looking at you.'

'Tell what?' asked Miss Cook.

'Our dear Alice,' said the missionary with a sympathetic smile, 'is carrying a child.'

* * *

At first Alice would not believe she was pregnant but George was so pleased at the idea that she was encouraged too. The ginger drinks helped calm her nausea and she developed a passion for bananas that seemed to coincide with her strength returning. After a couple more weeks the sickness began to wear off and Alice's spirits revived. She was full of guilt for her unkind words to her husband.

'George, I'm so sorry for the way I've treated you these past weeks,' she said. 'I've been monstrous.'

'No, dearest,' he said, pressing her hands between his, 'it's I who must apologise. I should never have subjected you to Major Jenkins and his wretched leeches. I could have endangered you and our child . . .'

Alice saw the tears in his eyes. 'There is no harm done,' Alice assured him with a smile. 'I am made of hardy northern stock, remember?'

Now that pregnancy appeared to be a reality, Alice was secretly unnerved by the thought of being a mother. She worried that she might turn out like her own – devoid of motherly feelings and unable to love her child. Would she take one look at her baby and instantly want to give it away? She was ashamed of such thoughts, especially when the idea of them being parents had filled George with a renewed tenderness towards her.

Alice agreed readily to her husband's insistence that they should leave without delay for the hills.

'You will have the healthiest air possible,' George decreed, 'and we will travel before the monsoon makes the roads impassable.'

'Simla?' Alice cried in hope. 'Please can we go there?'

'Yes, Simla.' George grinned. 'I've already written to the Aytons to see if we can lodge with them at Daisy Cottage.'

Alice threw her arms around him and kissed him roundly. 'Thank you, George!'

* * *

The arduous journey upriver and across the baking Indian plains took three jolting, exhausting weeks. But Alice never complained once at the heat or the flies, her determination to get to the hills keeping her strong. When the Himalayan foothills finally came into sight, there were still several days of hair-raising travel up narrow winding paths on the backs of mules. But the higher they climbed, the clearer the air became, until they were riding through pine-scented trees.

Alice laughed, gulping in breaths of the sweet air. 'I haven't smelt such wonderful fragrance since leaving Northumberland.'

Her first sight of Simla was a hillside thick with mighty cedars and firs and dotted with bungalows whose windows glinted in the evening sun. Soft plumes of smoke arose from chimneys into a blue-grey sky.

When they arrived at the Aytons' wooden bungalow, nestling into the slope with a view that dropped away to the hazy plains, Alice couldn't contain her emotion. She fell into Emily's arms – her friend's belly already large with child – and burst into tears of relief.

Chapter 14

In the damp mist of the Choor mountain, John huddled in a blanket under a dripping awning and waited. His fellow surveyor, Hodgson, was trying to light a wet cigar at the stove. They were bearded and unwashed but triumphant at having completed the thirty-foot-high pyramid of stone for their theodolite at the top of Choor. If a sudden storm – an early precursor of the monsoon – had not caught them on the peak and marooned them in a cloudbank, they would have finished this section of the trigonometrical series and been on leave.

But the cloud hadn't lifted for days. They waited in frustration for it to clear enough for them to send a signal from their heliotrope or receive flashes of light from the triangulation points on the neighbouring mountains.

'Have some more claret,' John said, pouring out the wine with numb fingers.

His servant Rajban was attempting to brew up coffee in the thin atmosphere; John had developed a passion for the drink since coming to India seven years ago. He admired the hillsmen who worked alongside him, carrying the heavy survey equipment and provisions, digging and hacking with pickaxes and sleeping in the open muffled in their blankets. He could hear their talk and laughter just below on the stony slope and smell their aromatic pipe smoke.

'What will you do on leave?' Hodgson asked, sucking hard on his disintegrating cigar. It was a question that had occupied John's thoughts during the frustrating hours of waiting.

'Join my artillery friend MacRae for a month of hunting up the Sutlej River,' said John.

'Into the unknown, eh?' Hodgson nodded.

'Not for Rajban. He comes from the Bushahir district so knows those hills and speaks the language. He'll be my guide.'

'You'd put your trust in that wily old devil? He'll sell you into slavery to the Tibetans or Chinese.'

'I'd trust him with my life,' John retorted. 'He's a Highlander like me – and not much older, for all he has a face like leather.'

'Well, be careful is all I'd say.' Hodgson gulped at his wine. 'You don't want to stray beyond British-held land – don't want to upset the Sikhs, or the Tibetans for that matter. If you do, the Company won't come to your rescue.'

John felt a flicker of unease at his friend's words; they strangely echoed the secretive conversation he'd had the previous month in Dehra Dun, the Survey's headquarters. A political agent, sent by Colonel Wade from Ludhiana on the banks of the Sutlej, had come to sound him out. Over several glasses of wine and port, the man had flattered him about his work with the Grand Trigonometrical Survey and his ability as a mountaineer.

'Your superior officer, Everest, speaks highly of you – one of his most able triangulators. You need strong lungs and a cool head to climb the mountains that you do and carry out your work.'

'I grew up with mountains,' John had said, wondering where the conversation was going. The man had called himself Captain Smith but John doubted that was his real name.

'Some of our political officers are keen to know what lies beyond the Himalayas – what the routes through might be,' the man continued. 'Trade is of vital importance to the Company – especially as our sources in Persia tell us how Russia is flexing its muscles in our direction. We want to explore possible new markets – the Tibetan trade in *pashm* is of particular interest. But,' Smith cautioned, 'nothing must be done to upset the Sikh ruler in the Punjab, Ranjit Singh. We need him as an ally of the British and he has designs on certain of the Himalayan states.'

'So what are you suggesting?' John had asked.

'A foray into the mountains to the east of the Punjab, mapping out the trade routes.' Smith gave a charming smile. 'You are a keen hunter, I hear, and could make that your excuse for exploring the region. We would provide you with money to do so – cover your expenses.'

'And travel permits?'

'Ah,' Smith had said with a regretful shrug, 'I'm afraid not. You would have to rely on your wits. But if you come back with information that is valuable to the Company, you will be richly rewarded.'

John had replied, 'Rewards don't interest me but a hunting trip in the mountains is a more tempting offer.' He had contemplated the other man. 'Still, I'm sceptical about how far I would get with just a hunting gun and a Company uniform. If you gave me a legitimate trading mission – to buy horses from the Ladakhis, for instance – and a letter of introduction from the Company,' John bargained, 'then I could go much further.'

Smith eyed him shrewdly. 'And if you didn't get these things would you refuse to go?'

'Then I would simply go hunting' – John smiled – 'and stay the right side of the Sutlej River.'

By the time they had finished off another bottle of port, Smith had promised him a limited trading role as cover for his exploration and John had agreed to the venture.

'The letter we send with you,' Smith had warned, 'will specify that your interest is only in horses. You cannot promise political alliance or British protection to any of these hill kings.'

John had readily agreed to that, having no interest in political intrigue. He relished the horse-buying trip and the chance to map mountain passes unknown to the British; and both would provide him with plenty of opportunity to hunt.

At the end of a long night's drinking, Smith had said, 'Just one last thing. Unofficially, I encourage you to go as far as you can this summer. But if you get caught straying beyond the bounds of British influence and are accused of spying, you're on your own. The Company won't come to your rescue. Is that understood, Sinclair?'

John had given a dry smile and nodded.

In the morning the mysterious Smith had gone but a week later a package of money had been delivered to John's quarters with a vaguely worded letter bearing the Company's seal, attesting to his good character and stating that his business was to buy horses.

'. . . and the Annandale Fair is supposed to be a lively occasion with fancy dress and horse racing.'

John's attention was brought back to the present. He realised Hodgson had been talking about his own plans for recreation once they got off the mountain.

'The Eden sisters are supposed to be full of fun,' Hodgson said. 'Simla has never been as full of social events as this year's hot season.'

'The Eden sisters?' John queried.

'The new Governor General's sisters,' his friend cried. 'Goodness, Sinclair, don't you hear any of the gossip?'

'Not stuck up a mountain with you,' John joked. 'I don't know how you manage to hear of such things.'

His friend laughed. 'Because I bother to write and receive letters. I never see you write to anyone.'

'I've never been much good at writing – unless it's mapping or filling in plane-table charts.'

John felt a stab of guilt at his lack of letter-writing to Hercules or his Aunt Morag. He thought about them often – and his dear friend Azlan – but he was a hopeless correspondent. He had lost the appetite for writing letters and expressing his thoughts when Alice had ignored his love letters. How long ago that seemed now and yet he could still conjure up her fair face and pretty eyes too easily.

Over the years, on the long journey up the length of India, working for Everest's mapping survey, he had thought of Alice. On hot nights in jungle camps he had lain awake plagued by memories of her. He would imagine her riding the bridle paths of her father's estate or attending balls in Newcastle. She would be married off by now and probably the mother of several children. John would clench his teeth and screw his eyes tight to stop himself remembering the feel of her cool hand on his face or the taste of her lips.

He had known other women since Alice but none had excited him or made him as sore at heart as she had done. That had been a relief, for John's life was a rootless one, moving on from place to place and never calling anywhere home. He loved his job in the survey team; the painstaking and ambitious project of mapping India in a grand arc – a series of triangles – from Cape Comorin in the south to the Himalayas in the north. Early on in his army career he had seized the chance to travel the length of the sub-continent and was one of the few engineers who had been able to withstand the temper and exacting standards of their superior officer, Everest. John took tongue-lashings with good grace and often diffused outbursts with wry humour because he respected the man for his dedication to science and passion for discovery.

'So is that where you're meeting MacRae?' Hodgson asked.

'Where?' John said, dragging his thoughts back to the mountain once again.

'Simla! I think the altitude is turning your brain to porridge, Sinclair.'

John laughed. 'What I wouldn't do for a bowl of porridge just now.'

'Simla would be the best starting off point for a hunting trip up the Sutlej,' said Hodgson. 'Plenty of mules and coolies for hire to carry your kit. And a spot of socialising before you go, eh?'

'Aye, why not?' John grinned. 'Meet these Eden sisters. Do your gossips say whether they are bonny?'

* * *

It was the end of June before John and his survey team were finished on Choor Mountain. Once the fog had lifted, the nights had been cold and the slopes had dazzled in silvery moonlight like polished pearls. To the south spread the sweltering plains of India, while to the north, in a series of dark waves, lay the foothills and Simla.

Returning first to Dehra Dun, John sent a message to Colin MacRae at the barracks in Subathu to meet him in Simla. By the time he and Hodgson and their entourage of servants had wound their way into the hills again, Colin was already established at the house of fellow Scots officer, Captain Charlie Nairn. As political agent to the hill kingdoms, Nairn had set up home in Simla and had a reputation for generous hospitality and long, raucous dinner parties.

John and Colin thumped each other on the back and exchanged Gaelic greetings.

'Look at you with your brown face and black beard,' Colin teased. 'You could pass for an Afghan!'

'I've got used to not shaving when out on survey.' John laughed. 'And I hope you've been keeping your guns primed and your eye trained for the game we're going to be hunting.'

John bathed and shaved off his beard. They had a long, leisurely dinner, catching up on the past year, eating well and drinking late into the night.

'There's only one bit of bad news,' Colin said, as the brandy bottle was passed around. 'Vernon Buckley's on Auckland's staff. I've seen him strutting around the sports' ground at Annandale with his cavalry sword clanking.'

John snorted. 'Doesn't surprise me. He always did have a long tongue for licking the boots of the rich and powerful.'

Colin nodded in agreement. 'Just the type to get himself a comfortable, well-paid position while we do the dangerous work. He's a captain now, so we lieutenants have to bow to the insufferable man.'

'Good luck to him,' John said, 'I wouldn't want to trade places. Give me a frozen mountaintop and a mutton curry over a life of governor's dinners and gout any day!'

* * *

It wasn't long before John came across Vernon. The European population of Simla swelled in the summer to several hundred but the social activities – card parties and soirées – were held in a dozen of the more spacious houses or recreation was taken outdoors. If it wasn't raining, the British took leisurely rides along the wooded tracks and picnicked at Annandale, a picturesque glade below the town that was big enough to hold sporting events such as archery and horse racing.

After two days of continuous rain and mist hanging over the trees like smoke, the sky had cleared and word had gone round that there would be racing and a charity fair at Annandale.

'Well, well,' Vernon crowed as he spotted John and Colin riding into the grassy arena, 'if it isn't the Scotch boys. Come to gape at the real horsemen?'

'Buckley.' John smiled, dismounted and went to shake his hand. 'As charming as ever, I see.'

'Captain Buckley to you,' he said with a satisfied smile, briefly touching John's extended hand. 'Still measuring bits of desert with your chain links, Sinclair?'

'No, the survey has progressed into the mountains,' John replied, ignoring his sneering tone. 'We climb with ropes as well as our theodolites. Not a chain link in sight.'

'Well, you wild Scotchmen are as surefooted as mountain goats, aren't you? I'm glad you've found your purpose in life.'

'And you are dancing attendance on the new Governor General, I hear,' John said with a wry smile. 'Congratulations on becoming one of Auckland's aides.'

Vernon's smug expression faltered, unsure if he was being slighted in some way. He turned and called to a fellow officer who was standing nearby in the entrance to a refreshment tent.

'Ayton, come here! Let me introduce you to two of *your* kind.'

A ruddy-faced man, a few years their senior, ambled over.

'Two fellow Scotch for you, Sandy – from the Bombay Presidency. There'll soon be enough of you for one of your savage reels, eh?' Vernon laughed, clapping Sandy on the back. 'Ayton here is from Edinburgh and has one of the prettiest wives in the service.'

John and Colin exchanged bows and pleasantries with Sandy.

'Where is Mrs Ayton?' Vernon interrupted. 'Stitched together with the delightful Mrs Gillveray no doubt. Where one fair lady goes the other must follow, eh?'

'They're in the exhibition tent with George,' said Sandy. 'Mrs Gillveray's watercolours are selling well. Why don't you come over and take a look?'

The men entrusted their horses to the *syces* and followed Sandy, John thinking that the name Gillveray sounded familiar. The tent was crowded with bonneted women and their uniformed husbands, and noisy with their chattering as they exclaimed over the displays of embroidery and paintings in the charity sale. Vernon stopped at a table of lacework to compliment some young women.

'Oh, there you are!' a petite woman called to Sandy. Frizzy blonde hair escaped her bonnet and she was heavily pregnant. 'Nearly all of Alice's paintings have sold already. Isn't that marvellous?'

'Emily, here are two fellow countrymen,' beamed Sandy, 'who have come to bid for the rest. Lieutenants Sinclair and MacRae.'

John bent over the hand that Emily held out. 'Mrs Ayton.' As he straightened up he asked, 'Are you one of the artists?'

'Goodness no.' She laughed. 'I was always hopeless at drawing. But my friend Alice has a real talent for it. Alice!'

On hearing her name called, the tall woman with her back to them broke off her conversation and turned. John's immediate thought was that she was pleasantly full-figured and her smiling face under the bonnet was attractive. Her cheeks were well-defined and rosy, her mouth pink and sensuous. Then their eyes met and his heart stopped. Even shaded by the bonnet he could see they were as vivid a blue as the sky outside. He knew those eyes.

Alice? He smothered a gasp, stepping forward.

His heart began to pound. He found breathing hard. How was it possible for her to be standing in front of him in this tent in one of the Company's remotest outposts? For brief heady seconds, John felt a rush of euphoria. He had found Alice again. The same desire he had experienced as a young cadet surged through him.

Then she froze, her smile dying. She looked around in panic. For a moment John thought he must have been mistaken but the flush that rushed into her neck and cheeks reminded him at once of his time of convalescence in the lighthouse. Alice had blushed so prettily then at his amorous teasing.

'George,' she said, putting her hand on the arm of an elderly man who had come quickly to her side.

George smiled at the young officers as Sandy introduced them once more.

'George Gillveray,' said the older man, shaking each firmly by the hand. 'And this is my talented wife, Alice.'

John stared in stupefaction. He must have misheard. This man could not possibly be married to Alice; he looked twice her age. He felt the blood drain from his face. Disappointment engulfed him. Of course she would be married – but to a man so much older?

Colin kissed Alice's hand. John hesitated and then, bracing himself, did likewise. It was sweet torture to press her slender fingers to his lips. He could feel her trembling. As he pulled back, their eyes met fleetingly. Was he just imagining the warmth of emotion in hers?

George was talking about his work at the botanic gardens in Calcutta but John hardly heard a word as he fought to control his feelings and hide his shock. Colin made conversation, aware that something had shaken his friend. Suddenly it struck John that he knew who Gillveray was. He found his voice.

'I believe we have met, sir,' said John. 'Long ago at Ramanish Castle. You were on tour with Stevenson, reviewing lighthouses. Hercules MacAskill is my foster father.'

'Hercules?' George exclaimed. 'He's a good friend of mine from my first days in India! How is he?'

'Very well, thank you.'

'But I don't recall . . . ?' George said, puzzled.

'I was the young boy who spoke nothing but Pashto.' John smiled. 'I was a wee bit rude to you – ran off as I remember. You never knew it but you helped me to speak again – Gaelic and English, that is.'

'Heavens, did I? I'm glad I was of some use on that trip. I remember you now – a handsome boy. Hercules was immensely proud of you.' George smiled. 'And here you are an officer in the Company army. I bet that pleased old MacAskill.'

John laughed. 'It did.' He liked Gillveray, even though the thought of Alice being his wife made his guts twist with jealousy. He listened as George reminisced about his time sailing around the Western Isles reviewing lighthouses over twenty years ago. John waited for him to bring Alice into the conversation and mention how she had once lived in one. Then John would be gallant and praise her for saving his life from the storm-lashed rocks beyond her lighthouse home. It gave him a stab of pleasure to think how it would remind Alice of how she had forgotten her promise to him and treated him so carelessly once she was famous. He watched her but she wouldn't look at him.

Abruptly, George changed the subject, asking the men about their work. He grew enthusiastic when John told him he was a surveyor with Everest.

'Dear boy, I'm eager to hear more. You must come and dine with us and tell me all about it. Promise me you will?'

'Won't Mrs Gillveray find such talk tedious?' John said, unable to resist a jibe.

'Not at all,' George answered for her. 'Alice is very knowledgeable about all sorts of matters. Her father kept a vast library and encouraged her learning. That's why my wife is so keen on native girls being educated – the paintings are raising funds for a school for the daughters of Gurkha *sepoys*.'

John glanced at Alice. She was blushing furiously and seemed incapable of speaking for herself. How she had changed! So this was how she was presented to the world – as a rich man's daughter who was bountiful towards lowly Indian girls. It dawned on John that neither Alice nor George wanted to mention her own lowly upbringing with her simple foster family. John thought of the kind and compassionate Browns and felt distaste that Alice should turn her back on them so readily. He would never disown his humble origins. John turned to go.

'Lieutenant Sinclair,' Alice said, 'surely you won't go without buying something for the charity?'

Turning back, he saw her challenging him with a bold look; a flash of the strong-willed woman he remembered. His stomach clenched.

'Forgive me – of course not,' he replied, reddening at the rebuke. He followed her to the table where three watercolours remained, propped up on roughly made easels.

He expected them to be of typical rustic Simla scenes; bungalows on Jakko Hill, the ravine at Combermere's Bridge or pine-fringed Annandale. But to his surprise they were of people rather than views; a porter carrying firewood in a basket strapped to his forehead and a mother with her baby bound to her back in gaily coloured cloth. There were farmers with mules, pipe smokers squatting in the bazaar, children splashing in puddles. Strangely they reminded him of the village at Ramanish; she had caught the essence of the people going about their everyday lives.

'These are very good,' John said. 'So lifelike – colourful.'

'And that surprises you?' Her mouth twitched in amusement.

John regarded her. 'It surprises me,' he murmured, 'that such a high-born lady thinks to paint the commonplace.'

116

Alice gave him a sharp look, her mouth tightening in annoyance.

'I'll take the one with the boys playing,' said John. 'It reminds me of my childhood running around barefoot and half naked.'

'Don't you mean running away?' Alice challenged.

John frowned. 'Meaning?'

'Nothing of course,' Alice said lightly, taking the painting off its easel and wrapping it in cloth. 'Thank you for helping the girls' school.' She held it out to him.

John fished out money, puzzled by her strange remark.

At that moment, Vernon returned from flirting with the women at the embroidery table and called over. 'Sinclair, there's a shooting match about to begin. I wager you a jorum of champagne that you can't beat me!'

'Well, if you can afford it,' John quipped back, 'then I'd be happy to win a jorum off you, Buckley.'

* * *

Alice gripped the table as she watched John go. Her pulse raced and head pounded. She thought she would faint. The suddenness of his appearance had completely winded her and left her floundering to speak. Her fingers still tingled where his firm mouth had brushed them with a kiss. At first glance she had thought him one of those swarthy French or Italian mercenaries who came to India to seek their fortunes. He looked older, his face leaner and more rugged, his jaw already darkening with stubble after the morning's shave. But then their eyes had met. She would have known those lively green eyes anywhere. Her heart had flipped in her chest.

'My dear, are you unwell?' George asked in concern.

Alice dragged her gaze away from the departing soldiers. 'It's just the heat in here. I'm all right.'

'I thought this might be too much for you,' he fussed. 'You've been overdoing it with your painting. Let's get you into the refreshment tent and sat down. Some tea will restore you.'

'Yes,' Alice said, still breathless, 'tea would be good.'

But when George got her into a camp chair and she sipped at the hot drink, she felt a familiar wave of nausea rise in her throat. Alice had been unwell for the first week in Simla, exhausted after the journey, and had taken to bed. Only after a heavy downpour had cleared the thundery air did her energy begin to return. She had spent the following fortnight roaming the town on foot, George at her side, sketching the hill folk.

'Why do people say that Simla is just a few dozen houses on a hill,' Alice had mused, 'when there is this native town below absolutely bursting with life?'

George had laughed. 'That's because they aren't looking for it.'

Alice was enjoying sharing a house with the Aytons – Emily was the only other person she had confided in about being pregnant – but she had lost the appetite for socialising. She was always sick after dinner parties and found it hard to stay awake at musical recitals. Even tea parties were a chore, whereas Emily seemed to thrive on Simla society. Her friend could eat anything and was ballooning like a ship's sails in her summer dresses. Pregnancy appeared to suit Emily and both she and Sandy were delighted to think their first child would be born in the hills away from the miasma of fevers on the plains.

The one house Alice liked to visit was that of Miss Wallace, who had set up the girls' school at Subathu. Her dark looks showed her Indian heritage. The gossip in Simla drawing rooms was that her grandmother had been a wealthy Hindu merchant's daughter who had married a Company sea captain, Wallace. Alice found her lively and welcoming in the way that Miss Cook had been in Calcutta.

'Come and watch the shooting,' Emily urged, finding Alice in the refreshment tent. 'Sandy's having a go too.'

'Alice is not feeling well,' George said. 'I'm thinking of taking her back to the house.'

'Oh, don't do that,' Emily said in dismay. 'The fun is just beginning. And you said you wanted to enter the archery competition, didn't you, Alice?'

'She certainly won't be doing that,' George decreed.

Alice stood up, irritated. She sighed. 'Don't mollycoddle me. I'm not an invalid, George.' She saw his hurt look and immediately regretted her words. Yet she didn't want to let Emily down either. 'Thank you for your concern but I feel fine now I've rested.' She smiled. 'Come on, let's go and watch Sandy beat the arrogant Captain Buckley.'

* * *

The target was an upside-down brass jug impaled on a pole. Gunfire rang out on the makeshift range and the air was tinged with acrid smoke. The crowd of onlookers clapped and cheered when they heard the metal ping of a bullet hitting the jug. John was level with Vernon with six shots each on target; they were the last two contestants still in the competition. Sandy and Colin had withdrawn after missing their last attempts.

'Stick to field guns,' Vernon had told Colin with a patronising wink, 'you can't fail to hit something with those.'

As John stepped up to the mark again, he caught sight of Alice and her talkative friend at the front of the throng. No doubt she had come to cheer on Vernon – all the women seemed to be doing so – and the thought unsettled him. He took aim and missed for the first time. Excited gasps rippled around him.

Vernon made a big show of taking his time and theatrically positioning himself for his shot. If he hit the target then he would win. The onlookers held their breath. He fired and the metal jug jerked as the bullet struck home. Cheering broke out.

Vernon turned and gave John a satisfied smile. 'Bad luck Sinclair; champagne's on you tonight.'

John stepped forward and shook his hand. 'Well done, Buckley.'

'I'll be round to Nairn's to claim my prize,' Vernon said with a pat on John's back, 'and take you on at cards.'

'I'm sure Captain Nairn can't wait for the honour,' John said dryly.

As he walked off to join Colin, he glanced over at Alice. She was watching him, her arm linked possessively with her husband's. He frowned in annoyance that her presence had made him lose concentration. His time in Simla was going to be purgatory if he was to come across her at every turn – though she had not been at any of the riotous, liquor-fuelled dinners that his host, Nairn, had thrown since John had arrived in the hill station. He would keep to the company of bachelor officers and avoid any chance of social intercourse with Alice. John also determined that he would speed up his plans to venture north.

Chapter 15

'Do we have to invite those Scottish lieutenants?' Alice asked, trying to hide her alarm at George once again making the suggestion they entertain John and Colin. It was several days since the Annandale event and Alice had managed to avoid John. 'I'm sure they would much rather be dining at Auckland House with the Edens.'

'I know you tire easily, my dearest,' said George, 'but it would just be a simple supper. And I did promise young Sinclair. Besides, I'm very keen to hear about the Trigonometrical Survey; it's the most astonishing feat of engineering. Would you like the Aytons to be there too so that you have Emily to converse with?'

'It's not that,' Alice said. 'But wouldn't you rather go over to Nairn's and discuss it with Lieutenant Sinclair over a bowl of tobacco and a glass of port? He might find that more congenial.'

'In my experience,' said George, 'young officers crave a little bit of domesticity and female company. I certainly did as a young man. Spending all your time in the mess grows tiresome.'

'From what I hear they have all the female company they want at Nairn's,' Alice retorted. 'Dancing girls after dinner, that's what Emily says.'

'Don't listen to gossip,' said George.

'Not gossip, the truth,' Alice replied. 'Miss Wallace is most concerned about these *nautch* girls. She thinks the men take advantage of them when they've had too much to drink.'

'My dear!' George exclaimed. 'Miss Wallace shouldn't be talking to you about such things.'

'So you know it goes on?' Alice demanded.

George looked pained. 'I don't make any excuses for such behaviour. But isn't that all the more reason to invite the young officers into this genteel home and give them some civilised entertainment? They are far from home and I would like to show them friendship. Is that so very onerous?'

Alice felt ashamed of her reluctance to give hospitality. As usual, her kind husband was only thinking of others while she was selfishly trying to protect her feelings. Was it possible that George had forgotten the names of the people she had saved on the night of the storm? It would seem so. If she explained to him now that John had been one of them, George might call off the supper party. He was very protective of her past.

When they had become engaged, they had agreed not to mention her heroism as Alice Brown or the gossip about her scandalous mother. She had not sought the publicity and it had brought untold strain on her family. In India she had felt unshackled from her past by becoming Mrs Gillveray. John threatened that harmony in her new life. She might already be the talk of the mess. What if he had boasted about how she had nursed him and given her kisses so readily? Or was his ungentlemanly conduct of promising marriage and then deserting her keeping him silent on the matter? Perhaps it would be best to get the ordeal of seeing him over. Then she could make it quite plain that she expected his discretion on the matter and wanted nothing more to do with him.

'You are a good man, George.' She smiled. 'You see nothing but the best in people. Of course we must make the officers welcome here.'

* * *

John downed two brandies before setting out for Daisy Cottage. Earlier he had cut himself shaving.

'Let's keep this as short a visit as possible,' he muttered to Colin as they made their way along the narrow path from their billet on Jakko Hill down towards Combermere Bridge.

'I don't know why you're so reluctant,' Colin said, lapsing into Gaelic as they always did together. 'The Gillverays seem a pleasant couple.'

'Looks can deceive.'

'What's that supposed to mean?'

'Nothing.'

Colin stopped and grabbed John by the arm. 'Friend, tell me what's preying on your mind. You've been out of sorts this past week – drinking till you pass out. I've had to carry you to bed every night. And picking arguments with Nairn over *nautch* girls . . .'

John shook off Colin's hold. 'I don't think much of Simla society, that's all. I'm impatient for us to be off into the mountains.'

'It's more than that,' said Colin. 'I know you too well. You haven't been yourself since you set eyes on Mrs Gillveray.'

John reddened. 'Was it that obvious?'

'To me,' Colin said with a pitying smile. 'You've met her before?'

John let out an impatient sigh. 'Before she was Mrs Gillveray she was Alice Brown and then Fairchild. Doesn't that name mean anything to you?'

'No, should it?'

'She was the Alice who saved my life – the lighthouse heroine of the broadsheets.'

'*That* Alice?' Colin exclaimed. 'The one you wanted to marry?'

John nodded, his jaw clenching.

Colin let out a low whistle. 'Why didn't you say anything?'

'Because it's obvious she doesn't want to be reminded of it – of her former life, or of me.' John gripped Colin's shoulder. 'You mustn't say anything. I don't want her to blame me for any gossip that might spread about her.'

'I don't see what harm it would do if people knew she was the lighthouse heroine.'

'Because they printed all sorts of lurid stories about her notorious mother giving birth and abandoning her in the lighthouse. Some even said she wasn't Fairchild's daughter at all – that she was a sea captain's bastard. I don't know where they got such tales.'

'If that's the case then of course I won't say anything,' Colin promised.

'Good,' said John. 'Let's get this over with quickly and then head for the mountains. Agreed?'

Colin clapped him on the back. 'Agreed.'

* * *

Under cover of the soft lamplight, Alice studied John. He was in deep, animated discussion with George about triangulation and measurements allowing for the curvature of the earth. The light fell on his strong-featured face and made his dark hair glint like a raven's wing. She listened to the cadence of his Highland voice and felt a tug of longing deep inside.

At the start of the evening, the conversation had been stilted and a baffled George had been extra jovial, filling the awkward pauses with chatter about the botany of the Himalayas. Alice had the impression that John must have told Colin about their past entanglement for he had seemed just as embarrassed to talk to her as John had been.

But after a supper of tinned Scottish salmon that George had ordered specially for their guests, along with potatoes and peas from their garden, washed down with three bottles of claret, all the men had become relaxed and talkative.

' . . . and they're very appreciative of your efforts, Mrs Gillveray.'

Alice was suddenly aware that Colin was talking to her. She had only been half listening.

'Sorry,' she said. 'My efforts?'

'For the *sepoys*' daughters. The school at Subathu. I know some of the Gurkhas there.'

'Oh, yes, of course,' Alice said hastily. 'But it's really Miss Wallace who deserves the credit. I just sold a handful of paintings.'

'Charming paintings,' John said, taking her by surprise. Had he been listening in to her conversation as she had to his? 'Your picture of the boys by the watering hole has pride of place on our wall – though I fear the rain that leaks through the ceiling might damage it.'

Alice smiled. 'Well, I'm glad it's covering up the damp marks.'

'What do you intend to paint next, Mrs Gillveray?' John asked.

'I have yet to visit the monkey temple at the top of Jakko Hill,' she said. 'I've heard you get the best view of Simla from there.'

'You do indeed.' He nodded. 'Especially at sunrise. The peaks of the Himalayas are clearest then – before the clouds cover them. I would recommend an early morning ride.'

He held her look, his eyes gleaming fiercely in the candlelight. Alice felt a slow thudding in her chest. Was he challenging her to meet him there? The atmosphere between them had shifted subtly during the evening; his initial frostiness to her had thawed. She had to remind herself that he had no reason to be curt with her, as it was she who was the wronged one. Yet Alice was grateful that he had made no mention of how they had once known each other.

Colin said, 'I'm eager to see the mountains close up when we go on our trip.'

'Trip?' queried George.

'We're travelling up to Bushahir province in a few days,' explained John, 'as part of the cavalry's mission to buy horses for the Company remount at Dehra Dun. Colin and I hope to do some hunting while we're there.'

Alice felt a stab of disappointment. 'How long will you be gone?'

'Till we return to our regiments,' said Colin, 'at the end of the hot season.'

'Well, I wish you both good luck,' said George enviously. 'I've always wanted to visit the high plateaux and see Himalayan goats in their natural habitat – see for myself how they extract the *pashm* from their coats. I've always promised Alice a shawl made of pashmina. If I was ten years younger, I'd be joining you like a shot.'

'Your wife might have something to say about that,' John said dryly.

George chuckled. 'Alice would be there like a shot too if she wasn't carrying—' He stopped abruptly.

Alice flushed. He had been about to let slip that she was expecting their child. There was an awkward silence. She turned away from John's keen look.

'Lieutenant MacRae, you mentioned you would like to buy one of my paintings. Would you care to come back tomorrow and view them in daylight? I keep them in the summerhouse.'

'I'd be delighted,' said Colin.

'And I could show you around the garden,' said George, stifling a sudden yawn.

John stood up. 'Thank you for a very pleasant evening. We must let you get to your bed.'

Alice led them onto the veranda; the trees were dripping after a fresh downpour but the clouds were clearing to reveal a star-studded sky.

'That's the Choor, the mountain we were measuring,' John told them, pointing south. A solitary snow-tipped peak was emerging, a glittering outline in the starlight. 'The name means the Bracelet of the Moon.'

'How beautiful,' gasped Alice.

He turned and a look passed between them. Was he too thinking of the moment nearly ten years ago when he had declared his love for her?

'Aye, it was,' he said, his voice sounding deep with regret.

Suddenly Alice didn't want him to go. 'I hope you will come and see us before you leave Simla,' she said, holding out her hand.

'I would like that,' he answered. Stepping towards her, he took her hand and pressed it to his lips. 'Goodnight, Mrs Gillveray.'

'Goodnight,' she answered, hoping her voice didn't betray her hammering heart.

* * *

Alice lay in bed, sleepless. George was snoring loudly, unused to drinking so much claret. She was furious with herself for allowing tender memories of John to resurface. She was betraying her husband with every treacherous thought – the man whose baby she carried! Yet she could think of nothing else but John. She imagined him returning to Nairn's house to join in the revelries, torturing herself with visions of him lying in the arms of some beautiful dancing girl. She had no claim on him and shouldn't care what he did. How she despised herself!

John had come into her home and deliberately stirred up old feelings with his desirous glances. He was just the same flattering deceiver as of old. Alice tossed and sighed with frustration and anger. Then she thought how unfair she was being. He had merely answered a supper invitation and had made no attempt to see her until that night. She had read too much into his looks and words. It would be best if she never set eyes on him again.

* * *

In the pearly half-light of pre-dawn, Alice crept out of bed, dressed and went out. A sleepy-headed *syce* saddled up one of the ponies that Sandy had hired for the summer. George did not like her to ride in her delicate condition but she was tired of being treated like a porcelain doll. She missed her morning rides. She would go at walking pace. She needed the cool morning air to clear her head, which was fuzzy with lack of sleep.

Alice pretended the route she took up Jakko Hill was done on a whim but she knew deep down it wasn't. She wanted to glimpse the mountains that were drawing John away from Simla; she wished to feel their pull too. Above all, she wanted him to be there.

The air was filled with the resinous scent of the long-needled *deodars* that overhung the twisting track. Early fires sent up vertical columns of smoke from the bungalows hidden among the trees. She wondered which one was Nairn's. At the top of the hill there were no other early-morning riders and Alice felt a pang of disappointment. Yet the place was entrancing. Monkeys scampered around a weathered wooden temple with a steeply sloping roof. The trees were alive with the flapping and screeching of birds heralding the dawn. The noise masked the soft tread of hooves approaching so that Alice gasped in alarm as a rider pulled up beside her.

John smiled and her heart swelled. He had come! He didn't seem at all surprised to find her there.

'I hoped you'd be here,' he said.

She smiled back, too emotional to speak.

He nodded and said, 'The best view is from over there.'

She followed until he stopped his horse at a gap in the forest where trees had been recently felled. The sky was beginning to lighten to the east. As they watched, a rose-red dawn spread like fire behind a dark mass of indistinct ridges. Alice held her breath and waited, as if to breathe might break the spell of intimacy that bound them. Then she saw them: the mountain peaks. They emerged from the night as if waking from sleep, turning from pink to orange to gold and finally to a soft fluffy white.

Her mouth fell open in wonder. She had witnessed many splendid dawns from the lamp-room of the lighthouse but never one as magical as this. Alice felt tears of emotion sting her eyes.

'Why did you never reply to my letters, Alice?' John startled her with his question. It broke the spell at once.

'What letters?' she demanded. 'Don't pretend now that you bothered to write.'

He looked at her sharply. 'Indeed I did! I wrote many times.'

'I don't believe you,' she retorted. 'I never received any. I waited for months. It was I who wrote to you but got no reply. You promised you would write to my father—'

124

'I did,' John said indignantly. 'I asked for your hand in marriage. I sent gifts to your parents – clothes and books – I spent a small fortune on you all. That silk dress. But I suppose it wasn't fancy enough once you were claimed by Colonel Fairchild.'

Alice gaped at him. 'Silk dress?'

'Aye, it was sky blue,' said John, 'to match your eyes.'

Alice looked at him, stunned.

'When you never replied – not a word month after month,' John said, 'I went half out of my mind.'

Alice felt sick. What if he was telling the truth? A terrible doubt clawed at her insides. Was it possible that someone much closer to home had betrayed her and not John? She closed her eyes in pain. All these years of blaming John – loving and hating him in equal measure – all the wasted years!

'Thomasina,' she hissed, 'and Danny.'

'Your brother?' John asked, putting his hand on her arm.

Alice flinched and opened her eyes. 'Thomasina had a new blue dress. She helped her mother run the post office – she must have taken it for herself, and all the other gifts.'

'Why would she do such a thing?'

'She hated me,' said Alice bitterly. 'Thomasina was always jealous over Danny. When I got all the attention after the rescue she hated me all the more. She turned Danny against me too.' Alice felt winded by the betrayal. 'I gave him a letter to post to you but he must have destroyed it.'

John's anger turned to bafflement. 'But why would Danny do that?'

'Because he was frightened that you were special to me,' Alice said in distress. 'He didn't want me going off with a soldier when there were far more rich pickings. I half suspected they read some of my post but not that they withheld any of it . . .'

She looked at John, nauseated by the thought of Thomasina and Danny's scheming.

'They did it for greed! They even made money by selling the story of my birth to the newspapers.' Alice let out a howl of anger. 'Greedy devils, the pair of them! Why did I never think they might have done such a thing?' She doubled up in pain, unable to stem her tears of outrage.

The next minute John was out of his saddle and lifting her down from hers. He carried her to a patch of soft grass, spread out his jacket and pulled her close. She sobbed into his shoulder. He kissed her forehead tenderly.

'So you do care for me?' he asked.

'So v-very much.'

'And I for you, sweet Alice. Not a day goes by without me thinking of you – no matter how hard I try to put you from my mind.'

'It's the same for me,' she cried. 'If only I had known you still loved me the way I did you . . .'

He held her in his strong arms. She felt his heart drumming close to her cheek. How often she had longed to feel his arms around her again! But the moment was bittersweet. It had come too late.

'I tried to see you,' John said. 'Before I left for India. But you seemed too far out of my reach by then.'

'The Spanish coin,' Alice gasped. 'So it *was* from you?'

John nodded. Alice told him how she had only been given it years later by Josiah's widow.

'I still wear it,' Alice admitted, 'even though I know I shouldn't. Not now I'm another man's wife.' Her words seemed to anger him.

'You should be mine!' John cried. 'Not that old man's.'

Alice pulled away. 'I feel so guilty. George is a good man.'

'You're carrying his child, aren't you?'

Alice's eyes stung with fresh tears. She nodded, unable to speak. They looked at each other in misery, overwhelmed by the tragedy of their misunderstanding.

John let go his hold. He raised her to her feet and stood facing her.

'I have never loved any woman as much as I love you, Alice,' he said, his green eyes feverish. 'Never! Yet I have to accept that you are Gillveray's wife. I know he is a fine man but I cannot bear to see you with him. It's like a sword in the guts. We can't see each other again.'

Alice reached out and grabbed his hands. 'I can't bear not to,' she whispered. 'Please let me see you before you go!'

She saw the tension in his face as he struggled with his conscience. She was beyond all such scruples. She was about to lose him again. The pain at the thought of never seeing him was suffocating.

'I love you, John. Don't break my heart a second time!'

His eyes blazed. 'Woman, you are carrying his child. If we can't be together as man and wife, then it's better to be parted. I would never be content just as your lover, so don't ask it of me.'

'I'm not—'

'There is no future for us,' John said harshly, 'only heartache.'

He almost dragged her to her pony and lifted her roughly into the saddle. 'Go, Alice,' he rasped.

She gripped onto the reins, blinded by tears of anguish, and kicked the pony into a trot. It bumped and jarred her down the hillside, but she cared nothing for the pain. The agony in her heart was tenfold.

* * *

Alice was not sure how she got through the rest of the day. George chided her for her early-morning ride and ordered her to rest.

'You look grey from the effort, my dearest. Please, never do that again without taking me with you.'

Later, she woke to hear voices in the garden below. George was being firm.

'I'm afraid my wife has been overdoing things. Perhaps you could come back another time, Lieutenant?'

'Of course,' a Scottish voice answered.

Alice struggled out of bed and rushed to the window in panic. George was sending John away. Peering out she saw it was Colin retreating down the garden path. Her spirits plummeted. How guilty she felt at her yearning for John and yet

126

if she had known the truth that he had always loved her and wanted to marry her she would never have accepted George's proposal. She should be Mrs Sinclair not Gillveray.

But what could they do about it now? She was filled with resentment towards George, though none of it was his fault. How she cursed her selfish brother Danny and his heartless wife. Alice sank back on the bed in despair. She had to admit that John was right; it would only bring them further pain to see each other and not be able to be together.

Yet the next day Alice insisted on going out with her paint brushes and water-colouring paper hoping for a glimpse of John. George protested but she wouldn't be stopped, so he insisted on going with her. She chose Annandale, thinking that the Scottish officers might be exercising their horses in the glade, but there was no sign of them.

It rained for the next four days, torrential downpours that kept most people indoors. Alice sat with a book opened but unread in her lap as Emily chattered about the Eden sisters and a garden party that was being postponed. Rain drummed overhead and drowned out the conversation while servants hurried around with bowls to catch drips from the leaky roof.

By the end of the week the skies cleared and warm sun returned. The garden was lush with flowers and new growth. The forests around Simla were dank and sweet smelling with ferns and pink lilies. The paths steamed as they dried and the residents resumed their carriage rides and picnics.

On Sunday, George and Alice joined the Aytons at church.

'We've been starved of society,' said Emily. 'Church is the best place for picking up news.'

Sandy chuckled. 'Tittle-tattle you mean.'

There was talk of building a grand church for the town but for the moment the British had to make do with occasional services in a thatched building along the ridge. It was inadequate for the numbers attempting to cram inside and soon Alice was feeling faint and unwell. George took her back to Daisy Cottage.

When the Aytons returned for lunch, Alice couldn't help asking, 'Have the Scots officers left on their horse-buying trip yet?'

'Yes,' said Sandy, 'they left as soon as the rain stopped. Quite a procession by all accounts. Enough pack horses and porters for a military campaign. You would think it was Auckland going on tour.'

'That surprises me,' said George. 'They didn't seem like the sort of gentlemen who bothered about home comforts when travelling.'

'No, it wasn't Sinclair and MacRae who took so much baggage,' Emily joined in. 'It was Captain Buckley.'

'Buckley's gone with them?' Alice was astonished.

'Major Raine has taken ill with pleurisy,' Sandy explained, 'so Buckley's been put in charge of the expedition.'

Emily laughed. 'Put himself in charge most likely so he can lord it over Sinclair and MacRae. You know what he's like. Apparently they were all terrible rivals at Addiscombe. No doubt they'll be trying to outdo each other shooting bears and leopards.'

'No doubt,' agreed Sandy.

'I thought MacRae would come back for one of your paintings,' said George, looking at Alice. 'I'm sorry if I put him off – but you really weren't well the day he called, were you?'

'No.' She blushed.

'A pity they didn't come to say farewell before they left,' he added.

'Oh, but they did,' said Emily. 'I quite forgot. You were out. At Annandale I think. I can't remember which day.'

'Why didn't you say so?' Alice exclaimed.

'I'm sorry, it went right out of my head. They didn't stay long. What was it they said, Sandy?'

'I wasn't here,' Sandy reminded his wife. 'But you told me that Sinclair left a message.'

Alice felt her heartbeat skip. 'What did he say?'

'Something about *pashm*,' said Sandy.

'That's it,' Emily cried. 'He said to tell George that he would send back some pashmina so that you could have a new shawl made for your wife.'

'How kind of him.' George smiled. 'Isn't it, my dear?'

Alice fought to bring her emotions under control. 'Yes, very kind.'

She excused herself quickly and escaped upstairs to lie down.

What did it mean that John had come round to the house? Had he weakened at the last minute and wanted to see her or had Colin forced him to come out of politeness? Why did he mention having a pashmina shawl made for her? It could indicate that he really meant the gift to be from him or it might be a reproof to her that she should remember she was George's wife and no other man's. What would he have said to her? Alice would never know.

She turned her face into the bedcover, stuffed her mouth with it to muffle her cries and howled in misery until she was spent of all emotion.

Chapter 16

Bushahir Province, August 1836

John finally lost all patience with Vernon. 'You may be content to fritter away the summer at the raja's expense but there's work to do. Did you secure the deal?'

John and Colin had come into Sanpore from camp to see if Vernon had made good his promise to pay for fifty sturdy ponies at the horse fair. Through Rajban, John had done the bartering with the Tibetan horse-dealers and then gone exploring high into the foothills towards the Tibetan border, leaving Vernon to finish the transaction. Vernon had tired of frugal camp life almost immediately and elected to stay downriver with the hospitable raja. John and Colin had been more than happy to leave him there but John now wanted the dealing to be over so he could be free to explore into Ladakh.

'I've been working hard,' Vernon said, dissolving into a fit of giggling. His eyes were glazed and unfocused. His lodgings in the rambling riverside palace reeked of opium smoke and liquor; a clawing, sickly smell that turned John's stomach.

Vernon lay on a dirty divan, half-naked. As the Scots officers had arrived, a girl had scurried from the room, pulling a veil over her head.

'So where are the horses?' John demanded.

Vernon wafted a hand at him. 'All in hand, Scotchie. Just come back later.' He lolled on the grubby cushions.

John strode across the room and hauled him up by the arms. 'Have you bought any horses at all while we've been away?'

Vernon tried to struggle free. 'Still negotiating. Can't rush these matters.'

'Then give me the money and I'll do it myself.'

Vernon laughed. ''Fraid not, Scotchie. Had to spend it. Got to live.'

'You've spent it but got nothing to show for it?' John cried.

'Wouldn't say that.' Vernon grinned. 'Had a different girl in my bed every night. You should have stayed and joined in the fun.'

John pushed him away in disgust. 'That's Company money you've stolen.'

'Leave him to stew in his own filth,' said Colin.

'Don't pretend you're a saint, Sinclair,' Vernon sneered. 'Going after married women.'

'What's that supposed to mean?'

Vernon's bleary eyes lit with triumph. 'Saw you coming down Jakko Hill following pretty Mrs Gillveray. I was on my way home from Barrett's billiard room but you were obviously up with the lark. So don't criticise me for my tastes.'

'Nothing happened between us,' John said, flushing with anger.

Vernon sat up, sensing advantage. 'That's what you say,' he smirked. 'She seemed quite upset to me. Now you wouldn't want Gillveray to find out you'd been playing with his wife's affections, would you?'

'You leave her alone!'

'Or what?'

John lunged across the bed but Colin grabbed him and held him back.

129

'He's not worth the bruised knuckles,' said his friend. 'Come on, John. Let's go.'

John stormed to the door, shaking with rage and annoyed with himself for letting Vernon antagonise him so easily.

'Why are you so upset at the mention of Mrs Gillveray?' Vernon called after him. 'Spurned your advances, did she? I bet I'd have more success.'

Colin turned at the door. 'Go back to Simla, Buckley, and explain to Major Raine why you've bought him so few horses but spent all the money. You'll get no more help from us.'

* * *

By the end of August, John and Colin were in the high Spiti valley, a mountainous semi-desert of beige cliffs and grey-green rivers.

'By the start of the cold season,' warned Rajban, 'the passes into Ladakh will close and not open again for six months.'

Colin thought it was time they turned south again. 'My regiment leaves Dhera in November. Why not explore a way back via Rohru – down the Pabbar and Yamuna rivers – so we don't have to return to Simla?'

They both knew what Colin was alluding to: avoiding having to see Alice again. But John was determined to press on into Ladakh in search of more supplies of pashmina and to document the high mountain passes. Delayed by Vernon's antics in Sanpore, he knew that time was running out before the snows came and the passes closed.

'Why not go further?' urged John. 'We've got two whole months left.'

'It's too risky,' Colin warned. 'That Company letter you carry won't protect you from jealous Tibetan traders if they get a sniff you are after their pashmina trade. No one will believe we are merely after sport – there is precious little to shoot even here.'

John grinned. 'I'm just a simple mountaineer after ibex and mapping a few high passes as I go.'

'And if they catch you with your telescope and plane-books,' replied Colin, 'they'll hang you as a spy.'

'My friend,' said John, 'you have done more than enough for me. I'm forever in your debt for you coming with me this summer. We've had a grand time at the hunting and I've enjoyed your company more than I can say.' He clapped Colin on the back. 'I'm grateful of your offer to go back via the Yamuna – perhaps another time. It's selfish of me to ask any more of you,' John continued, 'but I'm going to carry on. I'm at home up here and I'd rather spend the rest of my leave in the mountains. That way you can return to Simla if you wish.'

Colin gave him a pitying look. 'If I do see Alice, is there anything you want me to say to her?'

John felt the familiar tension in his jaw at the mention of her name. Colin knew the full story. 'What use are words? The past can't be undone,' John said resignedly. 'I can't settle for being Alice's friend and nothing more – nor can I watch her nurse Gillveray's child.'

'I understand,' said Colin.

130

Two days later, Colin departed with most of their porters as not many of them wanted to travel as far as Leh in Ladakh and John knew he could cover ground more quickly with fewer men and less equipment. On the spur of the moment, John gave Colin a package.

'It's the pashmina we got from the shepherd in Pangmo. See that Alice gets it.'

His friend gave him a long look.

John shrugged. 'It means nothing. She can do with it what she pleases.'

Colin did not press him. They clasped hands and wished each other good luck.

* * *

John struck camp with Rajban, taking a handful of porters and four yaks to carry his survey equipment and tents. They rode swiftly north-west, stopping only to snatch sleep, eat and barter for supplies at tiny hamlets. Pushing on, they crossed the Zanskar mountain range at a high pass where the past winter's snow still clung to the barren peaks. John's head ached and he found it hard to breathe. As they climbed to another dizzyingly high pass, light bounced off the bald rock and dazzled the eye.

Finally, on a bright autumnal afternoon, they descended to the broad fertile valley of the Indus – that fabled river he had read about in Hercules's dusty history books – and saw the town of Leh in the distance. They passed a flat-roofed monastery on the hillside, the sound of gongs and horns reverberating through the thin air. They had reached Ladakh!

Chapter 17

Simla, August 1836

John had been gone two weeks when Alice felt the first flutters of movement in her womb. Since his departure, she had been consumed with a private grief that she could tell no other; all these years John had loved her but was now lost to her for good. He had made it quite plain that he would do nothing to break up her marriage to George and that they must both live without each other.

George treated her warily, afraid to be too solicitous in case she rebuffed him. Did he suspect her attachment to the young Sinclair? Alice felt guilty that she might be hurting her husband's feelings but could not shake off the grief she felt at the thought of never seeing John again.

The strange butterfly movements inside her made Alice gasp and put her hands to her belly. Could these be the stirrings of her unborn baby?

She sought out Emily, who was stretched out in a long cane chair on the veranda, fanning herself. Her friend was now huge with child and needed help getting out of a chair. Alice told her what she was feeling.

'Of course it's the baby,' Emily said, smiling. 'You'll feel something every day from now on. My wee bairn is doing somersaults. Look at this.' Emily smoothed down her gauzy dress and Alice saw a movement ripple underneath.

'How amazing,' gasped Alice.

'It's a foot or a fist.' Emily laughed. 'He's going to be a man of action like his father.'

Alice's hands went protectively back to her own stomach.

'It's exciting, isn't it?' said Emily.

'Yes,' Alice said in surprise, 'it is.'

For the first time she felt a stirring of anticipation. She really was going to be a mother! The idea filled her waking moments and lessened the ache of emptiness when she thought of John. Alice determined she would try harder to be kind to George and confided in him that she could feel the baby. He looked ridiculously pleased and began to whistle again around the house.

A few days later, the air grew oppressive as a thunderstorm threatened. Alice cried off a trip to the Assembly Rooms. Her head ached and her stomach felt oddly tight.

'I don't feel well,' Alice told George.

'What do you mean?' he asked in alarm.

'Just the atmosphere,' Alice said. 'I'll feel better once there's been a good downpour.'

'Shall I get the doctor?'

'There's no need.' She winced as her stomach cramped in pain.

Upstairs in their attic bedroom, Alice lay listening to the storm break beyond the shuttered window. As it darkened, she got up and threw open the shutters to allow air into the stuffy room. She leant over the window sill and tipped her face to the refreshing rain, as if it could wash away the anxiety that nagged her mind. Something was wrong. She had felt no movement in her womb since the day after she had spoken to Emily about it and told George. George found her shivering by the window and chased her back to bed.

'What foolishness is this? Your hair is soaking,' he chided.

Alice curled up and hugged her knees, glad of her husband's reassuring presence beside her. She drifted into a fitful sleep.

In the middle of the night Alice woke to a strange sensation. She had wet the bed. George, roused from sleep, lit a lamp.

'My God, it's blood!' he cried.

The sheets were damp with it, as was Alice's nightgown. She froze in horror.

'What's happening?' she gasped.

'I'll get the doctor,' said George, his look terrified. He scrambled into his clothes.

Emily and Sandy, woken by the clatter of George on the stairs, came along to help. Emily shooed Sandy out. She held Alice's hand as she lay petrified in the bed.

'Am I losing the baby?' she whispered.

For once Emily was speechless and unable to offer reassurance.

If Alice had not been so distressed she would have been mortified with embarrassment as George returned with a doctor. She could hear servants having hushed conversations beyond the door.

Shortly afterwards, Alice felt something pass between her thighs – more than just the cramps – and then the mess was being bundled into a sheet and the sweeper called to remove it from sight. For the rest of the night she lay aching, stunned at the speed of the miscarriage. George did not know how to comfort her.

'I'll leave you to sleep, my dearest,' he mumbled and went below. She heard sombre male voices talking quietly – perhaps Sandy or the doctor staying up with him to commiserate over a stiff brandy.

The next day, George said not a word about it. No one came to visit. Why should they? No one but the household knew and it was a subject never to be raised in polite society. George insisted she stay in bed to rest for a week. Alice wondered if he found it easier to have her out of the way or whether he was protecting her from awkward conversations around the dinner table.

Emily came to sit with her but Alice could tell she found it difficult.

'It happens to such a lot of women, even this far on,' Emily said, 'but you'll go on to have another one. The main thing is that you have been spared.'

Alice put on a brave face; Emily was trying to be kind. Alice guessed that the miscarriage might have increased her friend's anxiety about her own baby's imminent birth. It was a hazardous ordeal for both mother and baby. She put out her hand and squeezed Emily's.

'Thank you, but you don't have to stay with me. Go and rest yourself,' said Alice.

What she couldn't say to her friend was how upsetting was the sight of her distended belly. It represented everything that had been so abruptly torn away from her. Only now, as she lay weak and tearful, did Alice realise how much she had wanted her baby. She had been so unwell at the beginning of her pregnancy and anxious about whether she would make a fit mother that she had not allowed

133

herself to enjoy her pregnant state. Then had come the shock of seeing John again and the misery of his going.

Had she brought on the miscarriage with her impulsive behaviour? Perhaps if she hadn't ridden out to meet John that morning she would still be with child. George had cautioned against any riding. Or what if she had caused it by allowing the rain to soak her hair the night of the storm? She had overheard George saying to the doctor that she had got chilled by opening the window. Did he blame her too?

Alice tortured herself with guilty thoughts until she could no longer bear to lie confined in the bedchamber. Ignoring George's protests, she took to going for long walks around the hillside paths and up Jakko Hill to stare out at the far mountains and wonder where John was.

* * *

In the middle of August, Emily gave birth to a lusty baby boy with fair downy hair and a loud querulous yell. His cries filled the small wooden house both day and night. An *ayah* was employed to look after him when Emily wasn't feeding him. He was christened Alexander Robert, after Sandy and also Emily's father, and the Aytons grew besotted with their new son.

'He's got Sandy's colouring,' pronounced Emily, 'and my eyes. And my father's long nose. Just look at his strong legs. He'll be an excellent horseman just like his father.'

When he wasn't being paraded around the drawing rooms of Simla, baby Alexander lay in a cradle on the veranda being rocked to and fro by his *ayah*.

Alice tried her best to show interest and joy in the new arrival but the very sight of his squalling red face left her winded. His presence reminded her how hollowed out her own insides felt. She tried not to flinch when Emily was handed the baby for suckling. The house smelt of baby, of milk and posseting. The washing that hung drying in the servants' compound was joined by swaddling clothes and tiny lacy robes, which tugged at Alice's bereaved heart.

Emily never tried to make Alice hold Alexander, sensing that her friend found it difficult having the baby in the house. For that, Alice was grateful. But George was not so reticent. When the baby cried, he would seize him from his cot and stride about the veranda, joggling him till the wailing subsided. Alice found the sight of this even more upsetting than when Emily or Sandy took the baby in their arms. She despised herself for her resentment towards George for his delight in the Aytons' son but could do nothing to stem it. It was only when disappearing with her sketch book or riding out along the ridge – she had taken to early-morning riding once more – that she found temporary relief from her sense of failure.

* * *

For a month, George slept in the tiny dressing room off the bedchamber and kept away from Alice at night-time. This pained her but she did not blame him.

Perhaps he was frightened of making her pregnant again or was punishing her for the miscarriage. Yet she knew he wanted children as much as she did.

One night, after hours of lying sleepless, she got up and padded across the moonlit room, opening the door to the dressing room. George was sprawled on an army camp bed, his limbs flung out over the frame. She gazed at his face in repose; he looked younger than in the daytime when his face furrowed into worry lines whenever he looked at her.

She went over and gently shook him awake. He sat up startled.

'What is it? Are you all right?'

She felt a pang at his ready concern. 'Yes.'

'Then what is it?'

Alice spoke before her resolve deserted her. 'I want . . . Will you come and lie beside me, George?'

He hesitated. She saw his habitual frown return. When had her husband begun to frown so much?

'I'm not sure that we should. Is it not too soon after . . . ?'

Alice felt a wave of sadness well up inside. There was a chasm opening up between them. She bowed her head, tears prickling her eyes.

'I'm so lonely, George,' she whispered. 'I want you to love me again like you used to.'

He climbed off the camp bed and went to her, putting his arms gently about her shoulders. They hugged each other.

'I'm sorry, my dear girl,' he murmured. 'I thought you no longer cared for me.'

Tears spilled down her cheeks. 'I do. And I want us to be parents. I yearn for that more than anything. Seeing you holding Alexander so tenderly breaks my heart.'

George kissed her forehead. 'I want that too.'

'Then be a husband to me, George,' Alice pleaded, 'and sleep in our bed again.'

'If that's what you really want?' George asked.

Alice nodded and then, taking his hand, led him back to bed.

* * *

Emily heard the news first, rushing back from a party at the Governor's house. It was late September and people were preparing for the long trek back to Calcutta for the cold season.

'Buckley's back from Bushahir.'

Alice broke off from her book. Her heart began a treacherous thudding. 'Oh?'

'There's been a hoo-ha about horse trading. Hasn't brought nearly enough ponies with him apparently.'

This was of little interest to Alice. 'And are all the officers back now?'

Emily shook her head. 'No, that's what's got tongues wagging; the Scots lieutenants aren't with him. As a matter of fact, Buckley's blaming them for the failure to buy horses. Said they squandered the money on the temptations on offer in Sanpore and then took off to go hunting.'

'I don't believe that.' Alice was indignant.

'Well, that's what he's saying. Said he had to use his own money to buy Tibetan horses from the raja. He's very annoyed about it all.'

'And do people believe him?' asked Alice.

Emily shrugged. 'They're beginning to wonder. After all, Sinclair and MacRae are nowhere to be seen, are they?'

Over the next few days of packing up and hiring baggage handlers, there was a fervour of gossip in the town about the missing officers.

'It seems most out of character,' said George.

Sandy also defended them. 'It's just Buckley's word against theirs. Once they return from their hunting trip it will all be explained.'

Alice worried about what had happened to them. She felt a stab of unease. John had been deeply angered and upset when they had parted. What if he had acted recklessly – selfishly – in an attempt to put the past behind him? But surely the sensible Colin MacRae would not have allowed him to misspend Company money?

The town buzzed like a hive with wild speculation. Sinclair had succumbed to opium addiction. The two officers had gone east and north to line their own pockets with lucrative deals in pashmina. They were still in Sanpore living like rajas with a *zenana* full of mistresses. They had escaped to Tibet with Company gold. Alice refused to believe such ludicrous tales. Buckley was far more likely to be the kind of man who might give into temptations of the flesh than John or Colin.

* * *

In mid-October, on the eve of departure for Calcutta, a package was delivered to Daisy Cottage for the Gillverays. George had just returned from organising the conveying of his precious plant samples back to the botanic gardens, in particular some rhododendrons.

'It's from Colin MacRae,' said George, letting Alice unwrap the present of pashmina wool.

'How kind!' She pressed the soft beige-coloured wool to her cheek. Its animal smell brought a whiff of the mountains.

George read the accompanying letter. 'He's back with his regiment in Dehra Dun.'

'Thank goodness,' Alice said in relief. 'So they haven't run off with Company money after all.'

'It seems he came back a different way than through Simla,' George said.

'And John Sinclair too?' Alice felt herself blushing as she mentioned him.

George gave her an odd look. 'No, I'm afraid not. He stayed on in the mountains. MacRae said he planned to go on to Leh in Ladakh.'

'But that's beyond British-held territory, isn't it?'

George nodded.

'Well, at least it shows Buckley's wrong and he's not living a life of debauchery in Sanpore,' Alice pointed out.

George frowned. 'But it's not good. It worries me that he didn't return with MacRae.'

'What do you mean?' Alice asked, feeling anxiety grip her.

'Well, if Sinclair doesn't report back to his duties in Dehra Dun by the end of this month, it will be seen as desertion.'

'Desertion?' Alice echoed in alarm.

'He'll be court-martialled,' said George gravely.

'But that's terrible,' she cried. 'It would end his army career and it means everything to him.'

'Let's hope our fears are wrong,' he said. 'But it would seem to be an act of recklessness to remain in the far mountains this late in the season. Only a man who has nothing to lose would do that. So perhaps there is some truth in what Buckley says.'

'How can you say such a thing?' Alice was indignant. 'John Sinclair is an honourable man.'

George gave her a long assessing look, which made her blush deepen. 'I believe you are right, my dear.' He got up and passed her the letter to read. As he made for the door, he turned and said, 'Your pashmina was not from MacRae. He was merely passing it on. It was Lieutenant Sinclair who wished you to have it.'

* * *

The Gillverays and Aytons left Simla on a bright, cloudless October morning with the peaks of the Himalayas clear and dazzling against an azure sky. Alice gave them a last longing look – her pashmina mountains as she thought of them now – and wondered what had become of John. Perhaps he too had chosen to journey back to Dehra by another route. Or had he deliberately decided to cock a snook at the Company and seek his fortune elsewhere?

Either way, by the time they were wending their way out of the foothills, John Sinclair had not returned to Simla.

Chapter 18

Leh, Ladakh, September 1836

John was fascinated by Leh. That first time he had entered, stepping his pony over a high doorstep in the surrounding stone wall, he'd expected to find himself in a courtyard of a large homestead. Instead there had been a wide road lined with mud-built houses and a bazaar with artisans' shops selling metal pots, furs and precious stones. Crowning the cliffs behind was the solid fortress of the king and a monastery, keeping a benevolent eye on the settlement, and its gardens, which stretched down to the sandy plain and the river.

Lamas dressed in red robes and pigtailed men in belted coats mingled freely with women wearing girdled tunics, sheepskin cloaks, soft wool boots and hats bedecked in bright turquoise stones. Both men and women wore black fur earflaps. People were friendly and greeted them politely with bows and salutations.

Rajban had found them accommodation in a low-roofed dwelling down a side street, with stabling for their ponies. The porters had been paid off and departed with their yaks.

They had rested for several days and then John had begun to take an interest in the trading in the town, going to view the livestock. Wherever he went the tall broad Highlander attracted a crowd of onlookers and eager children. There were other non-Ladakhis in Leh – merchants from Gilgit and Afghanistan whose features and clothing marked them apart from the locals. John made friends with a Kashmiri wool merchant called Wahid who could speak Hindustani. They shared a water-pipe and compared travel stories. He was a fount of information about the trade in pashmina.

'The Ladakhi goats are superior to our ones in Kashmir,' said Wahid. 'The higher elevation produces a finer winter coat. That is why I come here to barter for their wool.'

One day, royal guards in yellow capes and caps knocked at John's door. Rajban explained that they were summoned to the king's palace. Riding on a squat Yarkandi pony with his feet nearly scraping the ground, John was escorted up the steep hillside into the forbidding-looking castle. To his amazement the inside was richly adorned with carved-and-painted pillars and doorways. He was met by a fanfare of horns and cymbals and led into a large audience chamber. The king, who was dressed in a highly embroidered silk robe of green, blue and red, greeted him warmly. John thought they were of a similar age; the monarch's genial smiling round face reminded him of his childhood friend Donald.

They sat on low divans while servants brought dishes of apricots, bowls of curds and thick brown buttered tea. The audience chamber smelt pleasantly of aromatic incense burning in recessed niches. Rajban interpreted.

The king was honoured to have a British officer in his capital. He was welcome to go where he wished in Leh.

'But you must get permission to travel beyond the valley,' said Rajban, 'as there are bad men who might wish you harm.'

'Thank him for his concern,' said John. 'Ask him who the bad men are.'

Rajban relayed the reply. 'Gulab Singh and Zorawar Singh. The Sikh aggressors from the west.'

John raised his eyebrows. 'Ranjit Singh's protégés?'

'His Majesty says they have already sent raiding parties this summer,' said Rajban.

'Tell him I will be careful but would like to explore more of his country – that I wish to hunt for a couple of weeks before returning back to India.'

'He says he is not much interested in hunting but will be happy to provide you with an escort.'

John feared for the young ruler. It seemed to him on first impressions that this was a peaceable land. Buddhists were renowned for their lack of aggression and reluctance to resort to violence to resolve conflict. However, if they were being threatened, then the priest-king would have no alternative.

They talked to and fro, the king eager to hear all about India and the world beyond his realm. He seemed fascinated by John's family and background.

'So you too are the son of a ruler!' he cried. 'And are you related to your British king?'

John laughed. 'No.'

'But you are an important man,' said his host. 'You wear the colours of your king's guard and you come with a letter bearing his seal.'

'I am just a hunter with an interest in horses,' John insisted.

They were entertained by masked male dancers, and the court astrologer was called forward to divine when would be an auspicious day for John to go hunting. John handed over gifts that he had brought to smooth his way with officials: a picture of a sailing ship, a tin of sardines and a pocket watch. The king was delighted.

Before John and Rajban left, they were shown around the castle with its warren of dark passageways and stairs, every gloomy room hung with silk banners. The king had a library lined with wall hangings depicting gods and Buddhist symbols and deep shelves storing ancient texts and scrolls. The heart of his rock palace was the altar room, its dark recesses hardly penetrated by flickering butter lamps. The rancid smell was tempered by incense, which burnt in front of a large image of Buddha alongside offerings of flour and water in little brass bowls.

From here they were led up to the top of the castle and emerged onto the flat roof into sharp, clear air and vivid light that dazzled after the gloom of the castle. The view was dizzying. Far below were the mud houses of the town and the ochre sandy plain stretching to the green strip of the Indus valley. Towering all around were rocky mountains in endless ranks, disappearing off into purple shadows and gleaming white peaks.

To the north, John saw a dirt track winding its way into the mountains.

'Where does that go?' he asked.

'To Yarkand,' the King replied, 'and far beyond.'

John and Rajban exchanged looks. Was this the old trading route to Turkestan and China? The Company would be very interested to know if there was a viable way through from India to Yarkand.

* * *

139

Whenever John and Rajban rode out to hunt, they were accompanied by the king's guards. John wanted to explore further than the valley and into the mountains but he was always politely persuaded not to do so. Bears would kill him or bad demons would bring sickness.

Tired of being followed, John decided it was time to retrace their steps back to India. Fresh snow was appearing on the far peaks and would be descending to the mountain passes by the end of October. Rajban set about hiring new porters.

Two days before departure, John emerged from their lodgings to find guards posted at the door.

'What are they doing here?' he asked Rajban.

Rajban had a heated argument with one of them. He told John in frustration, 'They say we can't leave until the next full moon. The king's astrologer says it's inauspicious to travel at the moment.'

'The next full moon?' John said in exasperation. 'That's nearly a month away. The passes could be blocked by then. We must be allowed to travel sooner. Tell him I wish to speak to the king.'

But an audience was not granted. Messages were relayed from the palace with predictions from the astrologer and good wishes from the king. As days went by and clouds amassed over the mountains, John's patience snapped.

'We must leave today,' he ordered, 'else we will be stuck here for the winter and my army career will be over.'

Rajban came back from arranging the transport with an anxious face. 'The porters will no longer agree to come. They have been told not to obey your orders.'

'Says who?'

'Officials at the palace.'

'Why on earth do they want to keep us here?'

Rajban shrugged helplessly.

John's unease grew. Soon their ponies were confiscated and the guards were not allowing him to venture beyond the town.

'They say it's for your own safety,' Rajban reported.

'This is unacceptable!' John cried. 'They can't keep me hostage. I demand to see the king.'

Finally, John was given another audience at the castle. He was received with the same courtesy and smiles. John pleaded for his release and to be allowed to travel on.

The king seemed hurt. 'Do you not like my country? Are you not being treated with respect?'

'I do like your country,' John said. 'All I ask is that you allow me to return to India before the winter comes.'

'It is not safe to travel,' said the king. 'I will not put your life at risk – you are my guest.'

John tried a different tack. 'I have other gifts that I can give Your Highness if you let me go.'

The king smiled. 'I do not want earthly rewards.'

'I can offer you friendship from the British,' John urged, even though Captain Smith had warned that he must not promise political allegiance to anyone. But he could offer a trading relationship. 'We can give you a ready market for your pashmina. Just tell me what it is that you want.'

'My astrologers predicted that you would come. You will save my kingdom.'

John looked at Rajban in disbelief. 'How is that possible?'

'The Sikhs will not attack us if they know that an important emissary of the British is staying in Leh. I have sent out messengers to tell them. You and your British king will protect us.'

John was dumbfounded. How could he tell this naïve young monarch that his kingdom was far too remote for it to be of interest to the Company or its government beyond being a trading outpost?

'You put too much faith in the British,' John said. 'We won't fight the Sikhs on your behalf. We are allies with the Sikh ruler, Ranjit Singh.'

The King spread his hands in a fatalistic gesture. 'But if the Sikhs attack and kill you, your British king will avenge your death. I have heard how the British army believes in an eye for an eye.'

'I am not important to the British army,' John protested.

'I have seen the letter you carry with the king's seal. You are indeed an important man.'

John silently cursed ever having agreed to Captain Smith's ploy. He tried one more time to change the ruler's mind. 'I would be of more use to you if you allowed me to return to India. Then I can alert my superiors to the troubles you are having with the Sikhs. I could speak up on your behalf.'

The king looked thoughtful. After a pause he nodded. He would meditate on John's words and consult with his priests and astrologers.

John left with raised hopes. But the guards remained at his door and continued to follow him around the town.

* * *

Days slipped by and no permission to leave came from the palace.

'They are keeping me here as a bargaining counter,' he said to Rajban in frustration. 'I am sorry, my friend. It means you are stuck here too.'

Rajban smiled and joked, 'It's the most comfortable prison I've seen.'

John sat down and wrote three letters explaining his predicament; one to Colin, one to Everest and one to Captain Smith. In the latter he warned the political agent about an invasion brewing.

The King of Ladakh is a peaceable ruler but lives in very great fear of being invaded by Gulab Singh from Kashmir. I urge that pressure be made to bear upon the Sikhs not to carry out aggression to their easterly neighbours. It would cause great instability in an area that is ripe for greater trading links. I have made good contacts among the traders in pashmina here and their wool is far superior to that in Kashmir. I also have seen with my own eyes the beginning of a route through the mountains to Yarkand.

Yet I fear I will be held hostage here indefinitely – or until the Sikhs carry out further raids. I do not remain here willingly and am greatly pained at being unable to return to my regiment and carry out my duties to the Honourable Company.

I remain your loyal servant

Then he went to seek out Wahid. The Kashmiri was preparing for the trek back home. Most of the traders had already gone or were about to leave.

'My friend, will you take these letters for me and have them sent on when you get to Srinagar?'

'Of course,' Wahid agreed. 'I am sorry that you are being prevented from leaving. But the Ladakhis are gentle people – you will come to no harm among them.'

They embraced and John wished him a safe journey.

'I shall look for you when I return in the spring,' said Wahid. '*Inshallah!*'

A few days later, from the top of his flat roof John watched the last caravan of pack animals and merchants wend their way down the sandy path and turn upriver. The sky was crystal clear. He could still hear the sound of the animals' hooves even after they had disappeared from view.

He thought with frustration of the months of confinement stretching ahead. He should have returned with Colin while he had the chance. Why had he been so reckless and insisted on exploring as far as Ladakh? Deep inside he feared he knew the answer. In India he would always be at risk of running into Alice in one of the army cantonments; his life there would be full of reminders that she was another man's wife.

Here in the mountains he was free of all the painful associations of the past summer and his angry parting with Alice. There was no Company, no Simla gossip, no superiors ordering him about, just the freedom to ride and explore and pit his strength against the elements. Perhaps he had always intended to escape, leaving it too late to make the journey back.

John mocked himself. Except he now had less freedom. Here he was in Leh, a prisoner to a benign captor, but a prisoner nonetheless.

'We'll just have to see what the astrologers have in mind for us,' he told Rajban as they sat by their smoky stove and warmed themselves with a drink from John's precious supply of brandy.

A week later, the snow and winds came and turned the landscape into an icy desert.

Chapter 19

Calcutta, April 1837

'Please, Mrs Gillveray, will you tell us the story about Wellington the sheep again?'

Alice smiled at the eager-faced schoolgirl. 'Perhaps another day – if you work hard at your letters. But now it's time for you to go home. I look forward to seeing you all tomorrow morning. Class is dismissed.'

As they handed in their slates and pencils, Alice felt a wave of affection for her young Bengali pupils, whom she had got to know well over the past months. They left with a cheerful chorus of goodbyes. She smiled to herself as she returned the slates to the chest in the corner of the schoolroom. The school and its girls had been a lifeline for her that winter back in Calcutta.

The cold season had been busy with social events and much entertainment at Governor's House, instigated by Auckland's gregarious sisters. Emily had thrown herself into it all with enthusiasm and insisted on Alice taking part in everything from picnics at Barrackpore Park to masquerades in Fort William.

Alice had put on a brave face of enjoying Calcutta society, knowing that her friend was trying to make her forget the upset of losing her baby, but her heart wasn't in it. George was equally tepid in his enthusiasm. Her husband had never much enjoyed dances or grand dinners, much preferring to stay at home sipping a brandy on the veranda and reading by lamplight after a busy day at the botanic gardens.

Her fondness for George had returned and he had been full of concern and affection for her when she had suffered a further miscarriage – this one at only a few weeks – the knowledge of which they had kept to themselves.

Alice had determined to find a way to fill her days with more purpose. George was completely absorbed in his work; she should do something more worthwhile too.

Alice had turned to her friends Miss Cook and Mrs Meadows and volunteered her help once more at the school. What began as an assistant's job of handing out slates and showing the younger ones how to thread needles soon progressed to teaching her own class in reading, writing and arithmetic. And stories. Alice smiled. The girls all loved stories.

Now the hot weather was starting again and soon Auckland and his staff, including the Aytons, would be setting off on the long journey back up to Simla.

That afternoon, Emily appeared at their bungalow to take tea, bringing baby Alexander with her. Alice's initial pain at the baby's presence had soon turned into affection. He was a sunny-natured infant with a shock of fair hair and a gummy smile. They laid him on a rug on the veranda and let him wriggle.

'You will be coming with us to Simla, won't you?' Emily asked. 'You know how ill you became staying in Calcutta last May.'

'I have my duties at the school,' Alice reminded her friend.

'Surely the missionaries can cope without you for a while? They seem impervious to the heat.'

'It depends on George,' said Alice, sitting on the floor and letting Alexander stuff her finger in his mouth.

'You could come ahead with us and he could join you later, couldn't he?'

'What could I do?' George appeared on the steps. 'Are you ladies plotting something?'

Alice laughed and stood up to greet him. 'Emily is always plotting. I wasn't expecting you back so soon.'

'I thought we could go for a ride before it gets dark,' said George, kissing her on the forehead.

Alice smiled. 'I'd like that.'

'I'm pleading with Alice,' said Emily, 'to come to Simla with us. Don't you think that's a good idea? Alexander and I will miss her far too much if she doesn't. And you could join her later, couldn't you?'

'I could,' George agreed. Alice could see his indecision. Few people could withstand Emily's entreaties for long. She seemed so mild natured but was one of the most persuasive people that Alice knew. She usually got her way.

'We'll talk about it on our ride,' Alice said, not wanting him to be browbeaten into a hasty decision.

'Oh, do come!' cried Emily. 'Simla just won't be the same without you.'

Alice knelt down and tickled Alexander. 'Your mama just won't take no for an answer, will she?'

The baby giggled and threw back his hands in delight.

* * *

Alice and George rode across the Esplanade and watched the sun sinking behind the fort. The air was filling with the noise of birds and the call to prayer at a nearby mosque. They dismounted and went to sit by one of the water tanks; the orange sky was reflected in its tranquil surface.

'Do you want to return to Simla?' George asked.

Alice thought back to the previous year and of how much she had hated Calcutta in the heat – how she had turned into a person she had disliked and George hadn't recognised. It worried her that she might come across John in Simla – the place would be full of memories of him – but such a meeting was unlikely. She had picked up no rumours that he had ever returned from the mountains and, if he had, he would no doubt avoid Simla in case she was there.

She had resigned herself to a life without John and her thoughts about him had lessened until she felt only a dull ache of disappointment when he came to mind. Alice hoped that wherever he was he was safe, but her life was with George and she would make the best of it she possibly could.

'I do want to go to the hills,' she answered, 'but not without you.'

What she wanted above all else was for her to be able to carry a child to full term and for them to be parents. But she didn't have to say that aloud as she knew that George felt the same.

'Your health is paramount,' said George, taking her hand in his. 'I don't want to see you become sick again – and the air in Simla suits you. I'd be happier if

144

you went with the Aytons rather than delaying and waiting for me. I have work I must finish at the gardens – the tea trials – before I could join you.'

Alice knew it was no use arguing – as she had last year – that he had no need to work and that he could spend as much time in the hills as he wanted. For she understood that George's work was what gave him purpose and that it would be selfish to insist that he travel with her.

'I'll go if you promise me you'll join me as soon as you can,' said Alice.

He raised her hand and kissed it. 'Of course I promise, my dearest.'

* * *

On the eve of Alice's departure, a letter arrived. It was from Colin MacRae. George looked visibly shaken as he read it.

'Tell me what it says,' Alice urged.

He looked up, his face troubled. 'It's about Lieutenant Sinclair. MacRae has only recently heard the news because he has been moving about with his regiment.'

Alice's heart began to hammer. 'What news? Is it bad?'

'Sinclair sent a letter last October saying he was detained in Ladakh against his will.'

'Lieutenant Sinclair's a prisoner?' Alice gasped, her hand flying to her mouth.

'It would appear so.'

'Then he can't be accused of desertion.'

George looked sombre. 'He has got himself involved in some political plot between the Ladakhis and the Sikhs. He shouldn't have been there. I don't think the Company will look favourably on such recklessness, especially if it has embroiled them in trouble with the Sikhs.'

Alice felt nauseated at the thought of John being captive.

'Does it say under what conditions he's being held? It would be terrible if he were suffering. Surely the Company will do something to have him released!'

'I'm very sorry, my dear.' George gave her a pitying look. 'I know you hold him in high regard.'

Alice flushed. 'I just don't wish to see any harm befall him.'

She saw his eyes glistening with sorrow. 'Alice,' he said quietly, 'I know who John Sinclair is.'

'What do you mean?' Her heart drummed uncomfortably.

'He's the young man you saved from the *Berwickshire*. I didn't remember at first. But when I saw the two of you together I knew that you weren't strangers to each other. Then it came back to me how fondly you talked of him when you spoke of the rescue – how you had nursed him out of danger.'

Alice felt her insides twist. She put her face in her hands, unable to deny any of it.

'I think John Sinclair holds an equally high opinion of you.'

'Don't, George,' Alice whispered.

'Was there an understanding between the two of you when you were younger?'

Alice was going to deny it but the look of compassion on her husband's face gave her the courage to admit it. George deserved the truth.

145

'Yes, there was. But Thomasina and Danny withheld our letters to each other – out of spite and greed I believe – and so we thought the worst of one another. It was only in Simla that we found out what must have happened.' She looked at him unhappily. 'I'm so sorry, George. I never meant to hurt you. And John would never have come between us – he admires you and he doesn't want to see me again.'

'I don't blame either of you,' he said. 'When you love someone you can't help how you feel. It must have taken great willpower for the two of you to resist your attraction to one another. I will always be grateful for that, Alice – that you chose to stay with me.'

'I would never have left you!' Alice's eyes smarted with tears. 'I'm your wife, not his.'

George said, 'I hope he has not rushed into trouble because of finding you married to me. I would feel responsible for his plight if that were so.'

'Oh, George!' Alice looked at him in anguish. She held out her arms. He hesitated and then went to her.

He encircled her in his wiry hold, his jacket smelling comfortingly of camphor and tobacco.

'Why didn't you say anything before about knowing who John was?' Alice asked.

'I could see how hard you were trying to resist your feelings,' George said frankly, 'and I loved you for it. It's enough that you are fond of me. At my time in life each day with you is a delight and a gift I don't deserve.'

Alice said tearfully, 'I don't deserve *you*. I couldn't have asked for a better husband.' She looked into his craggy face. 'I do care for you very much.'

He smiled. 'I know.' He kissed her brow and held her gently while she wept on his shoulder.

Alice wasn't sure if she shed tears for their marriage, which would always be one of companionship rather than passion – or for John in exile; the only man she would ever truly love.

* * *

'It's charming!' Alice exclaimed as Emily showed her around Carrick Lodge, the house that Sandy had rented for the season in Simla. 'And the views of the mountains from the veranda . . .' She caught her breath at the sight of snowy peaks rising above the clouds like a fairy-tale island afloat in a pearly sea.

'Much better than Daisy Cottage, isn't it?' said Emily.

'Much better,' Alice agreed.

She was thankful that they weren't returning to the cramped, damp cottage of the previous year with its painful associations. Daisy Cottage had been to the south of the ridge whereas Carrick Lodge was high on the Elysium spur to the north, with a breathtaking view of the Himalayas.

'And it's so close to Auckland House,' Emily said, 'so we'll be handy for all of the Edens' parties.'

146

It wasn't long before the round of social engagements began: picnics at Annandale, dances at the Assembly Rooms, musical soirées and dinners at Auckland House.

Wherever Alice went, she tried to glean more about the situation in Ladakh and what might be happening to John. Both Alice and the Aytons were concerned about his fate and Sandy endeavoured to find out more through his position on Auckland's staff.

'Colin MacRae has been putting in a word on his friend's behalf,' Sandy reported, 'but Auckland's not very sympathetic.'

'Why on earth not?' exclaimed Emily. 'Sinclair shouldn't just be abandoned. Better to face a court-martial in India than a worse fate in Tibet or wherever he's being held.'

'It's complicated, dear,' said Sandy.

'Please tell us,' Alice pleaded.

Sandy frowned. 'There's trouble stirring among the Afghans again – their amir, Dost Mohammed, is threatening to go to war with the Sikhs over Peshawar. The Afghans want it back. Auckland doesn't want anything to upset our good relations with the Sikhs but he also wants co-operation from the amir. There're fresh rumours that the Russians are behind unrest in eastern Afghanistan so we need the Afghans as allies too.'

'What's all that got to do with John's plight?' Emily asked in confusion.

Sandy sighed. 'I'm afraid that the capture of one solitary Company soldier, who had no business to be where he was, is just an extra irritation for the Governor General when there are far more pressing concerns demanding his attention.'

Alice swallowed her disappointment, trying not to show how anxious she was for John. Perhaps if the Sikhs were being threatened by the Afghans then they would abandon their attempts to take Ladakh.

Powerless to do anything for John, Alice threw her energies once more into helping with girls' education. Alice went most days to the rudimentary schoolhouse close to the bazaar run by her friend, Miss Wallace, to teach sewing and basic reading and counting.

She wrote to George telling him all about her work and enjoyed receiving his affectionate letters. As always he enthused about his experiments at the botanic gardens. She was glad that there was no bad feeling between them after their frank conversation about John.

'When is he coming to join us?' asked Emily.

'He says at the end of August,' Alice said, 'when the worst of the rains are over.'

'Well, at least there is no shortage of officers to partner you at the dances,' Emily said. 'George has only himself to blame for leaving you a grass widow when so many handsome captains are falling in love with you.'

Alice winced at Emily's unintended barb. Her friend knew nothing of George's sadness at Alice's love for John.

'What nonsense,' Alice retorted. 'I've given no encouragement to anyone.'

'No you haven't' – Emily laughed – 'but Sandy says that many of Auckland's staff talk of the pretty Mrs Gillveray. It piques them that you prefer to spend more time with native urchins than them.'

Alice dismissed Emily's chatter but she had noticed that Vernon Buckley was particularly solicitous towards her at social functions. Alice was cool with him, angered at his part in damaging John's reputation among the British in Simla the previous year. Gossip saying that John had indulged in drinking and wenching and then run off with Company money was still circulating around the town a year later.

So when Vernon asked her to dance, she would feign tiredness and stay seated. She got a small flicker of satisfaction to see how his handsome, patrician face frowned in annoyance when she accepted the hand of other officers to dance. But her disdain for him had the opposite effect from that which she intended. Vernon remained attentive, bringing her refreshments and making flattering comments.

'I'm full of admiration for your work with the native children,' he told her.

'Are you really?' Alice replied, her tone disbelieving.

'Of course. It's very Christian of you and to be applauded.'

'Then perhaps you would like to contribute to the school's funding?' Alice challenged.

'I'd be delighted to,' Vernon replied.

Nobody was more surprised than Alice when Miss Wallace told her gleefully that Captain Buckley had sent over his tailor to make new shirts and tunics for the pupils.

'You shouldn't be so hard on poor old Vernon,' Emily chided. 'It's just in his nature to want to please.'

'In his nature to flirt,' said Alice. 'He knows I'm a married woman yet it doesn't seem to make any difference to him.'

'Has he done anything improper?' Emily asked.

'No,' Alice admitted.

'And he's given generously to the school, hasn't he?'

'Yes.'

'Then is there any reason why you can't allow him the occasional dance?'

'I suppose not,' Alice conceded with reluctance.

When Alice did agree to put Vernon on her dance card he was so pleased, blushing like a boy in excitement, that she found it almost endearing. He danced exceptionally well and Alice noticed the envious glances from the young unmarried daughters of staff officers eager to make a match with the eligible captain.

But she treated him with mild indifference, not wanting to encourage any false rumours that might cause George embarrassment. She was puzzled as to why Vernon showed her attention at all.

One day, as she was leaving the school to return home to Carrick Lodge, she found him waiting outside with a hired *jampan*.

'It's such a fine afternoon,' he said with a smile, 'that I thought you might like an excursion to the top of Jakko Hill for the view.'

Alice's astonishment was quickly replaced by annoyance. She had balked at returning to the wooded hilltop where she had parted so acrimoniously from John. She certainly had no intention of going there with Vernon.

'No thank you, Captain Buckley,' she said, stepping past him. 'I am having tea with Emily and Alexander.'

'Please, Mrs Gillveray,' Vernon said, putting a hand on her arm to stop her going.

She glared at him and he quickly dropped his hold.

'Why do you dislike me so?' he asked, baffled.

'Why do you show so much attention to another man's wife?' she challenged.

'I'm sorry if I offend you,' said Vernon, 'but I cannot help admiring you. You are quite unlike any of the other women in Simla, whose only talk is of dresses and gossip.' He towered over her. 'You have such spirit – you do as you please and don't care about what people think. I like that in a woman.'

Alice was momentarily thrown by his bold words.

When he saw her hesitation, he smiled. 'So will you allow me the honour of accompanying you up Jakko Hill?'

'Certainly not,' said Alice.

'I'm not responsible for what's happened to Sinclair,' he said. 'Sandy has told me how worried you are about him.'

Alice's mouth fell open. 'W-we all are,' she stammered.

'But you perhaps more than most.'

'You are impertinent,' Alice said, flushing.

'I saw you last year with him,' Vernon said in a low voice. 'On Jakko Hill. It worried me. He has a bad reputation with women – I've known him long enough.'

'Some say the same of you,' Alice retorted.

'I admire women,' he said. 'Sinclair falls in and out of love all the time – leading girls on and then discarding them like soiled clothing. He prefers the lower sorts – servant girls at Addiscombe and natives—'

Alice rounded on him in fury and slapped his face. 'I don't want to hear your hateful words! Stay away from me.'

She turned and fled up the path, leaving Vernon rubbing his stinging cheek.

Chapter 20

Ladakh, spring 1837

John waited impatiently for Wahid's return. Being cooped up in Leh and inactive for most of the winter had sent him nearly mad with frustration. To expend his pent-up energy, he had taken part in wild games that the Ladakhis played on horseback in the centre of town, chasing after a stuffed animal skin with sticks.

Once the valley had become sealed in by winter blizzards, the guard on his house had been relaxed and John and Rajban had managed a few forays beyond the town walls. The dazzling snow had been blinding and John had never experienced such penetrating cold. They bartered camping equipment for thick seamless, ankle-length Tibetan coats, sheepskins and fur-lined boots. John's beard grew thick and his face turned as brown and weathered as that of the locals in the fierce sun.

'You could be mistaken for a Yarkandi merchant' – Rajban laughed – 'if you didn't have such a long nose! Maybe a Tajik or an Armenian.'

John chuckled, surveying Rajban, who was bundled up in sheepskin, a fur hat and earflaps so that his face hardly showed.

'And you, my friend, look like a Himalayan bear. Careful they don't shoot you and serve you up for the king.'

John could not have borne the tedium and anxiety of the past months without the cheerful hillsman. Rajban had changed from his role as servant into John's confidante and comrade-in-arms. While the king had sent them food, drink and fuel, it was a distant kinsman of Rajban's who had provided them with rugs and blankets to keep their lodgings warm and a water-pipe for their tobacco.

They had made many friends in Leh and were often invited into the houses of hospitable merchants, sitting on cushions in their large upstairs reception rooms to drink butter tea and chat. John picked up enough of the language to have rudimentary conversations. There was worry that a summer incursion from Gulab and Zorawar Singh might badly damage the all-important pashmina trade.

'Their ambitions go further than our kingdom,' one merchant said gloomily. 'They won't stop until they have conquered Tibet too – then they will have all the wool trade to themselves.'

* * *

It was late May before the snow retreated, the passes opened and new green growth sprouted beside the rushing torrents of melting glacier. Within a week, Wahid's caravan of yaks and ponies appeared in the valley below. John went out to greet him and help take the animals into the compound.

Later, after dark, Wahid came to John's lodgings and they sat on rugs while Wahid told him news of the outside world.

'There is tension in Kashmir,' he said gravely. 'The amir of Afghanistan is flexing his muscles at the Sikhs. He wants control of the Khyber Pass and Peshawar again. There is worry that the British will back his claim.'

'The Khyber.' John smiled on hearing the name. 'My uncle is an Afridi from there.'

'Your *uncle*?' Wahid exclaimed.

'Azlan married my Aunt Morag,' John explained. 'If he's anything to go by, then no one will ever rule over the Khyber except the Afridi.'

He drew out the jewel-studded dagger that he always kept on him and showed it to Wahid.

The wool merchant whistled in admiration and handed it back. He grinned. 'So you are an Afridi brother.'

'I wonder what Azlan would do in my situation?' John mused.

'Escape,' said Wahid at once. 'I have met a few Afridi tribesmen in my travels and none of them would let some princeling keep them tethered like a goat waiting to be sacrificed.'

John felt irritation at the comparison. Yet it was true; he had made no serious attempt to leave the valley. Where would he go if he did manage to elude the king's guards? Back to India and beg for his army job or seek his fortune elsewhere – perhaps with the Afridi?

As if reading his mind, Wahid said, 'This might help you make up your mind.' He pulled a letter from deep inside his coat. 'I didn't want to be seen handing this to you in broad daylight. It came just before I left Srinagar.'

John's stomach clenched at the familiar handwriting: Colin's. The letter was written in Gaelic to evade censorship. After comradely greetings it grew sombre.

. . . by the time I returned to Dehra a whole six months had gone by and the attitude of our superiors had hardened. Everest was furious that you had turned your back on his great survey and said he would refuse to ever have you work for him again. Hodgson has been promoted.

Wade in Ludhiana is adamant that you had no authority to go beyond British India. I am endeavouring to fight your corner, John, but the political situation is becoming difficult. We are backing Ranjit Singh in the Punjab but also trying to keep our influence in Afghanistan. Do you remember Lieutenant Burnes from Montrose who wrote that racy book of his travels in Afghanistan and beyond? Well, he's been promoted and sent to Kabul as part of a trade deputation to make sure Amir Dost Mohammed isn't tempted to befriend the Russians instead of us.

There are some on Auckland's staff who are obsessed with the idea that the Russians are about to strike into the heart of India through Afghanistan – they are making martial noises. No surprise that Buckley is one of them. Just the type to shout for a military escapade while staying safely under the wing of the Governor General in Simla or Calcutta.

I'm sorry, but the brutal truth is that no one is going to send troops to rescue you. In fact, Buckley has done his best to blacken both our names by putting about rumours that we were the ones living a life of debauchery at the Company's expense. I'm doing what I can to redeem us both.

Good luck, my friend, and may God go with you.

John sat for a long time staring at the pattern in the carpet. His jaw ached as he clenched it in fury. Buckley the blackguard! He had done his utmost to ruin John's career. Why did Vernon hate him so? But then John had to admit that the arrogant cavalry officer had not been the one to encourage him to explore beyond the Sutlej River or to delay too long in Ladakh. He had only himself to blame for that. He had been far too eager to carry out Captain Smith's challenge after his traumatic parting with Alice in Simla. He had been reckless but he had found solace in the mountains – just as he always used to as a boy on Skye.

John studied the letter again, looking in vain for some mention of Alice or hint of what she might be doing. But Colin did not mention her. Why should he? His friend knew about his unhappy affair and would not want to upset John further by telling him of Alice's life with Gillveray. They would have a child by now. He wondered if it was a girl or a boy.

John let go a cry of anguish. Why torture himself further?

'There is nothing to be gained by going back to India,' John said bitterly, 'even if I were free to do so.'

'So, do you want to sit here and let others decide your fate?' asked Wahid, his dark eyes challenging. 'Or do you want to take your fate in your hands like an Afridi?'

John was stung into replying, 'I want to act! Do you have a suggestion?'

* * *

A week later, before sunrise, Wahid's caravan of pack animals set off down the sandy slope to the Indus River. He let it be known that he was making for Kashmir. He took with him half a dozen unkempt porters, the ends of their turbans wrapped across their faces in the pre-dawn cold.

A couple of hours later, two men were seen slipping out of the town and making off with two ponies from the compound and riding rapidly southwards towards the high passes that led to India.

By the time it was discovered that the guards at John's lodgings had been found inside, drugged and tied up, the two riders were long gone. The king sent men in pursuit, who rode all day but didn't catch them up. Three days later, the men were found exchanging their exhausted ponies for fresh ones down by the Chenab River. To the consternation of their pursuers, they turned out not to be the two fugitive British officers that they had expected; they were merchants from Leh who had kin in Spiti and were going to visit a sick relative.

* * *

From the rocky path John looked back down on the large *caravanserai* at Kargil where they had spent the previous night under willow trees next to green fields of unripe corn. Behind was Ladakh; ahead lay sheer cliffs and desolate border country inhabited by autonomous tribes, and beyond that was Baltistan. Below, traders and farmers milled around the bazaar. Wahid had stocked up on supplies there – and it was there that he had parted from John and Rajban with embraces and blessings. Wahid and his convoy were heading west into Kashmir; John was striking north to Baltistan and its Muslim ruler at Skardu. From there he planned to travel to Afghanistan and perhaps offer his services to the maverick fellow Scot, Alexander Burnes, in Kabul. He planned to steer clear of Kashmir and the

Punjab where he might yet again become a pawn in a bid for power in this volatile region.

He turned to Rajban. 'It would appear your cousins must have done a good job of drawing the Ladakhi guards after them. I hope they won't suffer as a consequence.'

'They can talk their way out of anything,' said Rajban with a grin.

John clapped him on the back. 'Thank you. One day I'll reward you properly for your loyalty.'

Turning their backs on Ladakh, they pushed on towards Baltistan.

Chapter 21

Simla, summer 1837

'Clever boy!' Alice cried, holding out her hands to Alexander, who staggered into her arms. 'Look, Emily, he can do five steps without falling over.' She pulled him close, hugging and tickling him.

Alexander threw back his head and let out a delighted giggle. Alice thought there was no more joyous sound than that of a child laughing.

The rain pounded on the roof, and the mountains had disappeared into mist.

Emily sighed. 'When will it ever stop raining?'

A month ago Emily would have clapped her son's achievement and fussed over him. But Alice noticed how tired and pale she was looking, how she visibly gagged at the smell of curried food. Her friend was pregnant again, Alice was sure of it. Nothing had been said, but she could tell. Alexander had not yet turned one. Emily was going to have her hands full; or at least her *ayah* was. Alice felt a twinge of envy that it wasn't she who was with child.

Alice pulled the boy onto his feet. 'Come on, try again.'

'You're not supposed to make them walk too soon,' Emily fretted. 'Get Ayah to put him back in his cot.'

Alice gave an exaggerated expression of shock. 'Do you hear that, Alexander? Your mama wants you banished to your room instead of having fun with your Auntie Alice. What do you want to do?' She leant forward, cheek to cheek with the boy. 'What's that? You want to carry on walking! Of course you do.' She laughed and kissed his soft plump cheek.

Emily lost interest in trying to assert control. 'I wonder if they've managed to clear the landslides yet?' she said, staring out listlessly at the unceasing rain. 'How many days have we been stuck indoors now? And they say it rains a lot in Scotland . . .'

Alice glanced beyond the veranda. 'It'll dry up soon,' she said. 'Then George will be able to join us. He's probably already reached Kalka and is twiddling his thumbs there, waiting till the hill roads are passable.'

She thought of her husband with a fond pang. They had never been apart like this since they had married and she missed his company. There was so much to tell him about the school, and he would notice such a change in Alexander. She wanted to hear about Calcutta and her missionary friends, and she wanted George's opinion on whether Auckland should support the Sikhs or the Afghans.

The Aytons never wanted to discuss politics but she knew George would have a sensible view. He was one of the few Company men still in India who remembered Elphinstone's grandiose trade mission in 1808 to meet a previous Afghan ruler, Shah Shuja. In those days, according to George, the British had courted the Afghans with gifts and money so that they would resist an alliance with the French. Once Napoleon had been defeated though, Afghanistan had diminished in importance to the British.

Alice ordered tea and gingerbread. By the time it came, the rain had abruptly stopped and the mist begun to lift. Within half an hour, the sun was breaking through and steam was rising from the garden.

'See, I told you,' Alice said. 'Here, eat some gingerbread. It'll make you feel better.'

'I don't want to eat anything,' Emily said, grimacing.

Alice eyed her. 'Go on. Ginger stops you feeling queasy.'

Emily blushed. 'You know . . . ?'

Alice nodded.

'I haven't told Sandy yet,' Emily said. 'How did you guess?'

'I remember the nausea.'

Emily bit her lip. 'Of course. I'm sorry.'

'There's no need to be,' Alice assured her.

'You and George,' Emily said hesitantly. 'I'm sure you'll be blessed with children soon.'

Alice felt a familiar stab of disappointment. 'I hope so,' she said, allowing Alexander to clamber over her. 'In the meantime I'm happy being a doting pretend-auntie to this one.'

Sandy appeared at the garden gate, looked around at the view for a moment and then strode towards the house.

'Just wait till you see how many steps your son can walk,' Alice called out to him. 'Come on, Alexander, let's show papa.'

The boy chortled as Alice stood up and hauled him to a standing position. He staggered forward as if the veranda was a pitching ship deck, laughing at his father. Sandy leant forward and scooped him up. He buried his face into the boy's neck and then quickly set him down.

'Ayah,' he ordered, 'take Alexander to his room, please.'

Ayah rose from sitting on the floor and padded forward, lifting the boy. Alexander let out a wail of indignation as he was carried away.

'There's no need,' Alice said, disappointed. 'He wants to play.'

'Alice,' Sandy said, looking at her directly for the first time. 'I think you should sit down.'

Alice felt her insides lurch at the look on his face. 'What is it?'

His ruddy face was harrowed. He began to speak and then clamped his mouth closed as if he couldn't trust his own words.

'Whatever is the matter, Sandy?' Emily asked. 'Please tell us.'

Sandy cleared his throat and swallowed hard. He pulled a letter out of his breast pocket.

'This came from Calcutta with the office *dak*,' he said, thrusting it at Alice. 'There's been cholera. I'm sorry. Very sorry.'

Alice felt her chest constrict with fear. 'Is it George?' she whispered.

Sandy nodded, his eyes welling up with tears. 'He – he was taken swiftly . . .'

'When?'

'Over a month ago.'

'He can't be.' She could make no sense of what he said. 'I got a letter a week ago saying he was preparing to leave.' But even as she said it, she knew that the letter had been written in July, six weeks ago.

'He's buried in the cantonment cemetery,' said Sandy. 'Miss Cook was taken in the outbreak too.'

155

Alice let out a howl of disbelief. Emily jumped out of her seat and threw her arms around her, bursting into tears. Alice clung onto her friend, dry-eyed with shock.

* * *

The hardest part was having no funeral to arrange. What hasty rites had been performed at George's burial? Had anyone attended? Or had he been unceremoniously dumped in the ground by overworked low-caste gravediggers, their scarves wrapped around their faces to ward off the deadly miasma. The outbreak had swept through parts of the city – the docks especially – killing hundreds. Poor Miss Cook too! Had George gone to pay her a visit – collect letters to take to Alice – and caught the disease?

Alice tortured herself with guilty thoughts. She should have stayed with George and looked after him, instead of enjoying herself in Simla. Or she should have insisted he join her much sooner. Why had he not? He had thought his work more important than her. It was he who had been selfish by staying down in Calcutta. He hadn't loved her enough!

She seesawed between guilt and anger, hating her impotence to change a thing. But underlying her mix of emotions was her grief for George and the death of their short, tender marriage.

'We'll take you back to Calcutta early if you wish,' Sandy offered.

'You must come and live with us at Fort William for a bit,' said Emily. 'I won't let you be on your own. At least till you decide . . .'

When Alice tried to think of the future she could picture nothing that would make her happy. Was she expected to return to Britain? Tolland Park seemed like a different world – a distant life that a much younger Alice had lived. She would be lonely there in the dower house, attempting to fill in endless hours with riding, embroidery and taking tea with the gentry.

Yet how long could she stay in Calcutta as a widow? She could hardly bear the thought of returning there without George. She had made the long journey to India to be with him. Calcutta was his city, the botanic gardens his passion. Had their charming home been fumigated and boarded up? She could never bear to live there again.

Would she be expected to swiftly remarry? Widows of officers frequently did, especially if they had young children.

'Oh, George!' she wept aloud in her room. 'If only you had given me a child to love, I could bear this emptiness more easily.'

At night, sleepless and numb with grief, she would wrap herself in her warm gauzy shawl – made from the pashmina that John had sent – and sit on the veranda. Staring out at the Himalayan peaks, Alice would allow herself to think of John. Only in the dark of the Indian night did she admit that she was now free to marry him. She felt disloyal for even contemplating it so soon after George's death but it plagued her waking thoughts.

But where was he? A month ago a rumour had been circulating Simla that he was no longer in Ladakh. Kashmiri traders had brought news that they had helped him escape. If that were so, then why was he not back here in India? It was probably untrue, yet it gave her hope. Sandy had written to Colin MacRae to ask if there was any truth in the rumour but had heard nothing back.

Yet, a worm of doubt had burrowed into her mind about John ever since Vernon had said those terrible things about him. Could John really have been so callous in his treatment of women? She had hated Vernon for saying such things – had avoided him since and ignored his flowers and letter of condolence – but what if some of what he'd said was true?

How well did she really know John? She had fallen in love with him during ten intense days while she nursed him in the lighthouse. But she had only been seventeen years old and completely naïve about men. She had agreed to marry him on a romantic impulse, not because she knew him well. She had thought about him constantly since but had no idea how he had lived his life until they had come across each other in Simla.

Even then, they had been unable to talk to each other frankly until the final painful morning when John had declared his love once more but decreed they must not see each other again. What if he had never really written letters to her and her father and just made up the story to excuse his behaviour? Perhaps he had received her letters to him but had ignored them – enjoying himself too much with the maids at Addiscombe. And yet he had made the journey to Tolland Park to try to see her; the Spanish coin was proof of that.

Restless, Alice went to her jewellery box and retrieved the tarnished coin. She had consigned it to the bottom of the box since her heart-to-heart with George before leaving Calcutta. She fingered the coin and tried to shake off her doubts about John. He did love her; she was sure of that. If John knew she was no longer another man's wife, would he not come rushing back to be with her? She would write to Colin herself to see if he could help her find him. She hung the chain around her neck and dropped it beneath her nightgown. Then Alice felt a fresh wave of guilt that her mind was preoccupied with John and not with George.

* * *

'I'm not going to go back to Calcutta with you,' Alice told the Aytons. It was the end of September and her friends were making preparations for the long journey down to the plains.

They gaped at her.

'But you must,' said Emily.

'We can't leave you here on your own, my dear,' said Sandy.

'I won't be,' said Alice. 'I'm going to live with Miss Wallace and carry on working at the school. It's all I want to do at the moment. I feel I'm being useful here.'

'But you can't!' Emily cried in dismay. 'I'd miss you too much and so will Alexander.'

'I'll miss you all too,' said Alice, 'but you'll be back next spring and we can take up where we left off.'

'I really don't think we can leave you,' Sandy said, flustered, 'not a young woman on your own—'

157

'I won't be on my own,' Alice pointed out, 'I'll be with Miss Wallace. If it's safe in Simla for her, then it is for me.'

'But how will you manage financially?' Sandy asked.

'I am well provided for,' said Alice. 'George made out his will in my favour. He has no other relatives to make a claim on his estate.'

She did not add that the combined wealth from Tolland Park and Black Harbour was considerable. She was a wealthy widow and was determined to use her money to help girls' education in the way that George had helped hers. She had already arranged for a donation to be given to Mrs Meadows to keep the mission school going in Calcutta.

Nothing the Aytons could say would dissuade her. She could tell by their shocked looks that they were a little scandalised by her stubborn wish to live independently and reject the security of the British enclave. But Alice did not care what people thought. To stay in the hills with kind Miss Wallace and the schoolchildren would give her life purpose and bring comfort to her sore heart.

Alice moved her belongings into Miss Wallace's airy bungalow on Jakko Hill the week before the Aytons left for Calcutta. She went to bid them farewell.

'I'll miss this boy the most,' said Alice, hugging Alexander to her.

'If you change your mind,' said Emily, 'you must come and live with us.'

Alice smiled. 'Thank you.' She kissed Alexander and handed him over to his *ayah*.

She didn't stay to see them leave, preferring to go to the school and keep busy instead. A sudden panic gripped her that she was being reckless in staying. How isolated she would be in Simla over the long winter months. Loss for George engulfed her anew.

But when she saw the smiling faces greeting her at the school, she felt a surge of optimism. She was doing the right thing. It was best not to think too far ahead; life in India was so uncertain. She would cope with the future one day at a time.

Chapter 22

Baltistan, summer 1837

John and Rajban followed the River Indus north, at times climbing above sheer black cliffs when the gorge became too narrow for a path. They crossed mountain spurs between dark pinnacles that reminded John of the Cuillins – hard peaks of gneiss with crevices filled with ice.

When they reached the next plateau they would search for shade from the harsh white light under sparse clumps of willows or apricot trees. There was little vegetation anywhere except for where triangular fans of alluvial soil had been washed down from the mountains. They came across occasional fields of barley clinging to the contours of mountain slopes and irrigated by hardy farmers who gave them refreshment. Sitting in the shivery gloom of dark mud houses, John and Rajban would be offered handfuls of crisp toasted barley.

'This reminds me of toasted oats,' said John. 'We used to take bagfuls with us when we went up to the shieling with the cattle in summer.'

But they never lingered, preferring to push on towards Skardu where they could rest and refresh their supplies before heading to Afghanistan.

The only other people they saw were occasional bands of nomads with flocks of sheep, roaming in search of pasture.

There was a stark beauty to the countryside, with its rock and sand of different hues from rusty red to bleached white and green-grey rushing water from the melting glaciers. John was amazed by the number of birds that managed to survive in the harsh landscape: hoopoes, water wagtails, linnets and redstarts. The men shot antelope and used the dung from their two ponies and one yak as fuel for their fire.

They rose before dawn and travelled until early afternoon when the sun grew too fierce, then made camp and slept with their turbans wrapped over their faces to protect them from the sun and wind.

John had never experienced such sand storms. The wind never stopped blowing, whipping sand into their eyes and shredding the skin on their faces. Where they could they followed goat or deer tracks higher up the slopes.

Finally, they came over a pass and glimpsed in the distance an imposing fortress dominating a dazzling blue lake. John knew this must be Skardu, the fortress capital of Baltistan. What he had learnt of the Baltis was largely from Wahid. They were fellow Muslims, ruled by the ageing Ahmed Shah, who was fiercely independent. In looks they were like their Tibetan neighbours.

'It's too far off to reach today,' said John. 'Let's make camp and arrive there in daylight tomorrow.'

From their vantage point on the hillside, overlooking the broad plain ringed on all sides by mountain ranges, they now had a good view of the fortress.

'Looks like the rock at Gibraltar,' John mused. It thrilled him to think he was one of the very few Europeans who could have come this way. 'Do you think there's really a way through from here to Yarkand like Wahid said?'

'There must be,' said Rajban. 'If Wahid is right, then Afghan traders still use it.'

159

As the light faded they wrapped themselves in blankets, brewed coffee over John's spirit lamp and ate apricots. It was Rajban who spotted the caravan of camels in the setting sun, crossing the plain below.

'Nomads?' he queried.

'No flocks with them,' said John. 'They must be merchants.'

They watched with interest as the travellers stopped to set up camp. John took out his telescope for a closer look.

'They have women with them,' he said in surprise. 'There's one getting out of a box-like contraption on that camel.'

'A Balti woman?'

'Looks more like an Afghan.' John passed the eyeglass to Rajban.

'Perhaps they are pilgrims?' the hillsman speculated. 'Certainly followers of Mohammed. Some of them are praying.'

They continued to observe the setting-up of tents, fetching of water and fires being lit for cooking and keeping wild animals at bay. John felt comforted by the sight of others peaceably resting in the clear, dry atmosphere of this remote valley. If they had come from Afghanistan and were moving east then they must be familiar with a route through the Himalayas. It might be worth trying to speak to them to find out what they knew. He hadn't used his Pashto or Persian for a long time but was sure he could communicate with them somehow.

The sun sunk quickly and a bright full moon rose, flooding the rocky plain with silver light. John and Rajban wrapped their blankets over their heads and slept.

Rapid hoof beats woke John. The moon was gone but the sky was littered with stars. Shots fired out. Yells from below had him scrambling to his feet. Rajban was instantly beside him. Animals bellowed and the campers shouted out in confusion as a dozen riders were suddenly amongst them.

John saw sabres drawn and glinting in the ghostly light. A shrieking rider tore into the camp and slashed about him. Others followed. People tried to flee on foot but were cut down. Their screams filled the night.

'We have to help them,' John cried, seizing his rifle.

Rajban did the same. They grabbed swords and knives too and mounted their ponies – hardly horses of war but they would have to do.

The men exchanged glances. They knew that two of them against the robbers below would soon be outnumbered. The look that passed between them said everything; they would be comrades-in-arms until they took their last breath.

'When we get within range, start firing and not before,' John ordered. 'It doesn't sound like they have many guns between them.'

They kicked their ponies forward and down the slope.

The raiders had not expected a counter-attack from that direction out of the dark and were quite taken by surprise. John and Rajban's shots sounded deafening, ringing around the bald rock. Two riders fell from their saddles. The others turned their horses in confusion. John and Rajban brought down two more before the raiders worked out where the firing was coming from. Some of the travellers struck back, plunging knives into the fallen attackers. Two of the robbers drew out pistols and began firing indiscriminately about them. John and Rajban rode at them, swords unsheathed. They clashed. John unseated one and slashed the arm of another.

160

Abruptly the attackers wheeled around and began to retreat. One of them seized a woman standing petrified by the camp fire and threw her onto his horse. She screamed in terror as he galloped off with her.

John turned and went after them. John caught up with the first rider just as he was gaining the entrance to a narrow pass. The robber slashed wildly with his sword and caught John on the arm. His thick Tibetan coat took the worst of the blow but his sword clattered from his grip. John pulled out Azlan's dagger and, lunging forward, threw himself at the kidnapper's horse and plunged the dagger into the man's shoulder.

With a cry of anguish, the man pushed the woman from the horse and kicked the animal forward. He sped off, leaving the woman sprawled on the ground. John dismounted quickly and went to her aid. She was unconscious, blood sticky on his hand from a head wound. He pulled off his turban and made a bandage of it. Lifting her as gently as he could onto his pony, he mounted and led it away from the gulley and into the shadows. Half a dozen riders came clattering past. John waited till the sound of hoof beats had died away. He led his pony back to the camp, holding firmly onto the unconscious woman. There was carnage. People lay dead or dying in the flickering firelight. The camels had scattered across the plain.

John found Rajban nursing a young boy. 'He has a bad sword wound to his leg,' his friend said.

John looked about him, stunned by the brutality that had come so swiftly in the tranquil night. As he did so, he heard horses returning. Grabbing his knife, he turned to face the enemy. He would defend this woman and child with his life.

The horsemen appeared out of the dark and quickly surrounded them. They were not the same men; they looked like soldiers.

John shouted out a salaam before he and Rajban could be mistaken for attackers.

The front rider saluted him back with a hand to his heart. 'I am sent by Ahmed Shah. Tell me who you are!'

'I am Lieutenant John Sinclair of the East India Company. These people are badly wounded and need your help.'

* * *

It was after sunrise before the few survivors were safely within the walls of Skardu's fortress, and the wounded had been seen to. Ahmed Shah, the amir of Baltistan, welcomed an exhausted John and Rajban into his dining hall. He addressed them in the courtly language of Persian.

'Eat, eat, Lieutenant!' he encouraged. 'My men will fetch your yak and possessions. You will tell us what brings you to my kingdom – but first we must see to the others.'

The Balti-speaking soldiers could understand nothing that the survivors said, until John discovered that they spoke Persian. From the distraught boy, Aziz, that Rajban had saved, he learnt that they were a group of Kazilbashis from the Kohistan region of Afghanistan. Aziz told him that they were on their way to Kashmir to trade and attend a wedding. The boy's sister, Sultana, the

161

unconscious young woman being tended in the next room, was the bride-to-be. Apart from a wounded uncle, all the male relations escorting Sultana had been murdered, among them their father and two other uncles. Only a handful of servants had survived.

Ahmed Shah assured the boy that they were safe and he would protect them while they remained in Baltistan.

Later he told John, 'I fear for the boy and his sister. Their uncle may not survive his stab wounds. And the robbers appear to have made off with most of the dowry along with the raisins that the travellers were bringing to sell in Kashmir. It's a terrible business – and to happen right under my nose!'

'Who was it who attacked them?' John asked. 'They did not look like Baltis.'

The amir said disdainfully, 'The robbers are bad men from neighbouring Kafiristan – they hate us Muslims. Their greatest trophy is the severed head of one of our brothers. Or to abduct one of our young women.' He spat into the fire.

* * *

John slept an exhausted sleep in a dark chamber that was simply furnished but comfortable with a padded bed roll and cushions. He awoke not knowing where he was or the time of day.

It was already evening.

In the main hall, Ahmed was playing a board game with the young Kazilbashi boy.

'Aziz is a skilful player,' said Ahmed with a wink. 'He can already outwit a king. Perhaps you will be a better match for his keen young mind than an old man like me?'

John saw from the boy's red-rimmed eyes that he was in pain from his leg wound and deeply in shock. The kind ruler was trying to divert the boy's mind from the horror of the previous night's attack.

'I can try,' said John. 'I used to beat my chief at backgammon – this looks similar.'

While they were playing a new game, a servant who had survived the attack and was keeping watch over Sultana came hurrying in.

'She's awake!' the woman cried.

Aziz leapt to his feet, spilling counters to the floor in his haste. The men kept back. A few minutes later, Aziz returned, his face tear-stained and smiling in relief.

'She can speak – she knows who I am.'

* * *

Over the following days, Sultana grew in strength. Her servant and Aziz were very protective of her and no one else was allowed in to see her.

'She is desolate at our father's death,' said Aziz, trying hard not to cry, 'and weeps for our dear uncles. Like me, she can't get the thought of what happened out of her mind . . .'

162

Word was sent to the Kashmiris about the massacre of the wedding party and to ask them to send an escort for Sultana. Ahmed Shah delayed sending word to the Kazilbashis; he did not want to provoke a feud on his doorstep.

A week later, as they waited for news from Kashmir, their one remaining uncle from the wedding party died of his wounds too. He had babbled incoherently about Sultana and Aziz as fever overtook him.

'Perhaps he wants revenge,' said John grimly.

'Or for us to take care of his nephew and niece,' countered Ahmed Shah.

The uncle was buried in the cemetery on a hill outside the fortress. The amir worried about what should become of the young Kazilbashis in his care. Twelve-year-old Aziz was trying to be brave and assume the role of protector to his sister but he followed John everywhere, limping beside him, reluctant to let him out of his sight. He told John all about his village in the mountains of the Hindu Kush, with its apple orchards and mulberry trees that gave shade from the hot sun and how his father had taught him to hunt with a hawk.

'I have an uncle, Azlan, who taught me to do the same.' John smiled. 'Do you have a hunting dog too?'

Aziz nodded.

'Tell me about your dog,' John encouraged.

One day, John took him up to a high roof in the fortress and gave him his telescope to look through. Aziz was fascinated.

'I can see birds as big as dogs!'

'Not that big.' John laughed. 'They are ordinary birds. You just see them magnified – as if they are closer.'

The boy took to sleeping at the foot of John's bed. Rajban grinned and said he, Rajban, would soon be demoted to sleeping with the servants around the kitchen fire.

'You have become his uncle,' Ahmed Shah said, commenting on how Aziz depended on John. 'It is because you are a man of the mountains like us.'

* * *

Perhaps because of Aziz's complete trust in John or because Sultana knew that it was John who had prevented her abduction by the robbers, she asked to see him.

He went reluctantly, not knowing what he could say to this reclusive and traumatised young woman.

She was standing by the narrow window looking out on the scene in the courtyard below. Her servant hid her face from him as he approached but when Sultana turned, he saw that she was unveiled. She had pale auburn-tinted hair and a slender fair face under her bandaged forehead. To his surprise she looked at him directly and not with downcast eyes. He jolted under her steady gaze; she had startling blue-grey eyes. Something about her reminded him of Alice – not the sophisticated woman who was Gillveray's wife but the young Alice without guile with whom he had fallen so deeply in love all those years ago.

After a stilted exchange of greetings, John asked, 'Are you feeling better?'

She nodded.

163

'Does your head still hurt?'

She shook her head. John wondered if she was going to say anything and if not whether he should withdraw quickly from the room.

Abruptly, Sultana said, 'I want to thank you for saving my life. I cannot bear to think what would have happened . . .'

'I am glad to have done so,' John said. 'I'm only sorry that we could not save your father and uncles.'

He saw the pain in her eyes but she replied with dignity. 'You did what you could – you and your friend. Aziz has told me how much. I don't know how we can repay your bravery and kindness.'

'There is nothing to repay,' John assured her, startled by her eloquence. 'It is enough that you and your brother are safe and will be able to travel on soon.'

He saw a shadow cross her pretty face. 'It was my uncle who arranged the marriage. He has traded in Kashmir for years. My father wanted me to stay in the Kohistan and marry within our people. I wish that I had.' Her expression was full of anguish.

'Oh,' John said, embarrassed by her frankness. 'So why didn't you?'

'My uncle is the eldest – was the eldest,' she said with a shudder. 'He wanted to strengthen our links with the merchants in Kashmir.'

'And what did you want?' John asked.

She looked at him startled, her eyes widening. 'I want what my elders think best,' she said.

It struck John how the blue of her eyes was made more vivid by the darkness of her lashes – surprisingly dark for one with pale-brown hair. He saw the colour rise into her cheeks and realised he was staring. He quickly looked away.

'What do you think will happen to Aziz and me?' she asked.

'You are under the amir's protection,' said John, 'so you must not worry. He will see you safely to Kashmir or back to the Kohistan if that is what is decided.'

Even as he said it, John wondered who it was who would make that decision for the young Kazilbashis now.

'We're very grateful,' she replied.

Glancing at her, he saw how young and trusting she was and was once again reminded of a seventeen-year-old Alice.

'I am glad you are feeling better,' he said. With a bow, he hastened from the room.

* * *

A fortnight later a message came from Kashmir. The marriage would not be going ahead. Sultana should return to her family.

Ahmed Shah was scathing. 'The cowards! They are only thinking of their purses. They don't want a girl who comes without riches or trading agreements. And they call into question her honour,' he cried. 'How dare they suggest I would have let her come to harm!'

John said, 'No one could doubt that you would defend her honour like your own daughter's. But there are no men of her clan to speak on her behalf. The word of Aziz – a mere boy – is not going to satisfy them.'

164

The amir's anger quickly deflated. 'You speak wisely,' he said.

John had come to greatly respect the Balti ruler over the past few weeks; he was a man of peace and good humour who was trying to hang onto sovereignty in the same way as was the King of Ladakh. The amir's son, a handsome, jovial young man, had confided that they feared that the Singhs of Kashmir had designs on their territory too. The news filled John with dismay; he didn't want a repeat of his treatment in Ladakh.

'The Kazilbashis' fate is in the hands of Allah,' said Ahmed Shah. 'It will become clear what must be done.'

While pondering what to do with the young people under his protection, the ruler took his other guests hunting. John and Rajban were keen to see beyond the castle walls.

'Why not take Aziz too?' John suggested. 'He can still ride, despite his bad leg, and it will take his mind off his troubles. He tells me he is an expert with a hawk.'

The amir agreed at once. 'You see how quickly you have become his uncle,' he teased.

They all enjoyed the morning's hunting, going out at break of day, before the sun grew too strong. They shot ibex and water fowl.

As they returned, Ahmed Shah spoke his thoughts to John. 'There is rumour of war breaking out in Afghanistan between Dost Mohammed and rival chiefs in the west and also with the Sikhs. Are you sure you want to go there? You are welcome to stay here as long as you want.'

John was touched by the generous offer but was also aware that the amir might want to keep him as insurance against attack from the Sikhs.

'I know a fellow Scots officer in Kabul, Alexander Burnes, who might be able to give me work,' said John. 'Speaking Pashto and Persian I could be of use to him as an interpreter. And I know much of the ways of the Afridis from my uncle, Azlan, who I told you about.'

'You could certainly pass for an Afghan.' Ahmed grinned. 'You look like one of the brothers with your dark beard and your light eyes.'

John laughed. Watching Aziz thrusting out his arm for the returning hawk, he said, 'Perhaps I could accompany Aziz and Sultana back home to Afghanistan when I leave? If that would be a help.'

'It might well be, my friend. Better to travel in a small group and attract less attention than with a camel train of spoils.'

* * *

John could hear the shouting from along the dark corridor. Aziz was arguing with his sister. He was about to intervene when Rajban said, 'Best leave them alone. This is a matter for the amir.'

Nonplussed, John retreated to the hall below. Ahmed Shah appeared distracted. Only much later did he send for John to join him in his private chamber. It had a large balcony that jutted out over the cliff side, and its shutters were thrown open to admit the cool evening air.

165

They stood together looking out at a fiery sunset that was turning the shadowed peaks purple. John had never seen such a blaze of colours in the sky.

'Sultana is fearful of returning back to her people,' the amir confided. 'It is causing bad feeling with Aziz. He is keen for you to take them home – and show you off to his cousins.' The ruler gave John a wry smile.

'She is bound to be afraid of the journey,' John sympathised, 'considering what has happened.'

The older man fixed him with a look. 'She has more courage than you give her credit for,' he said. 'It is not the journey that daunts her but the reception of her family. She fears they may also reject her as dishonoured – the way the Kashmiris have done.'

'Surely not?' John was dismayed. 'Aziz would speak up for her.'

'She says that his word will not carry enough weight, even with their own people.'

John sighed impatiently. 'Is that why they have been arguing?'

'It is,' said the amir with a nod.

'Well, I will explain everything to her family when I deliver her home,' John pointed out.

'She believes that will not be enough. And I have sympathy with her plight. There is one solution I can think of . . .'

'What is that?' John asked.

'That she returns as your wife.'

John gaped at him, thinking he must have misheard.

'It is a good solution, don't you think?' Ahmed Shah smiled. 'She goes home with honour and you secure a pretty young wife. You British leave it too long to marry. You should have the comfort of a woman.'

John exclaimed, 'I couldn't possibly!'

'Why not? You wish to make your home in Afghanistan anyway. It does not stop you choosing another wife from your own people as well, if the need arises.'

'That's not quite how our women see it,' John said. 'Besides, she is a Mohammedan and I a Christian. The Kazilbashis would never accept me.'

Ahmed Shah was not to be put off. 'You are both believers of the Good Book – such a marriage is allowed as far as I am concerned. And I'm sure Sultana could be persuaded too. Aziz says she has taken a liking to you.'

John was astounded. 'But – why can't – wouldn't it be more suitable for one of your own people to marry her?'

The amir was dismissive. 'No Balti would trade living here for Afghanistan.' He gripped John's shoulder. 'It is the only solution that will reconcile Sultana and her brother. Aziz would be proud to have you as his kin – and you already know the ways of the Afghans.'

'Of the Afridis, not the Kazilbashis.'

The amir waved away such a trifling difference. 'At least give it some thought.'

John swallowed down his frustration and nodded in agreement.

* * *

Sleep eluded John. Marriage to Sultana was a ridiculous idea. It would tie him down to a fresh set of obligations just when he had shed his old one to the Company army. They didn't know each other. She was much younger than he; they had nothing in common. He wondered what Azlan or Hercules would have done in his situation. He rather thought that they would just have gone along with it.

Had Azlan not been in a similar position years ago, arriving as a stranger in Ramanish thousands of miles from home? Yet he had embraced his new life and taken a local woman for his wife, even though they could hardly speak a word of each other's language.

He knew that Azlan loved his Aunt Morag and that she adored him. In time, perhaps, could he grow to love Sultana? He could not deny that he had felt an attraction for her on the one occasion he had been allowed to visit. Again it unsettled him that she had reminded him of Alice. The light-coloured hair and the mesmerising eyes . . .

John's insides clenched at the thought of Alice. She was like a fever that had entered his bloodstream. Would he ever be cleansed of thoughts of her? Perhaps marrying Sultana would help rid him of his desire for Alice once and for all.

It struck him that he would like the companionship of a woman, someone with whom to share his life in the way that Azlan shared his with Aunt Morag. He could settle with her in the Kohistan – in time they would have a sweet daughter like Ariana or a son to carry on the name of Sinclair. Or he might take her to Kabul where she would keep house while he worked for Burnes or at the court of Dost Mohammed. Dost's mother was a Kazilbashi so he might find favour with Afghanistan's amir if he were married into their clan.

'What should I do?' John asked Rajban, his thoughts in conflict.

Rajban shrugged. 'Only you can decide. I will come with you, either way.'

'Thank you,' John said gratefully, wondering what he would do without his loyal friend.

By morning, with only snatched sleep, John had made up his mind. He would be firm and say no. He didn't want to be burdened with a wife. An itinerant life, roaming Central Asia as an interpreter, was no life for a married man. He would keep his word to deliver Sultana and Aziz safely home to the Kohistan but after that his obligation to them would be over.

He found the brother and sister together in Sultana's small chamber, the pair peering disconsolately out of the narrow window. With a pang of pity, John thought of how deeply they must be grieving for their father and uncles.

Aziz's face lit up at his appearance.

'Uncle John, you've come! Isn't it a great thing that the amir has suggested? Have you come to say yes?'

John's heart sank. He braced himself for the boy's disappointment.

'Aziz,' he said, 'could you wait outside for me? I wish to speak to your sister first.'

Aziz hesitated, unable to judge if this was good or bad. 'But I am her only male relative here so you must speak to me.'

'Well, if that's what you wish . . .'

'No, Aziz.' Sultana spoke up. 'We should do as the lieutenant asks.'

167

Her brother seemed about to protest but he went, his face anxious.

John could not look at Sultana; he stared over her head at a cracked tile in the mosaic around the window frame. He had rehearsed his speech; his words of refusal would be softened by the promise to speak on her behalf to her people.

'I have given the proposal much thought,' John began, 'but I think you will agree that marriage between us—'

'*Please*,' Sultana said.

He was stopped by her voice. John looked at her. There was an intensity in her gaze that set his heart thudding. She had such beautiful eyes. What did 'please' mean? That he should not have come at all and his presence pained her or that she wanted to marry him?

She stepped towards him. He found it impossible to look away. She held her head up proudly but her pale lips trembled and her eyes glittered with tears.

'Please,' she whispered, 'don't leave me. My father would have wanted me to marry you, I am sure of it.'

John's resolve melted. She looked so lost and unhappy, and yet beautiful and brave.

He reached out and took her hand. She flinched as if he had scalded her but did not snatch it back.

'Then I will marry you,' said John, hardly believing his own ears.

Tears brimmed over her lids and slid down her cheeks. He bowed his head over her hand but did not kiss it. Then he swiftly let go, unnerved by the effect that touching her had on him. When he looked up she gave him a wan smile.

He left the room wondering what on earth had possessed him to change his mind.

* * *

John and Sultana were married without delay and a message was sent to her family. John could hardly comprehend that it was still July yet in two short months since escaping Ladakh, his life had changed completely. He had to admit that he had not been happier for a long time. It made him realise how alone he had felt all those years as a bachelor, missing Alice and determined to live a solitary life. Finding Alice again in Simla, married to Gillveray, had been sweet torture. It reinforced how much he had longed for her and left him all the more determined never to let his feelings rule his future again.

But Sultana had broken through his emotional defences with her beauty and trusting adoration. He still thought of their first night as husband and wife with tenderness. She had unbound her hair, which fell to her knees, and he had gasped as the long strands had glinted like copper in the lamplight. John had pushed from his mind how it made him think of Alice's hair. He had filled his hands with it and buried his face in its smoky scent.

Sultana had been nervous and shy at the beginning but John had been gentle and loving. Now, every night after a day's hunting with the amir, he was impatient to get back to his new wife and be alone with her in their bedchamber. He relished their lovemaking and her company. She knew little of the outside world but had an enquiring mind and a sense of wonder about the stories he told her. She never tired of hearing about Ramanish and his people, and it made John feel closer to home to be able to repeat his family tales.

The amir was so hospitable that John delayed taking Sultana and Aziz back to Afghanistan. He was enjoying the freedom to hunt and explore into the mountain passes as well as his married life. But he knew that at some point he would be obliged to take her back and face her family. He hoped they would accept him as easily as Sultana and Aziz had done.

Then, in September, as the Baltis were harvesting their crops of wheat, barley and peas, Sultana broke the news to him.

'I am carrying our child,' she said, blushing but unable to hide a smile of triumph.

John picked her up and swung her round. 'That's wonderful!' he cried, kissing her roundly on the lips.

'I will give you a son,' she promised.

'I don't mind.' He grinned. 'A daughter with your beauty would bring me just as much happiness.'

'Are you happy, John?'

'You must know I am,' he answered. 'And you, Sultana, are you happy here?'

'Yes, you make me very happy,' she said, and then her smile faded. 'But . . .'

He tilted her face to look into her eyes. 'But what?'

'I miss my home,' she said, her eyes flooding with tears. 'I know I have no right to ask anything of you – or the amir, who has been like a father to Aziz and me – but when our child is born I would like him to grow up among my people.'

John brushed the tears from her cheeks with his thumbs. 'Don't cry. I understand. My own mother felt the same way. She wanted me to be brought up among her kindred too.' He kissed her forehead. 'When the baby comes I will take you back to the Kohistan.'

Chapter 23

Simla, summer 1838

'We won't really be going to war against the Afghans, will we?' Emily asked in alarm.

'It won't come to that,' Sandy reassured her. 'At the very most we might help fund an attempt by the old Amir Shah Shuja to march on Kabul – if the Sikhs will back him. But we won't get involved.'

'Don't be so sure,' said Vernon. 'Dost Mohammed must be ousted. He's thrown in his lot with the Russians – the man can't be trusted. We have to have control of who is in charge of Afghanistan – and if Shah Shuja is pro-British then we must give him all the help he needs.'

Alice listened to the arguments going to and fro between the men around the Aytons' dinner table. She had welcomed the return of her friends that spring and they had brought Sandy's amiable younger sister, Helen, recently arrived from Edinburgh, with them. Earlier in the year, Alice had been greatly saddened to hear by letter that Emily had suffered a miscarriage shortly after the Aytons' return to Calcutta. Her friend doted on Alexander even more than before and Helen was cheerful company for Emily too. Alice had spent most days seeing Emily, Helen and Alexander since.

Alexander was a robust and lovable boy, rushing about on sturdy legs and beginning to talk. Alice adored him and delighted in spoiling him. Her winter of teaching children and living quietly with Miss Wallace in the snowbound hills had given her the time and tranquillity needed to grieve for George. By early May when Auckland arrived with his entourage from Calcutta, she was ready to be sociable again.

But the Aytons' dinner party was proving difficult. Colin MacRae and Vernon had been sparring all evening and clearly disliked each other; they had fallen out badly after the failure of the horse-trading trip the previous summer and the accusations over John's absconding. Colin had only recently arrived in Simla, and Alice was desperate to get him alone to ask about John. The only letter she had received from Colin after her enquiry after John had been to say that he was now living in Baltistan and had no intention of returning to India. She listened with impatience to the fractious conversation.

'That's not the information that Burnes is telling us from Kabul,' said Colin MacRae, arguing back at Vernon. 'He says that Dost Mohammed would prefer to be in alliance with the British and we'd be fools not to back him. Burnes says he's the most able ruler Afghanistan has ever had.'

'Burnes!' Vernon was contemptuous. 'He's just saying that so he can stay on in Kabul with his harem, satisfying his—'

'Buckley, you forget yourself,' Sandy interrupted. 'There are ladies present.'

'Please forgive me,' Vernon said at once, throwing Alice an apologetic look.

'Burnes has already left Kabul,' said Colin. 'The trade mission has been a failure because of all this suspicion we've cast over the Afghans seeking to do deals behind our backs with the Russians. But I hear Dost Mohammed still wants to make a pact with us and not the Russians.'

'Burnes is discredited,' Vernon said with a dismissive wave.

'I've heard that from a more reliable source,' said Colin.

'Really?' said Sandy.

'And who might that be?' asked Vernon.

'John Sinclair,' said Colin.

'Lieutenant Sinclair's in Afghanistan?' Alice gasped, her heart thudding. Around the table people were looking at her.

Alice blushed furiously. 'I – I'm just surprised to hear it,' she stammered.

'We all are,' said Emily quickly. 'What is the Lieutenant doing there?'

'Hardly a lieutenant,' said Vernon, 'seeing as he deserted the army.'

'He's providing intelligence for the British,' said Colin. 'Burnes recommended him as he's a brilliant linguist.'

'Two Scotch rogues together, eh?' Vernon said with a contemptuous laugh.

'Two men who know the ways of the Afghans well,' Colin countered. 'John's uncle is an Afridi.'

'So he's a political agent?' Sandy mused. 'Perhaps he's been offered an amnesty by the Company if he keeps his ear to the ground on our behalf.'

'How long has he been there?' Alice asked, clasping her hands in her lap to stop them shaking.

Colin gave her a sympathetic look. 'I don't know. He sent a message with Burnes. He believes a British invasion of Afghanistan would be disastrous. It would be the surest way to get the Russians involved – and to turn Afghan friends into deadly enemies.'

'Afghan friends?' Vernon was incredulous. 'None of them can be trusted. The only way to deal with them is with the gun or bagfuls of money to buy them off.'

Emily rose. 'I think we ladies have heard enough talk about guns and Afghans. We'll retire to the sitting room for coffee. You gentlemen can join us for cards after your port.'

Alice followed with reluctance, throwing Colin an anxious look. She wanted to hear more; especially any news about John. He gave her a slight nod to indicate he would talk to her later.

* * *

Alice sat half-listening to the conversation around her. Emily had made new friends among the Calcutta officers' wives and she was enjoying giving them, as well as her spinster sister-in-law, Helen, advice about life in Simla.

What had taken John to Kabul? Colin had as good as called him a spy for the British there. Had he done it in order to seek a pardon and return to India as Sandy thought? Had he received Colin's message that she was now a widow? She could hardly bear to sit there listening to the talk about servants and the imminent monsoon or what the Eden sisters would be wearing at the forthcoming ball at the Assembly Rooms.

It was a relief when the men came to join them. Vernon tried to engage her in conversation. He had been very attentive to her since his return to Simla – had written her amusing letters from Calcutta, which she had ignored – but the more she tried to put him off, the more compliments he paid her.

'I'm sorry, Captain Buckley, but I'm too tired for cards. I shall be leaving shortly.'

'Let me escort you back to Miss Wallace's,' he offered.

'Thank you, but I know that Lieutenant MacRae is going in that direction and has offered me a lift in his *jampan*.'

Alice threw Colin a pleading look.

'That's right,' said Colin, coming quickly to her side. 'Would you like to leave now?'

Alice nodded. 'If you wouldn't mind?'

'Not at all.'

They said swift goodbyes to their hosts. Alice could see Emily was disappointed that the handsome lieutenant was leaving early; Emily had told her that she thought Colin would be an excellent match for Helen.

Making their way along the narrow garden path to where the *jampan* waited, Alice said, 'I'm sorry to drag you away. It's selfish of me.'

'I'm not sorry,' Colin grunted. 'I couldn't have taken any more of Buckley's rash remarks. He's treating this whole Afghan escapade as if it were no more dangerous than the Annandale races. And he's not the only one. Auckland seems to be surrounded by young bloods who can talk of nothing but invasion and giving Dost Mohammed a bloody nose.' He made an impatient sound. 'Even Fane, our commander-in-chief, is talking about sending a grand army to put Shah Shuja back on the throne. No half measures – that's what he's advising Auckland.'

They stopped on the lane. The pines were swaying and sighing in a strengthening breeze.

'I'm sorry,' said Colin. 'That's not what concerns you, is it?'

Alice's heart beat rapidly. 'It concerns me greatly that we might be contemplating a foolish rush to war – especially if John is in Kabul. He'd be in great danger, wouldn't he?'

Colin nodded but seemed reticent to say more. He helped her into the *jampan* and climbed in next to her. They set off on the short run to Jakko Hill in silence. When they disembarked, Colin led her through the picket gate to Miss Wallace's veranda.

'May I sit with you for a moment?' he asked.

'Of course,' said Alice, almost bursting with wanting to know more of John. Any slight titbit of news would do. They sat down, facing out at the view of the Himalayas. Pinpricks of light came from bungalows nestled in the trees on adjacent slopes, the mountains beyond reduced to an indistinct dark mass.

'At dinner you said you'd got a letter from John through Burnes?' Alice prompted. 'Did he mention me at all? Does he know about George?'

Colin gave her a pitying look. 'No, he didn't say anything personal. It was purely about intelligence. He wanted me to try to speak to Auckland or his advisors about the folly of backing Shah Shuja.'

'So he might not have got your letter about me?' Alice asked. 'But now that I know he's in Kabul I could write to him, couldn't I?'

Something about Colin's look made her insides go leaden. She felt suddenly cold.

'What is it you know, Colin?'

He cracked his knuckles, a sign of his nervousness.

'Please tell me,' Alice urged. 'Whatever you say can't be worse than this not knowing.'

'There was a letter from John waiting for me when I passed through Dehra in April,' he said. 'It was more than six months out of date.'

'From Baltistan?'

'Aye, he was still there then. He must have written it soon after the one I received saying he was staying as the amir's guest.'

'So what news did he have that made him write again so soon?' Alice pressed him. Her chest was tight with dread. He was holding something back that he knew was going to hurt her.

'I didn't just want to tell you in a letter,' he said, 'as I knew I would be seeing you soon in Simla.'

'Tell me what?' Alice's heart was pounding now.

'That John had got married,' said Colin, 'to a young Kazilbashi girl.'

Alice found it hard to breathe. 'Kazilbashi?'

'An Afghan tribe from the Kohistan in the Hindu Kush,' he said. 'It appears he saved her life from some robbers.'

Alice felt an ache at the thought. How ironic that she had saved John's life, only for him to save the life of another woman – a woman who had taken him from her. Shock engulfed her.

'Perhaps he felt obliged to do so,' said Alice, floundering for an explanation, 'to save her honour?'

She could hardly bear the look that Colin gave her. It was full of sadness for her.

'Perhaps he did. But it has grown into more than that. John said he loves her and . . .'

'And?' Alice whispered. 'Say it.'

'And she was bearing his child. He was overjoyed at the thought of becoming a father. I'm very sorry, Alice, but I don't want you to hold out any false hope for my friend.'

She felt desolate. All winter she had daydreamed about John receiving her message and rushing back to be with her. Now that would never be. Even if he had got word that she was free to remarry, he would not have come. How many other women had he had relations with since leaving her bereft in Simla? Vernon's words came back to taunt her. John was always falling in and out of love; he was a womaniser who flattered to get what he wanted. But now he had really fallen in love. This time he loved someone enough to marry them and father her child. The gut-wrenching jealousy that she felt at that moment for the Afghan woman made her want to scream.

Bile rose in her throat as further realisation dawned. 'That's why he's gone to Kabul, isn't it? Because he's married to an Afghan.'

Colin reached out and covered her hand in his, giving it a squeeze of comfort. 'I think that must be so,' he said. 'I'm very sorry, Alice. I know you cared for him and that he cared for you—'

'Don't say that!' She snatched her hand away. 'Please don't make excuses for him. I've been such a fool – loving him all these years when I've never really meant that much to him.'

'You did,' Colin insisted. 'I knew him at Addiscombe. He never looked at another woman. It was always you he talked about.'

'That's not what Vernon says,' Alice said, her tone scathing.

'You don't want to believe a word that man says,' retorted Colin. 'He has the morals of a pariah dog.'

Alice stood up. She couldn't bear to hear any more. 'Please go, Lieutenant.' Her eyes stung with angry tears. 'I'm sorry to have involved you in my ridiculous daydreams. I feel nothing but shame to have put you in such an awkward position. John is your friend and I don't want to say anything more that might offend you, when you have been so considerate and kind to me.'

Colin stood and bowed. 'It is I who am sorry,' he said. 'I wish I had been able to bring you the news that you wanted. But in my friend's defence, he probably married this girl thinking you were still Gillveray's wife.'

Alice was stung by the gentle reproof. She faced him, her nails digging into her palms to stop her breaking down in front of him. 'It doesn't matter now, does it? All I wish for is to forget I ever knew John Sinclair and to make the best of the life I have here.'

She watched the Scots officer walk away through the trees. An owl hooted; far off a jackal made a barking howl. She hugged her barren stomach and gritted her teeth. She waited until the creaking of the *jampan* and the thud of runners' feet faded into the distance. Then Alice crumpled to her knees and wept in distress.

* * *

It felt like a second bereavement, losing John after George. Except that this time Alice was plagued by the thought that John still lived beyond her reach, enjoying life with another woman and becoming a father. She tortured herself with the thought of this Afghan wife bearing John a child. How she yearned to be a mother! Her anger that he had so easily fallen for someone else turned her love for him to bitter resentment.

At times, as she lay tossing in bed, listening to the monkeys clattering on the roof, she cried out, 'I hate you!' She wasn't sure if she shouted at the irritating monkeys or at John.

A small part of her chided such thoughts; was Colin not right to suggest that John had married this woman thinking Alice was still George's wife? The last he had known of her was that she was carrying George's baby. Alice smothered the painful memory of her miscarriages. But she was too distraught at John's marriage and fatherhood to allow him that excuse. For all she knew, he had received Colin's letter about her widowhood and had chosen to ignore it. Even if Vernon had exaggerated John's weakness for women, Alice had to face the brutal truth that John could not have loved her as much as she had loved him all these years.

Alice felt drained from her nocturnal bouts of anger and tears. It left her listless and numb. Emily, full of concern that Alice had shut herself away, came round.

174

'Miss Wallace is very worried,' said her friend, marching straight into Alice's bedroom. 'You haven't been to the school all week and you've not answered any of my notes. Are you sick?'

Alice tried to rally. 'I'm fine. I just needed to be alone for a bit.'

'Are you grieving for George?' asked Emily, sitting down and holding her hand. 'I know it must get you down at times.'

Alice's guilt that she had hardly thought of George this past week brought fresh tears to her eyes.

'Oh, Emily, I've been so foolish.'

'Tell me. Is it something Colin MacRae has done? Vernon thinks it is. He says you haven't been out in Simla since MacRae took you home after my dinner party. Has he acted ungallantly towards you?'

'No, of course not,' Alice said, aghast at the accusation. 'Colin is a good man. But he did tell me something upsetting.'

'What?' Emily asked, squeezing her hand.

Alice unburdened herself to her friend. It was a relief to admit aloud how much she had deluded herself about John.

'Married to an Afghan?' Emily said, quite shocked. 'Well, who would have thought it? Vernon was right about him after all; he said that Sinclair had a liking for native girls.'

Alice flushed.

'Oh dear, Alice, it's not your fault at all. You were just taken in by a handsome young officer. Sinclair was wrong to make advances to you when you were married to Gillveray.'

'It wasn't like that,' Alice said in distress. 'We'd known each other years before I came out to India. We'd had an understanding . . .'

Emily's eyes widened. 'What do you mean?'

Alice told her about the rescue from the wreck of the *Berwickshire* and nursing John back to health. Emily was dumbfounded.

'You are the lighthouse heroine?' she cried. 'I remember my papa reading aloud from the newspaper. Why have you never told me?'

'I've never told anyone in India,' Alice admitted. 'George and I decided that we would keep quiet about it. I hated all the fuss that it brought. I just wanted to be known as Alice Gillveray out here.'

'Well, what a dark horse you are!'

'Please don't go telling everyone,' Alice said, regretting confiding in the talkative Emily.

'Of course not,' Emily said, 'though if I were you, I'd be boasting about it all over Simla. To think you saved Sinclair's life and this is the thanks you get – a broken heart.' Emily patted her hand. 'Well, we're going to mend it. You will come as our guest to the ball at the Assembly Rooms on Friday. I won't have you moping on your own. This is when you need your true friends.'

Alice gave her a teary smile. 'Thank you.'

* * *

After Emily's visit, Alice made an effort to enter into the social life of Simla. Her friend was on a mission to cheer her up. She attended the ball and took a day off from the school to go to the races at Annandale. She went to musical evenings and suppers with charades. Colin was polite but avoided groups where she was conversing. Vernon redoubled his efforts to be kind and solicitous.

Alice was hardly surprised when word quickly spread through Simla about John's scandalous marriage to an Afghan girl. She knew Emily wouldn't have been able to keep such a secret. Perhaps that was why Colin kept his distance, blaming her for the gossip about his friend.

Vernon came round one afternoon and sought her out. 'I am organising a night picnic at Mahasu. It's a full moon tomorrow. I'd be honoured if you would agree to come.'

Alice was surprised. 'Emily hasn't mentioned such a trip.'

He gave a conspiratorial smile. 'It isn't for the Aytons. I never get to speak to you properly when Emily is around. She's very protective of you.'

'Then who will be there?' Alice asked, feeling a flicker of alarm. He was an imposing man with his great height and charm. She knew he was the kind of man who was used to getting what he wanted. But she would not be forced into anything with which she felt uncomfortable.

'A few friends from the Governor's staff,' he said, 'and Auckland and the Edens too, of course.'

Alice gaped at him. 'Are you really so high up in the Governor General's staff?'

Vernon laughed. 'I admit I get along very well with Auckland – and his delightful sisters. And I know the best places around Simla for romantic picnics. Mahasu is a charming place – a meadow of wild flowers among cedars with a view to the mountains.'

'Don't you mean *deodars*?' said Alice. 'George said that was the Indian name for the trees.'

'I stand corrected,' he said with a bow. 'So will you say yes? There will be fireworks too.'

Alice gave in with a reluctant smile. 'Well, if there are to be fireworks, then how can I say no?'

* * *

Sitting under the stars, watching the fireworks shooting overhead, Alice felt she was in a magical land. They had dined by candlelight in a sweet-smelling glade to the haunting music of a sitar player. Vernon was as attentive as ever, not drinking too much like some of the other officers but making sure that her champagne glass was never empty.

Alice enjoyed the feeling of slight inebriation, so that her thoughts were pleasantly numbed and her body relaxed. She laughed and joined in the conversation more than she had done in months. On this enchanting Indian hillside in the soft flickering light, she felt that given time she could be happy again.

176

'Thank you for a lovely evening, Captain Buckley,' she said to Vernon when he dropped her back at Miss Wallace's bungalow.

He raised her hand to his lips and pressed it with a firm kiss. 'The pleasure was all mine, Mrs Gillveray,' he said, holding onto her hand.

She felt a pleasant stirring of desire deep inside; a sensation that she had not experienced for a long time.

'May I call on you tomorrow?' he asked.

She hesitated. Was it wise to encourage this man? Opinion seemed divided on Vernon. Some said he was a hedonist who did everything to excess, others that he was gallant and misunderstood by lesser men who envied his rapid success on the Governor General's staff. It was rumoured he would be a major before long; Alice had noticed how Auckland listened to whatever Vernon had to say. What was the harm in seeing more of the handsome captain?

'I will be at the school until mid-afternoon,' said Alice. 'You may call for tea after four if you wish.'

'I'd like that very much.' He kissed her hand a second time. As Alice mounted the steps to the veranda she knew he watched her. It gave her a frisson down her spine. She turned at the top. He smiled, made a short bow and then walked off into the dark.

* * *

Alice saw Vernon every day for the following two weeks. They took tea on the veranda and went for walks along the ridge to watch the building of the gleaming Gothic Christ Church, which was close to completion. He took her to musical soirées and plays. They went out riding together in the cool of the evening and he organised night-time picnics with a few chosen friends.

Word soon spread around Simla that the dashing captain was courting the spirited widow with the striking fair looks. Some were scandalised that she should be encouraging such attention when she had not been in mourning for a full year. But the Aytons defended her.

'George wouldn't have wanted you to spend the rest of your life as a hermit,' Emily said stoutly. 'Let them say what they will – gossip soon blows over.'

Yet it gave Alice pause for thought. She knew her own motive for seeking out Vernon's company was largely to quench her anger at John's marriage. How hurt she had been to hear John loved another woman! Allowing the handsome, sophisticated cavalry officer to court her was her attempt to bury the past and to prove to herself she could live without John. But what was Vernon's motivation? She had overheard a snide remark.

'He's obviously after her money. Gillveray left her a wealthy woman.'

Alice had been tempted to tell the gossips, hiding behind their fans, that a large part of her fortune was her own. It troubled her that this might be why Vernon was pursuing her so relentlessly.

'Why do you wish to spend so much time with me?' Alice asked him as they sat on her veranda one evening, watching thunder clouds building beyond the trees. The monsoon was imminent. 'There are prettier, younger and more eligible women in Simla this season. I hope it's not because you're feeling sorry for me.'

177

Vernon reached over and took her hand, squeezing it in his large one. 'How could you think such a thing?' he protested. 'I care nothing for the silly girls newly out from England. You are the most fascinating and desirable woman I've ever met.'

Alice could not help being flattered. But she needed to be sure.

'You must know that we are the talk of Simla drawing rooms this summer?' she said. 'Some say your interest in me is only because of my wealth.'

He flinched. It reminded her of how she had once slapped him for being impertinent about John.

'My dear Mrs Gillveray,' he said, his expression pained. 'I hope you don't think such a thing?'

She hesitated. He grew indignant and stood up. 'I can see that you do. I thought we knew each other better than that. I care for you deeply – more than any woman I've ever met. But if you think so little of me and my intentions, then I shall not stay!'

Alice was startled by his reaction; she stood up quickly. 'Please, don't be offended,' she said, reaching out to stop him. 'It's not what I think.'

'But you have doubts,' he said. 'I can see it in your eyes.'

'I enjoy your company, Captain Buckley. Isn't that enough for now?'

'Not for me,' said Vernon. 'You mean more to me than a passing summer fancy. I don't need your fortune – my father is a very wealthy man and I will inherit everything in due course.'

'I'm sorry,' Alice said, 'I just need to be sure of your intentions. I have been a bad judge of men in the past.'

'Do you mean Sinclair?'

'Yes,' she admitted, glancing away in embarrassment.

'Did I not warn you about that scoundrel?'

Alice bit her lip, not wanting to be reminded of her foolishness.

'I know why you trusted him,' said Vernon, his tone softening. 'He made promises to you that he did not keep.'

'How do you know that?' Alice felt annoyance. 'Emily told you, didn't she? She should not have done.'

'Don't judge her harshly,' said Vernon. 'She only told me out of concern for you.'

'Did she tell you everything?' Alice asked in alarm. 'About me knowing John years ago?'

'Yes,' he said. 'I must say it came as a shock to know you were the Alice of the lighthouse – and Colonel Fairchild's daughter.'

'I didn't want it known—'

'It just makes me admire you more,' insisted Vernon. 'And makes me all the angrier at Sinclair. The things he used to say about you . . .'

Alice's insides clenched. 'What things?'

'No, I can't repeat them. They are too callous. And he was just a foolish young buck trying to impress his peers at Addiscombe – boasting about his conquests. You were just one of the names—'

'Stop it!' Alice said, feeling winded. 'I don't want to hear any more.'

At once he was full of concern. 'Please forgive me.' He pulled her round to face him. 'I would never mistreat you like that. You do believe me, don't you?'

She looked up into his handsome, concerned face. Alice wanted to believe him. She had felt so alone this past year and she wanted to be able to trust a man again. 'Yes, I think I do.'

'Then marry me, Alice!'

She was taken aback. 'Marry?'

'It's the only way I can show you that my intentions are honourable – that I care only for you,' he insisted. 'Say you will be my wife.'

She pulled away. 'I think we should get to know each other better first.'

'What is there to know?' he said with impatience. 'I think about you all the time – I desire you, Alice. It must be obvious?'

His words were so seductive – and the way he was suddenly using her first name – that she felt herself weakening.

'I can't make such a decision until my year of mourning is up,' she said. 'Ask me in a month's time, Captain Buckley, if your feelings are still as strong.'

'My God, you are as infuriating as you are desirable,' he exclaimed. Abruptly, he bent and clasped his hands around her face, bringing his lips so close to hers that she thought he was about to kiss her.

Her heart drummed in sudden excitement. But he pulled away.

'If that's your wish, then I shall respect it,' he murmured, 'however hard I find being kept at arm's length from you.'

Abruptly, he spun on his heels and clattered down the veranda steps. In agitation she watched him go into the dying sun. Her feelings were so confused towards him. She was strongly attracted to Vernon and felt the physical desire that he professed for her. But were his words just flattery – the famous Buckley charm – or did he really care for her? Alice was deeply hurt to think that John had boasted about her in crude terms of conquest. Was it true or was Vernon saying it to make her hate John all the more? Colin had said quite the opposite. But what did it matter now?

A rumble of thunder sounded nearer. Alice paced the veranda in the growing dark, glad that Miss Wallace was out at a bible meeting and hadn't been witness to Vernon's outburst. Alice could never have John but she could make a new life with Vernon. Was it such a bad match? They had interests in common, such as riding and dancing. Vernon had a good ear for a jaunty song. He didn't have much patience with reading or literature but then he was a man of action. He was very good-looking and he made her feel desirable even when dressed in the widow's purple of half-mourning.

Being with him made her realise how much she missed the physical side of marriage. Despite having kind friends like the Aytons, Alice yearned again for intimacy with a man who could be loving as well as a soulmate. Above all, marrying Vernon would mean that she would have another chance of becoming a mother.

Alice went to the balcony rail and turned her face up to the first fat drops of rain. How she yearned for a child! She knew that George would have been a good father. With a twist of pain she imagined that John was a devoted father to his child. Would Vernon be one too? Alice had seen him being playful with Alexander, tickling him till he giggled and bringing him sweets from the bazaar.

As lightning lit the sudden darkness, Alice allowed herself to imagine what a child of hers and Vernon's might look like, a sweet-faced child with golden curls.

* * *

Vernon stayed away. Alice missed his daily calls to the house after her work at the school. She looked out for him at social functions but there was no sign of him.

'Have you seen Captain Buckley?' Alice finally asked Emily.

'Sandy says he's taken himself off to Sanpore to visit the raja on behalf of the Governor General. Did you have words?'

'Not as such,' Alice said. 'But I know you told him about my past with John Sinclair when I told you that in confidence.'

'Only because I could tell the captain cares for you,' said Emily.

'He thinks I don't trust him,' said Alice.

'And don't you?'

'I'm not all together sure.'

Emily said, 'You shouldn't judge him so harshly. Not all men are as fickle as John Sinclair.'

Alice was tempted to tell Emily about Vernon's sudden proposal but stopped herself. It would be announced all over Simla before she had come to a decision – even supposing Vernon hadn't had a change of heart.

The monsoon arrived and the school was closed. Alice spent many hours cooped up at Miss Wallace's with too much time on her hands for thinking. She couldn't get Vernon out of her thoughts. His absence had increased her desire for him. She missed his attentive presence. She tried to paint but couldn't concentrate. The only time she managed to stop fretting over whether she wanted to marry Vernon or not was when playing with Alexander. Alice spent as much time as she could over at Emily's keeping the little boy entertained.

Then one day Alice received a note.

My Dear Mrs Gillveray,

I wish to invite you to a luncheon at Mahasu this coming Friday. I will meet you at Combermere Bridge at twelve noon and we shall ride out together. I do hope you will accept.

Your devoted servant,

Captain V Buckley

Alice was at once nervous and excited by the short invitation. What did it mean? It was almost commandeering in tone and yet solicitous. The only way to find out what intention lay behind it was to accept and go.

* * *

It was a day of bright sunshine, one of those clear fresh days after a deluge. The mountain peaks were visible for the first time in a week. It was a year and five days since George's death in Calcutta. For the first time since coming out of mourning Alice eschewed sombre clothing and dressed in a pale-green riding frock with creamy lace trim and a bonnet to match, and rode out to Combermere Bridge with a servant in tow.

Her heart thumped to see Vernon waiting for her, dressed immaculately in his army uniform, astride his horse. His fair face was freshly shaven and his blond sideburns trimmed. He smelt strongly of spicy cologne. He smiled in delight but didn't try to take her hand and kiss it as she had expected. It was a month since she had set eyes on him and, from the curdle of excitement in her stomach, she realised that she had missed him. The strength of her feelings took her by surprise. Until that moment, she had not appreciated how much she had come to rely on his company.

They chatted as they rode towards Mahasu. Vernon brushed over his time away in Sanpore.

'Boring duties for the most part,' he said. 'Endless dinners and fawning over the raja. But tell me, what you have been doing?'

'Precious little,' said Alice, 'since the monsoon came. If it wasn't for Alexander keeping me entertained I would have gone mad with being confined by the rain.'

'How is the little scamp?' Vernon chuckled.

'Growing fast. He can say whole sentences now – in English and Hindustani and sometimes mixed together.'

'You're very fond of him, aren't you?'

'Yes,' said Alice, 'I am.'

As they drew nearer to the Mahasu glade he asked her abruptly, 'Have you missed me?'

Alice reddened. 'I was worried I had offended you and that's why you'd left Simla.'

'That's not what I asked, Mrs Gillveray.'

'Yes,' she admitted. 'I have missed your company.'

'And I yours,' he said, smiling.

* * *

Riding into the glade, Alice gasped to see that a canvas pavilion festooned with garlands of flowering creepers and ribbons had been erected at its centre. The sides of the tent were draped with gauzy muslin and its carpeted entrance lined with pots of ferns. A small band of three musicians struck up and played as Vernon lifted her down from her side-saddle.

'How beautiful,' she cried as he gave her his arm and they walked into the pavilion.

Low tables were laid out with bowls of food, and around them were piled soft cushions to sit on. As Alice wondered where the other guests were, Vernon snapped his fingers and a bearer came forward with champagne. When two flutes had been poured, Vernon clinked his glass with hers.

He smiled. 'To us!'

'Is it your birthday?' Alice asked in bemusement.

'No, it's a more important day than that.'

181

'Oh?' Alice was intrigued.

'It's a day of celebration.' He knocked back the glass of champagne. 'Come on, drink up!'

Alice took a large mouthful, the bubbles frothing on her tongue. It made her instantly relaxed. She took another as he ordered the bearer to top up their glasses.

'Are we waiting for others to arrive before you tell me?' Alice guessed.

He moved closer. 'There are no other guests. This luncheon is just for you.'

Alice blushed. 'That will get the tongues wagging in Simla,' she said dryly.

'There's one way to stop that,' said Vernon. 'And that's for you to agree to marry me.'

Alice felt her insides somersault. 'This is a marriage proposal?'

'You said I was to ask again in a month's time,' said Vernon. 'The only way I could bear to keep my hands off you was to remove myself from Simla. That's why I volunteered to go to Sanpore. Now the month is up and I'm glad to see that you are out of mourning.'

Alice felt her flush deepen at his blunt words.

'So there is nothing now to prevent our getting married.' Vernon fixed her with his blue eyes. Up close they looked a little bloodshot. She wondered if he had been losing as much sleep over her as she had over him.

'All this,' he said, with a sweep of his hand, 'is to show you how serious I am in courting you.'

He took her glass from her and handed them both to the bearer. Then Vernon went down on one knee and took her hand in his. 'Alice, please say you will be my wife.' He kissed her fingers.

She was quite overcome. He had gone to such lengths to show his love for her. No one had lavished attention on her quite like this before; it was extravagant and generous and made her feel very special. Up till then, Alice had still been unsure about Vernon. But what more could he do to reassure her that he was serious in wanting her as his wife? Too many times in her life she had lost the ones she loved and happiness had been snatched away. Now here was this eager and ambitious officer, full of a zest for life, offering her a future. Why not take it?

'Yes, Captain Buckley, I will.' She smiled.

His eyes widened in a flash of surprise and then he was on his feet and pulling her face up to his. He planted a robust kiss on her lips.

'That's settled then,' he said with a triumphant look.

Seizing the champagne glasses again, he bade her drink.

'Let's not delay our wedding,' he said eagerly as they settled on the cushions. 'We'll marry here in Simla.'

'If that's what you want,' said Alice, lightheaded from champagne and the speed of his plans.

'It's all very uncertain about Afghanistan at the moment,' said Vernon. 'So we might as well enjoy ourselves while we can.'

Alice felt a twinge of unease at his cavalier words. But wasn't that what she liked about Vernon – his spontaneity and ability to live for the moment?

The sun was dipping before the long luncheon was over. Alice was almost too intoxicated to ride home. She had had to keep his exploring hands at bay and he had laughed good-naturedly.

'So coy for one who has already known the marriage bed.'

The next day Alice tried to remember half of what Vernon had said but it was that little jibe that came back to her. He had meant nothing by it; it was just his eagerness to be intimate. And wasn't she guilty of the same impatience? As the day for their hasty marriage grew nearer, Alice was consumed by thoughts of sharing the marriage bed with the lusty officer.

* * *

On a sultry day in late July, Alice and Vernon were married in a quiet ceremony, with the Aytons and some of Vernon's bachelor friends in attendance. Alice caught her breath at the sight of the tall, curly-haired Vernon awaiting her in full military regalia. Despite Alice wanting no fuss, most of Simla society came out onto the Ridge to view the spectacle and comment on Alice's dress of pink taffeta and lace as they made their way to the Assembly Rooms.

Here there was a lavish dinner with much feasting and drinking. Alice had felt that too much celebration was somehow disrespectful to George so soon after his death, but Vernon had been quite put out at the suggestion of a simple afternoon tea. Alice had quickly relented. This was his special day too and she would do nothing to spoil it.

It was late by the time they returned to Arden House, which Vernon had rented as their first home; a charming stone-built dwelling with a terraced garden and a view of the mountains. He had spent a small fortune furnishing it and staffing it with servants, insisting that she must have the best of everything.

Captain Nairn and a group of Vernon's cavalry friends escorted them along the path with ribald comments about the night ahead. The men drank a bottle of brandy between them before leaving the newlyweds alone. Vernon poured himself another large brandy and took it up to their bedroom. His bearer pulled off his boots while Vernon loosened his collar. His regimental jacket had been discarded downstairs.

It occurred to Alice that he might be nervous. It was the end of his bachelor life. Perhaps he was not as familiar with women as the gossips had said. She tried to reassure him.

'You don't need to drink yourself senseless on my behalf. Let's just enjoy our first night together.'

She went towards the dressing room where a maid that Vernon had hired was waiting to help her but he blocked Alice's way.

'Stay and undress here,' he slurred. 'I want to watch you.'

He called the maid through to help Alice undress and then lay on the bed slugging his brandy, eyeing Alice. The lamps blazed so that she felt as if she were on stage.

'Shall we turn down the lamps?'

'No. I've waited a long time for this.' He smiled. 'I want to see you in all your beauty.'

Alice felt uneasy but began to remove her wedding dress. The maid helped untie her stays and take off layers of petticoats. Alice was acutely aware of Vernon watching them, his breathing growing more rapid as she shed her clothes.

'Pass me my nightgown,' she bid the girl.

'No, take everything off,' said Vernon.

Alice felt acutely embarrassed. 'Go now,' she told the maid. 'I can manage from here.'

When the girl had gone, Alice hurriedly stepped out of her under-shift. Finally, she stood naked before him. He gazed at her, then drained off his drink. She moved towards the bed, pulling back the covers.

'No,' he rasped, 'lie on top. I want to see every bit of you while we consummate our marriage.'

He fumbled out of his own clothes. Alice could see at once that he was already aroused. He straddled her.

'Please kiss me first,' she said.

He covered her mouth with his, sucking at her lips. He kissed and nibbled his way down her face and neck. She felt desire flare at last. Then suddenly he bit her breast. Alice cried out in pain but he quickly silenced her with another wet, smothering kiss on the mouth. He squeezed her breasts. Then he was pressing his way between her thighs and entering her. Alice gasped in pain. Then it was over. With a grunt of satisfaction, Vernon rolled off and sank back, throwing an arm across her. Moments later he was snoring.

She lay in shock. Her body throbbed. She could feel his sticky seed congealing on her. He lay like a Greek god, his blond hair tousled and his strong limbs carelessly flung wide across the bed. All the anticipation she had felt for weeks about lying with a man and once more sharing sweet intimacy shrivelled in that moment.

Alice got up and went to the washstand. She washed and dried herself and pulled on her nightgown. She slipped under the bed covers, shivering and trying not to cry. This was only one night; it would get better. Alice squeezed her eyes shut and tried not to think that she had made a terrible mistake in giving up her freedom for this man.

Chapter 24

'You give the best parties in Simla,' Emily said to Alice. 'It's so nice to see you having fun again.'

They were taking tea in the Arden House garden and Alexander was in a swing suspended from a tree that Vernon had had made for the boy. One of the many *malis* that they employed was pushing the swing.

'High! Higher!' Alexander kept shouting. 'You do it, Auntie Alice!'

Alice's head pounded. She was too exhausted to get up and play with the boy. The latest dinner party had gone on until four in the morning. Before passing out, she remembered Charlie Nairn and Vernon stripped to the waist and arm wrestling on top of the table. Luckily the Aytons and their other married friends had long gone by then.

'In a minute, Alexander,' she said, leaning back in the wicker chair.

'Not getting much sleep?' Emily asked with a grin.

'No,' Alice admitted.

'Lucky you,' said Emily.

Alice closed her eyes as Emily gossiped about some new arrivals on leave from the plains and whether they would be suitable for Helen. Colin MacRae had returned to his regiment without showing any interest in Sandy's sister.

Alice wondered how much longer she would be able to keep up the pretence of being happily married to Vernon. It had been the strangest month of her life. Outwardly he was still the same charming, attentive cavalry captain who had wooed her. They were popular among his peers, attending every social function that they could and always accepting any invitations from the Edens to Auckland House.

They went on an endless round of dinners, picnics and dances; they attended horse racing and archery competitions. If Alice said she was too tired to go to a function, Vernon would attend anyway, rolling back drunk as the dawn light broke over the trees. The dinners she dreaded the most were the ones that they put on at Arden House. They were long and raucous with crate-loads of champagne and wine consumed, as well as port, brandy and whisky.

Sometimes, when just a few of Vernon's bachelor friends were left, water-pipes were produced and they would smoke something pungent and strong that left them all giggling and uninhibited. Vernon would make Alice smoke too. On one occasion, the party ended with a show of dancing girls that Charlie Nairn had somehow conjured out of the night. Alice had been made to watch that as well.

But she didn't complain. Delay and intoxication were preferable to what came after their guests had staggered home. Alice found being inebriated or drugged helped get through the ordeal in the bedroom.

Vernon had his rituals; he liked her to dress up as a *nautch* girl and bought her veils, pantaloons and anklets to dance in before she undressed in front of him. She would only do so when she was very drunk, so her husband always plied her with alcohol throughout the evening.

He was rough during lovemaking; she was covered in teeth bites and purple marks where he'd sucked her till her skin bruised. Alice had to wear dresses that covered her chest and arms. Sometimes she wore a scarf around her neck to hide the marks he made.

Vernon had laughed when she'd complained. 'They just show how much I love you.'

He was always quickly aroused and swiftly sated, whereas she was left frustrated and tearful at his lack of attempt to satisfy her. Lying awake, head and body throbbing, she yearned for him just to put his arms around her and kiss her lovingly.

But Vernon seemed to see sex as a contest. He goaded her to bite and scratch him back. They would wrestle on the bed while he cried out, 'You're a vixen! Come on, my wildcat!'

Once, when she was intoxicated by whatever it was they smoked in the water-pipe, she scratched his face and bit his bottom lip till it bled. Yet it didn't feel as if she were really present at this bout of fighting with Vernon. It was as if she were watching herself and Vernon from beyond the bed, seeing her anger at him turning to lust. She had got the better of him that night, pinning him to the bed with a strength she didn't know she had while he was almost comatose with drink and drugs. Alice had shouted foul things at him and ordered him to pleasure her.

In the morning she had been consumed with shame at their debauched behaviour and wondered what the servants had made of the screaming and cries. Vernon had touched his swollen lips and scratched cheek and smiled as if he wore battle scars. She was sure that he had boasted about his uninhibited new wife to his bachelor friends for they gave her knowing looks when next they met.

Alice was thankful that Miss Wallace's school was closed for the summer; she certainly didn't have the energy for teaching. Her self-disgust – and that for her husband – had grown throughout the month. She avoided Miss Wallace and the families of the girls she had taught and wondered if she would be able to face them come September. She was tempted to confide in Emily about her unhappy situation but was too ashamed. She didn't want to risk losing Emily's friendship and dreaded that the kind Aytons might hear salacious gossip about her.

It amazed Alice how Vernon had the stamina for his work on the Governor General's staff when he got so little sleep and drank so much, but he appeared to thrive on it.

He would come home and talk excitedly about the growing likelihood of a British invasion of Afghanistan.

'I think Auckland is nearly persuaded,' Vernon had said. 'We're going to give Dost Mohammed a bloody nose and restore Shah Shuja to the throne.'

'Is that what the Afghans want?' Alice had asked.

He had looked at her in astonishment. 'Enough of them want it that matter. Shah Shuja has strong support in the country. Anyway,' he'd said bullishly, 'it's what the British want that matters. We're doing it for the peace and security of the whole area.'

As August had waned, the clamour for action among Auckland's young staff had grown ever louder, until the momentum seemed unstoppable. Still the Governor General dithered, seemingly paralysed with indecision. The Board of Directors of the East India Company were sending frantic messages for Auckland not to back such a risky and costly escapade.

'They're a bunch of cowards,' Vernon had sneered. 'All they can think about is their precious money and not wanting to pay for the invasion, even though it's in the British interest.'

'Well, I can see their point of view,' Alice had said. 'Sending an army big enough to invade another country is going to cost a fortune.'

'The Company has deep coffers; they can afford it.'

Alice bit back a retort that their own personal coffers were not so deep. Vernon was spending money – her money – as fast as he could. All his lavish entertaining was at her expense. She thought he had been wealthy in his own right but it turned out that he was deeply in debt to family and friends. His father, disapproving of his extravagant lifestyle, had refused to give him more than the most basic allowance. She had begun their married life by honouring his debts. Now Vernon was talking about them selling the dower house at Tolland Park to pay for the coming season back in Calcutta.

Secretly, she began to hope that if the invasion took place then Vernon would be chosen to go; that way he would have to live a more frugal life – and they would have a time apart.

* * *

'So do you think I should encourage Captain Nairn to court Helen?' Emily asked.

Alice realised she had not been listening to a word her friend had said for the past quarter of an hour.

'No, I don't,' Alice said, sitting up. 'He's a terrible womaniser.' She pressed her fingers to her throbbing temples.

'Are you all right?' Emily asked.

'Do you think we really will invade Afghanistan?' Alice blurted out.

'Whatever made you think of that?'

'It's all the men are talking about,' said Alice.

Emily's fair face creased in sudden worry. 'Sandy thinks we will.'

'It would be madness, surely?'

'You mustn't worry about Vernon,' Emily said. 'He and Sandy are unlikely to get sent there. Auckland will want to keep his best men on his staff here in India.'

Alice sighed. 'Yes, I suppose he will.'

* * *

By mid-September, in was common knowledge that Auckland was going to give the order for an Afghan expedition. A fever of excitement gripped the British in Simla as they waited to hear which brigades and staff officers would be chosen to go. Information leaked out that three forces were to be amassed: a Bengal army, a Bombay army and an army to be led by the ageing exiled Shah Shuja.

Vernon threw a party in celebration, boasting that he expected to be among the elite picked to go. Arden House and garden overflowed with officers, officials, their wives and dependants as they toasted the success of the expedition. There was feasting and dancing, fireworks and drinking late into the night.

187

No one noticed Alice slip away to the edge of the garden and sit under a *deodar* tree watching the revelries from afar. Vernon was flirting with a group of young unmarried women but she didn't care. She was hardly speaking to him. They had argued all week about whether she should return to teach at the native school. Alice had been shocked by his disdain.

'Why do you want to go and teach those wretched heathens?'

'I thought you admired my work at the school?'

'It might have been all right for a widow to do such a thing. But you are a cavalry officer's wife now and such work is beneath your dignity.'

'Don't be such a prig,' Alice had said.

He had seized her by the arms and shaken her. 'Don't you speak to me like that! You will do as I say on this matter.'

Alice had been determined not to, but when she went to the school in defiance, Miss Wallace had turned her away.

'Captain Buckley has made it clear you are not to help out.'

Alice did not know which of them was the more embarrassed. She wondered what threats Vernon had made to the kind-hearted woman.

'I'll send a donation,' Alice had promised.

As she sat in the shadows, Alice seethed at the memory. She prayed for two things: that Vernon would be sent to Afghanistan and that she would fall pregnant before he left.

* * *

On the first of October, Governor General Auckland issued a manifesto from Simla: the power of Dost Mohammed and his Barukzai tribe in Afghanistan were to be destroyed and the rightful amir, Shah Shuja of the Suddozai royal house, was to be given back the throne of his ancestors. Dost Mohammed had forfeited his throne by his unprovoked attack on Ranjit Singh of the Sikhs in 1836 and his intriguing with the Russians and Persians. The British would escort Shah Shuja to Kabul and reunite him with his loyal subjects. The Persians, who were threatening Herat, would be repulsed. Once the unity and prosperity of the Afghan peoples had been restored, the British would swiftly withdraw from Afghanistan and leave it to be governed by its own people.

The Governor General delayed his return to Calcutta. Rumour spread that he was reluctant to face his older advisors, who were cautioning against military intervention. Officially, it was so he could be nearer at hand to issue orders to the army that was being assembled on the plains below Simla – along the banks of the rivers Sutlej and Indus.

Emily was in a state of anxiety.

'Sandy's been given orders to join MacNaughten's staff,' she told Alice. 'Do you remember him from last season? He's an amiable sort but his wife's a bit common.'

'Don't be unkind,' Sandy chided Emily.

'Well, she comes from a humble background is all I'm saying,' said Emily, 'but is full of airs and graces.'

'What will MacNaughten be doing?' Alice asked.

'He's the newly appointed envoy to Kabul with Lieutenant Colonel Burnes in support,' said Sandy. 'Smoothing the way for Shah Shuja – that sort of thing. Purely diplomatic, so there's no need to worry that I'll be in the firing line.' He smiled at his wife, trying to allay her fears.

'No doubt they'll give MacNaughten a knighthood for going,' said Emily. 'That'll make Mrs MacNaughten lord it over us all the more.'

'Don't you mean Lady MacNaughten?' Alice said with a wink.

* * *

Vernon returned home one crisp October day to find Alice being sick in the bedroom.

'Been at the champagne early today?' he teased.

She straightened up from the china washbowl, wiped her mouth and went to lie on the bed.

He frowned. 'Are you ill?'

Alice faced him. 'I'm with child.'

He came towards the bed and peered at her. 'Are you sure?'

'Yes.'

He seized her hand and kissed it. 'That's marvellous!'

'You're pleased?' Alice asked.

'Of course I am.' He smiled. 'My very own son and heir!'

'It's early days,' Alice cautioned. 'I've lost babies . . .'

'Not this one,' Vernon said, squeezing her hand. 'Buckleys are made of stronger stock than Gillverays.'

He leant and kissed her forehead. It was the first tender gesture he had shown her in weeks.

'Wait till my father hears of this. He won't be so quick to condemn me now, will he?'

Alice felt a pang of pity for her husband. What he wished for most in the world was for his martinet father to show his approval. Whenever he didn't get it, Vernon behaved even worse.

After that, Vernon was more considerate towards Alice, cosseting her and making sure she rested. He no longer forced her to join in his revelries. At first she felt so unwell that she could keep no food down but gradually the sickness eased. She developed a craving for sweet things so he ordered her sticky *jelabies* from the bazaar and had the cook make her sugary rice pudding.

To her immense relief, Vernon left her alone in the marital bed. Sometimes he would stretch himself out beside her and run a hand gently – almost reverently – down the curves of her body. But he never pressured her to have sex.

'We'll call him Richard after my father,' said Vernon. 'That should please the old tyrant.'

'And what if it's a girl?' asked Alice.

'It won't be.'

'We should choose a name just in case. What is your mother's name?'

'Charlotte.'

'That's the same as my mother's!' Alice cried.

'Hardly the same,' Vernon was dismissive. 'My mother didn't whore with a foreign sailor and abandon her brat.'

Alice flinched at his sudden cruelty. How she regretted confiding in Vernon about her birth when she had been the worse for drink, confirming the rumours he had already heard.

'But you're not like your mother,' Vernon went on, unaware she was upset by his words. 'I've seen you with Alexander. You will be a wonderful and loving mother to my child.'

* * *

Their marriage entered a calm phase with Vernon being affectionate and possessive towards Alice. She felt a stirring of optimism that their future together could be happy. He would be a doting father and learn to curb his excessive appetites; he was already a more loving and considerate husband. There was rumour that the whole Afghan expedition might be abandoned as the Persians, who had been threatening in the west, had withdrawn.

'No military reason for us to invade now,' said Sandy cheerfully.

'What a relief that would be,' cried Emily.

So Alice met Vernon's announcement in early November with dismay.

'I'm to be called up for field service after all,' he said, his eyes shining. 'Cavalry brigade under Colonel Arnold. Bengal Army. I'm to report to Ferozepur by the end of the month.'

'But I thought the invasion was being called off?' Alice said.

'Not at all,' said Vernon. 'It might be scaled down a bit but there's still a need for us to put a ruler on the throne in Kabul who favours the British.'

'But I thought you wouldn't have to go? Auckland needs you here, doesn't he?'

'He's letting me go,' said Vernon. 'Knows how keen I am to do my bit.'

'So you begged his permission? How could you do that now you know about the baby?'

Vernon looked impatient. 'I can't stop being a soldier. I have a duty to go.'

Alice felt a wave of disappointment. She knew it wasn't duty but the thrill of being part of a campaign that drove him. He was infused with excitement at being included. Home life was too humdrum.

'I don't want you to go,' Alice said, feeling suddenly tearful. She cried easily these days.

Vernon sat down beside her and put an arm about her shoulders. 'And I don't want to leave you.' He kissed the top of her head. 'But it'll all be over soon. We'll march on Kabul once the snows melt. It'll all be done and dusted by the spring. I bet I'll be home in time for the birth.'

* * *

Vernon and Sandy left a week later with a large procession of pack animals and porters.

'Dry your tears and kiss me,' Vernon said to Alice on the morning of departure.

190

He gave her a lingering kiss and touched her belly. 'Look after my son. I've instructed Emily to keep an eye on you and not to let you do anything you shouldn't.'

'I'm not the one who needs to be told,' Alice said with a wry smile. 'You must take care of yourself too. Promise me you won't do anything rash? I don't want this baby to grow up without a father.'

'He won't. I promise you that.' Vernon pulled her to him for one last kiss – a fiercer one that left her lips feeling bruised.

Emily and Alice waved their men away.

Over the next few days they kept each other company and spoilt Alexander, trying to hide their anxiety and sadness. They had decided to winter in Simla in case there was any chance of joining their husbands before they set off for Afghanistan.

Alice was surprised by how much she missed Vernon. Two months ago she would have gladly seen the back of him. But he had shown a more caring and considerate side since knowing she was pregnant. Settling down as a family man would be the making of him; Vernon was learning about responsibility and love for people other than himself.

As Christmas came, Alice waited for word from Vernon. Emily received letters from Sandy about the extraordinary sights at Ferozepur; the pomp and ceremony laid on by their ally Ranjit Singh for the British army that was camping on his border.

'*Tents of crimson and gold,*' Emily read out loud, '*gun salutes and elephant processions. We went across the river to watch the Sikhs put on military displays. They were all dressed in magnificent scarlet-and-yellow uniforms with chain armour and steel helmets – and mounted on stallions. They have learnt tactics from French instructors to great effect. I'm afraid the evening entertainment was more unseemly. Old Ranjit Singh appears to be rather too fond of dancing girls. It doesn't do to criticise his ways so we have to remain silent on such matters.*'

Emily frowned. 'I don't like the sound of dancing girls, do you?'

Alice felt a stab of disquiet. She wished she could erase from her mind the time she was made to watch the cavorting of *nautch* girls with Vernon's bachelor friends. The girls had hardly been older than the children she had taught. Miss Wallace had set up the school to give native girls an alternative to such exploitation. How had she allowed such a thing in her own home? Alice felt a wave of shame. And the things she had done in drink just to please her equally drunk husband . . .

Alice tried to banish the memory. She would never allow her senses to be so out of control again.

Just when she thought she would never hear from Vernon, a parcel arrived with an array of expensive presents for Christmas: a peacock-blue shawl, a necklace of gold medallions, a sapphire ring and a tiger skin for the sitting-room hearth.

'Vernon knows how to spoil a girl,' Emily said in envy. 'All I got from Sandy was a gaudy jewellery box made of papier-mâché.'

Alice kept to herself that it was she who was paying for Vernon's extravagance.

'But you get such lovely letters,' Alice pointed out. 'I'd trade all these gifts for some proper news.'

191

A week later, she felt the first thrilling flutter in her womb. She could do nothing about her husband's profligate ways but at least Vernon had given her this baby that she carried – and for that she could forgive him a great deal.

Chapter 25

Simla, May 1839

Alice's baby pushed its way into the world on a warm sunny day in May and gave a piercing wail. Emily was with her.

Alice tried to sit up, panting and sweating from the exertions, which had gone on all night.

'Let me see! Is it all right?'

The doctor, whom Vernon had insisted must attend the birth, smiled and said, 'Well done, Mrs Buckley. The baby is fine.'

He cut the umbilical cord and the baby was wiped down and wrapped in a cotton sheet.

'What a bonny bairn!' Emily said, tearfully handing the mewling bundle to her friend.

Alice clasped her baby in triumph and wonderment. Never before had she seen such a sweet pink face, with bright eyes open and trying to focus on her.

'Hello, my beautiful boy! Won't your daddy be pleased—'

'It's not a boy,' Emily said. 'You have a daughter. Aren't you the lucky one? Sandy and I long for a girl. I'm quite jealous of this wee thing.'

Alice stared at the baby in confusion. She had been so sure that it was a boy; Vernon's conviction that he would have a son must have swayed her too. Throughout the pregnancy, when she had felt the boisterous kicks in her womb, she had known it was a boy. How many times had she written to Vernon and told him so? The only two letters she had received from him in six months – two short notes – had been taken up with excitement about their son and how he was going to teach him to ride as soon as he could walk.

Alice could not help her disappointment. She felt suddenly nauseous. She had failed Vernon. He would be upset to find it was only a girl. Tears leaked from her tired eyes.

'Vernon so wanted a boy,' she said, utterly drained.

Emily stroked the baby's cheek. 'Alice!' she chided. 'You know what it's like to lose a bairn. So you know how precious this one is. It doesn't matter if it's a girl or a boy – she's alive and healthy. That's what counts, surely?'

Alice felt a twinge of shame. Poor Emily knew what it was like to miscarry a baby and to long to be with child again. 'Yes, you're right.' She looked closer at the baby. She had stopped crying and her tiny bud-like mouth was opening and closing as if she wanted to speak.

'She wants her first feed,' said Emily with a smile.

Alice asked, 'Will you show me how?'

'Of course.'

'Thank you,' Alice said gratefully. 'I don't know what I'd do without you, Emily Ayton.'

* * *

Each day, Alice grew to love her daughter more. She called her Charlotte after both the baby's grandmothers and wrote to Vernon's parents to tell them so. It made her realise how much she missed her own papa and the mother that she had never known. How good it would have been to share her news with them – her papa would have delighted in his new granddaughter, of that she was sure.

Alice wrote instead to the Browns. For a long time she had blamed them for keeping the truth of her birth secret from her; the shock of the discovery had caused a rift between them. But now that she was a mother herself and felt deep emotions of love and protection towards her child, Alice could see how much the Browns had loved her. Effie may have fussed and scolded but more often she had been kind. How many times Alice must have tried her patience! Arnold had fostered in her a love of learning and nature; he had favoured her over his own sons and shown her deep affection.

So Alice wrote them a tender letter, telling them of baby Charlotte and sending a tiny lock of the baby's downy blonde hair.

'I'm mad with love for this tiny creature,' Alice said to Emily as she marvelled at her daughter. 'Everything she does delights me. Even being kept awake half the night when she's demanding to be fed doesn't seem like a chore.'

'Not so tiny anymore.' Emily laughed. 'Look how plump she grows. A picture of health.'

'I know, isn't she adorable?' Alice smiled, lifting the baby and covering her face with kisses, making Charlotte gurgle with pleasure.

Alice sighed. 'I just wish I knew if Vernon had got my news. Lotty is nearly two months old. He hoped he'd be back for the birth.'

'That was never going to happen,' Emily said, 'not with such delays all through the winter. But at least they're making progress now. You'll hear from Vernon soon, I'm sure.'

Word had come through shortly after Charlotte's birth that the British forces had reached the city of Kandahar, somewhere in the south of Afghanistan. Sandy's most recent letter, written in April, had come from there. He had alluded to some resistance through the mountain passes between Quetta and Kandahar but mostly he had made entertaining comments, such as the one about Shah Shuja's insistence on royal gun salutes, which had set panic among the baggage train and caused camels to bolt.

Both the women knew that he was keeping a lot from them for they heard talk in other Simla drawing rooms.

Mrs MacNaughten, who had joined them in Simla that spring along with Lady Sale, wife of a brevet-colonel with the 13th Regiment of Foot, seemed to be an authority. Dysentery had decimated Sale's Infantry, servants had deserted, there weren't enough camels to carry all the luxuries some officers insisted on taking and the army had been hampered by the huge spread-out baggage train.

'Me husband says it's like a city on the move,' said Frances MacNaughten. 'It's an 'eadache trying to find provisions along the way for such a number. It's not just soldiers, don't you know? There are thousands of servants and camp-followers and their families. Who would have thought an army needed so much?'

Alice thought of the money that had flowed out to cover Vernon's expenses in Ferozepur that winter: crates of champagne and wine, boxes of cigars, tinned luxuries from Europe; bills from tailors, meat merchants, cobblers, metalsmiths, barbers and saddlers. She knew that he alone had hired ten camels for all his camping needs and provisions. She was uncomfortable at the thought that Vernon's love of possessions could have added to the slowness of the army's progress.

'Some of these young officers think they're going on a picnic,' said Florentia Sale with a wry laugh. 'They've grown accustomed to far too many luxuries in India. The Afghans will show them how it's done – they ride with a gun and sleep in a blanket.'

Alice had a sudden image of John Sinclair. He was the kind of soldier who would travel light and not care for comfort. She felt winded by how vividly he came to mind. What on earth had made her think of him? Was it all this talk of Afghanistan? She wondered if he was still in Kabul and whether he was working for the advancing British.

Colin had said how John had been against invasion. But she had not heard from Colin since her marriage to Vernon. She had been piqued by his blunt message at the news; he wished her well and hoped she knew what kind of man she was taking on. Alice had no idea if Colin was on the expedition or not.

'Don't look so worried, Mrs Buckley,' Florentia said, reaching out and patting her hand. 'Our men are still the best soldiers in the world – and the best armed. Any day now, we'll hear news that they've taken Kabul.'

Alice smiled and tried to smother the long-buried yearning that thinking of John had rekindled deep in her belly. She liked the lively and straight-talking Florentia Sale. Her husband was a veteran infantry commander who had been knighted for heroics in Burma and was known affectionately among his men as Fighting Bob. Alice had made friends with Lady Sale's daughter, Dinah, who was betrothed to a British officer, Johnny Sturt. Both Florentia's husband and Dinah's fiancé were on the expedition to Kabul.

'And then we'll be able to join them,' said Dinah eagerly.

'Join them?' Alice said, startled by the idea. 'But won't they be returning as soon as the old amir is back on the throne?'

Florentia shook her head. 'That could take at least a year. Our men won't be able to leave until they are sure Shah Shuja is secure and the country is calm.'

'They say that the mountain air is invigorating,' said Dinah, her slim, pretty face lighting up. 'Much more healthy than India. I think it would be jolly if we could join our men up there.'

'It depends if the men want us, don't you know,' said Frances MacNaughten. 'If my William sends for me, I'll go – as long as I can take all me gowns and home comforts. I'm not one for camping.'

'Well, I'd join Sandy like a shot,' said Emily. 'He's missed so much of Alexander growing up already. The boy won't know his father if we're parted for too long.'

'You must be desperate to see your husband, Alice,' Dinah said, smiling. 'And for him to see baby Lotty.'

Alice flushed. 'Of course.'

But it wasn't the thought of seeing Vernon that was suddenly making her pulse quicken, it was the idea that she might come across John in Kabul. The thought both filled her with dread and excitement. He had been the cause of so much heartache and yet the chance of seeing him again made her heart leap. She mustn't think of him! For Lotty's sake she must redouble her efforts to make her marriage to Vernon work.

* * *

It was September before the joyful news reached the women that the British forces were triumphant. They had arrived in Kabul in August, having taken the stronghold of Ghazni on the way. After years in exile Shah Shuja had entered his capital to the ecstatic welcome of his adoring people. At least that is what the British newspapers in India were reporting.

'Sandy says it was more like a funeral procession,' Emily told Alice. 'He'd never seen such a solemn crowd. But perhaps the Afghans are less demonstrative than the Indians.'

By the end of the month, just as the wives in Simla were wondering whether to return to Calcutta or not, word came through that all was calm in Kabul but it looked as if the British would be needed for a few months to help with the transition. They would be settled in for the winter. At last, Alice received a letter from Vernon.

The relief at finally hearing from her husband after months of silence made her lightheaded. She opened the letter with trembling fingers.

'Daddy's written to us at last, Lotty,' she told her daughter breathlessly. The baby shook her rattle and beamed at the sound of her mother's voice. She gave Alice a gummy smile and jammed the rattle in her mouth with a happy shriek.

Alice's anticipation turned to dismay at the sight of the short message, barely covering one page. The news was paltry and Vernon's final comment made her eyes flood with tears.

. . . the Afghans are an ungrateful lot. They smile to your face then lie and scheme behind your back. Even the supporters of Shah Shuja can't seem to agree among themselves. Kabul is dirty and smelly. And I didn't even get a promotion out of it all, despite fighting like a lion and skewering plenty of the devils. I wanted you to be upsides with Emily and married to a major. But you'll have to wait.

I'm sorry to hear we have a daughter. You know how I had hoped for a son. I don't know why you bothered to write to my parents. My father will see it as further proof of my failure as a son. But never mind, we'll make a boy next time. An enjoyable prospect – once I get home to you!

I send my love,

Vernon

Later that day she went round to Emily's bungalow, still sick inside at her husband's callous remarks about Charlotte; he hadn't even mentioned her by name.

'I've heard from Vernon,' Alice blurted out. Her friend had given up asking so as not to embarrass Alice.

'That's wonderful!' cried Emily. 'What does he say?'

196

'He didn't sound in very good spirits,' Alice admitted. 'He seems to have missed out on promotion.'

'Plenty of time yet,' said Emily. 'And does he ask after Lotty?'

Alice felt her insides clench. She gave a bleak laugh. 'He acknowledges her existence at least. But, as I feared, he's disappointed she's not a boy.'

'He'll feel differently once he's met her,' said Emily, 'and held his own flesh and blood. You'll see.'

'Yes, I'm sure you're right,' said Alice, encouraged. 'Who couldn't love her?'

She leant down and plucked Lotty from the floor. The baby was able to sit up now and her hair was growing into soft curls. To Alice she was like a happy cherub.

Emily said, 'I hear Frances MacNaughten has agreed to join her husband in Kabul. He's encouraging her to go – says it's perfectly safe.'

'Yes,' said Alice, 'and Dinah says she and her mother are thinking of doing the same. Florentia thinks it would be good for the men's morale if we make the effort – set up home for them and make life seem normal again.'

'The men must miss simple domesticity after all this time, mustn't they?' said Emily. 'I know Sandy does. And he's so eager to see Alexander again.'

Alice felt leaden. She doubted if Vernon missed her much – and he was certainly in no hurry to meet his new daughter.

'So will you go?' asked Alice.

'If it's safe and we have a proper escort to protect us while we're travelling,' said Emily, 'then yes I will. Helen has decided to return to Calcutta with the Edens – there'll be more society for her there.' She eyed her friend. 'What about you? I wouldn't blame you if you decided against it. It's more hazardous with such a wee infant.'

Alice sat cradling Charlotte. 'If you're going, wild horses won't keep me away,' said Alice. 'I couldn't bear to be left behind here without you and Alexander.'

'That's what I hoped you'd say.' Emily grinned. 'Och, our men are going to be so pleased to see us!'

* * *

It took all of October and most of November for the convoy of women and children to reach Afghanistan. Some, like Alice, rode on horseback while others, like Emily, sat in large panniers strapped to camels. Charlotte and Alexander travelled in a basket on top of a mule that trotted along beside Alice's pony. The motion seemed to lull the baby for she slept a lot, whereas many of the other children were made queasy and sick by the swaying of the animals. Sometimes Alice would let Alexander sit in the saddle in front of her to give him relief from the tedium of the journey and they would chatter about what they could see. The boy was bright and articulate for a three-year-old and Alice enjoyed his company greatly.

They went by way of the ancient city of Lahore and the frontier town of Peshawar with its low mud-built houses and *caravanserai* teeming with camels and traders. In the bazaar, open stalls hung with dripping carcasses and mounds of colourful spices were sold from sacks. Tribesmen in loose clothing, huge white turbans and matchlocks slung over their shoulders swaggered down the dusty lanes and eyed them with curiosity. Alice wondered if some of these tribesmen were Afridis like the uncle that John had talked about with such admiration.

Escorted by a regiment of cavalry under the command of Captain Edward Connolly and with the protection of Afridi guides, they wound their way up the Khyber Pass into Afghanistan, through narrow defiles amid towering cliffs. Fortresses, which reminded Alice of Northumbrian peel towers, were perched on impossibly sheer mountainsides and she knew that they were observed and followed.

'Don't worry,' said Frances MacNaughten. 'We pay the tribes well to keep their distance, don't you know. William says he's spending a small fortune in bribes and on guides.'

'Not his personal fortune, I suspect,' Florentia Sale said dryly.

'Some of 'em look like they'd cut your throat for a sixpence,' said Frances.

'Or a camel-load of crystal chandeliers,' said Florentia tartly. She had made no secret of her disapproval at Frances's cumbersome amount of baggage. 'Who would blame them for carrying off booty from the back of the camel train when you put such temptation in their way?'

'It's not my fault if I've got such good taste in furnishings,' Frances said, her face growing red with indignation.

Florentia raised an eyebrow. 'The taste of the seraglio,' she murmured to Dinah.

'Mama!' Dinah chided but smothered a giggle.

Alice had grown used to the bickering between the two commanders' wives. They had been too long on the road thrust together at close quarters. Arrival in Kabul couldn't come soon enough.

* * *

They reached the walled Afghan town of Jalalabad at the beginning of December. A sea of army tents was encamped under the walls; a large contingent of the Bengal army was on its way back to India. Alice was encouraged by this sign that the country was tranquil and hoped that Vernon might be among them.

'Then Lotty and I could travel back with him without having to go to Kabul.'

But they soon discovered that it was largely infantry being withdrawn and Vernon's regiment was still in Kabul.

To the delight of Frances MacNaughten, her husband William was there to receive them. Shah Shuja had decreed that he and his court would winter in the more temperate climate of Jalalabad; Kabul was too teeth-chatteringly cold at that time of year.

'He's grown soft living for so long in India,' said their escort, the cheerful Captain Connolly.

To Emily's huge joy, Sandy had also come south with the envoy's staff. The Aytons had an emotional reunion. Alice's throat tightened to see the joy on their faces. Sandy's eyes swam with tears as he picked up Alexander and clasped him in a fierce hug. The boy squealed in excitement and alarm, hardly recognising his father. Sandy was thinner and the skin on his fair face was rough and flaking from the harsh winds.

'How is Vernon?' Alice asked. 'Is he well?'

Sandy looked uncomfortable. 'There are hundreds of us at Kabul – I hardly see him. He lives near the Balla Hissar; I've been in the camp.'

'The Balla Hissar?' queried Alice, her stomach knotting.

'It's the amir's fortress in the city.'

'Why is he living near there?' Alice asked, puzzled.

'Some of the young officers choose to do so. Burnes lives there and they – well – I suppose it's more comfortable.'

'So why don't you live there?' Emily asked. 'You're on the envoy's staff, after all. You should be the one living in comfort.'

His face reddened with embarrassment. 'Well, MacNaughten is taking the lead in setting up house in the new cantonment, so I'm supporting him. It's showing the Afghans that we're not trying to take over the citadel – and it's going to be more spacious.' He smiled at his wife. 'You'll enjoy it there more than the overcrowded city.'

Alice persisted. 'I don't understand why Vernon should choose—'

'You mustn't concern yourself over it,' Sandy said hastily. 'I'm sure that as soon as you arrive he'll want to move to the cantonment. No doubt he's just trying to fill in time with his bachelor friends because he's starved of a home life.'

Alice was not reassured by his words. Images of her husband acting in a drunken and debauched way with his officer friends plagued her thoughts. The sooner she got to Kabul the better.

Alexander grinned. 'I want to go to Kabul now!'

'Oh, so do I,' said Alice.

But it was decided that the party of wives and children should rest in Jalalabad too, in case they were caught by snow in the mountain passes that separated them from Kabul. Alice was frustrated by the decision but settled as best she could into their temporary surroundings.

* * *

It was April before the royal party decamped to Kabul. Over the winter Alice had learnt that all was not as peaceful in the country as MacNaughten liked to portray – or Shah Shuja as popular. Dost Mohammed had not been completely defeated; he had withdrawn into the mountains of the Hindu Kush. It was rumoured that MacNaughten wished to send a force after him and annex the northern lands that bordered Russia to consolidate Shah Shuja's power. But Auckland in India wished the withdrawal of troops rather than sending more.

Dinah had letters from her fiancé; Johnny Sturt was an army engineer in Kabul.

'He said we should have insisted on keeping the army stationed in the city,' said Dinah. 'They'd already started to repair the lower Balla Hissar as a barracks. Now that's been given to the amir's harem.'

'It'll be nicer for the families in the cantonment,' said Emily brightly.

'But not as safe,' said Dinah, 'or as easy to defend.'

Her mother agreed. 'Especially with Dost Mohammed and his sons still on the loose,' said Florentia.

'Well, Sandy said they had to move out of the city,' said Emily, 'as a sign of good faith to the Afghan chiefs.'

'Yes,' said Alice, 'he said that Shah Shuja has to be seen to be in control.'

Emily changed the subject; she hated pessimistic talk. 'So what do you think of Auckland being made an earl? It shows that the government thinks the liberation of Afghanistan has been a success, doesn't it?'

'And MacNaughten's got his knighthood,' said Alice with a wry smile, 'so Frances is happy.'

'Don't we all know it.' Florentia rolled her eyes and laughed.

* * *

A week later, Alice caught her first sight of Kabul; a brown stack of buildings and battlements against a backdrop of mountains across a beige-coloured plain and a grey river. At the top of the stack, dominating the city, was the Balla Hissar fortress. Smoke rose in vertical spirals into the thin air, the sky above a dazzling blue.

Away to the left lay the new cantonment. It was a hive of activity with scores of workmen completing the building of orderly lines of squat houses, barracks, stables and sheds, which spread out across the open plain. Coolies were carrying mud from the river banks in baskets suspended from poles across their shoulders and dumping it at the brickworks. The sounds of sawing and hammering rang out in the clear spring air. An encampment of tents and mud huts had sprouted on the periphery to house the hundreds of servants, labourers, camp-followers and their families who served the army.

As they drew nearer, horsemen in scarlet uniforms rode out to meet them. Alice felt nervous anticipation. Surely Vernon would be among them? She had written from Jalalabad but had no reply.

Dinah spotted her fiancé and kicked her horse forward with a cry of delight. Colonel Sale had also come out to welcome Florentia. Alice searched among the riders but it soon became apparent that Vernon wasn't there.

All the way to the city, Alice smiled bravely as if she too shared in the general happiness. She swallowed down tears. Inside, her anxiety mounted at the thought of being with Vernon again. Surely he would be pleased to see her? She had come all this way for him.

200

Chapter 26

There was a chaotic entry into the cantonment as quarters were found for the new arrivals. Sandy had to go with MacNaughten into the city to accompany Shah Shuja back to the Balla Hissar with all the ceremony that a returning monarch demanded.

'I'll get word to Vernon that you are here,' Sandy promised.

'You must share our house with us,' Emily insisted, 'until Vernon secures one of your own. Ours is already furnished.'

Alice unpacked enough of their possessions as would fit in the small spare bedroom and busied herself making it homely with rugs, a colourful bedspread and muslin drapes to give them privacy. Lotty had grown too big for her cradle over the winter so Alice had had a cot made in Jalalabad, which one of the servants now assembled. As evening came, Alice and Emily sat with their children while they ate their supper and waited for the men to come. Even from four miles away they could hear the gun salutes and fireworks in celebration of the amir's return.

'They probably won't be able to get away,' Emily said. 'Partying all night by the sound of it.'

Alice knew her friend was trying to calm her anxiety but she could hardly bear the wait. She just wanted the moment to be over when she would meet her husband again after a year and a half of separation.

An exhausted Sandy arrived late in the night, rousing the women from sleep.

'I couldn't find Vernon – it was bedlam everywhere in the city with the return of the court. I left a message. I'm sure he'll come tomorrow.'

He could hardly look Alice in the eye. She suspected that he wasn't telling her the truth but nodded in agreement.

'Thank you,' she said, and retreated to bed again.

She could hear the Aytons talking heatedly in the bedroom next door, Emily firing questions and Sandy sounding defensive. Alice knew they were talking about Vernon but couldn't hear distinctly. She would not demean herself by pressing her ear to the wall to eavesdrop.

The next day, Alice said to Sandy, 'Will you take me into the city to find Vernon? I don't think I can bear to wait any longer.'

He looked alarmed by the suggestion. 'I don't think that's a good idea. The city isn't terribly safe for foreign women – you'd stand out—'

'Sandy will fetch Vernon,' said Emily firmly. 'Won't you, dear?' She fixed her husband with a look.

'I shall do my best,' Sandy said, trying to hide his worry with a smile.

* * *

As the sun was setting in a ball of fire across the plain, Vernon walked into the cantonment house. Emily quickly took Alexander by the hand.

'We'll go and help feed the horses,' she said to the boy, 'and leave you in peace.'

Alice's heart drummed as she faced her husband. She was shocked at the state of him. He had shed weight – his jacket loose on his shoulders – and his face was gaunt and scored with lines around the mouth. His eyes looked glassy and bloodshot, the skin below bruised. His wavy blond hair had thinned. It looked dry and unkempt.

'Vernon,' she gasped, and held out her arms.

He stood for a moment looking disorientated and then smiled and stepped towards her.

'Alice,' he said, his voice rasping. 'You look well.'

They hugged briefly, then stood holding hands; his were shaking. His whole body was trembling and his breath smelt sour.

'Have you been ill?' she asked in concern.

He muttered, 'This place makes me ill.' He stared at her. 'I can't believe you've come all this way.'

'I wanted to be with you,' she said, 'and be a family together. I'm desperate for you to meet Lotty. It's nearly her first birthday and you've never even seen her—'

'You've brought her here?' Vernon exclaimed.

'Of course.' Alice smiled. 'Didn't you read any of my letters? She's in her cot. Come.' Alice took him by the hand and led him into the bedroom.

Lotty was lying on her back, her arms thrown up as if in surrender, her face pink in sleep.

'Isn't your daughter beautiful?' Alice whispered.

Vernon was suddenly overcome. He nodded, his eyes flooding with tears. Alice went to put her arm around him but he shook her off.

'You shouldn't have brought her here!' he hissed.

Alice flinched at his sudden mood change.

'It's a godforsaken place. There's fever and danger – the country's full of villains who would jump at the chance of carrying off a *feringhi* child and selling her into slavery – 'specially a fair-haired one.'

'Stop it, Vernon,' said Alice. 'You're frightening me.'

'You should have thought about that before dragging our child here – you could have been butchered on the way. Good God, you stupid woman! How am I supposed to protect you both?'

His raised voice woke the baby. Her eyes opened in alarm. Lotty's mouth began to tremble and then she let out a yell. Alice swiftly picked her up.

'Shush, now. It's all right,' she crooned. 'This is your daddy. He didn't mean to wake you.'

But the sight of Vernon made Lotty wail louder.

'Say hello to her,' she urged her husband.

He stood shaking with anger – or was it fear? Alice was not sure.

'I can't bear the noise,' he cried. He put his hands over his ears and, turning, lurched from the room.

* * *

Alice didn't see her husband again for the next two days. She had no idea where he'd gone but he appeared again on the third day looking more presentable; his shirt was clean and his face scrubbed and newly shaved. Alice was sure that Sandy had given him a talking to and told him to see to his wife and child.

Vernon was subdued but rallied at the sight of Lotty trying to pull herself up on the furniture and stand. He bent and picked her up, putting his face close to hers.

'As pretty as your mother.' He grinned and kissed her on the nose.

Alice held her breath but Lotty squealed with pleasure and grabbed his nose in return.

He played with her for a minute or two, then grew bored and abruptly set her down. She protested and tried to grab onto his legs. He stepped away looking irritated.

'I've had our things moved into the house at the end of the street,' Alice told him. 'Come and see.'

She thought he would protest but he nodded in agreement. Alice scooped Lotty from the floor and walked out of the Aytons' house.

Vernon was at once critical of the modest furnishings and two paintings that Alice had done in Jalalabad.

'I'll order better chairs, and we must have a bigger dining table – we'll hardly get more than six round that one. And grander pictures for the walls. They sell or make everything you could possibly want in the Kabul bazaars – it's the city's one saving grace.'

Alice's heart sank. 'We won't need to have lavish dinner parties here; it's hardly Simla.'

'Of course we will,' he snapped. 'It's the only thing that keeps up morale. At least I'll be away from the blasted citadel and having to kowtow to that jumped-up amir and his awful family. If he wasn't so useless we wouldn't be stuck here for God knows how long.'

'If it's that unpleasant in the city, then why have you spent so much time there?' Alice retorted.

He gave her a mirthless smile. 'Because I have friends there – people who keep me amused. Now I'll be able to entertain them here.'

He walked into the bedroom and saw the cot next to the bed. 'I'm not sleeping with a baby in the room,' said Vernon. 'We'll get no peace.'

'Lotty's a good sleeper,' Alice assured him, 'and I like to have her close in case she needs me.'

'Are you still feeding her?'

'No,' she admitted.

'Then the *ayah* can see to her in the night.'

'She doesn't have an *ayah*.'

Vernon looked shocked. 'Then she must have one. I'll not have my wife behaving like a common nursemaid.'

Alice summoned all her patience; she didn't want them to argue like this.

'Let's go to the bazaar together and choose some new things for the house,' she suggested. 'We could go tomorrow. I'd like to see the city.'

'Certainly not,' said Vernon. 'It's no place for a white woman.'

'I've travelled across India and through tribal lands as a white woman,' Alice pointed out, 'without coming to any harm. I'm not frightened of shopping in a bazaar – in fact I *like* buying in bazaars.'

He gave her a cold look. 'Not as my wife, you won't. You will stay safe in the cantonment – there are shops here too. Anything you want from the city I shall bring you.'

Alice didn't argue back. She would bide her time. When they had got to know each other again he would relent. She could see how the time apart – the long campaign, sickness, combat and marching under a scorching sun – must have all taken its toll on her husband's health. It was obvious to her that he was ill. He had lost his ability to charm or laugh at trivial everyday things. She must help him. She wondered if he was suffering from melancholia as well as an exhausted body and, if so, who she could turn to for help?

That night, they dined with the Aytons. Vernon drank a lot of wine and port. Alice was distracted by the thought that they would soon be going to bed together for the first time since Vernon had left Simla. Alice found it hard to believe he was the same person as the handsome, eager officer who had kissed her goodbye with affection and set off on his adventure. It had been longer still since they had been intimate; her pregnancy had put a stop to that. What would sex be like for her after having given birth to Lotty? She dreaded the return to the old combative sex of their early marriage. Perhaps if she kept Vernon from drinking too heavily, he would not be rough with her.

'Shall we leave these good people and go home?' Alice suggested, with a hand on Vernon's arm. 'It's late and I'm tired.'

He drew away from her and poured himself another glass of port. 'You can go if you like. Ayton and I are going to finish the bottle – and maybe have another, eh, Sandy?'

Alice saw anxious looks pass between the Aytons.

'Drink up, Buckley,' said Sandy, 'and get away to your bed. You must be looking forward to your first night back with your family. And I have to be up early for a briefing with MacNaughten.'

With a belligerent look, Vernon drained his glass, pushed his chair back and got unsteadily to his feet. Alice thanked them and followed him to the door, taking his arm to stop him staggering.

'Can manage,' he said in irritation, throwing off her hold.

'Just say if you need anything,' Sandy said with a knowing look at Alice.

Her stomach clenched. Did the Aytons fear Vernon might be violent? She had no idea how her husband was going to behave once she got him home. He was like a stranger to her. She nodded and put on a brave smile.

Back in their house, Vernon went straight to the wall cupboard and pulled out a bottle of brandy. He opened it and swigged straight from the bottle. Bracing herself for his anger, Alice took the bottle from him.

'That's enough for one night. Keep it for when we entertain.' She put it back in the cupboard.

To her amazement he didn't protest, just stood there with a look of confusion, swaying. She guided him into the bedroom. Lotty's cot had been removed to the small second bedroom that was to double as a dressing room. She helped him undress. Alice tried to hide her shock at his emaciated body; his ribs stuck out and his once broad chest looked sunken. His skin in the lamplight had a yellowish hue. His face glistened with sweat.

He lay down on the bed, shivering even though the night was balmy. Alice wrapped a blanket around him and stroked his forehead. It was clammy and her touch made him flinch although her fingers were warm. By the time she had undressed, put on her nightgown and climbed into bed beside him, Vernon was asleep.

*　*　*

As the days passed, Alice could do nothing to please Vernon. He criticised the menus she prepared, the clothes she wore, the style of her hair, the servants she employed. The latter came and went, unwilling to put up with his sudden angry outbursts and having plates and knives hurled at them.

Luckily the *ayah* that she had employed seemed able to handle his rudeness with a calmness that Alice envied. Gita was the wife of one of the Hindu *syces* at the cantonment; Gita and Ravi had travelled all the way from Ludhiana with the Army of the Indus and their two young sons, Adeep and Bali, and had been put to work as grass cutters bringing in fodder for the horses.

Alice gave in to Vernon over his wish for lavish entertainment and encouraged him to invite his friends for dinner. He behaved better when others were around, managing to be full of bonhomie towards his fellow officers and their wives. But afterwards, when she was alone with him, he shouted obscenities and slammed doors.

His behaviour in the bedroom was even more baffling. She had expected his sexual appetite to be undiminished. She knew he desperately wanted a son – when drunk he repeated his demand for one and castigated her for only producing a girl – but the drink seemed to diminish his ardour.

Vernon appeared impotent. As the hot weather arrived, they lay naked under muslin drapes to keep out the flies and mosquitoes but the sight or touch of Alice's body no longer aroused him. While he slept fitfully, she lay wondering if she would ever make love again, feeling a mixture of loneliness and relief.

Despite Vernon's complaints about boredom and having to dance attendance on the amir, he spent most of his time in Kabul. While he disappeared off on vague duties, Alice turned her energies to creating a garden.

With advice from Florentia and Dinah, who were equally keen on their gardens, Alice planted flowers for colour as well as vegetables. Lotty would crawl around and eat soil while Alexander helped Alice water the plants. Both children usually ended up giggling, soaked and muddy.

The women shared news. Emily hated talking politics but Alice found ready listeners in Florentia and Dinah. They discussed the trouble unfolding in the west of the country; the chief in Kandahar was once again in league with the Persians, plotting against Shah Shuja.

'And I bet the Kandahari chief is still taking our bribes at the same time,' said Florentia indignantly.

'According to Sandy, yes,' said Alice. 'MacNaughten wants to send a force to deal with the troublemaker but Auckland says just give him more money. The Governor General refuses to send extra troops.'

'I hear it's not safe to travel between Kandahar and Kabul now,' said Florentia.

'That's what I heard too,' said Alice. 'There's unrest among the Ghilzais.'

'I thought they were being paid to keep the highways open?' said Dinah.

'They are,' said Alice, 'but some of them so hate being told what to do by foreigners that no amount of money is going to satisfy them.'

'Is that what your husband says?' asked Dinah.

Alice reddened. 'No, Vernon's not interested in what the Afghans do. It's what Sandy Ayton says – and Sir William. Emily and I sometimes take tea over at the MacNaughtens' house. I keep my ears cocked for news.'

'And how is Lady MacNaughten?' asked Florentia. 'Enjoying her exalted position?'

'Don't be unkind, Mama,' said Dinah.

'I'm simply asking,' said her mother with a wink.

As Alice was on the point of rounding up the children she said, 'Do your menfolk find it difficult having so much time on their hands?'

'What do you mean?' asked Florentia.

Alice felt a sudden urge to unburden her worries over her husband. 'Vernon is going mad with boredom and says his duties at the Balla Hissar are tedious. He disappears for hours roaming the city. And he's spending lots of money – even that doesn't seem to bring him pleasure. And when he's at home he's so listless he won't do anything. Never shows the slightest interest in Lotty.'

The women exchanged glances. 'Johnny and his engineers are always busy,' said Dinah. 'There's been so much to do getting the cantonment built. And Papa has his hands full seeing to the needs of his men, doesn't he, Mama?'

'Yes,' said Florentia.

'Perhaps the cavalrymen have less to do,' said Dinah with a sympathetic look.

Florentia decided to be blunt. 'Listen, it doesn't do to let them hang about the city being idle. Burnes leads them astray – he lives like a *pasha* in the old citadel, getting our men a bad name with his womanising. The Afghans don't like it – especially not with their women.'

Alice flushed. 'Are you saying that's where Vernon is going?'

'I don't know for certain, my dear,' said Florentia. 'But one does hear rumours.'

'What rumours?' Alice's heart began to thud. When Florentia looked reluctant to say more, Alice pressed her. 'Please say. If my friends can't be honest with me then I have no one to turn to.'

'We hear that he keeps a house in the old citadel close to Burnes and spends a lot of time with that man and his, shall we say, household.'

'You mean other women?' Alice asked, her stomach knotting.

'Some men,' said Florentia, 'seem to think that sort of thing is acceptable when they are on campaign and their wives are far away. Your husband may have fallen into that habit.'

'And the cavalry had a hard time of it on the expedition,' said Dinah, trying to find excuses. 'Johnny says that they had some bloody clashes – hand-to-hand combat with tribesmen who take no quarter. Johnny says that's why some of them smoke opium, to try to forget.'

'Opium?' Alice gasped.

The women looked at her pityingly.

Florentia said, 'Surely it's obvious to you that Captain Buckley smokes it?'

Alice was stunned. 'I – I didn't know. I suppose I should have . . . ?'

Why had she not known? She thought of his emaciated state, his restlessness and mood swings. All the signs were there. She had seen opium addicts in Simla – some of the children she had taught had been left fatherless because of the drug. Perhaps she had even smoked opium herself at the all-night parties that Vernon had thrown in Simla? Alice felt nauseated.

'I'm sorry,' said Dinah. 'We thought you must have guessed.'

Florentia grew brisk. 'He's not to blame. Captain Buckley needs to be doing something healthy. He's a horseman. Get him out riding. Remind him of what he enjoys doing best.'

The women departed, leaving Alice shaken by their frank words. No wonder he didn't want her going anywhere near the city – he hadn't wanted her to come to Afghanistan at all. Vernon had blamed her for endangering Lotty's life by bringing her to Kabul, but he had not wanted either of them there for quite a different reason. Vernon had been indulging his base passions and didn't want to stop.

How long had it been going on? Was it just since the army had arrived in Kabul and he had been driven to it by the rigours of the campaign and being lonely without his wife? Or had Vernon started being unfaithful to her as soon as he left Simla? Doubts about him turned her insides leaden. Perhaps he had always slept with other women even when they had first been married.

A vague memory resurfaced of seeing Vernon kissing one of the *nautch* girls that Charlie Nairn had brought to their dinner party. Alice had passed out soon after, and later had dismissed the memory as a bad dream. She had refused to believe him capable of seducing another woman in front of her.

Then she thought of the fortune he was spending; it wasn't just on their army quarters. He had a house in the city. Who else lived there with him? Did he have a mistress? Perhaps, like Burnes, he kept a whole harem? Alice tried to stem the nausea that was rising inside. He disgusted her. She picked up Lotty and hugged her close. But what was she to do? She was stuck in Afghanistan; this was her home. She was Vernon's wife. For Lotty's sake, she was going to have to make the best of it. Alice kissed the girl's soft pink cheek. She would put up with almost anything as long as she had her daughter.

* * *

Alice smothered her resentment and distaste for her husband's behaviour and resolved to try to help him. For a time, Florentia's suggestion worked. Alice cajoled Vernon out riding in the cool of the early morning, leaving Lotty in the care of Gita.

His colour and appetite improved. Vernon began to put on weight again. Alice revelled in the dawn rides; the stark mountains looked at their most beautiful as the rose-coloured light struck their peaks and the valley was flooded with golden rays.

She liked to see the villages and their orchards emerging out of the dark – green clumps on the pale, dusty plain – and hear the calls to prayer and the creak of buckets being hoisted from wells.

One morning as they rode back she said, 'I think this place has a wild beauty, don't you?'

He grunted. 'No, I don't.' Then he briefly touched her hand. 'You are the only wild beauty as far as I can see.'

Alice laughed. The remark was so unexpected. It was the first compliment he had paid her since she'd arrived; a flash of the old Vernon. Then she thought of how he still spent half his time absent in the old city and felt her distaste return. The suspicion of what he was doing was poisoning their marriage. She couldn't trust him. Yet she didn't have the courage to confront him about the rumours. Only by not knowing for sure could she contemplate keeping up this charade of a marriage. Alice moved away from him.

'Race you to the river!' she challenged. She kicked her pony into a gallop.

She heard him laugh behind her and make chase.

* * *

As the summer peaked, disturbing rumours began to circulate that Dost Mohammed was amassing a huge force in the Hindu Kush, backed by Uzbeks. The mood in Kabul grew feverish and panic spread to the cantonment as the news was confirmed.

A British force was hastily assembled of Gurkhas, native infantry, horse artillery and cavalry. Vernon was among them.

Alice watched the preparations with anxiety but, once the decision had been made to go, her husband seemed almost relieved. Perhaps action was preferable to the destructive life he was leading. She could not deny the relief she felt at the thought of him going.

To her annoyance he stopped their early morning rides. When she protested, he grew angry.

'It's not safe you being out there with only me to guard you. I don't trust any of these Afghans – even the ones who pretend to be our friends. And I forbid you to ride outside the cantonment once I've gone. They might attack you just as a way of getting back at me.'

'And why would they want to do that?' Alice asked, resentment stirring.

'Because they despise us as much as we despise them.'

Alice itched to ask him if the reason he was so disliked by the Afghans was because he took advantage of their women. But she didn't want to cause an argument on the eve of his going. She swallowed down her accusation with difficulty. Let him have his way for the moment. Once he was gone, he wouldn't be able to control what she chose to do.

At the end of August, the British force wended its way out of the cantonment and into the mountains of the Hindu Kush. Alice stood with the other women on the cantonment wall to wave them off.

'The Lord help us if they're not successful!' cried Frances MacNaughten, clasping her husband's arm.

'Of course they will be!' said Emily.

They stood and watched for hours till their backs ached – and the convoy of uniformed soldiers was just a distant thread of red.

Chapter 27

Kabul, autumn 1840

News reached them in late September of the Battle of Bamian in the Hindu Kush. The British superior fire-power had overwhelmed Dost Mohammed's men and his Uzbek allies had fled the battlefield.

'The cavalry pursued them,' reported Sandy. 'It was a rout. Vernon might get his promotion to major for this. You should be proud of him.'

Alice nodded but her feelings were mixed. She was still plagued with dark thoughts about him; a small part of her secretly hoped that he wouldn't come back. Guilt clutched her. How could she wish ill on the father of her beloved child?

Later, they learnt that Dost Mohammed and his sons had managed to elude the pursuing British by fleeing on swifter horses. The fugitive amir appeared to have magical powers of escape.

Sandy was optimistic. 'He can't do much harm now that his army's defeated. One man with his sons is hardly a match for the British army. And the chiefs of the Kohistan in the Hindu Kush have agreed not to harbour him in the future – for a handsome price, of course.'

'Goodness me,' said Emily. 'With the amount of treasure we've paid out to these tribesmen they should jolly well be our friends.'

'John Sinclair has been negotiating on our behalf,' said Sandy. 'He appears to know the people of the Kohistan well.'

Alice's heart stopped at the sudden mention of John's name. Heat flooded her face.

'John Sinclair? Have – have you – are you in touch with him?' she stammered.

'Not in person,' said Sandy, 'but he's been sending reports to MacNaughten.'

'Is he in Kabul?'

'I don't think he's been there for some time. I've never seen him. He travels in the mountains picking up intelligence. I believe it was Sinclair who first warned us of Dost Mohammed's counter-attack.'

'That's brave of him,' said Emily, giving Alice an awkward glance. 'It sounds very dangerous. But then he knows these people well, doesn't he, being married to one?'

'That's why he's so useful to MacNaughten,' said Sandy. 'He can pass for a native – goes about dressed like one and lives the life of one, so I'm told.'

Alice felt breathless. She had tried so hard to put John from her mind. But many times when she had looked towards Kabul – a forbidden city to her – she had wondered if he lived there and walked its streets daily. Did his family live with him or were they out in the countryside? Perhaps his wife was from the Kohistan and that was why John was able to be a negotiator between its chiefs and the British.

She imagined him living a simple life in the mountains; he would be in his element among the hills with a pastoral people just like his own kind. Alice felt a wave of bitter longing. What if Vernon had lied to her about John? What if his poisonous words about John's philandering and his disregard for her had been

210

untrue? The men obviously detested each other and had been rivals since Addiscombe. Had Vernon said such things to make sure she extinguished any lingering thoughts of love for John? It was Vernon who was the womaniser if the rumours were true.

Suddenly Alice had to know. She couldn't continue to ignore the doubts that clawed inside and left her sleepless. The idea of visiting the city while Vernon was away had occupied her thoughts all month. Now that he might be on his way back, she was all the more determined to do so before he returned to prevent her. She had not defied him by riding out alone in the early mornings; the Aytons too had been aghast at the idea. But she wouldn't be stopped from going into Kabul. She needed to see for herself the Balla Hissar and the places Vernon frequented. She had to find out the truth about his life there.

Emily had changed the subject; she was talking about a firework display that was being planned in the cantonment. But Alice had only been half listening.

'Is it safe to go into Kabul do you think?' Alice interrupted.

'Why would you want to do that?' Emily asked.

'We've come all this way but can only gaze on the city from afar,' said Alice. 'Aren't you curious to see it too?'

'I hear it's crowded and dirty,' said Emily, 'so not really.'

'I'd like to buy a present for Vernon's return,' said Alice, inventing a reason. 'For Lotty to give him. And get some warmer clothing for the winter. They say it can be bitter here.'

'Well, that might be a good idea,' said Emily. 'What do you think, Sandy?'

'Would you take us?' Alice pressed. 'You know the city well from visiting Shah Shuja.'

Sandy was easily persuaded once he could see that his wife wanted to go too.

* * *

The following day, accompanied by Sandy and three of his men, they crossed the wooden bridge that the British had built over the river and rode towards Kabul. On the rocky slope behind the city, Alice noticed defensive walls and a crenelated parapet where guards were on duty. This was a well-defended capital.

Riding through the gateway, they found themselves in a warren of lanes and open-fronted stalls. The streets grew narrower the further in they ventured. It was so crowded with people, animals and carts that their ponies could only go at a slow walking pace, two men in front of the women, two behind.

Around them, a jumble of flat-roofed houses of differing heights seemed to lean over the lanes and block out the autumnal sunlight. Up they went, climbing towards the citadel. Alice was astonished by the size of the place. They passed numerous bazaars.

'Wait till you see the Great Bazaar,' said Jamieson, the young lieutenant accompanying them. 'It's even bigger. The locals call it the Char Chouk.'

They dismounted when they arrived at the main bazaar. Sandy led them inside. It was a vast indoor market made up of four linking arcades, which stretched into the gloom. Its walls were decorated with brightly painted panels. Shopkeepers sat in front of huge displays of goods: heaps of fruit, spices and vegetables;

displays of armour and weapons, cutlery and earthenware; stacks of sheepskins and bolts of cloth; piles of dead unplucked fowl; and hanging from hooks were deer with staring sightless eyes.

For Lotty, Alice bought a quilted coat, a sheepskin hat and mittens, and brightly patterned woollen socks with leather soles. She bought herself a fur coat and hat. Unable to decide what to buy Vernon, she asked Sandy to choose.

'What about one of those fine woollen waistcoats?' he suggested. 'He can wear it under his uniform or in the house.'

'Thank you,' said Alice, 'that's a good choice. He's always liked smart clothes.'

Emily bought enthusiastically too. 'I can't believe you haven't brought us here before, Sandy – it's fascinating.'

They had their purchases wrapped and left instructions to have them delivered to the cantonment.

'I'm exhausted,' declared Emily. 'Can we get some refreshment before we go home?'

Sandy led them to a teashop; the owner beckoned them in and to sit on his carpet. Alice held back.

'With the time left I'd rather see the Balla Hissar,' she said. 'Perhaps Lieutenant Jamieson could show me?'

Sandy was doubtful but the young lieutenant was an eager volunteer, happy to show off his knowledge of the city. They agreed to meet back at the teashop in half an hour.

Alice and her escort wended their way higher, until they passed through the walls of the lower citadel where the amir's wives were housed.

'This is where we should have been staying if we hadn't built the cantonment,' said Jamieson, 'but I bet you're glad you're not.'

'No, I think this place has a certain charm,' mused Alice.

The houses were mainly of the same unburnt brick and mud roofs as elsewhere, but some had entrances of elaborately carved wood. Through them, Alice glimpsed sheltered courtyards with water tanks and fruit trees. The houses had enclosed balconies with shuttered windows running along the length of their upper storeys. She admired the intricate latticework. Some of the shutters were pushed open and veiled women leant out and watched them pass by.

Alice grew tenser the further on they went; was one of these Vernon's house? They passed into the main Balla Hissar; this was the fortress that crowned the city and where Shah Shuja had his palace. It was heavily guarded by Gurkhas and Afghan troops but they let the visitors pass through.

Jamieson led her up to the very top of the citadel. Alice gasped at the view out over the rooftops. Not only could she see the whole of the city with its patchwork of mud roofs, balconies and domed mosques, but far beyond to distant forts on the road to Jalalabad. In the other direction – towards the Hindu Kush – the cantonment lay in full view, basking in the sun. Alice could even pick out her own house, so neatly laid out were the lines – like rows of children's toy bricks. Kabul appeared impregnable; the army cantonment looked as if it could be swept aside by one swipe of a petulant child.

A ridiculous thought, of course, Alice realised. The cantonment was just as heavily guarded as the city.

'I'd like you to show me where Lieutenant General Burnes lives,' Alice told her guide.

He looked taken aback. 'I'm not sure . . .'

'Just out of curiosity.' She smiled. 'One hears so much about him. What's the harm in looking?'

Reluctantly, the young officer agreed. They doubled back the way they had come but once in the lower citadel they veered to the right along a street with substantial-looking houses surrounded by small mature gardens. The entrances were arched – in the 'Turkish style', as Jamieson pointed out. Balconies jutted over the street. There were teahouses and artisan workshops on the other side of the road. It all looked prosperous.

'That's the one,' Jamieson said, nodding at one of the houses. Alice felt tension across her brow as she gazed up at the windows, wondering how often her husband had enjoyed himself behind its shuttered façade.

She looked at the houses to either side. Was one of these where Vernon stayed? Did he rent a whole house or just part of one? Two women appeared on Burnes's balcony; they were unveiled but when they saw her staring up, they pulled their shawls over their faces and dipped from view.

'Have you ever been inside, Lieutenant?' Alice asked. 'You can be frank with me – I'm not going to tell anyone.'

His jaw reddened. 'Just once or twice. Burnes is very hospitable to us young officers. And he knows a great deal about Afghanistan – far more than the men in charge of our expedition.'

Alice was surprised by his outspokenness. 'So you think he was right in saying that Dost Mohammed should have been left in power?'

He looked uncomfortable, perhaps regretting his candour. He dropped his voice. 'Shah Shuja doesn't seem to command the respect that the previous amir did. But we're here to do the best job we can.'

'Do you know my husband? Captain Buckley?'

He gave her a guarded look. 'Yes, he's a good cavalry officer.'

'And a friend of Burnes's?' Alice asked.

'Yes, I believe so.'

'Which is his house?'

Jamieson went very red. 'I'm not sure I understand . . .'

'I think you do. My husband spends more time here than in the cantonment. I would like to know which is the house that he keeps here. You won't get into any trouble for telling me, I promise.'

Alice's heart was thudding at her own audacity. She felt humiliated by having to ask but she was not going to leave until she knew.

He hesitated, then pointed to a narrow building three houses down the street. It had a tall wooden door that was half ajar. Alice dismounted and hurried towards it.

'Wait!' Jamieson cried out. 'You can't go in there!'

Alice pushed at the open door and found herself standing in a small courtyard with a fountain in the middle. There was a carpet laid out under an almond tree.

A small baby was lying naked and wriggling on the carpet, half in shade and half in the warm sunshine. Alice dashed forward, her pulse drumming in her ears. The baby's soft blond curls were glinting in the sunlight. It was a boy.

There was a shout from the watchman who had been dozing in the doorway. A woman appeared from the house looking panic-stricken. She gaped at Alice, her shawl falling back from her head. She was beautiful, with a slim face and large dark eyes. Her breasts were engorged with milk. She looked very young.

The girl snatched up the baby and tried to shoo Alice away.

Behind, Alice could hear Jamieson trying to placate the watchman.

'Is it Vernon's baby?' Alice asked, holding the young woman's look. 'Is it Captain Buckley's baby?'

She stared back at Alice with fear and incomprehension. Alice repeated her question in Hindustani but the young mother gabbled back at her in a language she couldn't understand.

'She's speaking Pashto,' Jamieson said, pushing past the old man.

'Ask her for me,' Alice demanded. 'Ask her if that's my husband's child!'

Jamieson spoke to her in halting words. The Afghan girl looked tearful. She answered in agitation and then, pulling her veil over her and the baby, she fled indoors with him.

Alice grabbed Jamieson by the arm. 'What did she say? Tell me!'

'She said Captain Buckley is the father.'

Bile flooded Alice's throat. She thought she would be sick on the spot. She couldn't bear the look of pity on the young officer's face. Pushing past him, she ran out of the courtyard and back into the dusty street.

Chapter 28

Alice spent the next few days in a state of numbness. She could not speak of what she had seen – not even to Emily – and told no one about discovering Vernon's mistress and baby. She did not want to get Lieutenant Jamieson into trouble for taking her but she couldn't have found the words anyway; she felt as if she had been struck dumb.

Every time she looked at Lotty and touched her fair curls, Alice was reminded of the infant lying on the Afghan rug in the dappled sunlight, his long limbs, his honey-blond hair and his round contented face. His hair and skin had been a shade darker than her daughter's and his eyes may have been brown but he and Lotty looked like brother and sister – they *were* brother and sister!

What was the baby's name? How old was he? At a guess, Alice would have said he was about three months old – no more than four. He must have been born in early to midsummer at a time when Alice was despairing at Vernon's lacklustre health and spirits. Perhaps Vernon wasn't impotent at all; he just didn't want to be intimate with her. Had he lain there in their bed thinking of his Afghan lover, longing to be with her instead?

Did Vernon love this woman – this girl – who could be no more than sixteen or seventeen? Or was she just one of several mistresses? Was he like Burnes in keeping a harem of dependent women? And, if so, could there be other illegitimate children either born or on their way? Alice veered between queasy humiliation and bubbling anger. How little Vernon must think of her – or their daughter – to behave so callously. After two years of marriage Alice knew for certain that her husband had been unfaithful for at least half of it.

Who else knew about Vernon's other household? Was it common knowledge among the British officers or only those few who kept houses in the city? Surely Sandy Ayton and others on MacNaughten's political staff would not condone such behaviour? It would reflect badly on the British administration, just as Burnes's harem did. The British of the cantonment put up with Vernon's opium smoking and erratic behaviour in drink because he was a good cavalry officer. Would they be so forgiving if they knew about his Afghan mistress and child? Had Jamieson already told his fellow officers what they had discovered? Perhaps the men didn't care – saw it as one of the spoils of war – as long as wives and families didn't get to know.

But now Alice did know. The knowledge of what Vernon had done was like acid in her stomach, nauseating and corrosive. She found it hard to sleep or eat. Alice kept picturing the young mother snatching up her baby and clasping him protectively to her swollen breasts. Had she feared that Alice had come to take her half-*feringhi* boy away from her? The Afghan girl had been petrified and yet fierce in her determination to fend off Alice.

At first Alice had been full of resentment and anger at the other woman; Vernon chose to spend his time with her and her child rather than with Alice and Lotty. Yet the more Alice thought about the household in Kabul, the more she felt sorry for the Pashto-speaking girl. What bribery had Vernon used to lure her to him – what sweet promises and gifts? She must have gone against the wishes of her family, for the Afghans were renowned for defending the honour of their women and punishing those who transgressed.

But what would happen to the girl and her bastard baby when the British left Kabul – an outcome that was bound to happen sooner or later? Would Vernon abandon his mistress as easily as he had taken up with her? Alice suspected that he would. She began to feel pity for the young woman and her child. She despised Vernon for what he was doing. Whenever Alice thought of her husband now she felt revulsion. She had tried hard to love him and make his life happy but to what purpose? Vernon had tricked her into marriage by his relentless wooing of her after George's death. Why had he bothered?

Then it came to her that his main reason must have been her wealth. Vernon was in constant need of money to sustain his hedonistic lifestyle; Alice's fortune was paying for his indulgences in Kabul.

* * *

The men returned from the Hindu Kush in October but there was little jubilation. Fantastical as it seemed, Dost Mohammed was rumoured to have rallied another army to his cause – mainly hardy Ghilzais – and was exhorting them to rid their country of the hated godless *feringhis* once and for all.

'It's not safe for Shah Shuja to move his court to Jalalabad this winter,' said Sandy, confiding in Alice. Emily refused to listen to bad news so he often spilled out his worries to Alice. 'But we're having the devil of a job convincing him.'

Kabul was in open panic as word spread that Dost Mohammed was only forty miles from the city and that many of Shah Shuja's soldiers were deserting to the deposed amir. Hasty plans were being laid to defend the citadel. Even Emily could not ignore the tension. The next time Alice visited, Emily anxiously asked her husband, 'Will we have to move into the Balla Hissar?'

'It won't come to that,' Sandy insisted. 'It's unsettling for everyone, I admit – and it makes us British look weak to have Dost Mohammed snapping at our heels just outside Kabul. But he's no match for the British Army, my dear.'

'Sandy's right,' Alice reassured Emily. 'Sir Robert will fight back. Florentia has every confidence in her husband's ability to keep us safe.'

Alice knew from Florentia that her husband was leading forays into Ghilzai country to keep them in check. But, soon afterwards, Alice's optimism was dashed by the news that Captain Edward Connolly, who had brought the women safely to Afghanistan the previous year, had been killed in a skirmish with the Ghilzais. It pierced her emotional numbness.

'He was such a nice man,' Alice said tearfully, sitting with her embroidery untouched in her lap.

Vernon, who had told her the news, was irritated by her remark. 'Why are you shedding tears over a man you barely knew? I've been in bloody battle yet you've not given me the time of day since I returned.'

He looked stronger than when he had left a month ago and some of his old bullishness had returned. Alice had to admit that campaigning suited Vernon, even though she could hardly bear to look at him.

216

'The poor captain is dead,' Alice said with feeling. 'You have been lucky enough to come back unscathed.' She cast aside her needlework and got up. 'I'm going to see if Lotty has woken from her rest.'

He caught her arm as she tried to leave the room. 'I expected my wife to be more pleased to see me,' he said, his eyes narrowing. 'Forget Connolly; I'm the man you should be thinking about.'

'I do,' said Alice, disgust curdling inside.

'Then show it, woman,' he demanded. He pinned her by the arms and kissed her roundly on the mouth. It appalled her that his appetite for sex with her was returning. So far the excuse of her monthly bleed had kept him from touching her in bed. But any day now she knew Vernon would renew his demands.

Alice pulled away in revulsion. He must have seen it in her eyes because he held on and grasped a handful of her hair, tugging it hard so that she had to look into his face.

'I thought you liked my kisses,' he hissed. 'You used to hunger for them.'

Alice's jaw clenched. 'That was before I knew you didn't love me,' she said. 'Before I knew how little you thought of your own wife and daughter.'

'What do you mean by that?' he demanded.

Something inside Alice snapped. She would put up with his betrayal no longer.

'I mean that I know about your mistress in Kabul,' Alice accused him. 'That *girl* you have lain with longer than you ever have with me.'

His mouth opened wide in surprise.

'Don't deny it.' Alice looked at him in defiance. 'I've met her.'

'That's impossible,' he gasped.

'Not impossible,' she said, trying to push him off. 'I've been to your house in Kabul. So I know about her – and I've seen your bastard son!'

His astonishment turned to fury. He loosened his grip on her hair and slapped the side of her head. Alice was momentarily stunned. Vernon was shouting at her but her ears were ringing so she could not hear what. He looked livid. She put out her hand to steady herself on the back of a chair. Her hearing cleared though her ear throbbed in pain.

' . . . wouldn't have had to if you had given me a son like a dutiful wife.'

'Don't make that an excuse,' Alice replied, clutching a hand to her pulsing head. 'You've been living with that girl since you came here. You allowed me and Lotty to come—'

'I never encouraged you to come,' Vernon said dismissively. 'You're nothing but an encumbrance to me here. None of you women and children should have come – you put the army at risk. Now we're surrounded by the enemy. How are we supposed to defend this bloody cantonment? We're like sitting ducks. If MacNaughten hadn't encouraged his ridiculous wife to come here, we men would all be safe in the Balla Hissar, doing what soldiers have to do to get through war.'

She looked at him in contempt. 'Don't blame this situation on us women,' Alice said, 'and don't make the excuse that cheating on your wife is normal army behaviour. Good men like Sandy Ayton don't betray their wives like you do.'

'He doesn't have to,' Vernon sneered. 'He has a biddable wife who will do anything he asks. I remember the days when you would do anything I asked of you in the bedchamber.'

Alice felt nauseated. 'Not anymore,' she said.

'We'll see,' he said, his tone threatening.

'Go to your Afghan mistress,' said Alice with a defiant look. 'You're not welcome in my bed.'

She thought he was about to strike her again but abruptly he marched to the door. 'I will come to your bed when it suits me,' he said. 'In the meantime I'll sleep with a woman who takes pleasure in it – and satisfies my needs more than you ever will.'

Vernon stalked out, slamming the door and leaving Alice shaking with fear and relief.

* * *

Alice did not see Vernon again for days. He came home briefly to order his servants to prepare his kit for another march against Dost Mohammed. This time the British forces, commanded by Sale, were going to meet him head-on in the Parwan Valley to the north of Kabul before he could reach the city. It was early November and the first sprinkling of snow was appearing on the surrounding hills.

Alice spent tense days with Emily, the two mothers trying to keep their children entertained while confined indoors. Sandy wouldn't let them wander outside in case they were tempted to watch from the walls and were picked off by Ghilzai snipers. Alice was reminded of Vernon's words of accusation that the women being there made it unsafe for the men. Perhaps he was right and they should never have come. Was she not putting her own daughter at risk unnecessarily?

Grim news began to filter back to the cantonment that the British cavalry had been cut to pieces by Dost Mohammed's troops. The rebel Afghan leader had raised his blue standard and removed his turban as a challenge to the foreigners, before exhorting his men to chase the infidels from their soil.

Florentia and Dinah waited anxiously for news of their menfolk.

'You must be so worried about Captain Buckley too,' said Dinah.

Alice gave a short nod and turned away before her face betrayed her true feelings.

Then, suddenly, the gloom and dread were reversed. The troops began to return with astonishing news that Dost Mohammed, having had the upper hand, had stopped short of the British guns, flaunted his banner and then retreated. Amid the rejoicing was anxiety: several officers had been killed. Sale had sustained a sword wound to the face.

A message came for Alice.

'I'm afraid it's bad,' said Sandy, who had taken it upon himself to break the news.

Alice's heart began to pound and her throat dried. 'Is Vernon dead?' she whispered.

218

'No, not that, I'm glad to say. Sorry, I didn't mean to worry you unduly,' said Sandy, 'but he's badly injured. Sword wounds to the leg and arm. They're bringing him in from camp to the cantonment hospital. I'll arrange for you to see him as soon as possible.'

'Thank you,' Alice managed to say, her stomach twisting with both relief and regret.

She waited tensely to be allowed to see her husband but he was being operated on and in a critical condition. The following evening she was permitted a few minutes with Vernon.

'He's well dosed with laudanum,' the army doctor warned. 'Probably won't know who you are but it might do his morale good.'

She found him lying on a canvas hospital bed, one arm heavily bandaged, his face waxy and eyes feverish. He looked so vulnerable that Alice felt a pang of pity followed swiftly by guilt. She had prayed that he wouldn't come back and that she'd never have to see him again. What sort of person was she to wish such harm on anyone – even a man who had wronged her as Vernon had? She sat by the bed and took his hand; it was cold and limp. A man in the next door bed was moaning in pain but Vernon was silent.

'You'll be all right,' she soothed. 'You'll get better. They'll let you home soon and I'll help nurse you, I promise.'

He looked at her with confusion in his blue eyes. After a few minutes the doctor returned and nodded for her to leave. As she stood up, Vernon clutched weakly at her hand. He tried to say something. She leant closer.

'Please,' he whispered, 'don't let me die. I don't want to die.'

Her stomach tensed. 'You're not going to die.' She squeezed his hand. 'Lotty needs her father.' She forced a smile.

'Lotty?' he frowned.

'Your daughter.'

'Oh, yes.' He sighed and closed his eyes.

She left him with a heavy heart. Alice felt weighed down by the responsibility of being Vernon's wife. She did not love him – in recent times she had hated him with a passion – but they were bound together by Lotty. She would do everything she could to protect her daughter and try to make Vernon see what a joy the little girl could be to him.

Unsettled by her trip to the hospital, Alice went for a walk through the cantonment as evening descended. She climbed the steps of the wall that surrounded the envoy's compound and gazed across at Kabul. Lights were being lit and glowed in the descending dark like fireflies. The sun was setting in a glory of orange and pink in the western hills. It was so still that she could hear the bleating of sheep from a village over a mile away. How could this tranquil place be so near to where a bloody battle had raged two days ago?

Alice looked again at the distant city. Was Vernon's lover waiting anxiously for news of him? Who would come and tell her that he had survived the battle but was injured? She wondered for a moment if she should try to get word to the girl and then gave a sigh of impatience. She had not caused this intolerable situation; Vernon had. When he pulled through – *if* he pulled through – he would have to sort out the mess himself.

She was about to turn back and descend to the compound when she heard the sound of hoof beats across the plain, in the direction of where the battle had been. A small group of riders was approaching at a trot. Soon Alice could make out MacNaughten and Sandy; she knew from Emily that they had been out visiting the men returning from the battle who were still encamped a few miles off.

With them were a couple of Afghans, heads swathed in white turbans that glowed against their dark faces in the setting sun. They rode without saddles and looked dusty from travel. She stood and watched them as they neared the gateway below. Sandy called out for the sentries to let them in. Alice was intrigued. Perhaps these were envoys from one of the warring chiefs come to bid for peace. They carried weapons so did not appear to be hostages.

She watched until they were inside the compound and *syces* came running to take their horses. The Afghans were hurried into MacNaughten's house. Alice returned home, determined to find out from Sandy who the mysterious visitors were.

* * *

By the following day, the shock news had spread all over the cantonment.

'You'll never know who's turned up bold as brass?' Emily cried when Alice appeared at her door. She pulled Alice inside. 'Dost Mohammed himself!'

'What?' gasped Alice.

'Last night,' Emily said, hardly able to speak she was so excited. 'Gave himself up. Sent his henchman to talk to MacNaughten. Then put his life in their hands. Sandy just brought them back as if they'd all been out riding together.'

'I saw them,' Alice blurted out.

'Did you?' Emily was round-eyed.

'I thought it was some messenger on behalf of a chief.' Alice shook her head in disbelief. 'But I must have seen the infamous amir. He took a great risk coming here with only one guard. They might have shot them on the spot.'

'They should have done,' said Emily, 'after all the trouble he's caused us.'

'What will they do with him?'

'Sandy says MacNaughten's quite taken with him. They're supposed to be discussing the terms of his surrender but the envoy is spending hours chatting with the man in Persian. Goodness knows what about.'

Over the next couple of days, the officers of the cantonment queued up to be allowed in to visit the deposed amir. Word of his intelligent conversation and courtly manners had spread quickly and everyone wanted to be able to say that they had sat on the floor with him, drinking tea and talking.

Sandy reported daily. 'He is concerned for the safety of his large family. The only thing he fears is that they might all be taken to London as prisoners. It's their biggest worry; Afghans hate the idea of exile but to be sent over the seas to the land of the *feringhis* is the ultimate humiliation for a devout Mohammedan.'

'Is that likely?' asked Alice.

'Not if MacNaughten can help it. He's recommending to Auckland that Dost Mohammed and his family stay in India. He's suggesting that the amir is given a farm in Mussoorie in the foothills so that he can be kept occupied.'

220

'The ex-amir,' Emily reminded her husband. 'I don't understand why MacNaughten is being so kind to him.'

'Well,' said Sandy, 'he's really rather an impressive man. I think we were all too quick to believe the worst of him and put our faith in Shah Shuja. It would appear Dost Mohammed was the far more able ruler.'

'Burnes and John Sinclair tried to convince Auckland of that,' Alice reminded him. 'If only they had been listened to.'

Sandy gave her an awkward glance. 'Well, some on Auckland's staff were all too eager to go to war.'

'Like Vernon, you mean?' Alice said, tensing.

'Well, what's done is done,' said Emily, 'and we just have to make the best of things here. I do hope Vernon is improving?'

'A little bit better today, thank you,' Alice said.

'Funny you should mention Sinclair,' said Sandy.

'Why?' Alice felt the heat rise in her neck as it always did when John was mentioned.

'Well, he was the man who captured Dost Mohammed.'

Alice and Emily gaped at him.

'Why ever didn't you say so before?' asked Emily.

'The negotiations were delicate and Sinclair wanted no glory for doing so,' said Sandy. 'Captured might be too strong a word, but Sinclair was the man who brought him in. Rode up to us at sunset and said he would hand over the amir if we promised not to harm him.'

'Goodness!' cried Emily. 'Whose side is he on?'

'Ours, of course,' said Sandy. 'He managed to bring in our arch enemy without any further bloodshed. Now the amir is sitting meek as a lamb answering questions on his country and his faith as if he was giving a lecture at the Asiatic Society. That's largely thanks to Sinclair.'

Alice's heart began a painful thudding. 'So Lieutenant Sinclair was the other Afghan who rode in that evening?'

Sandy nodded. 'He certainly looks the part. I wouldn't have known him if he hadn't called out in greeting.'

'Is he still here?' Alice asked.

'Yes, he's staying with the MacNaughtens while they have the amir as their prisoner.'

'Sounds more like their guest than prisoner,' said Emily in disapproval.

'You should be thankful, my dear,' Sandy chided. 'The country is finally at peace. Word is already out that the Barukzai leader is in our hands and the hostile chiefs are now pledging allegiance to Shah Shuja. MacNaughten's even going to allow the amir to winter in Jalalabad as he wished. Everything has changed now Dost Mohammed has accepted defeat.'

* * *

Alice could settle to nothing, knowing that John was a stone's throw away from her house in the envoy's compound. She took Lotty for walks in the sharp November air in the hopes of coming across him. But there was never any sign

221

of him. The compulsion to see John grew stronger with each day. She thought of the turbaned and bearded rider who had accompanied the captive amir a few evenings ago. If only she had known it was John she would have paid more attention. Did he know she was in the cantonment? Or that she was married to Vernon?

The thought gave her pain. How he would despise her for that. Or perhaps he wouldn't care. He had made his own life here in Afghanistan and most likely never gave her a thought.

She heard from the Aytons how plans were progressing swiftly for taking Dost Mohammed out of the country. His family were already on their way to Peshawar and exile. Now that the threat of Shah Shuja being toppled was over, General Cotton was withdrawing further troops from Kabul and accompanying the prisoner south. Sale was to be left in charge until the new commander took over.

'Rumour has it that General Nott in Kandahar expects to get the top military post,' Sandy told them. 'Not sure that's a good idea – he's argumentative and well known for having a low opinion of Afghans.'

Sandy was to accompany MacNaughten to the court's winter quarters in Jalalabad so Emily had decided to go too.

'I wish you could come,' her friend said to Alice. 'I will miss you and Lotty a great deal. But I understand how you can't leave Vernon.'

'I'll miss you Aytons too,' said Alice, pulling Alexander into a hug and tickling his tummy. The boy squealed to be let go and then came back for another tickle.

* * *

On the eve of the move to Jalalabad, Alice walked back from the cantonment hospital lost in thought about Vernon. She knew he endured great pain but he was more querulous and demanding with each visit, ordering her to bring him brandy and criticising her for not staying longer. Never once did he ask after Lotty.

His arm wound was healing well but his leg was giving the doctors concern. The wound was weeping and they were fighting to make sure it didn't become gangrenous. Away from her husband's hearing, they were talking about amputation. Alice knew Vernon would never cope as an invalid; he prided himself on his manliness and being a soldier.

As she reached the mission compound, Alice was brought up short by the sound of a familiar voice and laughter in the half-dark.

'Colin MacRae, is that you?' she called out in astonishment.

The uniformed lieutenant stepped out from the shadowed archway. 'It is indeed.' Colin grinned, coming forward and kissing her hand.

'I didn't know you were in Afghanistan,' Alice said in delight.

'Arrived a few days ago. I've been with the horse artillery in the hills – came up from Kandahar during the summer.' He smiled. 'You are looking well. Marriage to Buckley must be suiting you after all.'

Alice flushed. She remembered how Colin had warned her about Vernon and disapproved of the match. How right he had been.

'My husband is severely wounded,' said Alice by way of an answer. 'I've just come from the hospital.'

'I'm sorry to hear that,' he said, his smile fading.

Alice was suddenly aware of a movement in the shadows. A tall turbaned figure loomed out of the dark, a dagger glinting in his belt. She gasped. 'Colin, careful!'

Colin half turned. 'Don't worry,' he reassured her. 'I know that tribesman well.'

The Afghan stepped into the dusk light. 'Mrs Buckley,' he said with a curt bow.

She looked into his swarthy bearded face and knew him at once. The familiar green eyes made her heart lurch. So he knew about her second marriage.

'Lieutenant Sinclair,' she said, her mouth drying.

For a moment, all three stood in a tense silence. There seemed to be so many questions hanging in the air between them that no one knew what to say.

'I – I saw you ride in with Dost Mohammed,' Alice blurted out.

John's eyes widened in surprise. 'You did?'

'I didn't know it was you, of course. Not with you dressed like that. But I saw your arrival with Sandy and MacNaughten. I was watching from the walls.'

'She'd make a better spy than you, John,' teased Colin.

Unexpectedly, John laughed. 'So she would.' He scrutinised her. 'Do you make a habit of wandering about the town after dark? I'm surprised your husband allows it.'

Alice was wounded by the remark. She wondered how much John knew about Vernon's double life – probably a great deal.

'He's in no position to tell me what to do,' said Alice. 'He's fighting for his life in the hospital.'

John glanced away. 'I'm sorry. I didn't mean to make light of his injuries. And I didn't mean to offend you, Mrs Buckley.'

Alice's chest tightened. His formality was worse than his mockery. She had dreamt of the moment when she would see him again and find out about his new life, but now they eyed each other warily like strangers. Too much had happened since their last meeting. Their emotional farewell in Simla seemed a lifetime ago.

'Can I offer you both some refreshment?' she asked, suddenly desperate to spin out this moment together.

'That's kind,' said Colin, 'but I'm on my way to dine with Sturt and Jamieson.'

Alice felt herself reddening further at the mention of Jamieson, the young officer whom she had forced into revealing where Vernon's Kabul house was.

'And I must return to the city,' said John. 'There is much to do before we set off tomorrow.'

'You are going to Jalalabad too?' Alice asked, unable to keep the dismay from her voice.

'I'm to help smooth the way with the unruly natives,' he said dryly.

'When will you return?' she asked.

He gave her a sharp look. 'That's not for me to say. Perhaps in the spring.'

Alice swallowed a lump in her throat. She felt suddenly very alone.

'That's a long time to be parted from your family,' she said. 'No doubt you will miss them.'

He gave her such a fierce look that Alice wished she hadn't mentioned them. Of course he would miss them; she was the unhappily married one, not he.

'Perhaps you will both come and dine with me – with us – when you are next in the cantonment?' she said.

'I doubt if Captain Buckley would want that,' said John.

Alice ignored this, glancing at Colin instead. 'Will you be stationed here now, Lieutenant MacRae?'

'For the short term,' he replied.

'Then I look forward to seeing something of you. You must come and meet my daughter Lotty – she'll be lost without young Alex Ayton to play with, so any distraction over the winter would be a help.'

Colin smiled. 'I'd be delighted to.'

The two men bowed at her as she made her way past. 'Good luck, Lieutenant Sinclair,' she murmured.

As she turned towards her house, she was aware that they watched her. She could hear them talking to each other in a rapid language she didn't understand – probably Gaelic. John's voice sounded angry, Colin's placatory. She could only imagine how John was saying something contemptuous about her being Vernon's wife and Colin was possibly defending her. Alice couldn't reach her door quickly enough. She hurried in and went in search of Lotty for comfort.

The girl was washed and ready for bed. Gita was singing her lullabies while Lotty sat on her knee having her wavy hair brushed. Both the songs and the rhythmic brushing soothed Alice's restless daughter. She sucked her thumb and gazed dreamily into space.

Lotty spotted her mother and scrabbled to her feet. Alice put out her arms and swung her up into a loving embrace.

'You smell so sweet I could gobble you up!' Alice said, kissing her cheeks.

Lotty giggled and thrust her fingers into Alice's hair, pulling at its loose coils. At eighteen months, the girl was parroting her words.

'Gobble you up.' She laughed and sucked on her mother's hair.

Alice buried her nose in her daughter's neck and breathed in her scent. Why had she mentioned Lotty to Colin? Was it because she wanted John to know that she was a parent too – that she was happy as a mother if not as a wife? He'd made no comment. Perhaps he didn't care. There was nothing in their short conversation that had indicated any interest on his part about her life. And why should he? They were both married to others and their lives had diverged so completely that there was no longer any common interest.

So why was it that her heart ached anew for John? Just seeing him again – looking into his lively green eyes – had made her deeply buried longing erupt inside like molten lava. How could she bear to see him again? How could she bear not to? As she hugged her daughter tight, Alice thought it was just as well that John was leaving for Jalalabad with the dawn. If this was the emotional turmoil she felt when meeting him then at least she would be spared it for the next few months.

Chapter 29

Kabul, spring 1841

Lotty learnt to skate that winter on the frozen river. She was a sturdy walker and was happy to slide and skid across the ice, holding on between Alice and Dinah Sale. Dinah was full of excitement about her wedding plans. Johnny Sturt had promised her that it would be this summer.

'As early as possible,' said Dinah. 'I can't wait for him to get back from Jalalabad.' She gave Alice a coy look. 'And we both want to get started on a family. I'd love to have a child as gorgeous as yours.'

Alice smiled. 'You will make wonderful parents. Lieutenant Sturt is such a kind young man.'

Alice had been grateful for the company of Dinah and her mother over the winter months. They had joined in or spectated at the cantonment activities of riding, horse racing, duck shooting and evening charades. Twice a week, Alice helped out at the cantonment school, giving lessons to the children of non-commissioned officers. She kept as busy as she could and away from the house as much as possible, where Vernon barked orders ill-temperedly from a truckle bed by the fire.

The doctors had saved his leg from amputation but Vernon could not hide the constant pain it gave him. He routinely drank brandy to dull it. It had aged him. He looked drawn and thin-faced, his eyes sunken and dark-ringed. His other leg had withered with lack of use and he needed the servants' help to get him up and onto the commode.

Recently, the news that Major-General Elphinstone (son of the Elphinstone who had wooed the Afghans into an alliance a generation previously) was to be their new commander in Kabul had galvanised her husband into making an effort to get out of bed and try to walk again. It was a surprise appointment for the elderly Elphinstone; though a hero of Waterloo, he had not served in India before.

'He knows nothing of India let alone Afghanistan,' Vernon fulminated. 'What are those useless politicians doing in London? I bet it's just because his father was a director of the Company. They say he's riddled with gout and can hardly walk.'

This seemed to be the impetus Vernon needed to prove that he was still soldier material. 'I can't wait to get back in the saddle,' he declared, with a lascivious look at Alice.

She ignored his double entendres, thankful that as yet his suggestive remarks had not been put into practice.

Alice had been sad that Colin MacRae had never come to visit. Either he had kept away because Vernon was always there or he had been sent out on duties elsewhere, for she had not seen him all winter.

Alice's life was largely confined to the cantonment, though as the snows receded and the spring flowers spread across the riverbanks, she started to take Lotty for picnics with other young officers' wives and their families. Some of the officers would attend too; once or twice Vernon came along. As his strength returned and he was able to ride again, he liked to flirt with the other women and teach cricket to their young sons. He walked with a slight limp, which provoked sympathy among the women, while his stories of battle drew admiration from the boys.

Vernon made a big show of being affectionate to Alice and Lotty in front of others, whereas behind the closed doors of their home he either ignored them or was coldly critical.

Lotty thrilled at the times her father made a fuss of her, giggling when he lifted her up to ride in front of him or when he gave her titbits of food from his meal.

'Me play 'ricket too, Daddy! Me too!' she would squeal, longing to join in the games of the older children.

'Girls don't play cricket, Lotty,' he would say with an indulgent smile. 'You just watch like a good girl.' If his daughter got in the way too much, Vernon would give Alice a sharp look. 'Keep an eye on her – don't want her getting hurt, do we?'

Alice's heart ached for her daughter; the little girl was baffled by her father's moods, which veered between affection, irritation and indifference.

* * *

In May, Lotty turned two. Alice held a birthday picnic at which Vernon distributed lavish presents to the other children and made a fuss of his daughter. Lotty was so excited she was sick. Afterwards, Vernon berated Alice for allowing such rich food and then disappeared back to the citadel for the rest of the week.

He seemed to be able to come and go as he pleased. His new commander Elphinstone's control was lax; the genial but ageing general was largely housebound with rheumatic fever and his second-in-command, Brigadier Shelton, often countermanded his orders. Or so Florentia told Alice. Sale was obviously irked at being caught in the middle.

As the heat of the summer grew intense, Alice resumed early morning riding, partly to enjoy the cooler air and partly to ease her frustration with being cooped up in the cantonment. She felt hemmed in by life in the mission compound. While Vernon was away indulging himself in Kabul she would do as she pleased, she decided. Their *syce*, Ravi, would ride out with her for protection.

Alice relished cantering out across the plain as the dawn light spilled over the eastern mountain tops, and she was reminded of her carefree life long ago at Tolland Park riding with her father before breakfast. She went as far as the King's Gardens, a pleasant oasis of trees and water tanks between the cantonment and the city, before turning back. She still took pleasure from the simple things in life, such as the wind in her face and the sight of a rushing river, and for that she was thankful.

As she was returning one early morning, Alice became aware of hoof beats behind. She glanced back and saw a lone turbaned rider gaining on her. She kicked her horse into a gallop and Ravi did likewise. But before she could reach the safety of the mission compound the rider had caught her up. Ravi turned to defend his mistress, raising his sword.

226

'I mean no harm to Mrs Buckley!' the man called out in Hindustani.

A jolt went through Alice. She reined in her horse. 'Lieutenant Sinclair?'

'Aye,' he answered, pulling up beside her. 'What are you doing out here with just one servant for protection?'

She could hardly breathe at his sudden nearness, let alone speak.

He frowned. 'It's too risky. What is your husband thinking of?'

Alice was piqued. 'My husband couldn't care less what I do and he isn't here to stop me.'

She immediately regretted her words. His look changed from concern to pity.

'Well, he should care,' said John. 'There is much unrest in the countryside. You could be a target for kidnap and ransom or worse. You are being very foolish, Mrs Buckley.'

Suddenly she couldn't bear his censure. It was bad enough being constantly criticised and belittled by Vernon but John had no right to tell her what to do.

'You exaggerate my importance,' she retorted, throwing him a defiant look. 'But it's a risk I'm prepared to take. I can only bear the rest of the day being in the stifling cantonment if I can feel the dawn breeze on my face. Not that it's any concern of yours.'

This momentarily silenced him. He held her look and then said, 'Not my concern at all. But you have a child. For her sake you should not take such risks.'

Alice was stung by the rebuke; all the more so because she did feel pangs of guilt at leaving Lotty to go riding. What would happen to her daughter if some accident befell Alice? Would Vernon palm the girl off on another family or send her home to England to relations she had never met? Either fate for Lotty distressed her.

Alice answered him hotly. 'Don't lecture me on how to look after my daughter. She is the one person in the world that I would walk through fire for. I will never let harm come to her and I don't intend leaving her motherless.' She saw him flinch but carried on berating him. 'Look to your own family, Lieutenant, and their welfare – but don't you dare lecture me about mine!'

She pulled on her reins to turn her horse away but he grabbed her gloved hand. 'Wait! Forgive me. I didn't mean to lecture you. I'm just troubled to see you out on your own.'

'Not on my own,' Alice pointed out. 'Ravi is with me.'

John nodded at the *syce* in acknowledgement. 'True, but one groom is hardly protection against marauding Ghilzais.'

Her hand was hot in the glove under his touch. He leant so close that she could see the pulse beating in his throat. The green of his eyes looked all the more vivid against his sun-darkened skin. Alice swallowed.

'Surely you exaggerate the danger? I've heard MacNaughten dismiss such talk as gloomy nonsense. He says the only trouble in the country is infighting between the tribes – it comes with the hot weather, and is not aimed at the British.'

'And I've come to try to warn him that he is wrong,' John said grimly. 'There is much resentment building against the British.'

'But why?' Alice asked.

'As many reasons as there are tribes.' John let out a sigh. 'The Ghilzais have been subjected to unprovoked attacks and now see their ancient forts being taken over and rebuilt by foreign invaders. The Douranee chiefs around Kandahar do not see why they should pay extra tribute to the King when they are already loyal to him. The Kazilbashis are furious; they were told that they would get paid for helping fight against Dost Mohammed but all the promises have been broken.'

'I thought we had paid them handsomely? Sandy certainly said so.'

'But I bet he didn't say that the Kohistan tribes had to raise taxes on their own people in order to fund that payment,' John said scathingly.

Alice blushed. 'That doesn't seem fair.'

'It's not,' said John. 'And it's time the British sat up and listened to their grievances – that's if they ever want to leave Afghanistan. Some of the chiefs are beginning to think the British have no intention of leaving.'

'You talk about the British as if you are no longer one of us,' said Alice. 'Is that how you feel?'

'I'm first and foremost a Highlander,' he answered, with a wry half-smile, 'and then a soldier of the East India Company. That is where my loyalties lie.'

'And not to your Afghan family? It seems to me that you are very sympathetic to the Afghan point of view.'

Abruptly, he pulled away, his smile vanishing.

'I'm sorry,' she said quickly. 'I have no right to assume such a thing.'

'I will see you back safely,' he said curtly.

They trotted back in silence, Alice berating herself for raising the subject of John's family. He obviously resented her prying, yet she longed to know more about them. Ravi followed. Alice wondered how much Gita's husband had understood of their exchange. But she trusted him not to tell Vernon of the encounter. Ravi felt more loyalty to her than to Vernon; she was a better employer to him and Gita than Vernon could ever be.

At the gateway, John stopped. 'I will leave you here, Mrs Buckley.'

Alice was hurt by his sudden coolness towards her. 'I hope I may see you again, Lieutenant. Perhaps you would care to visit me and Lotty?'

'Perhaps,' he said, turning away.

A moment later he was gone, disappearing into the shadows of the cantonment. Alice felt bereft and hurried home to breakfast with her daughter.

* * *

The following morning, while Vernon stayed in Kabul, Alice went out riding early. Her disappointment not to find John was overwhelming. Why should he come seeking her? He held none of the deep feelings that she did.

On the third morning, he was waiting for her in the shadow of the gatehouse. Alice could not keep the delight from her face.

'You came.' She smiled, then regretted her sudden presumption that he was there for her.

With relief, she saw him smile back. 'I see you are determined to carry on with your morning rides so I thought I would provide an escort.'

'Thank you.'

Her heart drummed faster than the canter of their horses as they rode to the river and followed its course to a sheltered orchard on the edge of the King's Gardens. She wasn't sure what his being there meant yet was joyful at his presence. She knew it could never be more than friendship but how she longed for any small gestures and signs that they were still friends.

At the orchard they stopped and dismounted. John asked Ravi to tend their horses while he walked a little way off with Alice.

'I'm sorry for what I said the other day,' Alice began. 'I had no right to pry into your family life and I could see that it upset you. I shan't ask again. Is it possible for us to be friends in spite of everything that has happened between us?'

John stopped and gazed out over the river where the early light was glinting off its surface. He turned to look at her, his eyes glinting with that fierceness she had seen in them at their last encounter. Her insides tensed; she had judged things wrongly again.

'I admit I was angry with you,' he said. 'The first time I saw you again – when I was with Colin – I thought you must have known. I thought you were deliberately trying to hurt me – get back at me for not being there to save you from Vernon. The way you talked about your daughter and goaded me about my family missing me . . .'

'I don't know what you mean,' Alice said, astounded. 'I would never try to hurt you or be disrespectful to your family—'

'That's what Colin thought,' John interrupted. 'And after you said it again two days ago, I realised that you didn't know. I assumed Vernon must have told you.'

'Vernon?' Alice queried. 'Told me what?'

She saw his jaw clenching as he tried to speak. The words came out between gritted teeth.

'I have no family,' he said. 'Not anymore. My wife and child are dead. They were murdered. In Baltistan. That is why I live the life I do, going where others will not go. I care nothing for my own safety for I have nothing left to lose.'

Alice was appalled. She saw his eyes glinting with tears of grief.

'John,' she whispered, 'that is terrible. I'm so sorry. You poor, poor man.'

She reached out and took his hand, pressing it between her own hands but he stood rigid, not responding to her gesture.

'When did this happen? Will you tell me?' she encouraged.

At first he said nothing but she held onto him until he found his voice. He began to talk about his arrival in Baltistan and saving Sultana, a Kazilbashi girl, and her brother Aziz from robbers; how he had been encouraged to marry the girl to save her honour and how she had given him a son. But then one day when he had been out hunting with the king, the robbers' kin had returned to wreak their revenge.

John looked harrowed as he told her. 'I had moved Sultana and the baby into a house in the village where she could have a garden to remind her of home in the Kohistan – I should have left her in the safety of the fortress or taken her back to Afghanistan sooner as I kept promising.'

Alice's sympathetic look and understanding silence helped him continue.

'I couldn't bear to stay in Skardu after that,' he said with a shudder. 'I left and took Aziz back to his people in the Kohistan. I lived with them for a short while – they were kind to me despite my failing to keep their daughter safe, or their grandchild—' John broke off, his jaw clenching.

'What was he called; your son?' Alice asked gently.

'Azlan Hercules Sinclair,' John said with the ghost of a smile, 'after the two men who brought me up at Ramanish.'

'A good name,' she said.

He broke away and drew his hand across his eyes, spilling the tears that had been brimming in them.

'You loved her,' murmured Alice. 'Your Sultana.'

He gave her an intense look. 'I married her out of pity but I grew to care for her. And when she gave birth to my son I thought I had never been happier.'

Alice nodded, her heart sore for him. 'You would have made a fine father.'

'Thank you,' he rasped with emotion.

Alice glanced away, unable to bear the raw pain she saw in his face.

'Did you . . . Did you ever get the message I sent to you through Colin?' she asked. 'Telling you that George had died?'

'Aye, I did,' said John.

Alice felt a wave of disappointment. So it had made no difference that she had been widowed; he would have married his Sultana anyway.

He took her by the arm and pulled her round to face him. 'But only long after I was married. Azlan had just been born when Colin's letter finally caught up with me.'

Alice tried to read the expression in his face.

'I came to Kabul to work for Burnes in the hope of being allowed back to India but I soon got to hear that you had remarried.' John's look was intense. 'I could hardly credit it. Once Buckley arrived in the city he was quick to boast to me how he had won you over so easily.'

Alice burnt with shame to think what Vernon might have said to John about her. Her hateful husband had never mentioned meeting his old rival but she could well imagine how Vernon would have gloated over John about his conquest of her.

'He lied to me about you,' Alice said indignantly, 'and about himself.'

'How could you have fallen for such a man?' John was incredulous. 'Colin said he warned you about what Buckley was like – how he mistreated women. You of all—'

'I'd heard you were married to an Afghan and had a child on the way,' Alice cried. 'What was I supposed to do? You were beyond my reach forever – and Vernon said such terrible things about you that I began to doubt you had ever loved me.'

'I have always loved you!' John said with vehemence. His grip tightened. 'Do you know why I agreed to marry Sultana? Because she reminded me of you! Her long auburn hair and her dimpled cheeks – if I tried hard enough I was able to imagine it was you . . .'

Alice gasped. 'Oh, John!'

'But you and Vernon,' he said, his voice hardening, 'it's like a dagger in the guts to think of you together. Him of all men!'

'I wanted a child,' Alice said, shaking under his hold. 'Longed for one. I'd miscarried twice with George. That's what Vernon offered me – a chance to be a mother. Is that so very wrong?'

John released his hold and let go an agonised sigh. 'Of course not. I'm sorry, Alice; I have no right to judge you. I just can't endure seeing you with that devil. The way he treats you—'

'I know what he's like,' she said with disgust. 'I know what he does in Kabul – who he lives with. I've met his mistress – she's just a girl – and I've seen the boy she gave him – the son he craves that I could not provide. There is nothing you can tell me about my husband that I don't already know – nothing that can shock me anymore.'

Abruptly, he pulled her into his arms and held her close.

'I could kill him for what he's done to you,' he declared.

Alice could hardly believe she was standing in the shadow of a mulberry tree in John's strong hold. She had never thought to feel his embrace again.

She looked into his vivid eyes and whispered, 'Kiss me. I don't care what happens after this. I just know that I can't leave without feeling your lips on mine. I've craved it for so long.'

She saw the surprise in his eyes turn quickly to passion. He bent and kissed her with a firm mouth, like a man who had hungered long for this moment too. He covered her face with kisses and then returned to her lips and embraced her till she was lightheaded with desire.

It was Ravi who came and warned them that the grass cutters from the cantonment were approaching; Alice and John were oblivious of anything but themselves. Life was stirring with the dawn. Alice tore herself away from John with reluctance.

'You must not be seen with me,' John cautioned. 'You should return first with Ravi before the sun is fully up.'

'Can I see you again tomorrow?' Alice pleaded. 'I'll ride out earlier.'

He raised her hand and pressed it to his lips for a last lingering kiss.

'Only come if it's safe,' he warned.

By that she knew he meant if Vernon was still from home.

Alice rode back feeling reckless and fully alive for the first time in an age. John still loved her; she knew that to be true with every fibre of her being. And the love she felt for him was like a wildfire raging through her and threatening to grow out of control. At that moment, in the orange blaze of dawn, she was exultant. She would not think of the future beyond her next meeting with John.

Chapter 30

Kabul, August 1841

John had his beard shaved off by a barber in the bazaar for Johnny Sturt's wedding to Dinah Sale. His chin felt raw from the cut-throat razor and the cheerful Indian barber soothed his skin by rubbing on musky-smelling oil. Back home in the small house he shared with Rajban and his family – John's servant had married a Hindu merchant's daughter in Kabul and now had two sons – John stripped off and washed in cold water. Then he dressed in the uniform that Rajban had laid out for him.

'Do you think the jacket still fits?' John asked his friend. The last time he had worn his best dress uniform was two years ago for the celebrations of Shah Shuja's arrival in Kabul.

'It will fit,' said Rajban, 'like a glove. A tight glove.'

John laughed. 'You think I have grown fat with sitting around in Kabul eating too much of your wife's curry?'

'Not fat' – Rajban grinned – 'but your appetite has been healthy since you met Memsahib Alice again.'

John's jaw reddened. 'Is it so obvious?'

'To me, yes,' said Rajban. 'To the outside world you are discreet. Not like that worthless husband of hers, flaunting his women and—'

'That's enough,' John ordered. He did not mind Rajban's outspoken comments – for years he had been more comrade than servant – but John didn't want to think of Alice's husband.

His stomach clenched as it always did when Vernon was mentioned. The man was odious. Alice's pre-dawn rides had come to an abrupt end in June. John suspected that someone had spotted them or had at least reported seeing Alice going out of the cantonment. Word must have got back to Vernon because, for two months now, Alice had not been able to meet him alone.

They contrived to see each other in passing; when John visited the MacNaughtens to hand on intelligence or at Sunday services at the cantonment church. But they could only exchange small pleasantries and longing looks. He would go over in his mind the few precious clandestine meetings they had had at the King's Gardens, sitting talking under the mulberry trees and stealing passionate kisses.

How he had longed to make love to Alice but it had been too risky and the snatched moments too short. She was nervous of Vernon finding out about their trysts and he had held himself in check. He suspected that, despite Vernon's ill-treatment of her, Alice still felt an obligation as Vernon's wife not to break her wedding vows. It infuriated John that Vernon should have any sort of hold over Alice, but for the moment all John could do was cherish the few sweet encounters with her in the cantonment.

Today they would see each other at Sturt's wedding in the cantonment church. John liked the young engineer; he was a plucky but level-headed officer and John had been touched to be asked to be his best man.

'Fellow engineer and all that,' Johnny Sturt had said bashfully.

232

In the early days of the British force's arrival in Kabul, Sturt had supported John when he'd advised MacNaughten to renovate the lower citadel to house the British. Both of them had thought it rash to leave the safety of the fortified city to build a cantonment on the plain as if they were in some peaceable part of India. But MacNaughten had ignored their warnings.

'Makes us look like we don't trust our Afghan allies,' the envoy had said. 'And they'll just accuse us of trying to manipulate the amir if we stay in the Balla Hissar.'

'Sir, they will respect us more if we fortify our barracks in the citadel and show that we are not going to be pushed around.'

'Listen, Sinclair,' MacNaughten had said with a polite pat on the shoulder, 'you understand these people well but I know Shah Shuja better than most. He thinks he looks weak if we keep all our troops here in the city. He wants his own guard to protect him, not foreigners. So we will build ourselves a comfortable residence outside the city walls, eh?'

It still worried John that the majority of the British were housed on the broiling plain in full view of all the surrounding forts and hilltops. Recently, over cups of wine in John's small courtyard, he and Sturt had discussed such matters while Rajban had strummed a guitar under the stars.

'It's madness that our supplies of grain and weapons are stored outside the cantonment in those old forts,' Sturt had said. 'Elphinstone couldn't believe it when he arrived. Not that the old boy's done anything to change matters since.'

'He's too ill for the job,' John had said.

'Perhaps you could try to speak to him?' Sturt had suggested.

'I'm here to advise the envoy, not the commander,' John had sighed. 'It would be nice if they would communicate with each other once in a while but I doubt my information is being passed on. MacNaughten likes to bury bad news.'

Sturt had looked so glum that John had changed the subject quickly.

'Let's drink to your forthcoming marriage,' he'd said with a smile, 'to the delightful Miss Sale. May you have many happy years together – you are well suited.'

Johnny Sturt had grinned. 'Dinah is a wonderful girl – she's got her father's courage and her mother's sociable nature. And I can't wait to be married.'

They had drunk to that.

* * *

Lotty was almost as excited as Alice. The girl knew something very special must be happening for her to be wearing her best dress and have Ayah Gita tie blue ribbons in her hair and fix a sun bonnet on her. She got her *ayah* to put a ribbon around her rag doll's plait and a new piece of muslin for a sari. The doll was called Gita too.

'Pretty Gita.' Lotty grinned, holding up her doll and waving it at her mother. Alice was wearing a white muslin dress with peach-coloured trimmings and bonnet. Around her shoulders she draped the soft feather-light pashmina shawl made from the wool that John had sent her from the mountains five years ago.

'Very pretty.' Alice kissed Lotty on the nose. 'And you are sweet as a pea.'

233

'Come Daddy now,' Lotty said, rushing up to her father and tugging on his braces, which were hanging down past his knees.

Vernon screwed up his face in irritation. Alice could tell he was hung over.

'Come on, Lotty,' Alice said, quickly pulling the girl away. 'We'll leave Daddy to get ready. Let's see if Alexander is outside.'

'Don't set off without me,' Vernon barked after them. 'Do you hear?'

Alice didn't care how irritable her husband was, she had been looking forward to this day for weeks, especially since hearing that John was to be Sturt's best man. Outside they were joined by the Aytons, who had returned in April. Emily was huge with child and hung onto Sandy's arm. Alexander was riding a hobby-horse and Lotty began running after him, so that Alice had to go after her. In the mêlée in the street, she ended up arriving at the church with her friends without waiting for Vernon.

John was standing at the entrance, immaculate in his uniform, his sword at the ready for the ceremonial sabre arch to honour the bride. He turned, caught sight of Alice and smiled.

Alice felt her insides melt. His dark hair was groomed and his face newly shaven. His eyes shone with desire for her. She had never seen him look more handsome. It was the John she had first fallen in love with – older and more rugged-looking – but with the same open, amused expression.

Her heart hammered as she and the Aytons filed past him and he kissed Emily's hand and then hers.

'Mrs Buckley,' he murmured, holding hers for longer than was necessary.

'Lieutenant Sinclair,' she said, feeling breathless. 'What a special day for our friends.'

'Indeed,' he said, lowering his voice. 'And you are in danger of eclipsing the bride with your beauty.'

Alice felt the flush rise from her chest into her neck and cheeks. Lotty tugged on her other hand. John crouched down to speak to the girl.

'Hello, Lotty. And who is this?' he asked, pointing at the rag doll.

'Gita,' said Lotty.

'Hello, Gita.' John grinned, shaking the doll's hand and tickling Lotty under the chin.

Lotty giggled and ducked her chin. Suddenly she spotted her father. 'Daddy, Daddy!'

Alice quickly stepped away from John.

Vernon pushed his way towards them, putting a proprietorial hand on Lotty's head.

'I thought I told you to wait for me, my dear,' he said with a cold smile at Alice.

Ignoring John's polite nod, he put his hand to Alice's back and steered her into the church. As they sat in the relative cool of the interior, Vernon pinched her arm. 'I hope you weren't making a fool of yourself over Sinclair,' he hissed.

She didn't reply. He was not going to spoil her enjoyment of the day. Today it was best to let Vernon have his say and not answer back; then he would let the matter drop. Too often she sparked back at him causing the argument to escalate.

234

She never won and often it ended in violence with him twisting her arm until her skin burnt or jabbing her in the breast, which was doubly painful.

Yet Vernon's moods were so contrary that on some occasions her silent contempt proved an even greater irritant than her defiant words. He would try to goad her into a response but she would not be provoked. Alice only had to let her mind wander to thoughts of John and she became immune to her husband's criticism and cruelty. It did not stop him inflicting small injuries – bruises that were invisible under her clothing – but she could bear anything as long as she knew John was near.

She watched him now, marching in with his friend Sturt, and her heart swelled with love. How she wished it was she and John who were marrying that day. Yet she was joyful for her friend Dinah, who was radiant with happiness in an ivory dress of muslin and lace and her dark hair bound up prettily in the style of young Queen Victoria. A picture of the monarch hung in the MacNaughtens' drawing room and Dinah had been very taken with it.

Afterwards, there was a wedding feast laid on at the Sales' house and the guests spilled out into their beautiful garden. There were Afghan friends there: the elderly Zemaun and his nephew Osman – Barukzai chiefs who were courteous and generous to the British officers in Kabul. Zemaun loved the Sales' garden and had sent them plants as gifts when the cantonment was being built. Osman was a friendly young man; he was doing tricks with a coin for Lotty, Alexander and the other children.

Alice, seeing her daughter occupied and knowing that Vernon was inside slugging back champagne with other officers, slipped away to the far end of the garden where a riot of perfumed pink roses hung down over a trellis, creating a discreet bower.

A few minutes later, John appeared around the trellis. He took her by the hands and pulled him to her for a rash kiss. Alice's heart thudded as laughter caught in her throat.

'We shouldn't,' she whispered.

'I can't help it,' said John with a grin. 'I've been driven to distraction seeing you and not being able to hold you.'

They kissed again quickly and then broke apart.

'What are we going to do, John?' Alice asked. 'I'm not sure how much more I can bear of these snatched moments.'

He seized her hand. 'When things are more settled in the country I shall take you away from here – you and Lotty – and you'll never have to live with that man again.'

'Where shall we go?' Alice asked in excitement.

'Anywhere you want. We could live in the hills near Simla. My bearer Rajban comes from the Bushahir district. It's a place of forests and meadows and rushing rivers. We could live simply but well.'

'Can you see the mountain peaks from there?' Alice asked dreamily.

'We'll watch the sunrise over them every morning,' he promised. He reached to loosen her shawl and traced a finger across her chest. 'I'll take you to where the pashmina goats graze.'

Alice felt a shiver of delight at his touch. 'My pashmina mountains,' she said with a smile. 'I used to look at them from Simla and imagine you there bartering for wool over a water-pipe.'

'A water-pipe?' John chuckled.

Alice's daydream was suddenly spoilt by a memory of Vernon forcing her to smoke something hallucinogenic from a water-pipe at one of his rowdy dinner parties in Simla. Her face clouded.

'But Vernon would come after me; I know he would,' Alice said anxiously, 'especially if it was you I'd run away with.'

'Then we'll go back to Britain – to Northumberland or Skye. You would be safe at Ramanish.' He raised her hand and pressed it to his lips. 'Have courage, my love. We'll find a way of being together soon.'

Alice's heart leapt. When she was with John she felt as brave as a lion and anything seemed possible. Before they could say more, they heard someone approaching and broke away, pretending to admire the roses.

It was Florentia. Alice knew she must be looking flushed and guilty.

'Alice, I thought I'd find you in the garden,' said the bride's mother. She gave John an assessing look as he bowed at her. 'I'm sorry to break into your horticultural conversation,' she said dryly, 'but your friend Mrs Ayton is in need of you.'

'Is anything wrong?' Alice asked in sudden concern.

'I think it's all been a bit much for her. It would appear her baby has decided to come on my daughter's wedding day.'

'Goodness,' Alice gasped. 'I'll go to her at once.'

* * *

Emily's second child was born in the early hours of the following day; a boy who they named Walter. Alice had stayed up all night to help. Her friend was exhausted by the birth but it had been uncomplicated and both mother and baby had survived the ordeal. Sandy was overjoyed at his second son and Alexander was curious to see his new brother.

'I'd have liked a sweet wee girl,' Emily confessed to Alice, 'like your Lotty. But Sandy's happy.'

'Walter is as sweet as they come,' Alice replied, cradling the newborn in her arms before taking him out to show him to his father. She felt a special bond with this baby from the moment she saw him emerge from between Emily's legs. What a miracle birth was! She gave a silent prayer of thanks when the baby uttered its first querulous cry.

Tired but exultant, Alice walked up the street in the dawn, pausing to look at the salmon-pink sky over the mountains. The citadel of Kabul sat brooding on its rock. She thought of John lying on a *charpoy* in the open air – he had told her he only slept indoors during the coldest weeks of winter – and wished she could lie down beside him. *Have courage, my love. We'll find a way of being together soon.* Would that ever be possible or were they just indulging in fantasy?

Entering the house, Alice hoped that Vernon had gone back to Kabul after the wedding. Her heart plunged to see him sprawled in a chair by the unlit fire, two empty bottles of brandy rolling at his feet. She tiptoed past but he couldn't have been asleep as the movement roused him. He reached out and grabbed at her dress.

'Don't try to give me the slip,' he growled. 'Where have you been all this time?'

'You know where – delivering Emily's baby,' said Alice. 'She had another boy. He's called Walter.'

'Bloody Ayton! He'll be lording it over me with two sons.'

'Of course he won't.' Alice sighed. 'Can't you just be happy for them for once?'

'Why can't you produce a son and heir for me, eh?' Vernon snarled.

'I'm tired and I'm going to bed.'

His grip on her dress tightened. 'Don't ignore me. Why am I the only married officer whose wife can't give him a boy? The other wives are breeding like rabbits.'

Alice's patience snapped. 'You've got a son, remember?'

'A bastard half-breed son,' he replied. 'He's never going to be acceptable to my father to carry on the Buckley name.'

Alice felt nothing but utter contempt for this man. She snatched her dress from his grasp. Vernon got to his feet.

'You'll not stay away from my bed any longer. I forbid you to sleep in the girl's room. You have a duty to give me an heir.'

Alice turned on him. 'I will never lie with you again,' she cried. 'Never!'

He came after her but his lame leg was stiff from sitting and he could only hobble. Alice hurried quickly to Lotty's room and barred the door. Vernon hammered on it.

'You'll do as I say! Let me in. You're nothing but a whore! I've been hearing about you and bloody Sinclair – seeing him behind my back. I bet you open your legs easily enough for that Scotch savage!'

Lotty woke and started crying at the noise. Alice gathered her daughter in her arms and tried to cover her ears.

'It's all right, my darling,' Alice crooned. 'Daddy's playing a game.'

'D-don't like it,' Lotty sobbed.

'No, he'll stop soon.'

Alice lay down and cuddled Lotty into her hold, stroking her hair as Vernon continued to pound on the door and yell obscenities. Her heart raced in fright that he would break in and subject her to a beating – or, worse still, harm Lotty. Vernon had never laid a finger on the girl up till now but he sounded so angry that Alice did not trust him.

She closed her eyes and tried to calm her breathing. She thought she would vomit from fear.

'You'll not deny me,' Vernon raged. 'You're my wife and you'll do as I say.'

Eventually, he grew tired and stopped his shouting. She heard him limping off and then his bedroom door slamming. Alice's relief was mingled with humiliation. What had Gita and others of the household thought of the commotion? The gossip would soon be all around the cantonment servants. From there it would spread to the officers' wives. But perhaps it was already common knowledge that Vernon was a boor of a husband and that Alice denied him his rights in the marriage bed. Some in the British community would see her refusal to perform her wifely duties as the greater sin.

Alice cared nothing for wagging tongues about herself but she did not want John's name to be bandied around as the cause of the friction. He was ten times the man Vernon would ever be, and she would not have him blamed for her rotten marriage.

Chapter 31

Kabul, autumn 1841

It worried John to distraction that he had not set eyes on Alice for weeks. Soon after Sturt's wedding, John had gone to the south-west to relay intelligence; fighting had broken out around Kandahar and Nott's troops had gone out from the southern citadel and engaged in battle across the River Helmand. The Douranee chief who had led the rebellion had fled and the other chiefs had been forced to come to Kabul to swear loyalty to Shah Shuja or be sent into exile. John had been interpreter for the Pashto-speaking leaders, who had come reluctantly to the royal palace.

By September, an uneasy truce had settled on the land and MacNaughten was sending optimistic letters to Auckland that all was peace and tranquillity, even though he was privately worried about the state of Shah Shuja's health. The amir was prone to bouts of fever and melancholy and was beginning to parrot those chiefs around him who voiced their growing resentment at the British.

John had made it his business to know what they discussed behind the thick wooden doors of the Balla Hissar. In the past month, he had also travelled among the Ghilzais and been away in the Kohistan visiting his dead wife's family. It was there that he had picked up the most alarming news.

In early October, he went to confront MacNaughten. The envoy had been avoiding him, cancelling meetings. John slipped into the cantonment late one night and caught MacNaughten readying for bed.

'Sir, this can't wait,' John insisted.

Reluctantly, the envoy showed him into his study. Like all the rooms in the mission house, it was richly furnished with carpets and polished furniture. Its bookcases were lined with large tomes on oriental history and language. MacNaughten was a cultured and intelligent man who thought the best of people; John had to convince him that the British were not nearly as well loved as the envoy thought.

John went straight to the gravest news first.

'Dost Mohammed's son, the sirdar Akbar, is back on Afghan soil. He's in the Hindu Kush gathering support.'

'Nonsense.' MacNaughten laughed. 'Sirdar Akbar's in exile.'

'He's in Bamian,' said John bluntly.

'This is gossip from the bazaar, surely?'

'I've heard it directly from Khan Shereen Khan, the Kazilbashi chief. He is a good friend to the British and wished to warn us.'

MacNaughten looked dashed. 'Even if it's true, Akbar has no following. The country is united now in loyalty to Shah Shuja.'

'The country may be growing in unity,' said John, 'but it's a confederacy against the British that unifies them. Akbar is watching and waiting to see how other rebellions go before making his move.'

'Other rebellions?' scoffed MacNaughten. 'There are no other rebellions. General Nott has ensured that all revolt in the west has been put down.'

'Not so,' John insisted. 'There's talk of invasion from Herat with Persian backing. There's trouble breaking out in east Ghilzai and that is giving heart to rebels in the Kohistan. Tribes in both areas are angry that the money they were promised to keep the peace has not been forthcoming.'

'Money!' the envoy cried. 'Don't talk to me about money. I've spent a king's ransom on these people.'

'Not as much as we pledged.'

'Well, there isn't any more to dish out,' MacNaughten snapped. 'I've asked for more and so has Auckland. But our new Tory masters in London have told us we must make economies. Afghanistan is costing too much. Some of these stipends to chiefs will have to go and the royal household will have to tighten its belt too.' He sighed loudly. 'Yet another difficult conversation I will have to have with the amir.'

John was dismayed. 'You must at least keep your word to the Ghilzais,' he challenged, 'if you want to keep the passes open between here and India. They could make life here impossible for us if they cut our supply lines.'

'You exaggerate the problem, I'm sure. They are far richer since the British came than they were before – they won't want to bite the hand that feeds them.'

'But we're no longer feeding them, sir,' John pointed out in frustration. 'I have heard what they are planning – the Ghilzai chiefs. They are not going to sit around in Kabul any longer paying lip service to Shah Shuja. They're plotting to occupy the passes to Jalalabad and raid the camel trains coming up from India. If we won't pay them, they'll take what's owed to them in the way they know best – by force.'

MacNaughten rubbed a hand over his tired face. 'My God, I can't wait to be gone from this job.'

John felt a twinge of sympathy. The envoy was a good man and he had worked tirelessly for three years to try to make a success of the rash invasion and keep Shah Shuja happy.

'We all look for the day when we can leave here,' said John, 'but it won't happen without a bloodbath unless we take heed of the chiefs' grievances.'

MacNaughten looked at him with sad eyes. 'I hope you're wrong, Lieutenant. As for me and Lady MacNaughten, the ordeal is nearly over.'

'Sir?' John frowned.

'I'm to be the next Governor of Bombay – I've just heard.' He gave a snort. 'It's my reward for our "glorious restoration of the rightful Afghan king to the throne".'

John's insides felt leaden. No wonder MacNaughten did not want to hear his message of doom; the man was already picturing himself enjoying the lush surroundings of the governor's mansion by a turquoise Arabian Sea.

'Congratulations, sir,' John said, with a short bow. 'Who will take over from you?'

'Lieutenant Colonel Burnes, of course. He's been itching to take over my position since I got here. Perhaps he'll make a better job of understanding what these tribesmen want.'

Silently, John agreed. Burnes had more friends among the Afghans than anyone. He knew them intimately – some too intimately – and that was where

240

his weakness lay. John had heard the threats of revenge made behind Burnes's back; some would like to cut the throat of the *feringhi* soldier for his licentious behaviour with their Afghan women.

As John left the mission house with a heavy heart, he thought grimly of Vernon, who also courted danger by keeping his Afghan mistress in the city and fathering her child. Rumour had it that the Ghilzai girl was pregnant again. Her brother, Chief Abdullah, was threatening to put out Vernon's eyes for dishonouring his sister. But Vernon was no fool; he made sure he was well guarded when he stayed in the city. That's why John knew that Buckley was in Kabul that night, for there had been two *sepoys* on duty at his gateway earlier in the evening.

That was John's other reason for visiting the mission compound; he was worried about Alice. Vernon had abused him drunkenly in the bazaar one day.

'Keep your filthy Scotch hands off my wife, Sinclair,' he'd slurred. 'She's done with you. Never wants see you again, you hear? She's mine – always will be.'

John kept in the shadows as he walked to Alice's house. The place was in darkness. He knocked gently at the door.

'Alice,' he called softly. 'It's John. Let me in.'

There was no answer and yet he knew that she must be inside. He could smell wood smoke from the chimney.

'Alice, please answer. I'm worried about you.'

John wondered if he should slip around to the servants' quarters and ask to be let in the house. But he did not want to cause Alice trouble. He stood gripped with indecision. It could not be possible that Alice had had a change of heart about him. He knew from her kisses and passionate words that she loved him – had never stopped loving him all the time they had been apart. The thought thrilled and sustained him in the moments of danger when he rode alone among the barren mountain passes, picking up intelligence or wrapping himself in a blanket to sleep under the stars.

Yet he had not seen her for nearly two months. Had she had second thoughts or given up on the idea of them having a future together? He refused to believe it. It was far more likely that Vernon had bullied her into submission. He knew Alice was a brave woman who stood up to her husband but what if he had made threats to her life? John felt impotent rage at the thought. Perhaps she had decided that the only way to have a peaceful life was to do as Vernon said – at least for the time being. Was that why Alice would not answer his knocking?

If Colin had still been in the cantonment, John would have sent his friend round to see how Alice was. But the artillery officer had been posted to a fort in the Khoord-Kabul, the first of many passes on the way to Jalalabad.

He tried one last time. 'Alice,' he whispered, 'I know you are there. If ever you need me you must send word with Ravi. Wherever I am, I will come to you, my love.'

Turning away with a troubled heart, John made his way back to the city.

* * *

Alice stood rigid with distress, listening to John's footsteps fading into the night. How she had longed to open the door and let him in! His loving words were like balm to her battered body.

The attacks had begun the day after Dinah's wedding when she had locked Vernon out of Lotty's room. He had waited for her to emerge and then dragged her by the hair into his bedroom, shutting the door in the face of a wailing Lotty. Vernon had punched and bitten her till she had collapsed on the floor, yet the worst torture had been her daughter's screaming.

'Mummy, Mummy, Mummy!'

Finally Ayah Gita must have managed to pull the girl away and calm her, for Lotty's distraught weeping had subsided before Alice had fainted. She had been covered in bruises, including to her face. Alice could not go out. She sent round a note to Emily to say she had fever and would not risk being near baby Walter.

'Look what you made me do,' Vernon had accused, blanching at her swollen face. 'If you would just be a dutiful wife . . .'

Alice's cut lips made answering too painful.

'You know I don't want to discipline you,' he said, 'but I had no choice. Just the thought of you being with Sinclair maddened me.'

He left, shamefaced, and did not return for two days. Alice wondered if he was violent towards Raiza. She knew the girl's name now; she had made John tell her. And she knew that Raiza called the boy Ali. Gita had tended Alice's injuries, bathing and rubbing ointments on her bruises and cuts. The *ayah*'s gentleness had made Alice weep far more than the pain had.

She had swallowed her fear of Vernon and decided to defy him on his return. But he had struck back in a way she had not thought him capable of. Grabbing Lotty and lifting her onto his lap, he had said to the girl, 'Mama has been very naughty. What shall we do with her?'

'Put her down,' Alice had pleaded, seeing the alarm in her daughter's face.

'Not until you promise to behave,' said Vernon. 'Otherwise I will have to smack Lotty. Like this.'

Abruptly, he put the girl over his knee and whacked her bottom. Lotty howled in shock.

'Stop it now!' Alice had rushed to intervene, seizing Vernon's hand. 'I'll do what you want – just don't touch Lotty!'

After that, Alice had submitted to Vernon. On the few occasions that he chose to stay at home she would share his bed and let him have his way. She would close her eyes tight and imagine herself somewhere else. It was too distressing to think of John so Alice went far back in her mind to a place of safety: the lighthouse. She emptied her thoughts of everything but the lamp-room with its view over the restless sea and the jagged rocks to the far horizon where a pink dawn divided the silver sky from the water.

There was never anyone else in the lamp-room – to think of the Browns and their kindness at such a time was painful – just the hiss of the bright lamp and the dazzle of the lenses. In this way she endured Vernon's hateful presence.

When he was absent in Kabul, Alice was overcome with self-loathing for allowing him to dominate and humiliate her. What had become of spirited Alice Fairchild? She would never have let any man treat her so. But she wasn't that

242

Alice; she was a fearful mother who lived in dread of her daughter being harmed by this unpredictable monster who ruled their lives.

Lotty was confused by her father; fearing him and yet wishing to please him – wanting his love.

Alice had stayed indoors for two weeks, until any lingering bruising could be disguised by powder. She resumed her visits to Emily and the baby but this seemed to annoy Vernon. He resorted to slapping her for imagined slights, a question asked or a roll of the eyes. After his initial assault on his wife, he had taken care not to cause injury to her face again.

But she lived with the queasy dread that he would beat her senseless and then there would be no one to look after Lotty. She could not imagine how she had ever had feelings for this man or he for her. Yet she saw how he could still charm and flatter women; her friends had little inkling of what he was really like. They knew he was possessive but she had confided in no one about the sudden increase in violence against her. Alice felt too ashamed to admit she had made such a mistake in her second marriage and deep down felt guilty that she had provoked Vernon's anger by seeing John behind his back.

Alice refused to give up going to see Emily and the boys but her visits to the Sales' home diminished. Vernon had the irrational conviction that it was there that she had clandestine meetings with John. Once, Florentia and Dinah had come round to see her unannounced, which had set Alice into a panic in case Vernon returned while they were there. He would interpret their concern as criticism of him and Alice's disloyalty. She had been on edge the whole of the visit, insisting that she was well, but Lotty had clung to her skirts and refused to talk to the visitors.

They had left, baffled by Alice's behaviour but pressing her to visit when she could. From them she had learnt of Sir Robert's concern at the worsening situation among the Ghilzai tribes. The military were pushing for action against them in case they threatened the trading routes to and from India.

Soon after the night where John had come seeking her out, Alice heard from Vernon that 'Fighting Bob Sale' was preparing to march from Kabul with the 13th Infantry.

'Clearing the passes to Jalalabad of tiresome Ghilzais,' Vernon said. 'Good luck to them.'

Alice thought of Florentia and how worried she must be about her husband – and Dinah about her father. She would go round and give them encouragement. When she made ready to leave, Alice was overcome with panic and had to sit down. Gita brought her ginger tea, which calmed her, but her nerve failed. Alice took off her bonnet and cape with trembling hands and did not go out.

* * *

John knew that trouble was brewing in Kabul when he saw the merchants of the Char Chouk removing their valuables. It was late at night on the first of November. He had not been home long when his friend Khan Shereen Khan, the Kazilbashi chief, appeared at his gate in person.

'You must leave the city at once,' he urged. 'British officers are going to be attacked. Burnes is the main target but I cannot guarantee your safety either.'

John was alarmed that the chief had not sent his *chaprassy* with the message; he must believe the rumour to be true.

'Where did you hear this?' John asked.

'My brother was at a meeting at the house of Abdullah the Ghilzai,' said Khan Shereen Khan. 'There is anger that the chiefs are being kept in Kabul like hostages. They blame the British and want to take revenge for other grievances . . .'

John knew that his friend was referring to the dishonouring of their women. He thought how Vernon would be at risk too. A flicker of revenge shot through John at the thought of Vernon getting his comeuppance. But it was quickly quelled. If Vernon was attacked then his household might also be in danger and they would be blameless victims.

'The British must go into the Balla Hissar or the cantonment,' his friend urged. 'It is not safe to stay in the city.'

'Thank you, my brother,' said John, clasping him in gratitude. 'Will you shelter my servant and his family tonight while I warn Burnes?'

'Of course,' said the chief.

John went to rouse Rajban and his family, telling them to make at once for the Khan's house.

'I will stay with you,' Rajban insisted.

'No, you must look after your family first,' John ordered. 'I will join you once I've alerted the other officers.'

Approaching Burnes's house, John could hear carousing from the open balcony. Instead of the street being deserted at that late hour, there were a dozen or so figures standing in the shadows, talking in excited whispers.

John slipped into the garden and up the back steps. Burnes and a handful of other officers were still sitting around on cushions, drinking and smoking.

'Ah, Sinclair!' Burnes greeted him. 'Join us. We're celebrating my new appointment as envoy.'

'Still enjoying dressing up as a savage, Sinclair?' Vernon mocked. He was sprawled on a divan with his arm around a young serving girl.

John, holding onto his temper, ignored the jibe.

'I have it on very good intelligence that you are all in great danger this night,' John said. 'Especially you, sir.' He appealed to Burnes. 'There's a plot to kill you. There are men already gathering in the street below.'

'There are always plots in this city.' Burnes smiled. 'I thank you for your concern but I don't think I'm at risk. I have too many friends here – they will protect me.'

'They have sent word to warn you,' said John, 'and that is how they are trying to protect you.'

Burnes's younger brother, Charles, went to the balcony and peered out. Someone shouted below at the sight of him. He returned looking anxious.

'There do seem to be men out there.'

'And they mean to do you harm,' said John. 'You should leave at once for the cantonment, sir. Staying here puts your whole household in danger.' John looked

244

around the room. 'The same goes for you all.' He held Vernon's look. 'You must all make arrangements to move your families and servants until it is safer.'

'How charming,' drawled Vernon, 'that the savage Scotchman is so concerned for us.'

'You can choose to heed my warning or not,' said John, 'but those who depend on you do not have that choice.'

'And what happens to our wives and servants is entirely up to us,' Vernon replied. 'And none of your business.'

John turned from him in contempt and urged Burnes to act. 'At least go tonight into the cantonment, sir. The mission house is practically yours anyway. The MacNaughtens are packed and ready to leave. And the threats were not idle ones – they come from Abdullah the Ghilzai.'

Burnes looked troubled for the first time. The others fell silent, waiting for his advice.

He sighed. 'I can't do anything to address the problems of the chiefs until I am officially in post as envoy. To scurry off into the cantonment at the first hint of a plot against me will be taken as weakness.' He gave a fatalistic shrug. 'And I cannot believe that my Afghan friends would seek to harm me – they know once I'm envoy here that they will get what they want from the British.' He swung an arm around John. 'Thank you, Lieutenant, for your concern. But I shall not be going anywhere.'

In frustration, John said, 'At least send word to MacNaughten of the threats made. Ask for extra guards on your house.'

'I'm sure that won't be necessary,' said Burnes with bravado. 'Will you stay and have a drink with us?'

'No, thank you,' said John. As he left he added, 'If you have need of me, I shall be at Khan Shereen Khan's house.'

To his surprise, Vernon followed him out.

'Sinclair, is it true that we're in danger?' he asked, no longer mocking.

'Aye, that's why I came to warn you,' John said. 'At the very least you need to put extra guards on duty.'

Vernon gave him a brief nod. As John let himself out into the street again, he saw Vernon limping towards the stables.

Chapter 32

Alice was woken in the early hours by Vernon arriving from the city. He looked dishevelled and his manner was edgy. He ordered Gita's son Bali to pull off his riding boots. His clothes reeked of smoke.

'What's happened?' Alice asked.

'I need a wash,' Vernon snapped, ordered a hot bath and went into the drawing room where he poured himself a large brandy, knocking it back in one.

After bathing and changing into his smartest uniform, he said, 'I'm going to see Elphinstone. There's trouble in the city.'

'What sort of trouble?' Alice asked anxiously, her first thought being for John's safety.

Vernon gave her a stormy look and left without another word. As the cantonment stirred to life, Ravi reported on rumours that there were fires in the city and a mob had attacked the house of Lieutenant Colonel Burnes.

When Vernon didn't return, Alice bundled Lotty into her winter coat and went round to the Aytons. Emily greeted her distractedly.

'Sandy's not here – he's at the envoy's house.'

Lotty perked up at the sight of Alexander, and the boy set about helping her build a tower with bricks. Alice eagerly took baby Walter from his worried mother and kissed his plump cheek.

'Sandy's very alarmed,' said Emily, her fair face puckered in anxiety. 'He's urging MacNaughten to order Elphinstone to send troops into the city. Is Vernon there?'

'No, he came home a few hours ago. What's happening?' Alice asked. 'Vernon rushed off to see Elphinstone without telling me anything.'

'Well, at least he's safe,' said Emily.

'From what?' Alice said, her stomach knotting.

'They say there's been an attack on Burnes's house – that the Afghans are rioting. There's smoke over the city.'

Alice was aghast. 'Why would they attack Burnes?'

'Sandy says we British are not as popular as MacNaughten likes to think. John Sinclair has tried to warn him but all that MacNaughten can think of is leaving for Bombay.'

'Have you seen John?' Alice tensed.

'No, but Sandy has. He's really worried about the other officers in the city.'

'Is John in danger?' Alice demanded.

Emily avoided her look. 'Elphinstone will send troops to put down any trouble – Sandy's sure of it. There's nothing we women can do.'

'There must be something,' Alice said, turning away in frustration.

* * *

Rumours flew about all day long. Alice left Lotty with Emily and went out to see what was happening. She found Florentia and Dinah watching from the low ramparts of the flimsy cantonment walls. To Alice's alarm, the road between the city and the cantonment was seething with people making a din.

'Who are they all?' Alice asked.

'Who knows?' said Florentia. 'Tribesmen from the surrounding villages, I suppose.'

'They've been pouring out of the hills all morning,' said Dinah, her eyes wide.

'Why is no one *doing* anything?' Florentia railed.

'If only Papa had not already set off for Jalalabad,' Dinah fretted. 'He would have acted by now.'

'MacNaughten is a frightened little mouse,' her mother exclaimed. 'He won't do anything without the say-so of the amir. And Elphinstone's no better. He can't even make up his mind what clothes to put on in the morning.'

'Hush, Mother,' Dinah said, glancing around. 'You're too outspoken.'

Late in the day, a troop of infantry was sent out and marched on the city but the gates were closed and the scenes were chaotic. Alice could hear gunfire and see the heavy pall of smoke hanging over Kabul.

She went back to the Aytons to collect Lotty and found Sandy trying to calm Emily.

'They say Burnes and all his household have been butchered!' Emily cried. 'Other officers too. How has it been allowed to happen?'

'Order will soon be restored,' Sandy said.

'Which officers?' Alice asked in fright.

Sandy shrugged. 'It's still just rumours. Until we get messages through . . .'

'What about us?' Emily said, on the verge of tears. 'Are we in danger here?'

'Of course not,' Sandy insisted. But his drawn face belied his words and Alice saw that Emily was nearing hysteria. Alexander had stopped playing to watch the adults with fearful eyes.

'I'm sure it's just an isolated act,' Alice said, 'so let's not alarm the children.' She took Lotty by the hand. 'If Vernon has any news, I'll let you know.'

It was late in the evening before her husband barged through the door, livid with the day's events and the lack of reprisals from the British army on the rioting Afghans.

'They murder British officers in their beds and we sit and twiddle our thumbs,' he fulminated. 'We should be setting the bloody place on fire!'

'So it's true that Burnes has been murdered?' Alice gasped.

'Yes,' he growled. 'I saw the savages attacking—' Abruptly he stopped.

'You saw it happening?' Alice was stunned. 'You were *there*?'

Vernon reddened. 'There was nothing I could do to stop them – they were like wild animals. I was lucky to escape.'

'Who else was there?' she asked, feeling faint.

He gave a cruel smile. 'Your lover, Sinclair, was. But he wasn't staying to save his fellow Scotchman. Last saw him running away.'

'Like you did?' Alice challenged.

He barged past her and slammed out of the house. Alice was left shaking and more troubled than ever. What had John been doing at Burnes's house? Had he even been there at all? She hardly believed a word Vernon said anymore. Was John safe? And what about Raiza and baby Ali? Had Vernon just abandoned them? She went to bed, her mind so much in turmoil that she couldn't sleep.

* * *

The days that followed unfolded like a nightmare from which there was no waking up. Word soon spread that the British had left their envoy-in-waiting to his fate – along with other officers who included his brother, Charles Burnes – and had then hesitated to punish the murderers. Emboldened by the timidity of the foreigners, Afghans flocked to the city – the numbers swelled daily – and vented their anger at *feringhi* rule by setting houses on fire, looting shops and murdering anyone who had dealings with the British.

Futile attempts were made to send out troops from the cantonment to stamp their authority on the city but it was too little too late; the numbers against them were overwhelming and the city impregnable. The amir was beleaguered in the Balla Hissar, protected by his own troops and a handful of British officers, including John Sinclair.

Alice was only able to piece information together through reports from Sandy, rumours from the servants, angry remarks from Vernon and witnessing for herself the scenes of distant fires and explosions. At least she had heard John was still alive.

Rebellion raged like wildfire. Within days, the surrounding forts that had held supplies of grain and weapons for the cantonment had been taken by hostile tribesmen and the British garrison soldiers killed. Alice worried for Colin MacRae, whom she knew was holding out in a more distant fort, as grim news reached them of rebellions breaking out all over the country.

Snipers with deadly *jezails* picked on grass cutters as they tried to gather fodder for the animals. Gita lived in daily dread of her sons being targeted. Supplies of grain were stopped and carried off before they could reach the cantonment and villagers who sold to the British were intimidated and set upon.

'A cat could jump over the cantonment walls,' Vernon raged, 'and we sit here cowering like pathetic mice! Shelton should be allowed full rein to attack the city but Elphinstone can't make up his mind about anything.'

Rationing was introduced. Troops were put on constant watch along the walls and reduced to half-rations. Soon soldiers and servants began to fall sick from fatigue and malnourishment. It grieved Alice to see how quickly the cantonment children were becoming dispirited and listless. Under pressure from Vernon, she had given up teaching at the barrack school but now she felt determined to help in some way, so went to volunteer at the hospital. Vernon could hardly complain at that.

She was appalled by the overcrowding from injured soldiers and the scores of *sepoys* who were succumbing to pneumonia. But their great need kept her from dwelling on her own fears.

Alice's nerves were ragged from lack of sleep and constant worry about keeping Lotty and the other children safe. Emily refused to leave her house or let Alexander or the baby out of her sight. She began to take laudanum for her nerves.

Their days were punctuated by gunshots and their nights fuelled by fear that the cantonment would be overrun by angry rebels. The authorities seemed to be

248

paralysed by the speed and savagery of the backlash; no one appeared to have a plan as to how to save the British.

What would John do in their situation? Alice wondered, lying awake, exhausted but sleepless at the tension. What was happening in the Balla Hissar? Messengers had been sent out for news but never returned. She had no idea if he was safe and the uncertainty ate at her insides like a parasite.

***

In the cantonment, there was endless division between MacNaughten and the military men. MacNaughten tried once more to buy off certain chiefs and set them against each other. When this didn't work, he urged Elphinstone to strike at the city – or at least regain some of the surrounding forts from where enemy snipers were taking potshots at the British sentries guarding the cantonment walls. Despairing of any action on Elphinstone's part, MacNaughten dispatched increasingly desperate pleas for Sale to halt his march to Jalalabad, turn around and come to their aid.

Finally, nearly two weeks after Burnes's brutal murder, a force was sent out under Shelton to capture guns that were firing on them from the nearby Behmeru hills. Delays and counter-commands went on all day so that it was almost dark by the time the infantry and cavalry were ready to set out, Vernon amongst them.

Alice watched tensely with Florentia and Dinah from the walls. One of the horse-drawn artillery guns got stuck in the canal as they crossed towards the hills. The women peered in the gloom at the ensuing chaos. The infantry pressed ahead up the hill but, to the horror of the women, Afghan horsemen appeared above like a cloud of roaring bees and charged through them, firing and slaying as they went. Alice clamped a hand over her mouth to stop herself retching, thankful that the battle was too far off to see distinctly.

'Our men are fleeing!' Florentia cried in disbelief.

Panic had set in and British troops were running back down the slope in complete disarray. Officers on the cantonment walls shouted impotently at their comrades to turn and fight. When all seemed lost, the watchers could just make out in the dying light the cavalry regrouping on the plain. To the frenzied shouts of encouragement from the cantonment, the British cavalry made a counter-charge up the hill.

It was hard to see quite how it happened, as darkness fell, but by eight o'clock that evening, the Afghan force on the hill had been driven off and their guns either captured or spiked. The exhausted men were greeted with wild cheers of relief in the cantonment.

But Vernon was not exultant. 'They should have sent us after them – butcher them like they would us, given half the chance.'

All night, he swigged back the last of his brandy and fulminated as they watched the torchlight flickering on the hillside. 'Look at the savages – coming back to bury their dead, and no one to stop them.'

The small victory meant that much needed supplies of grain and arms were brought back from the recaptured fort on the hill. There would be fresh bread for a few more days. Yet the cantonment hospital was now overflowing with wounded from the battle as well as the sick and feverish.

Alice continued to help with washing the bed-bound and changing their bandages, trying not to show how horrified she was by their injuries. There was at least fresh water from wells within the compound but winter was beginning to bite and the wards were cold. Gathering enough fuel to keep fires going for cooking and warmth was a daily deathly struggle. Alice stemmed her panic by keeping as busy as possible, only returning home to put Lotty to bed and tell her bedtime stories.

To her relief, Vernon stayed away from home as much as possible too, as he went on the lookout for drink in the houses of his fellow officers and danced attendance on Elphinstone.

There were nights when he didn't come home at all. Alice knew he could no longer be going to his other household in Kabul but she cared nothing for where he slept; she was just thankful it wasn't with her. She had gone back to sleeping next to Lotty.

'She's having nightmares,' Alice had told Vernon, 'and needs comforting. I don't want her waking you.'

To her surprise, Vernon had not objected. He was preoccupied and coldly distant; Alice realised that her husband was just as anxious as everyone else at their precarious position. So she lay awake, beyond exhaustion, and fretted about John. Would she ever set eyes on him again?

* * *

John slipped over the wall of the cantonment under cover of dark, dressed in the garb of an Afridi warrior, Azlan's dagger glinting in his belt. The young emaciated *sepoy* on guard had fallen asleep at his post. He spoke rapidly in Hindustani to the guards in the lane below, two of whom accompanied him to MacNaughten's house.

General Elphinstone was there, reclining on a sofa, hardly able to stand since falling from his horse at the beginning of the recent troubles. He looked in great pain. To John's dismay, Vernon was also there. He appeared to have the ear of the embattled general. An hour later, John was still trying to explain the gravity of the situation both in and beyond Kabul. The room was fuggy with pipe smoke yet chilly from the lack of a decent fire. They all sat hunched in their outdoor coats.

'But you must make a deal with Sirdar Akbar before he reaches Kabul,' John urged. He looked around at the anxious, exhausted faces in MacNaughten's study.

'Perhaps Sinclair is right and we should . . . ?' Elphinstone murmured. He looked haggard from the constant rheumatic pain he suffered.

'We can't be seen to be undermining Shah Shuja,' MacNaughten countered.

'This is a waste of time,' said Vernon. 'We should have nothing to do with this savage – and there's no proof he's anywhere near Kabul.'

'He's an Afghan prince and Dost Mohammed's favourite son,' John said with a withering look at his rival, 'and he's a matter of days away. Once he's here, he will assume power and Shah Shuja will have no say in it. Akbar is far more popular than the amir.'

'How come you know so much about him?' Vernon sneered.

'Because I met him at court when his father was in power – and again when I was negotiating for his father to hand himself over to the British,' said John. He would not rise to Vernon's baiting. The decisions that needed to be made were too vital to their people's survival. 'He's an educated and charming man. But he's also young and impetuous – prone to losing his temper if he doesn't get his way.' He turned to MacNaughten and pleaded, 'Don't make an enemy of Akbar – deal with him now and get him on our side.'

'On our side!' Vernon scoffed, 'He already is the enemy. You seem far too close to this rebel. Sometimes I wonder whose side you are on, Sinclair.'

John sprang to his feet. 'Don't you dare question my loyalty! I've risked my life to come here with this information. I didn't run away from the city on the night of Burnes's death like some—'

'That's enough,' MacNaughten snapped. 'Your quarrelling doesn't help us.'

John sat back down, glaring. Vernon gave him a smirk.

MacNaughten continued. 'Even if Akbar does come to Kabul, he won't threaten us British. We hold his father, Dost Mohammed, and his family in India. Akbar is not going to do anything to endanger them, surely?'

'Quite so,' said Vernon. 'And we shouldn't pander to such rabble-rousers.'

Sandy spoke up. 'Sinclair is not saying that we should.'

'It sounds like it to me,' Vernon retorted.

'I realise we are all at the end of our tethers,' said Elphinstone, shifting in discomfort. 'Shall we have a glass of sherry to calm things? I have some left.'

'Sherry?' MacNaughten sighed. 'Good God, man! We need to keep our heads clear and make some decisions.'

Elphinstone greeted this rebuff with a sympathetic smile but ordered sherry to be fetched from his quarters anyway.

John tried again to persuade his superiors. 'Shah Shuja wishes you to move back into the Balla Hissar for safety. Not just a small force but everyone in the cantonment – families and servants. He cannot guarantee the safety of the British out here on the plain.'

'Are you sure that's what the amir wants?' MacNaughten asked.

'Yes,' said John. 'It would send out a strong message to his rivals that they cannot have the run of the city. He says we must stick together – he fears Akbar's arrival.'

'Well, if we have his say-so . . .' MacNaughten's face brightened.

Brigadier Shelton spoke up. 'Impossible! We have over seven hundred sick and wounded. If we try to move such a number, we'll be attacked and cut to pieces.'

'Why should we rush to the aid of the old boy anyway,' said Vernon, 'when he has allowed us to be besieged for a month and reduced to starvation rations? You lot in the city have no idea of the hardships our families are enduring.'

John flinched at the barb. His mind had been plagued for weeks about Alice's well-being and how she was coping under the strain.

'And winter is coming on,' said Shelton. 'Our situation is only going to get worse. If we thought there was any chance of relief coming we might be able to stick it out.'

MacNaughten shook his head, his expression once again grim. 'Sale is besieged in Jalalabad. I've ordered General Nott to send troops from Kandahar but so far he's done nothing about it.'

'The Ghilzais are making trouble for him down there,' said John. 'We can't rely on help from that quarter. Going into the Balla Hissar is the only option. The lives of all our people are in danger by staying put.'

'I tend to agree with you on this, Lieutenant,' said MacNaughten. 'What do you say?' The envoy turned to Elphinstone.

The general was sitting with his eyes closed. John thought perhaps he had fallen asleep but then he opened his eyes and spoke.

'Our troops are dispirited. They are famished and not inclined to fight. We have thousands of people here in the cantonment who are looking to us for their survival. Going into the Balla Hissar can only be a temporary measure at best – and perhaps the time for that has already passed. As Shelton says, we risk being attacked by those chiefs who don't want us in the city. The amir has already lost control. And London and Calcutta won't send us any more reinforcements. So . . .'

There was a tense silence around the table.

'So?' MacNaughten prompted.

'We must leave Afghanistan. As soon as possible. You must negotiate our withdrawal – a safe withdrawal back to India.'

'But what about Shah Shuja?' MacNaughten demanded. 'We can't just abandon him. We encouraged him to take back the throne. A withdrawal now would be dishonourable in the eyes of the world.'

'The world has lost patience with us,' said Elphinstone. 'I don't want to risk any more British lives. You must try to get the best terms – honourable terms – and then we will leave.'

'I agree,' said Vernon. 'We've spilt too much good blood already in this godforsaken hole. Let's leave them to fight among themselves.'

'There speaks the man,' John said, 'who bullied Auckland into supporting Shah Shuja and pushed for the invasion.'

Vernon went red. 'That's before I learnt that no Afghans are to be trusted. Or the people who get too close to them.'

'Enough,' said Elphinstone, raising his hand. 'We have many good and honourable friends among the Afghans. These are the men we must appeal to now. A safe withdrawal for us; autonomy for them. We will take Shah Shuja back with us if he wishes.'

'Then it will all have been for nothing!' cried MacNaughten.

'And what about Akbar?' John reminded them. 'You need to deal with him now. Support Shah Shuja by moving a force into the Balla Hissar and then offer Akbar a position under Shah Shuja before he arrives. Whoever holds Kabul, holds onto power. Don't let Akbar sweep in and take over. At least if you move into the citadel we can hold out there until the spring and then have a phased withdrawal. It would be madness to attempt a retreat as we go into winter.'

'No one's talking about retreat,' Vernon said hotly. 'I demand you take back that slur.'

Arguments broke out around the table. MacNaughten was adamant that a hasty withdrawal would look weak and dishonourable. The generals refused a move to the Balla Hissar on the grounds of it being too risky. John gave up and left with no clear answers for the amir.

He hung about in the dark waiting for Sandy. His fellow Scot had kept quiet for most of the meeting, giving occasional encouragement for MacNaughten's point of view that sudden withdrawal would be disastrous.

'Thank you for speaking up for me, Ayton,' John said.

'Buckley really doesn't like you, does he?' Sandy said, lighting up the stub of a cheroot and offering it to John.

'I care nothing for Buckley's opinion,' said John with a grunt. He dragged on the cigarette and passed it back. 'How are the women coping?'

Sandy sighed. 'Emily is almost mad with worry. Nothing I can say pacifies her – and who can blame her. If it wasn't for Alice, I think my wife would have gone under. She's been a tower of strength to us all. And she helps out at the hospital too. I wish Emily would be like Alice and occupy herself more instead of . . . Oh God, where will this all end?'

John's chest tightened in pain to think of Alice. He would give anything to hold her in his arms and reassure her that all would be well. But he didn't believe it would be. Their superiors were at loggerheads and couldn't agree on anything. The repercussions of the rash invasion and ill-executed occupation were only going to get worse. Damn men like Buckley who had glorified in the escapade! To think of Alice shackled to the vile Vernon was more than he could bear.

He took a deep breath and put a hand on Sandy's shoulder. 'Give my regards to Mrs Ayton. And please tell Mrs Buckley that I was asking after her – and Lotty. I wish there was more I could do.'

'Aye,' said Sandy, 'don't we all?'

* * *

Later that night, wrapped in his blanket against the frost, John's anger at Vernon's destructive influence at the meeting reignited. He did not think his opinion of the cavalry officer could fall any lower. The night of Burnes's murder had been the final tipping point. John had been incensed by Vernon's cowardly actions. Buckley had fled the city, leaving his house to be ransacked and burnt – his guards and household massacred – and never returned. At daylight and despite the danger from a bloodthirsty mob, John had gone back with Rajban to see if they could help.

The sight of the carnage had made him want to vomit; it had conjured up anew the horror of seeing his own wife and child butchered in Baltistan – memories he had tried hard to bury. Vernon's *sepoys* had been beheaded and Raiza was lying in the mud disembowelled and with her throat cut. John had searched for baby Ali but there had been no sign of him; the infant had probably been burnt in his bed.

John tried to blot out the grisly images. If Vernon had been so callous as to turn his back on his mistress and child, then what hope was there that he would put Alice and Lotty's welfare first? The cavalryman was selfish to the core. He would save his own skin before that of anyone else, of that John had no doubt.

Chapter 33

Within a week, Akbar Khan was riding into Kabul to rapturous crowds. The British did nothing to stop him. Shah Shuja, isolated in the citadel, sunk further into his morose state, knowing there was little he could do to stop the tide of opinion turning against him. John could not help comparing the ecstatic welcome that the handsome young Akbar received to the resentful silence of Shah Shuja's return to the throne over two years ago.

Akbar was already receiving tribute from tribal chiefs as if he was their ruler. Soon the young Barukzai leader was harnessing the anger of the other tribes towards the foreign occupiers and at the same time courting the amir. John could not help but admire the young prince; he appeared able to charm both sides with promises and support. Akbar was conciliatory to the British officers cooped up in the Balla Hissar.

'I want to improve the situation in the cantonment,' he said with a look of concern. 'We will send in supplies.'

But John also picked up intelligence that Akbar was at the same time promising the opposite to the hardline chiefs. His Kazilbashi friend, Khan Shereen Khan, warned John.

'Akbar is saying that the quickest way to get rid of the *feringhis* is to starve them out. Don't trust him.'

Yet when John tried to get word to MacNaughten, he was prevented from leaving the citadel. Akbar flattered the officers and said he enjoyed their company but even going into the lower part of the city was now impossible. They were prisoners in all but name.

As December wore on and the first snow appeared on the hilltops, John knew they were running out of options. Akbar told Shah Shuja with glee that a brigade of *feringhis* marching from Kandahar to relieve the cantonment had been beaten back by bad weather. The day came when John was summoned to the river to be interpreter for Akbar and the chiefs at a meeting with the British.

John put on his officer's uniform and rode out. He managed a quick exchange with Sandy. The garrison was down to its last supplies and could hold out no longer; they had to make terms with the chiefs. John realised that none of Akbar's promises to provide food and fuel had been kept – either that or the provisions had been intercepted by others.

The British agreed that they would withdraw from Afghanistan as soon as the spring came. But the exchanges were short-tempered.

'We must have food and fodder,' MacNaughten insisted. 'Our flocks of sheep have been stolen from under the walls of the cantonment. Our people are being starved out.'

'You will have all that you need once you hand over your guns and give up the forts that you still occupy,' Akbar countered.

There was much dissension among the British. Elphinstone was inclined to be conciliatory but Shelton said it was madness to give up their weapons.

'We want to get out of here alive,' he muttered.

'We have to give them something,' Elphinstone said.

But even the mild-natured general drew the line at the demand for the women and children to stay behind as guarantee that Dost Mohammed and his family would be safely returned from India.

'Certainly not!'

'Then we want a high-ranking officer,' said Akbar. 'Shelton will do.'

Shelton refused. In the end, MacNaughten offered his own nephew, Lieutenant John Connolly, as a hostage.

'Fine,' Akbar consented, 'and I shall keep the officers that already live in the Balla Hissar.'

John caught Sandy's look of dismay. John gave a fatalistic shrug; he was already Akbar's prisoner. They retreated back to Kabul with the chiefs firing their *jezails* in the air, excited about the capitulation of the British. John felt bleak about his situation but at least a treaty was being drawn up that would be signed by leaders of all the major tribes. There should be temporary relief for the cantonment and, come the spring, a safe passage out of the country – as long as Akbar could keep control of the other chiefs.

But soon John was picking up rumours of British treachery and double-dealing; the *feringhis* were trying to drive a wedge between the Barukzai, Ghilzai and Kazilbashi. He did not believe it but even Khan Shereen Khan was wary.

'Akbar wants to meet alone with MacNaughten and do his own deal,' the Kazilbashi chief told John. 'He is promising to let Shah Shuja stay on as king if he is allowed to be chief minister – and the British pay him four hundred thousand rupees a year.'

'Is it a trap?' John asked in alarm.

His friend shrugged. 'I would not meet with Akbar unless I was well-armed – and certainly not alone.'

John put himself forward as interpreter for the meeting. It was a raw December day – two days before Christmas – when they rode out to meet the envoy and a handful of officers. John was uneasy from the start. Although the meeting was to be private, a large excitable crowd had gathered at the riverside where blankets had been spread on snow-sprinkled hummocks for the negotiating men. The tribesmen were heavily armed and seemed to know all about the meeting.

'We cannot speak while these men threaten us,' MacNaughten complained.

Akbar grew agitated. He began to set about the crowd with a whip. John saw the sudden frenzy in his eyes and knew they were about to lose control of the situation.

'Mount your horse, sir,' John ordered, 'and get back to the garrison at once!'

The envoy tried to calm the situation. 'Let us be reasonable. We have come here to speak with the Sirdar.'

'Ayton!' John appealed to Sandy. 'Get the envoy away now – I think he's been betrayed. This has been planned.'

As the officers scrambled to retrieve the horses, the crowds pressed in around them. John mounted and fired his pistol above the mob to draw their attention away from MacNaughten. But, as the others turned to ride away, Akbar grabbed at the envoy and pulled him to the ground.

'How dare you turn your back on me!' cried the Sirdar. 'Treachery! You wanted me killed, didn't you?'

256

MacNaughten lay sprawled on the ground. 'Of course not—'

John wheeled around to go to his aid. Akbar, furious, drew out a silver pistol. He aimed it at his adversary.

'No!' John bellowed.

'For God's sake!' MacNaughten pleaded.

Akbar fired point blank at the envoy's chest. In seconds, Afghan fighters were pressing around the mortally wounded MacNaughten and drawing out their long knives. John watched, stunned, as they plunged their blades into the prone figure and hacked him to death. John kicked his horse forward and drew his dagger, slashing about him while exhorting the other officers to retreat. Maybe it was the sight of Azlan's Afridi knife, but the attackers fell back in momentary confusion.

Then other Afghans were surrounding him, grabbing his bridle and forcing him back towards the city. Only later did John realise that they were Kazilbashis sent by their chief to keep an eye on him and save him from harm.

By that time, the blood lust had spread to the city and MacNaughten's dismembered body had been strung up in the Char Chouk as a grisly trophy. In the Great Bazaar, people stood in horrified awe at the sight but no troops came to avenge the murder. It showed more than anything that the mighty British were just men of straw.

John had no idea what had happened to Sandy and his fellow officers. He was locked up in the citadel with the other hostages – for their safety, Akbar insisted – and he could do nothing to help his comrades. Akbar now appeared full of remorse at the shooting in cold blood of MacNaughten.

'I only wished to talk to him,' he insisted. 'You must believe me.'

But the deed was done. John could only imagine the consternation and upset that the envoy's death must be causing in the cantonment. Their main negotiator – and the only man who seemed to show a degree of leadership in the garrison – was dead. What now would become of Alice and those he cared for? Frustration and dread clawed inside John at the thought of what lay ahead.

* * *

On Christmas Day, Alice insisted that the Aytons came round and spent the day with them. It was only two days after MacNaughten's horrific murder and everyone in the cantonment was still stunned. There had been bitter rowing between MacNaughten's staff and the military over the lack of action to save the envoy. No troops had been sent out to help, nor retribution taken against the city. It was thanks only to the intervention of two Afghan chiefs that Sandy and a couple of other British officers had been rescued and returned to the cantonment alive.

Captain Trevor had not been so fortunate; the crowd had cut him to pieces too. He left a widow and six children. Florentia had asked Alice to go with her to break the terrible news to both Mrs Trevor and Lady MacNaughten. Alice's heart still twisted at the memory of their howls of grief and the crying of the children.

'We've precious little to eat ourselves,' Vernon complained, 'without inviting others.'

257

'Our friends will bring what they have,' said Alice. 'Emily's in a terrible state. Sandy was very nearly killed too. The least we can do is share a meal with them – and the boys will be company for Lotty.'

The Aytons were grateful for the diversion but the conversation was tense around the meagre dinner of roast pigeon and kale. Gita's son Adeep had managed to barter for some sweetmeats at the cantonment gates, so the children had treats. Vernon made a big show of presenting Lotty with a doll's house that he'd had made in the bazaar, filled with miniature figures and furnishings. He was still adept at being prodigal with her money, Alice thought, but she did not resent it being spent on the children. Alexander and Lotty played happily with it all afternoon and Alice's heart was gladdened by the sight.

With the children distracted and a listless baby Walter asleep on his mother's lap, the adults talked in hushed voices about the future.

'Major Pottinger is taking over as envoy,' said Sandy.

'I thought he was still badly wounded from battle in the Kohistan?' said Alice.

Sandy sighed. 'He is, but he's our most experienced political officer and he's dragging himself out of his sick bed to help.'

'It'll all be over soon,' said Vernon, knocking back cheap spirit that he'd procured from the bazaar. 'Pottinger will just have to sign a treaty that guarantees our safe passage out of this barbarous place.'

'Do you mean we'll have to march down to India in winter?' Emily asked in alarm. 'What about the children?'

'It won't be till the spring,' Sandy reassured her.

Alice kept her doubts to herself. She saw no signs that Akbar and his chiefs had kept their promises to allow supplies into the cantonment. The traders and troops were harassed every day in their attempt to bring in food and fodder. But Emily spoke her fears aloud.

'How can we trust this Akbar,' said Emily, 'when he killed poor MacNaughten in cold blood?'

Walter woke up, snuffling with cold and fretful, and the question went unanswered.

* * *

At the end of the year, bitter winds brought snow to the valley bottom. It lay a foot deep in the cantonment streets. The last of the fruit trees in the compound's gardens were cut down for fuel. After that, there would be nothing to burn on the fires. The temperature plummeted at night-time to below freezing. *Sepoy* guards were regularly fainting with the cold and the numbers dying of pneumonia were rising. The women waited anxiously for daily news of Pottinger's negotiations with Akbar and the chiefs.

The major's initial suggestion that they fight their way into the Balla Hissar and hold it until the spring was roundly rejected by the military leaders. So he attempted to secure terms that would allow the British to stay on in the cantonment until the spring, with guarantees that they would be provided with food, fuel and medicines. The Afghans agreed, as long as they were paid the dues they were owed and the British gave up their guns. At first, Pottinger refused.

Florentia came to visit Alice, stamping the snow from her boots at the door, pink with indignation.

'The Afghans are demanding that we women and children be kept in Kabul as hostages until Dost Mohammed and his family are returned from India. Is there no end to their insolence?'

'You mean they will only allow our men to march and we will be left behind?' Alice asked in alarm.

'That's what they're saying,' Florentia said. 'But I've told the major in no uncertain terms that we won't be sacrificed. I said, "You men can do as you please but no one is going to order us women about."'

Alice laughed despite her fear. 'Oh, Lady Sale, I wish I'd been there to hear you!'

Florentia smiled. 'I suppose I was a bit high-handed on our behalf.'

'Good for you,' Alice encouraged.

Florentia said, 'I'm utterly ashamed of the way our commanders have been so spineless. The Afghan warriors put us to shame. We wouldn't be in this situation if our leaders had acted with more vigour months ago. I don't care for my own safety but I worry for you young women with your children and trying to keep them healthy and alive. And now Dinah . . .'

'What about Dinah?' Alice asked in concern. 'Is she ill?'

Florentia gave a bleak smile. 'No, she's with child. It should be good news but it just makes me worry all the more.'

Alice squeezed the older woman's hand. 'It is good news. Captain Sturt must be thrilled.'

Florentia sighed. 'Dinah hasn't told him yet. He's so fretful about her safety she doesn't want to burden him with more to worry over.'

'Poor Sturt,' Alice sympathised. 'He's such a nice man.'

Alice realised that this was the real reason for Florentia's visit; she needed to share her concern for her daughter with someone.

'We'll take good care of Dinah,' Alice assured her friend, 'and your future grandchild.'

* * *

In place of the women, several of the officers were offered up as hostages. To Emily's huge relief, Sandy was not one of them. Alice knew that John was already a prisoner and, according to Sandy, a valuable one because of his language skills. It was some small comfort to think that John would be kept alive as long as he was of use to Akbar and his insurgents.

On New Year's Day, 1842, a treaty between the British and the Afghans was ratified and signed by eighteen chiefs from all the major tribes.

'At least this means that the chiefs will keep their tribesmen in check,' Sandy said in hope, 'and we should see supplies being allowed into the cantonment.'

But the brief flare of optimism in the British compound was soon extinguished. Supplies were not forthcoming. The Afghans demanded that British guns should be handed over first. In desperation, Pottinger ordered the surrender of two guns each day, trying to delay their disarmament. Behind the scenes he was urging the military leaders to make a dash for Jalalabad, leaving behind all the baggage and moving out swiftly before the passes closed with snow. Staying would be a certain death sentence.

It was Vernon who told Alice of this desperate measure.

'I agree with Pottinger on this one,' her husband said. 'We could move much more quickly without being bogged down with all the baggage animals and camp-followers.'

Alice looked at him in dismay. 'But what would happen to them? There are thousands of servants and tradesmen – and all their families.'

'Precisely my point,' said Vernon. 'There are three times as many of them as us soldiers. They will only hold us back and make us more vulnerable to attack.'

Alice felt distaste at his callousness. 'We can't just leave them – they'll die of starvation or be slaughtered with no one to protect them.'

'We don't know that. The chances are they will get employment in the city, then come the spring they can make their own way back south.' Vernon frowned. 'Don't give me that look, woman. I'm sorry for these wretches but if it's a choice between saving them or my comrades and family then I wouldn't hesitate to leave them behind.'

Alice turned away, sickened by his cold-heartedness.

In the end, Elphinstone vetoed a quick dash to Jalalabad. There were too many lives at stake and he worried about the growing numbers of sick who would be unable to march. A bargain was made to allow the ill and wounded to be escorted to the Balla Hissar, along with two army doctors, Berwick and Campbell, who would stay behind to tend them.

The situation deteriorated rapidly. In a few short days, guns, ammunition, money, supply forts and hostages had been surrendered to the Afghans, yet nothing had been gained in return. The British were now under pressure to withdraw. If they went at once then Akbar would provide an escort to keep them safe from attack in the high passes towards Jalalabad. The hostages would be kept in Kabul until word had come through that the British garrison under Sale were retreating back to India.

Suddenly orders were flying around to prepare for quitting the cantonment.

'Everyone must travel as lightly as possible and leave their possessions behind,' Sandy came round to tell them, breathless with the news.

'Thank God,' said Vernon, 'and about time too.'

'As soon as Akbar sends an escort, we march,' said Sandy.

Alice couldn't tell if his feverish expression was from anxiety or relief.

'Let me know if Emily needs any help,' she said.

'Your first concern is packing up our house,' Vernon insisted. 'Ayton can look after his own household, I'm sure.'

Sandy gave a brief nod and left.

It soon transpired that Vernon intended to take all his personal furniture – his camp bed, tent, portable bath, armchair and dining table – along with his whole wardrobe of clothes, brushes and lotions.

Alice lost her patience. 'None of this matters. You can't expect Ravi and the boys to carry so much. All we need is our winter clothing and as much food as we can find.'

260

Vernon would not be swayed. 'If we have to travel with all our hangers-on then they might as well be useful. I've paid a lot for my possessions and you'll be the first to thank me when we have a tent over our heads when it drops below freezing.'

'It's more important that we take things to keep Lotty warm,' said Alice. 'What use is all this furniture? We've been told to travel light.'

Vernon hesitated and then called for Ravi. 'Make sure Charlotte's doll's house is dismantled and packed up too. It cost me a small fortune from those thieves in the bazaar.'

In frustration, Alice gave up and went to help in the hospital where they were preparing the transfer of the sick and wounded to Kabul.

* * *

Rumours of treachery swept through the cantonment like a fever. Akbar did not intend to send armed horsemen to escort them to safety; he planned to seize all the women and kill every last British soldier save one, who would be allowed to reach Jalalabad and tell the tale of massacre. Pottinger and his political officers tried to allay people's fears to no avail.

'These tales are wild nonsense,' Sandy insisted. 'We must wait for the escort. Zemaun has promised it will come and I trust him more than any of the chiefs. He says we mustn't move without an Afghan guard. It would be sheer folly to leave the cantonment without it. Akbar needs time to bargain with the chiefs who hold the mountain passes.'

'I don't trust any of them – least of all Akbar,' said Vernon, echoing the opinions of the military commanders. 'We need to go now and rely on our own forces to protect us on the march.'

Elphinstone and Shelton prevailed over the injured and beleaguered political officer, Pottinger. On the night of the fifth of January, Sturt and his fellow engineers were given the order to cut through the low ramparts of the cantonment to allow the flow of troops to leave with the six large guns the army had been permitted to keep.

'We march at moonrise,' announced Vernon, 'so there's no point in going to bed.' He sat huddled in his coat beside the empty grate and swigged at a bottle of local spirit.

Alice stayed dressed in her clothes and went to lie next to Lotty. She curled up under the chilly bed clothes and held her daughter close.

'Are we going on the big picnic tomorrow?' Lotty asked.

'Yes, my sweet,' Alice said, kissing her forehead. She stroked the girl's cheek, marvelling at its softness. It comforted Alice and yet made her acutely anxious. How much more vulnerable would her daughter be once they left the flimsy safety of the cantonment?

'Will Gita come too?'

'She will.'

'And Ravi and Adeep and Bali?'

Alice nodded.

'And Zander?'

261

'Yes, of course, Alexander.'

'And Daddy?'

Alice swallowed. 'And Daddy.'

'Then it will be the best picnic ever,' said Lotty, smiling.

She put her thumb in her mouth and sucked in contentment. Alice held her and watched her drift off to sleep, praying fervently that Lotty would be spared and reach the safety of Jalalabad alive.

Chapter 34

They should have left by moonlight but it was eight in the morning before the first baggage animals filed through the gap in the wall. Alice and the other families watched tensely as the snorting, whinnying beasts and their attendants ploughed through the glistening snow; it was ponderous progress.

'The poor drivers have hardly got a coat between them,' Alice fretted, stamping her feet for warmth in the bright, frosty, crystal-clear air.

The first baggage train was followed by the advance guard of cavalry and horse artillery pulling 6-pounder guns, along with the sappers and miners of the mountain-train. Then it was time for the envoy's entourage and the officers' families to leave before the main body of the army got underway.

'It's the safest part of the column,' Sandy assured a petrified Emily. 'The vanguard with Vernon is in front and Shelton and his infantry are protecting you from behind.'

He gave an encouraging smile as he helped his wife into a pannier strapped to a camel and handed her the baby. Alexander wanted to ride a horse like Alice and Lotty but was persuaded to climb into the second pannier. Emily continued to scan the hilltops for signs of tribesmen ready to attack. Alice thought how their labouring army of pack animals and scarlet-jacketed troops would be visible from miles away. She could see Emily getting worked up.

'Why aren't we moving?'

'We'll be through the Khoord-Kabul Pass and at Tezeen by tonight,' Alice said. 'Then after that we'll be out of the snow and descending to Jalalabad – you'll like it there. It'll be so much warmer and Alexander will be able to play outside again.'

'And me!' Lotty piped up, grinning at her mother. Alice kissed her cold cheek, amazed by how much her daughter understood.

They took all morning to jostle through the broken walls. Alice tried to distract Lotty from Emily's panicky comments by pointing out where Vernon was riding up ahead.

'And over there is Kabul, the big city where the king lives and where your nice thick coat came from.'

'Is that where the kind man lives?' asked Lotty.

'Kind man?'

'Lieutenant John.'

Alice's heart squeezed. How she wished that John was with them!

'Yes, Lieutenant John lives there too.'

'Can we say goodbye to him?'

Alice's eyes watered. 'I'm afraid not. Lieutenant John has to stay in the city.'

'I'll wave,' said Lotty. 'He might be looking.'

Alice kissed the top of her daughter's head. It was all she could do to hold her tears in check as Lotty raised a hand and waved at the distant citadel.

* * *

263

By early afternoon, half the cantonment force was still waiting to depart. There was a log jam at the Kabul River. Word came back that the gun wagons that were to be used as a bridge for the infantry had not been sent out early enough.

'Elphinstone was too busy eating breakfast to give the order,' said a frustrated Sturt as he rode by. 'Tore a strip off Shelton for interrupting him.'

Alice thought it was so unlike Sturt to criticise his superiors that she knew he must be under great strain. But the long delays began to cause unrest. Camp-followers who had been told to fall in at the rear started to pour out of their encampments and mill around the stranded soldiers, terrified of being left behind. Soon there was chaos by the river as thousands tried to cross at once. There was uproar. Camels bellowed in distress, men shouted in anger, children wailed and troops attempted to keep order.

Alice watched in agitation. About her, officers chivvied on the families. Emily was whimpering in fear and a frightened Lotty began to cry. Alice tried to soothe them both but resisted the order to cross.

'I'm not going without my servants,' Alice declared. She wheeled around and grabbed at the pony that was carrying Gita and the boys. She couldn't see Ravi and his mules, which were heavily burdened with Vernon's possessions, but knew that he would do his best to follow.

In a cacophony of noise that could probably be heard from the city, they clattered across the makeshift bridges. Others plunged into the icy water, trying to keep up.

All afternoon the convoy lumbered on, the overladen baggage cattle struggling through fresh snow and hampering progress. Behind, Alice could see that hundreds of troops still waited on the ramparts to depart. The whole withdrawal was a disorganised disaster.

Perhaps it was the sight of such slow progress or the temptation of rich spoils laid out for all to see, but before they had gone a handful of miles, the air was suddenly filled with the yells of plundering tribesmen.

They came out of the surrounding hills and orchards, the thunder of their hooves muffled by snow, and swooped on the startled camel drivers and *sepoys*. The screams of their victims filled the air.

The cavalry protecting the envoy's entourage rallied around the women and forced their horses into a canter. Glancing back, Alice saw in horror the snow stained red with blood. She pulled her cloak over Lotty's head so that the girl would not witness the carnage.

The army lines broke up in confusion and the troops scattered towards the village of Begramee and the way to the Khoord-Kabul Pass. By the time nightfall descended, they had gone six short miles instead of the planned thirty. Vernon managed to find them as they pitched camp in the snow. They looked back in horrified awe at the flames leaping in the frosty dark like a lurid sunset over the abandoned cantonment.

'The barbarians are setting fire to our houses,' Vernon said in fury. 'There's no going back now.'

Alice felt sick at the destruction: the homes and the lovingly tended gardens that their Afghan friends had admired, the hospital and school, the bazaar and native camps. A once thriving community reduced to burning embers in hours.

'At least we're alive,' said Alice, eyes smarting at the thought of the men cut down in the snow and left to die. 'I thank God for that.'

* * *

The morning brought stunned disbelief. The rear guard had caught up with the main army during the early hours of the morning, bringing tales of pillage and arson as they fled the cantonment. But worse was revealed by the daylight. Groups of *sepoys* and camp-followers, who had huddled together for warmth in the dark, lay dead in the snow or crippled by frostbite.

Alice and a frantic Gita went in search of Ravi. They found him crying with pain, keeping watch over his mules. They bound his frozen feet and ankles with strips of horse blanket from Alice's horse but the man could hardly walk. Alice told him to jettison the furniture and ride one of the mules himself.

Before the bugle call or order to march could be given, the mass of humanity began to move off in the same disarray as the day before. Camp-followers surged around the troops at the front, in a panic not to be left. Lotty was crying with the cold and Alexander with hunger. Florentia poured sherry into a tumbler and handed it round for the children to drink.

'Warms them and it'll dull the hunger,' she said before the children were bundled into panniers and lifted onto ponies.

Then the horror began again. The baggage train was once more targeted by snipers in the surrounding hills and Alice watched in helpless distress as cattle were driven off and their handlers butchered. Drivers deserted rather than wait to be picked off by the deadly gunshot. Panic ensued. The rear guard attempted to cover the most vulnerable part of the column but discipline was breaking down and guns had to be spiked and abandoned. Some of the troops were so debilitated by frostbite that they could not fire their matchlocks and watched, helpless, while raiders swooped and plucked them from their frozen hands.

Alice gripped onto a frightened Lotty and tried to comfort her with trite words as they pressed on, guarded by Sandy and others of Pottinger's entourage. She didn't believe her babbling words but saying them aloud was the only way to keep her gut-wrenching fear at bay.

By afternoon they had only covered another four miles and were barely at the mouth of the Khoord-Kabul Pass. Surprisingly, Elphinstone gave the order to halt. At this rate, Alice worried, they would take at least a week to reach Jalalabad, not the planned three days. A tense Vernon appeared and handed round a flask of brandy. Alice hadn't known he still had any but took a swig for courage.

Sandy came with news. 'Zemaun has sent word that we should stop here until they can disperse the fanatical tribesmen in the Pass. It's not safe to go on.'

'It's not safe to stay here!' Vernon argued. 'We need to press on and leave all this rabble behind. By the way,' he said, turning to Alice, 'where are my things?'

'I told Ravi to discard them,' she said with a defiant look. 'They were slowing us up. We've still got the tent and blankets.'

'How dare you—'

Then a cry went up that cut off Vernon's tongue-lashing. A fast-moving phalanx of Afghan riders had been spotted from the direction of Kabul. No one knew if it was the promised guard or a hostile band. But it had the effect of dispersing the bands of raiders, who melted back into the hills. While the officers and families attempted to get campfires going, Pottinger sent Sandy to meet the messenger being dispatched from the Afghan troop. He returned in excitement. Alice pressed forward to hear what the envoy and military leaders had to say to Sandy's news.

'I've spoken with Lieutenant Sinclair!' Sandy said. 'He says Akbar is offering six hundred horsemen to see us safely through the pass. The Sirdar will go ahead in person to restrain the more hot-headed Ghilzais to let us retreat.'

'What welcome news!' said Alice, her heart thundering to think of John so close by.

Vernon was dismissive. 'Another trap. Why would we trust anything Akbar or his hangers-on say?'

'Sinclair wouldn't be involved in anything treacherous,' Sandy retorted. 'He believes that Akbar is genuine in wanting us to leave safely. He knows that is the only way his father, Dost Mohammed, and family will be returned unharmed to Afghanistan. But Akbar wants something he can bargain with when dealing with the Ghilzais.'

'Good God!' Vernon swore. 'He's taken everything already.'

Pottinger held up his hand impatiently. 'Let the man speak, Buckley.'

'Akbar wants four more hostages – prestigious ones that the chiefs will respect.' Sandy turned to Shelton. 'They want you to be one of them, sir.'

'Out of the question,' Shelton protested. 'I'd rather die than abandon my men. Akbar is just trying to decapitate our army.'

Sandy said, 'Sinclair told me that Zemaun has gone to great trouble to persuade Akbar to give us protection. We have to give the Sirdar something in return so he doesn't look weak.'

'Well, I'm not going to play his underhanded little games,' Shelton replied. 'If any of the commanders give themselves up we'll all perish. Discipline is already going to the dogs.'

'I agree,' said Vernon. 'If there are any hostages to be sacrificed it should be from the political ranks.'

Pottinger looked grey with fatigue. Alice knew he was still in pain from his previous injuries. He asked Elphinstone what he thought. The general was sitting in a camp chair; he appeared even more ill.

'I think we should trust Akbar but perhaps not give him so many hostages?'

Argument broke out as to who should be handed over. Pottinger put an end to the wrangling.

'Let the military commanders stay. I'm injured and already a liability to the column. I shall go.' He looked at Sandy. 'Ayton, will you come with me?'

Alice saw Sandy trying to hide his dismay. She knew he wanted above all else to keep Emily and the boys safe but his duty was to his superior officer. He only hesitated a moment.

'Of course, sir,' Sandy said with a nod.

Emily crumpled at the news. 'How can I manage without you?' she sobbed. 'Please don't leave me and the boys.'

'You will be well protected,' Sandy said, putting an arm about her. 'My going should make it safer for you all.'

'I'll never see you again!' she wailed.

'Please, my dearest, be brave for the boys.'

Alice stepped in. 'We'll all stick together and help each other.'

Florentia joined in. 'Come, come, Mrs Ayton; you don't want to alarm young Alexander now, do you? We women must stay strong and show the men we are equal to them in courage.'

The words of the formidable general's wife seemed to calm Emily. She nodded and wiped the tears from her cheeks. Sandy gave the women a grateful look. Within the hour, the political officers had ridden off into captivity.

'You wish it was you, don't you?' Vernon accused Alice. 'Riding off to be with Sinclair and his savage friends.'

'Don't be ridiculous,' Alice snapped and turned away quickly. She blushed to think how easily her hateful husband could read her thoughts.

That night, the officer families shared the last of the food – cold fowl and flat breads that Zemaun had sent over on their departure – and tried to keep the children warm under the frost-covered blankets. But Alice could hardly eat; she was choked with guilt at the moonlit sight of thousands of *sepoys* and servants – women and children among them – moaning in pain as they crowded together in the snow to stay alive. They had no food or fires. In a desperate attempt to keep warm, the Indian soldiers were burning their caps and pistol cases and pressing around the temporary heat of the ashes.

Alice felt a huge weight of foreboding. How would any of them survive another night, let alone several? They should have been through the pass by now and below the snowline where food supplies might be more readily available. Fear smothered her. She hugged Lotty tighter. The girl gave a fretful whimper in her sleep. At least Gita and the boys were inside under canvas – Alice had insisted on that – and Vernon had taken himself off in protest to camp with fellow cavalry officers.

* * *

The third morning of the march began as chaotically as the others. This time, hundreds more ill-equipped soldiers and camp-followers had perished in the freezing night. Alice retched at the sight of stiff corpses half-buried in the snow.

'Are those people still sleeping?' Lotty asked.

'Yes,' Alice said, hating herself for lying. But how could she possibly begin to explain such horror to a girl not yet three years old? She turned Lotty away from the sight. There was a hurried departure. Alice was aghast at the pitiful state of their ponies; they were half-frozen and whinnying for food. Alice scooped up handfuls of snow and fed it to her pony, throwing her arms around its neck for temporary warmth.

The rush to get to the front of the column by desperate and half-crazed men made the progress slow and disorderly. The soldiers could hardly keep in their lines or hear the commands being barked at them by frustrated officers.

Soon the column was pushing its way into the Khoord-Kabul Pass. The way narrowed and the black icy cliffs of the gorge pressed in around them. No sunlight penetrated or melted the frozen slopes. They had to keep crossing mountain streams, the animals slipping on the banks and threatening to tip their passengers into the gorge. Dinah Sturt's pony went lame. Alexander jumped at the chance to give up his pannier for the engineer's wife and ride behind Alice. Earlier, he had wanted to ride with the young chieftain, Osman, but his mother had forbidden it.

'Hold on tight,' Alice ordered.

Just when Alice thought they would get through the dark pass without incident, the attacks began. Snipers appeared from above, picking off troops and followers with their long-range *jezails*. Screams echoed around the black rock. Bullets seemed to come from the very boulders themselves. Animals thrashed around in fright, throwing off their riders and trampling infantry.

Terrified, Alice gripped onto a shrieking Lotty and tried to shield both her and Alexander while keeping her pony steady. Then scores of tribesmen came rushing down the slopes to harry the back of the column and carry off the spoils.

The British officers made frantic attempts to protect the column and rally a counter-attack but they were dealing with a ghostly army that was ambushing them at every overhanging rock and twist in the gorge. There was nothing to do but try to press on and escape the attack.

The women rode on through a hail of musket shot, their horses and camels stumbling. Florentia cried out. Alice turned to see her agonised face. Her friend had been shot and was clutching her arm.

'Ride on!' she shouted at Alice. 'I'm all right.'

Alice lost sight of Emily's camel in the mêlée as they all tried to flee.

A moment later, Alice felt the sting of a bullet graze her hand, followed by another. Her pony reared up, shot in the neck. Alice felt no pain as blood appeared on her hand, just fear at how close Lotty had come to being hit. Alice screamed for help. She lost her grip on the reins as pain pulsed through her wrist. She thought she would faint. She clamped her knees into the flanks of the agonised beast to stop herself falling.

A rider came up alongside and took hold of the reins. Osman.

'Thank God,' she gasped. Her head pounded.

She felt Alexander's grip around her waist lessen. The boy screamed for his mother. Alice half-turned to see a turbaned horseman snatching the boy and lifting him onto his horse at full canter.

'No! Leave him!'

Then her own horse was being dragged forward and she almost toppled from the saddle. Clutching at a hysterical Lotty, Alice righted herself. Only then did she see that it was not Osman who pulled her pony forward but a Ghilzai bandit.

Alice struck out at him with her wounded hand. Indescribable pain shot through her. The wounded pony bucked and lurched in a frenzy of fear too. Leaving go of the reins, the attacker seized Lotty by the hair and pulled her from

268

Alice's slack hold. Alice saw the terrified look on her daughter's face. Alice was too shocked to utter a sound. Her daughter's screaming filled the air. Then the girl was gone, swallowed up in the chaos of fighting and fleeing humanity.

Chapter 35

Khoord-Kabul Pass, East Afghanistan, January 1842

Alice hardly remembered how she got to Khoord-Kabul. Later, she was told that it was Osman who found her hysterical beside her dying pony and, lifting her to safety, rode with her into camp. The British officers and families were sheltering in a cluster of overcrowded tents pitched in the snow below a brooding, half-derelict fort rumoured to be recently occupied by Akbar.

An army doctor extracted a piece of shot from her wrist and bound it up as best he could. From him she learnt that other women and children had been abducted.

'Alexander!' Alice wailed, as she remembered what had happened. 'They took him from me. It was my fault.' She buried her face in her hands and wept uncontrollably. How could she face Emily?

Vernon found her and forced her to drink the dregs of his brandy.

'Lotty,' Alice moaned. 'We must find her. A Ghilzai took her.'

Vernon was tight-lipped.

Alice's agitation grew. 'I must go and look—'

'You're not going anywhere. I've got my men searching.'

But Alice would not be stilled. She went out into the raw dusk – it was snowing again and visibility was bad – and she called and called for her daughter.

Eventually, Vernon, with the help of Gita and Bali, pulled her back into the meagre shelter of a damp tent. 'Stop making such a spectacle of yourself,' Vernon hissed. 'You're not the only one suffering. I've lost scores of my men. It was carnage out there. So much for your precious Sinclair and his savage friends with their promises of protection.'

Alice flinched at his harsh words. 'Don't you care about *Lotty*?' she rebuked him.

'Of course I care! When I find the men who have taken her I'll blow their bloody brains out! I can't bear to think of their dirty hands on her. But they won't get away with it – no one treats a Buckley like that.'

Angrily, Vernon marched off to be with his men, leaving Alice weeping with despair and guilt. Gita sat quietly with her, pressing something into her hand. Alice saw it was Lotty's favourite rag doll. With a stab of loss, she clutched it to her face and breathed in her daughter's scent. It gave her a flash of comfort.

Alice lifted her head and looked at Gita properly for the first time. Bali squatted close beside his mother, his usually cheerful face pinched with cold and anxiety.

'Where is Adeep?' Alice asked.

Gita dropped her gaze and shook her head. 'I don't know. He stayed to help his father in the pass. Bali has looked for them but nothing . . .'

Alice reached out and pulled Gita and Bali into her hold. The bereft women clung onto each other in comfort and Bali quietly wept. After a few minutes, Alice composed herself and went in search of Emily and Walter. She found them crammed into a tiny tent with Lady MacNaughten and the widowed Mrs Trevor and her seven children.

'I'm so sorry about Alexander,' Alice said tearfully.

Emily was mute with shock. She clutched a grizzling Walter to her breast.

'Our children will be returned to us,' Alice said. 'The men will see to that.'

Emily looked at her with eyes swollen from crying. 'I should have let Alexander ride with Osman, shouldn't I?' Emily whispered. 'Then he'd still be here with me.'

* * *

Alice could hardly sleep for the pain in her wrist and the anguish of wondering what had become of her daughter. Her mind was in turmoil at the thought of Lotty in the hands of a cruel enemy. She would be so frightened and wonder why her mother had let such a thing happen. Would some Afghan mother be put in charge of her? Perhaps she had been taken as a hostage for bartering. Alice would pay *anything* to get her beloved daughter back. Kidnap for ransom was the best she could hope for. Anything worse was unthinkable. Fear consumed her at the thought that Lotty might already be dead.

The moans of the other injured punctuated the night. People cried out for water. Brave Florentia had been wounded in the arm but she and her daughter were tending Johnny Sturt, who had been shot in the stomach. In the dim glow of a flickering lamp, the doctor had dressed his wounds but he lay feverish and shivering with cold.

Dinah was kissing her husband's brow and whispering into his ear. Alice swallowed down tears at her tenderness and the loving look that Johnny returned. Was she telling him about their forthcoming baby? From the deathly sheen on his skin, Alice doubted he was going to live long enough to see his child. She looked away, sore at heart for the devoted couple. Was it only five short months ago that they were embarking on married life together? Alice thought of that golden summer day when she and John had stolen kisses in the Sales' garden. It was the last time they had been intimate. If only she could get a message to John, she felt sure that he would do all he could to find Lotty and bring her safely back to Alice's empty arms. The thought gave her a flicker of strength.

Alice got up and went to help the officers who were tramping down to the stream to fetch water for the parched and delirious wounded.

* * *

Early the next morning, on the ninth of January, Johnny Sturt died of his wounds. They buried him under stones, sang psalms in the bitter air and prayed for his soul.

Dinah's distress shocked Alice out of her own worry over Lotty. She went to comfort her friend.

'You must stay strong for your baby,' Alice whispered. 'Do it for Johnny. The best way to honour him is to live and give birth to his child.'

As the sun rose, they waited for the bugle call to rally the column into marching, but it did not come. The snow was littered with the fresh corpses of those who had failed to find shelter and died in the night. Animals – those which had not already been stolen – had frozen in large numbers too. There had been no fodder to give them since leaving the cantonment three days ago. Alice was now without her pony and most of the camels had perished in the pass too.

Alice existed in a state of numbness, yet she thought she would never be able to rid her mind of the appalling sights in the snow. She looked around at her companions, the worn-out women and haggard officers. At least a dozen soldiers' wives had been abducted the previous day and half a dozen of their children were missing. How could they endure any more heartache? Would it not be better for them all to lie down in the snow and pray for a swift death?

Suddenly there was a flurry of excitement as a messenger rode in. He was swathed in a blanket but wore a British army jacket underneath.

'He's got a child sitting in the saddle with him!' someone shouted.

Alice and the other mothers picked up their skirts and staggered through the snow in their haste to see.

'It's Lieutenant Sinclair!' Florentia cried.

Alice felt her knees buckle. If Dinah hadn't caught her she would have collapsed in the snow in shock. John looked gaunt and unshaven as he threw off his blanket and dismounted but her heart filled with joy to see him. She pressed forward. Could he possibly have brought Lotty with him?

Another mother shrieked in relief as John lifted down a small boy into her arms. It was the son of Captain Boyd. Alice felt sick with disappointment. John caught sight of her and for an instant held her look. His eyes were full of compassion and her battered spirits lifted a fraction. But he was immediately ushered into Elphinstone's tent without a chance of talking to her.

* * *

'The Sirdar has been persuaded to take the British women and children under his protection,' John told them. 'If you agree, they are to be conveyed to the fort today. He has promised to keep them safe and return them when our garrison leaves Jalalabad.'

'Promise?' Vernon was scathing. 'You expect us to believe a word that barbarian says?'

'I believe he will keep them alive,' John replied. 'Surely that's what you want, Buckley?'

'Of course it is,' Vernon snapped. 'But I don't trust him an inch. He allowed that savagery yesterday.'

'He tried to stop it,' John insisted. 'It was Akbar who rescued the Boyd boy – along with an infantryman's wife and a private from the 44th.'

'Well, he didn't save my child from being carried off by some savage!' Vernon cried.

John felt winded. 'Lotty was taken? My God! I'm sorry, Buckley.'

'I don't need your sympathy—'

'Gentlemen,' intervened Elphinstone, 'we are all anxious about our families. Let us not argue amongst ourselves. We should consider what the Sirdar is offering.'

Vernon was adamant. 'We shouldn't let our women fall into the hands of these people without British men to protect them.'

272

'Akbar has agreed to take some of the most wounded officers,' said John. 'Osman said that Sturt was shot in the stomach. He can be rescued.'

'Too late,' said Shelton. 'Sturt died a few hours ago.'

John was appalled. Poor Johnny Sturt was dead? The young engineer was one of the bravest and most dedicated soldiers he had known. What a loss he would be. How was his sweet young wife coping? And Alice, she must be going out of her mind with worry over Lotty.

'What use will a handful of badly wounded officers be to our womenfolk?' Vernon asked. 'We must insist that their husbands go with them. Only we can make sure that no harm comes to them.'

John gave him a look of disdain. He knew how little Vernon cared for Alice. The cavalry officer was only interested in saving his own skin.

'I don't think Akbar will agree to that,' said John.

'Then we should tell him no,' Vernon said, with a challenging look.

John was sickened by the man's callous attitude; he was prepared to use the women as bargaining chips in a bid for his own survival.

'If you reject the offer,' John said impatiently, 'you are condemning women and children to death.'

Shelton said, 'I agree with Sinclair. We should hand over the families. They are an extra burden and worry on the march.'

'Sir,' Vernon appealed to Elphinstone, 'you cannot allow the women and children to go without their husbands. It would be dishonourable – and our wives wouldn't want it.'

John saw the general waver with indecision. Elphinstone looked as if he had aged another ten years in the short time since he had last seen him.

'I think Buckley's right,' said Shelton. 'Loath as I am to lose any more officers, we are just talking about half a dozen men plus some wounded. We have to think of the women's honour.'

'Very well,' Elphinstone said. 'Sinclair, go back to the Sirdar and say that we insist on the husbands accompanying the families. Let's hope to God he agrees.'

* * *

Later that day, Vernon sought out Alice.

'Thanks to me,' he told her, 'the British families are to be removed to the safety of the fort under the protection of their husbands.'

'All of us?' Alice gasped. 'To Akbar's fort?'

'Just temporarily,' he said. 'We'll be moved down to Jalalabad once it's safe.'

Alice put her hands to her face and swallowed down a sob of relief. 'Oh, thank the Lord!'

'Thank *me*, woman,' Vernon boasted. 'They wanted to abduct all the wives but I insisted that the husbands go into captivity too. At least that way, we can keep a protective eye over you.'

'And we can plead for the return of our children,' Alice said with a surge of hope. 'Lotty and Alexander.'

'We shall *demand* their return,' Vernon replied.

'But what of the others?' Alice asked. 'Our servants?'

273

'You will just have to do without such luxuries for a while,' he said.

'I don't care about my comforts,' Alice retorted. 'I'm thinking only of their safety.'

'That is none of my concern.'

'Well, I'm going nowhere without Gita and Bali,' Alice declared.

* * *

Camels were sent to transport the families to the fort – eleven women, sixteen children and eight men, including two wounded officers – and half a dozen servants. Alice got her way; Gita and Bali were among the latter. Alice listened to Florentia's indignation at Frances MacNaughten's overladen camel. Somehow, the murdered envoy's widow had managed to salvage basket-loads of possessions: clothes, furnishings, bedding and even her pet cat, Nabob.

'And a chestful of jewels!' Florentia muttered.

'Well, that might come in useful,' Alice murmured, thinking how Frances's treasure could be bartered for their missing children. Alice felt an agonising stab at the thought of her lost daughter. The pain was a hundred times worse than the throbbing in her wrist.

As they climbed higher, a flurry of snow obliterated the view below. By the time it had cleared, the army column was once more on the move. Alice prayed for their safety and survival.

They reached a circle of round Afghan tents – made of thick dark wool – and were taken inside for refreshment. Alice nearly fainted with relief to sit out of the cold and sip sweet black tea and eat dried apricots. She encouraged an unresponsive Emily to drink too.

'Let me take Walter for a few minutes while you rest,' Alice suggested.

Emily shook her head, clutching her baby tighter. He whimpered. Alice touched his forehead; it was cold and clammy. Dear God, don't let her lose Walter too! Alice unwound the heavy Afghan blanket that someone had put around her shoulders.

'Lie down then,' Alice said, gently pushing Emily onto a mattress. She tucked the extra blanket around the mother and child and left them to sleep.

As the light left the sky, Alice went outside, hoping to find John. The thought of seeing him and talking to him again had got her through the day. But she soon discovered that he had been taken with Akbar to negotiate in Pashto with the warring chiefs along the route.

'Thick as thieves, Sinclair and Akbar,' Vernon muttered. 'The Scotchman will make sure he survives whatever happens to us.'

Alice could not bear his snide remark. 'I heard it was Sinclair who persuaded Akbar to save us women, so we should be glad he has the ear of the Sirdar.'

She retreated into the tent before he could answer.

That night, the Afghans gave up their tents to the women and slept out in the open wrapped in their blankets. The next day, Vernon insisted that they should be housed in the fort and given hot food. Alice soon wished that they had stayed in the tents. The cell-like rooms in the crumbling fort were dark and dirty, and the food they were served was a thin soup of mutton bones and greasy rice. Yet she knew it was a feast compared to the starvation rations that the army on the move would be having.

* * *

The captives spent another day in the fort, wondering what was to become of them. The following morning, they were roused by the arrival of horsemen. Alice's heart raced to think it might be John returning. But they soon learnt that it was Sultan Jan, a cousin of Akbar's, who had come to move them on. They were not told where they were going.

They set off, bumping along in camel panniers, the wounded officers suffering at the jarring and jolting on the icy, rocky paths. Vernon and the able-bodied men rode on horseback alongside the Afghan escort, weapons at the ready to defend the small entourage.

At first, Alice thought the strange hummocks in the snow must be rocks but then the full horror of what they were passing hit her. Under the fresh snow were piles of bodies – bloodied limbs and uniforms – among abandoned guns and dead pack animals. They were following the tracks of the retreating army. Two days ago, as the British families had sat idle but safe at the fort, there must have been slaughter on a horrific scale. Some of the faces would still be recognisable to those who had known them; others had been mutilated and picked at by carrion.

Alice leant out of her pannier and vomited. A strange silence descended on the group. There were no words to describe what they saw. Each of them knew that, but for the intervention of Akbar, it could have been them who lay dead and unburied on the cold mountainside.

That day and the next, they followed the grisly trail of the doomed army. Alice became numb to the nightmarish sights. Part of her was thankful that Lotty was not witnessing such carnage, yet the other part shuddered to think what might be happening to her. If these tribesmen so hated the *feringhis* that they could indulge in such bloodlust, what hope was there that they would spare her child? And what of John? Despite what Vernon said, John was at high risk of being seized and murdered by the enemy tribes; only Akbar could prevent it and, so far, the young Barukzai leader appeared to have little sway over these vengeful chiefs.

At a huddle of huts called Seh Baba, they left the track and followed a riverbed. That night it snowed and they took shelter in a grain store; all of them crammed into one room where a local woman cooked them chapattis. The following morning, stiff and tired from a sleepless night, they carried on through the snow, climbing up steep mountain passes. The camels slid and bellowed in complaint. Wind whipped at the captives' faces and the sun, which bounced off the snow, burnt their skin. They muffled themselves in scarves and tried to shade their eyes from the glare of the snow. Some of the children cried at the pain in their eyes and screamed that they had gone blind. Their mothers tried to reassure them that it was only temporary and told them not to look at the snow.

'Better that they don't see,' said Florentia, with a tremble in her voice, 'it will only haunt them for life.'

As they descended the next slope they plunged into shadow again. Their eyes were adjusting when someone shouted, 'Army tents down below!'

275

Alice could not see them at first but as they grew closer she made out a couple of tents and a handful of men in scarlet tunics milling around them. Of the main force there was no sign. It was soon apparent that these troops – men of the 44th – were in the hands of Akbar's guards. Sultan Jan was greeted by his fellow Afghans.

Cries of relief went up as the soldiers set eyes on the families. To the astonishment of the arriving party, they found Elphinstone and Shelton inside one of the tents being attended to by Lieutenant Jamieson. Alice greeted the young officer enthusiastically, relieved to see him alive. Their initial euphoria at seeing their commanders soon turned to outrage and disbelief. They had been taken prisoner and Elphinstone was badly wounded in the leg.

'But where is everyone else?' Vernon asked.

Elphinstone was too overcome to speak.

'Butchered,' said Shelton, his face taut with fatigue. 'Or gone over to the enemy.'

'Surely not?' Florentia was indignant.

'Some of Shah Shuja's Afghan troops have deserted,' Shelton said, his voice drained. 'Some *sepoys* have fled. But most of our army has been wiped out.'

Alice covered her mouth to stifle a gasp of horror.

Elphinstone found his voice. 'Brigadier Anquetil has taken command of a remnant of a few score men. Yesterday, they fought their way out of Jugdaluk.' He nodded with his head. 'Down there in the pass.'

'We were tricked into going to consort with Akbar,' said Shelton angrily, 'only to be taken prisoner.'

'I wanted to stay with the men,' Elphinstone said, his expression riven with guilt.

'They might still get through to Jalalabad,' said Florentia. 'They will move more quickly without us as encumbrance.'

Elphinstone nodded and closed his eyes. Alice could hardly comprehend the scale of the losses. The cantonment had housed four thousand troops and three times as many servants and followers. Where were they all? Surely there must be more survivors? Perhaps in their exhaustion and in the chaos of retreat, the generals had underestimated the number who had escaped. Then Alice thought of the endless piles of bodies in the snow and her insides turned leaden.

* * *

At daybreak, they were roused and the punishing march continued. They drew a shred of comfort from the fact that they appeared to be heading in the direction of Jalalabad. If only they could reach the garrison town then there was a chance they would all live. Elphinstone was lifted onto a makeshift palanquin and carried by his faithful troops. Despite her injured hand, Alice made sure that she rode on a mule so that she could better see the landscape. Stuck in a camel pannier she would have less chance of spotting Lotty.

All day they scaled precipitous slopes and descended the far sides. Alice scoured the bleak hillsides for signs of life and whenever they came across an isolated dwelling her hopes would rise at the slim chance that she would miraculously see Lotty running down the path to greet her.

But the deeper they trudged into the mountains, the greater was the hostility towards the foreign captives. That night, the women were spat at and refused shelter at a fortified farm. Their escort persuaded the hostile locals to at least house the wounded officers in a cowshed.

Florentia galvanised the women. 'Let's not make trouble. We can sleep outside – it'll be healthier than wallowing in muck.'

So they bivouacked in the bitter wind, using saddles for pillows. Alice lay protectively against Emily and shielded Walter between them.

They were up and ready to march at daybreak and the punishing ordeal of ascents and descents began all over again. Alice's cheeks were peeling and red-raw from the blistering sun and icy winds, and her left arm throbbed continuously from the wound in her wrist. But the sight that greeted them on that day's journey made her ashamed of her self-pity.

As they rode past a steep defile in the snow-covered pass, they saw scores of skeletal figures crammed together taking shelter under the rocks. They seemed frozen into the landscape. But as the British column grew closer, some of the figures began to stir and stumble down the defile towards them. Alice could hardly comprehend what she was seeing; hundreds of camp-followers had somehow survived the slaughter of the past ten days.

They were half-naked and frostbitten – some had blackened limbs, and others were dressed in bloodied rags. There was a putrid stench in the air and a smell of burnt flesh, which Alice couldn't understand.

'Hindustanis,' gasped Florentia.

'My God, the poor bastards,' said Elphinstone.

Some struggled across the ice-compacted snow, trying to reach the camel train. Others, too weak to move, held out emaciated arms and begged for help. The escort and the officers drew their weapons to fend them off.

'Stop!' Alice cried out. 'Don't shoot them!'

'We can't stop,' Vernon hissed. 'They'll overwhelm us.' He raised his pistol in the air and shot above their heads.

The surge of desperate people halted a moment, frightened and confused. Then pressed forward again.

'Nobody is to fire on them!' Elphinstone ordered.

But the ones who reached them were so weak that they could not even grab hold of the passing animals. Alice watched in distress as shame overwhelmed her. Their beseeching voices cut her to the core yet the British were about to abandon them once more. There were so many of them. How could one decide whom to save?

Suddenly Gita started screaming. 'Adeep? Adeep!'

Alice saw a dark-haired boy, naked but for a ragged blanket, stumbling towards the mule that carried Gita and Bali.

'Wait!' Alice shouted. 'It's our servant!'

Gita scrambled off her mule and went to her son, sobbing with relief. Alice climbed down too and went to help. Adeep was shaking and wild-eyed in his mother's arms and hardly seemed to know her. Alice took off her woollen scarf and wrapped it around the boy. Vernon wheeled his horse around.

'Quickly, woman, get back in the saddle!'

He fended off other desperate men, while Lieutenant Jamieson helped the women lift Adeep onto Gita's mule.

'Bali can ride with me,' Alice said, encouraging the boy to scramble up in front of her.

Within minutes the column was moving away from the defile, leaving behind the mass of distraught and dying Indians to their fate.

* * *

The next day they crossed the Punjshir River in flood. Several of the Afghan escort lost their lives in the deep and rapidly flowing icy waters trying to help the convoy across.

'No great loss,' Vernon muttered.

Alice was sickened. 'How can you be so heartless? These men are trying to keep us alive,' she said tearfully.

'How do you know it wasn't one of them who kidnapped our daughter?' Vernon accused. 'I trust none of them.'

After that they descended below the snowline. To the relief of all, they saw a fertile valley stretching out below. Stopping to drink at a stream, Emily unexpectedly spoke.

'The Lughman Valley. I remember it from last year. We stopped at a pleasant wee town on the way to Jalalabad. Sandy bought me that blue shawl . . .' Emily's eyes welled with tears. 'Oh, Sandy! Do you think I'll ever see him or Alexander again?'

Alice put her arm around her friend. 'We must hope,' Alice encouraged. 'If I didn't think there was any chance of seeing Lotty again, I'd have curled up in the snow and given up. Look how Gita's son Adeep has survived against the odds.'

Emily's look changed; her dull eyes lit with a spark of defiance.

'Aye, he did, didn't he? It was a wee miracle.'

'So we must believe our loved ones will return to us too,' said Alice.

Heartened, they travelled on to the fortified town of Tighree. Optimism spread as the word went round that they were only twenty-five miles from Jalalabad and the sanctuary of Sir Robert Sale's garrison.

Chapter 36

Alice was astonished to learn it was Sunday. She had completely lost track of the days; all had merged into an unrelenting nightmare of terrible happenings. But here they were, resting in a modestly comfortable fort being kindly treated by their Afghan hosts and allowed to hold a religious service. Florentia organised it, commandeering a prayer book from one of the officers and delegating the reading of prayers. They muddled through a couple of hymns that they knew by heart and the children enjoyed joining in.

Dinah broke down sobbing at the singing but the other women – especially courageous Mrs Trevor – fussed over and comforted her. By the end, spirits had been lifted. Alice was grateful to the brave general's wife for somehow knowing what the sore at heart needed.

Despite being locked up, Vernon got hold of cheap liquor from a Hindu trader by bribing one of the guards. Alice suspected her husband had used a piece of her jewellery to do so, as he had insisted on carrying her most valuable jewels for safekeeping. He got drunk quickly, fell asleep and snored loudly, keeping many others awake.

Their night was also disturbed by gunfire beyond the fort's walls. In the early morning, they were roused by a guard and told to make ready to leave within the hour.

'Are we going to Jalalabad today?' Florentia asked. Alice knew she was longing to be reunited with her husband, Sir Robert, and thought that it would ease Dinah's grief to see her father again too.

But the Afghan just shrugged.

Outside it was hailing. Instead of heading down the valley, Sultan Jan ordered the party in the opposite direction. Shelton protested.

'You promised us we would be taken to Jalalabad. It was part of the agreement for us to leave your country.'

'It is not safe,' replied Akbar's cousin. 'Bad tribes attacked last night. My orders are to take you to Budeeabad.'

'Where in God's name is that?' Shelton demanded.

'You will see.' Sultan Jan turned away and kicked his horse into a trot.

Vernon hissed, 'Sir. Why don't we make a run for it now? There are too few of them to stop us all.'

Shelton gave him a withering look. 'And abandon our commander and the other injured?'

Vernon flushed. 'No, of course not. I meant we could fight off our guard and take everyone with us.'

'Within a whistle, their comrades would be pouring out of the hills armed to the teeth. We'll just have to bide our time, Buckley.'

Soon the party was once more scaling the steep sides of the valley and heading north-east back into the mountains. Alice felt a clash of emotions: dread that they were being subjected to another ordeal, yet hope that by doubling back she might have more chance of finding Lotty.

* * *

Budeeabad was an impregnable fort at the top of a remote valley, reached by the weary party at the end of a further two days' march. It appeared strangely deserted, save for a few servants and guards. Sultan Jan told them that it belonged to Akbar's father-in-law, Mohammed Shah, and that he was renovating it for his favourite wife. The fort was surrounded by ditches and high walls.

They settled in as best they could in a cluster of rooms around a central courtyard. Mohammed Shah made sure that each had a mattress and blanket against the cold and clean clothes were divided up from the salvaged baggage. Alice washed and changed her clothing for the first time in two weeks. She was sharing a room with Emily, Florentia, Dinah, and Mrs Trevor and her seven children. Alice was full of pity to discover that, like Dinah, Trevor's widow was also carrying a baby who would never know its father. How would the poor woman cope with an eighth child on her own? Vernon was the only man sharing their cramped quarters. Alice was thankful that he positioned himself across the doorway as their protector rather than lie next to her. There was little chance of him exercising his conjugal rights under such crowded conditions.

Two doors down was the room allocated to their handful of servants, where Gita nursed Adeep's frostbitten feet and kept busy showing the Afghans how to cook chapattis and make coffee from parching grains of rice and barley.

There was ongoing resentment between some of the women that Lady MacNaughten had managed to hang onto a large amount of her possessions, including fabrics, jewellery and her beloved cat Nabob, while others only had the clothes that they stood up in. Alice, distressed at the bickering, gave her locket to Lieutenant Jamieson, who had been put in charge of bartering for supplies. First she removed the precious lock of Lotty's hair and wrapped it carefully in a scrap of cloth.

'Please, exchange this for some material, thread and needles. Gita will help me make some new clothes – at least for the ladies and children.'

Within a week, Gita had made them comfortable clothes of drawstring trousers and long tunics with blankets fashioned into cloaks. Some of the men – Vernon included – were scandalised at their women wearing native outfits but Alice and her friends ignored the criticism.

'We'll go back into corsets,' announced Florentia, 'when we reach civilisation and you men bother to dress up for dinner again.'

The children were long-suffering but soon grew bored at their confinement. Alice and the other women tried to entertain them with games of hopscotch – the squares marked out in the snow – and Blind Man's Buff. The greatest problem though was not the monotony but the fear of not knowing what would become of them.

Alice lay awake at night listening to the sighs of other sleepless women and the babblings of those in fitful sleep. They rarely saw their leader, Elphinstone, who was confined to his bed and in constant pain. At least the children kept them occupied and stopped their minds from endlessly dwelling on the future.

One day, while a large number of them were sitting outside in the bright winter sunshine, Jamieson came to them in high spirits.

'We have a thousand rupees to spend on food and clothing. I won it from Sultan Jan in a wager,' said Jamieson with a wink. 'Two days ago he bet me that Dost Mohammed would be released by today.'

'What a stupid man,' Vernon scoffed. 'We wouldn't get to hear of it even if he was.'

'I rather think that was the point,' said Jamieson. 'He's letting us have funds without anyone losing face.'

'How kind of him,' Alice said, smiling at the captain.

'Kind?' Vernon snapped. 'You call being force-marched and incarcerated a kindness? What a ridiculous woman you are!'

Alice flushed at the public rebuke. 'I just meant in this situation—'

'How many times do I have to tell you that it doesn't do to let down your guard and trust these people?' Vernon said, interrupting her. 'That's what's got us into this mess – believing the empty words of the Afghans.'

'You overstep the mark, Major,' said Shelton.

'I meant no criticism of you, sir,' Vernon said quickly. 'But my wife has a weakness for these heathens and will forgive them anything.'

Florentia gave him a hard stare. 'Some say that it is you, Major Buckley, who has a weakness for the Afghan,' she said.

Vernon went puce at the waspish remark. 'Meaning?'

'I think you know exactly what I mean.'

Jamieson interjected. 'Best not to argue over the matter.'

Vernon got up and stomped away in the direction of the soldiers' quarters. Alice knew that he increasingly found refuge in playing cards and smoking hemp leaves with men who would not argue back. His fellow officers were finally tiring of his carping and dark moods.

* * *

Two days later, on a wet February afternoon, as Alice was agonising over whether she dared write a letter to John, a shout went up.

'Horsemen coming up the valley!'

Alice hurried outside where others were gathering in the sleety rain.

'Who are they?' demanded Shelton.

'Afghans,' shouted the officer on the lookout. There was anxious speculation as to what this meant. Others scrambled up the stone steps to see. Someone had a spy glass – battered but still usable – and this was passed around.

'There are Europeans with them, I'm sure of it,' Jamieson cried.

Alice's heart leapt. Was it Akbar paying a visit? If so, John would be with him.

Half an hour later, after feverish speculation, Sultan Jan arrived with three bedraggled prisoners. Major Pottinger led the way and was soon surrounded by fellow officers but it was the man behind him that caught Alice's attention.

'Lieutenant MacRae!' Alice gasped and rushed towards the Scottish officer. 'I thought you were—'

She swallowed down sudden tears. She felt ridiculously pleased to see him. He was like a cherished link to John.

He smiled at her, his face weather-beaten and scored with exhaustion.

'Mrs Buckley,' he said, 'what a sight to gladden the heart.'

Suddenly Emily cried out behind her. Alice spun round in alarm. Her friend was stumbling forward on shaky legs and throwing out her arms.

'Sandy? Sandy!'

Her husband, almost unrecognisable with his fair face swollen and peeling from sunburn, hurried towards the sound of her voice.

'My darling wife!' he rasped, as he flung his arms around her. 'Is it you?'

His eyes were so swollen they had closed up. Emily began babbling about Alexander and then broke down sobbing. Sandy held onto her, unable to speak. Alice's heart twisted to see the naked love on their tear-stained faces. How happy she was to see them reunited.

Later, after the new arrivals had pulled off their boots from swollen feet and been given food and drink, they told their news. Colin MacRae had escaped after his fort had been set alight and comrades slain; he had hidden out in a cave for two weeks, living off birds and eating snow. Pottinger and Sandy had been handed over by Akbar for safe-keeping; a lame Pottinger and a snow-blind Sandy were a liability as hostages. They suspected that Akbar was planning an assault on Jalalabad, impatient at Sale's refusal to leave the garrison town quickly enough.

'The Sirdar keeps Sinclair with him at all times,' Pottinger said.

Vernon exclaimed in disgust. 'Doing his dirty work, is he?'

Sandy spoke up for John. 'If it wasn't for Sinclair we'd have no idea what was going on. He goes to great lengths to find out news and at some personal risk. But he appears to have friends among the Afridi between Jalalabad and Peshawar who supply him with information.'

'What a surprise,' Vernon muttered.

'So what is the news from Jalalabad?' Shelton asked eagerly.

'Are we to be rescued soon?' Frances's querulous voice demanded.

The newcomers fell silent. Alice saw their tense looks.

'Tell us, for God's sake!' Vernon cried.

Pottinger spoke, his voice drained of emotion. 'Only one of us survived the march to Jalalabad – Dr Brydon, an assistant surgeon with the Bengal Army. Word has it the man arrived half-dead and with a head wound.'

There was disbelief around Elphinstone's room. 'Only one?' the ailing Elphinstone gasped. 'That's not possible! Surely others got through? Anquetil – others of the 44th – the gunners . . . ?'

Pottinger shook his head. 'No others of any rank whatsoever.'

Elphinstone let out an agonised groan.

'So there is no one coming to release us?' Frances said tearfully.

'Sir Robert is in no position to do so,' said Pottinger. 'Sinclair says he is fortifying the barracks as best he can so that the army keeps a foothold in Afghanistan and provides a springboard for any future rescue. At least, thanks to Sinclair, Sale knows that you all have survived.'

'But you think Akbar is planning to attack Sale?' Shelton said. 'Is there any indication that reinforcements are to be sent from India before such an attack?'

Pottinger sighed and shook his head.

Sandy tried to give them hope. 'We don't know that Akbar intends to take the garrison by force. He would rather the British left without a fight.'

'Of course he would,' Vernon said with disdain. 'But we shan't oblige him.'

Alice felt dread at the thought of John stuck in the middle of such an attack. 'But surely our best chance of survival is if the British agree to leave Jalalabad,' she said, 'and we are exchanged for Akbar's family in India?'

'We won't let that savage dictate terms to the British Army anymore,' Vernon said with venom. 'Even the government in London will want to avenge the deaths of our comrades when they hear what has happened. An eye for an eye – that's the only language these barbarians understand.'

Alice felt nauseated at the thought of further bloodshed. She clung to the hope that hostages could be exchanged – and their missing children returned – without any more killing. But deep down she knew it was a pipe dream.

Elphinstone mistook her harrowed look for fear. 'My dear, take heart. Once the Governor General hears that the women and children have survived they are bound to send troops to free us from captivity.'

A sob broke out in the smoke-filled room. 'Oh, Alexander!' Emily cried. 'Where is my bonny boy?'

* * *

For a short while, the prisoners were heartened by the arrival of letters from General Sale and other friends in Jalalabad, along with treats of tea and sugar, books to read and even chintz from which to make clothes and furnishings. Alice thought that life would be almost bearable if only she could hear some word of Lotty or Alexander's whereabouts.

Then abruptly, one early morning, the whole camp was roused and their rooms searched.

'You are to surrender all your weapons,' Sultan Jan told them curtly.

The officers protested.

'But the Sirdar promised we would not be disarmed,' Shelton said angrily, 'as long as our women need protection.'

'He has changed his mind,' the chief said brusquely.

'It's an outrage!' Vernon growled. 'An insult to the British. No Afghan would stand for such humiliation.'

Sultan Jan turned on him. 'Then you should have thought of that before you insulted the Sirdar.'

'What on earth do you mean?' Vernon demanded.

'Your letter to Sale was intercepted,' the Afghan replied. 'You told him not to trust Akbar or believe his promises that the women and children will be handed over safely. You encouraged him to use force against us.'

Vernon coloured. 'You've no right to read my letters,' he blustered.

The women looked on in dismay and the men cursed as the guards collected up the pistols and swords. Suddenly Dinah began wailing.

'Please don't take that!' she begged, running after a guard. He was carrying away a sword. 'It's my husband's. It's all I have left of his. Please let me keep it. *Please!*'

She grew hysterical and threw herself down on the ground, beating her fists in the dirt. Florentia rushed to her daughter. 'My dearest, don't upset yourself.'

Alice went after Sultan Jan. 'Please let her keep it. She will give birth to Captain Sturt's baby this summer but will have nothing to pass on to his child.'

'I can't,' said the chief. 'The Sirdar has ordered it – he no longer trusts you British.'

'Then tell the Sirdar to keep it for himself,' Alice pleaded. 'So I can tell Mrs Sturt that it is in safe hands and he'll return it when we leave Afghanistan.'

Sultan Jan hesitated and then nodded in agreement. Alice hurried to Dinah to reassure her of the sword's safekeeping.

'You don't believe him, do you?' Vernon was scathing. 'He'll most likely keep it for himself.'

Alice gave him a look of contempt. 'Your lack of trust has led to this. You shouldn't have written such a letter.'

'At least I'm trying to do something about getting us released,' Vernon snapped.

Colin spoke up. 'Looks like it's had quite the opposite effect, Buckley,' he said, and went to comfort a distraught Dinah.

* * *

The letters stopped and the prisoners turned anxious and despondent at the lack of news. Sultan Jan left and was replaced by a Ghilzai called Mirza who became their chief gaoler. He was meaner with their rations. One day he brought in some old newspapers sent from Akbar.

'That's a good sign, isn't it?' said Sandy. 'Perhaps the Sirdar is relenting and we'll be able to correspond again soon.'

'They're months out of date,' said Vernon scornfully. 'Ancient history. Completely useless.'

With little to do, Sandy and Colin began to leaf through them. After a few minutes, Colin looked up from his paper with a quizzical look.

'What is it?' Alice asked.

He beckoned her over. 'Take a look at this.' He pointed to a word and then another on the line below.

Alice was baffled. 'What am I looking for?'

Colin gave a watchful glance around the courtyard. The guards were squatting down and smoking, paying them no attention. Colin pointed again.

'Dots,' he said quietly, 'below the letters.' He drew out a stub of a pencil and tore off a piece of newspaper, writing down the dotted letters.

Alice stifled a gasp. 'Is it a code?'

Colin continued. After a few minutes he had deciphered a message. *Pollock gathering army in Peshawar*. The friends looked at each other. Alice felt her heart begin to race.

'Who is it from?' she whispered.

'Can only be John,' said Colin. 'He must have convinced Akbar that sending on old newspapers wouldn't cause any harm.'

Alice grinned. 'Oh, the clever, wonderful man!'

Colin smiled but put a finger to his lips. 'Let's see if there are any other messages.'

Eagerly they scoured the newspaper but found no further marks. Colin swapped journals with Sandy. There were some more dots in the second newspaper – no bigger than pinpricks – and Alice was amazed Colin had spotted them at all.

'Well?' Alice asked, hardly able to contain her impatience.

He looked up, a strange, intense look on his haggard face.

'What is it?' Alice felt her stomach clench. She braced herself for bad news.

Colin placed the scrap of paper in her hand. 'Read it.'

Alice peered at the message. *Fair child seen among Afridi, well treated. Will negotiate for return.*

Tears stung her eyes. 'Lotty,' she whispered. 'Do you think John's found Lotty?'

Colin covered her hand with his and gave it a squeeze of encouragement. 'Let's pray that he has.'

Alice felt a sob rise in her chest. She covered her mouth to stop a shriek of excitement escaping her lips.

* * *

Alice was helping Gita spread out washing on the roof to dry in the late February sun when she heard the thunder. She looked in puzzlement at the cloudless blue sky. A few moments later she heard it again, yet this time it sounded more like the rumble of heavy carriages. Alice shaded her eyes and peered into the valley in alarm. The snow was receding and the river looked swollen from melting ice but she could see no approaching force.

Suddenly the mud roof beneath their feet began to tremble. Alice saw a look of horror spread across Gita's face. The *ayah* grabbed at Alice's arm and pulled her towards the steps. People came to the doors of their rooms and the children stopped their play to cock their ears.

An explosion like a mine going off sounded in the distance.

'What's that?' one of the Trevor children called out. 'Is it the enemy?'

Suspended at the top of the steps, Alice saw a cloud of dust rise from the bottom of the valley. At that moment, the walls of the fort began to shake and buckle as if they shimmered in summer heat. Then Gita was pulling her down the steps.

Chapter 37

A scream tore through the tranquil air as people stumbled into the open.

Someone bellowed, 'It's an earthquake!'

'Get away from the walls!' Colin shouted.

People rushed about, grabbing their children and trying to keep their balance as the earth heaved and cracked and the walls rocked from side to side.

'Into the log room!' Jamieson ordered, pushing people towards the wooden cabin in the centre of the courtyard. 'It's furthest from the walls.'

The air filled with screams and terrified shouts as walls came crashing down and roofs caved in around the square. Thick dust enveloped them, making them choke and gasp for breath.

Emily screamed through the thick cloud. 'Where's Walter? I haven't got Walter!'

Alice stumbled towards the sound of her voice. 'Where did you leave him?'

'In his cot,' she wailed, grabbing at her. 'He's sleeping in his cot.'

'Stay where you are!' It was Colin's voice cutting through the dense cloud of dust. 'I'll find him.'

The women clung together. Alice thought the world was coming to an end. All she could think of was that Lotty was out there somewhere and she could do nothing to protect her. How widespread was the quake? She gave way to terrified tears.

Then abruptly the shaking stopped. The earth seemed to groan in pain and then it went quiet. A baby's crying filled the vacuum. Colin, caked in dust, stepped through the settling cloud like a moving statue, clutching a squalling Walter.

Sandy rushed to relieve him of his son. 'Thank you, MacRae!' he gasped, his eyes streaming from the gritty air.

Alice helped Emily step gingerly towards her husband. The couple clung to each other and their infant in palpable relief.

As the atmosphere cleared, Colin took charge, counting heads and assessing the damage. Miraculously, everyone appeared to have survived. Even the bed-bound Elphinstone had been hauled from his room by one of his devoted men. The general lay coughing and grey-faced on someone's coat.

The roof of the room Alice shared with her friends and the Trevor family had completely caved in and the hut had been obliterated. If Gita hadn't acted so quickly, Alice would have been crushed to death.

Frances started screaming. 'Where's Nabob? I can't find him!'

Colin tried to calm her. 'Cats have nine lives. He'll have leapt to safety.'

But she wouldn't be consoled. 'I can't bear any more of this terrible place! I must find him. Please help me, Lieutenant. Life won't be worth living without my Nabob!'

Colin set about organising the soldiers to clear the courtyard of debris.

'Best if we stay out in the open. There could be aftershocks. We'll bring out the bedding and rig up some awnings.'

Vernon, speechless until now, said, 'Well done, MacRae. Good to see the artillery doing some work for once.'

Colin grunted. 'You can lend a hand too, Major Buckley. Unless you don't want to get your pretty cavalryman's hands dirty.'

When Vernon didn't round on Colin for insubordination, Alice realised how much her husband was in shock.

As Colin predicted, there were further tremors throughout the day. The upper walls of the fortification had tumbled into the outer ditch, leaving a view down the valley. It was still blanketed in dust. The earthquake appeared to have been far-reaching; distant forts that they had passed a month ago were no longer on the skyline. A shocked Mirza and the other Afghan guards could tell them no more. They looked anxious and talked among themselves.

That night most of the prisoners slept outside but the single men gave up their room to Florentia and Dinah, who chose to stay indoors. Florentia was defiant. 'It's like a barrack-room out here. I'll not let an earth tremor turn me out of my bed.'

Alice was woken in the early hours by a squeal from Frances.

'Nabob! You're alive!'

The cat was sitting on top of its mistress, licking its paws as if it had merely returned from a night prowl. Alice lay back listening to Frances's gushing endearments and smiled. When everything else seemed so bleak, she was glad that the poor bewildered Lady MacNaughten could find comfort in the safe return of a missing cat.

* * *

The days that followed were punctuated by alarming earth tremors like a beast shuddering in pain. None were as bad as the original earthquake but they left everyone on edge. Mohammed Shah came to survey the damage to his fort and to make sure they had what they needed to survive. He sent men to help clear the worst of the rubble and supply extra blankets, for the nights were still intensely cold and the prisoners woke each morning with their bedding soaked in dew.

The old chief told them that there had been far worse devastation along the valley – whole forts had disappeared and scores of people had died. Mohammed Shah looked so harrowed that Alice wondered if the poor man had lost family close to him. The quake had ripped through the mountains as far as Jalalabad. It was rumoured the garrison town had collapsed.

Dinah was in a state of near panic at the thought that her father might be injured or dead. She could not bear to lose him as well as her husband. Florentia tried to pacify her but Alice could tell the older woman was equally as worried. As for Alice, her mind was filled with dark thoughts. Had Lotty been saved by the Afridi only to be devoured by the earthquake? What had happened to John? Was he alive? If the unthinkable had happened and he was not, who then would be able to rescue her daughter?

Even in the midst of his own concerns, Mohammed Shah was deeply worried about Elphinstone, seeing how frail and ill the commander had become.

'You will not survive in these conditions, my friend,' he said gravely. 'I will see about having you taken down the mountain where you can be properly tended to. I do not want it said that a sirdar of the British died while a guest in my home.'

Lady MacNaughten latched onto this. 'I must be taken too, Mr Shah,' she insisted. 'I've suffered too much. My husband was a sirdar too, don't you know? And murdered by your son-in-law. You must help me. I'm not like the other ladies – I don't have a husband to look after me like they do. It's intolerable for me.'

Seeing the look of annoyance on Florentia's face, Alice quickly intervened before the forthright woman pointed out to Frances that she was by no means the only woman there without a husband.

'I'm sure the chief will do all he can for you, Lady MacNaughten,' said Alice. 'Now, isn't it time for Nabob to be fed?'

Days of anxiety went by, the fear and not knowing what had become of Lotty and John eating away at Alice's spirit. No news came; not even precious out-of-date newspapers with their optimistic coded messages. It was the quiet, sensible Gita who kept her from losing all hope. She sat beside her and coaxed her into mending clothes, trying to keep her occupied. Her boys helped with the clearing up and building makeshift shelters. Alice saw that the way to ward off melancholia was to do mundane repetitive jobs and live each hour at a time. Small enjoyments kept her sane; the warmth of the midday sun on her limbs and the sound of Bali and Adeep teasing and laughing together.

* * *

March came and the aftershocks continued. The Afghan guards, who were kind to the children and often gave small treats to the captives, began to pass on news. There had been fighting to the south around Jalalabad and their chief, Mohammed Shah, was involved in it. Perhaps that was why the uncomplaining Elphinstone had not been moved: the situation was too unsafe. The news seeping back to the fort was alarming. Akbar, feigning a retreat, had ambushed some of Sale's men and then cut them to pieces.

'Well, at least it proves that my husband is still alive and taking the fight to the Afghans,' Florentia said bullishly.

But, by the middle of the month, the reports were turning Florentia's thin face ashen. Sale had been defeated and the garrison at Jalalabad had fallen into Akbar's hands. The prisoners began to argue about whether it could be true or not.

'Don't believe a word of it,' Vernon declared.

'But what about the coded message that General Pollock is on his way from Peshawar?' asked Emily. 'Won't he be able to save Jalalabad?'

'Maybe that's why Akbar has attacked now,' said Shelton, 'before reinforcements come.'

'We don't know that he has attacked,' Colin pointed out. 'It's all rumours and speculation. Best just to keep our counsel until things are clearer.'

But Vernon was spoiling for a fight. That night, fortified by local liquor, he baited their gaoler, Mirza.

'Why aren't you away fighting the good fight against the infidels, eh? Too scared? Rather hide behind the women's skirts, would you?'

Mirza didn't understand all his words but suspected he was being insulted. Colin and Sandy tried to pull Vernon away. Vernon struggled and continued to hurl abuse.

'Put us in a fair fight on the battlefield and the British will win every time! All you savages can do is hide behind rocks and shoot us in the back like cowards.'

'Shut up, Buckley!' Colin ordered.

'Don't speak to your superior officer like that,' Vernon growled. 'I'll have you whipped.'

There was a rapid exchange of words between Mirza and a guard who understood the gist of Vernon's words. Suddenly Mirza drew a long knife and lurched at Vernon. Colin instinctively put himself between the attacker and Vernon. The knife sliced at his arm. Colin doubled up with a grimace of pain.

Quickly, the other officers intervened, manhandling Vernon out of the way and going to Colin's aid. Mirza stood looking shocked. He gave a curt instruction to his guards to help the wounded officer and stormed off.

After that, Vernon was shunned by the other officers for putting all their lives at risk for no purpose. He sank into a morose state, drinking and smoking whatever he could lay his hands on.

A few days later, a trickle of Afghan fighters began to arrive at the fort – followers of Mohammed Shah. At first this seemed to confirm the captives' fears that the British had once again been defeated at Afghan hands. But word leaked out from the guards that Jalalabad had not been taken back by Akbar at all and that Sale's men were still in control.

Mirza came to them one day and asked them to sign a piece of paper.

'It's to say that you have been well-treated here,' he said. 'I have provided you with comforts and my men have looked after you, haven't they?'

It left the British in a fever of sudden speculation. Did it mean that Sale had scored a victory over Akbar or that Pollock had finally moved out of Peshawar and crossed the border? Did Mirza's conciliatory tone indicate that they would soon be handed over to Sale? Their hopes began to rise.

'Told you so,' Vernon said, his mood improving. 'I bet Akbar's on the run.'

* * *

A few days later, some more Afghans arrived and judging by their agitated state something momentous had happened. It was an outraged Mirza who broke the news, his previous solicitousness gone. Akbar had been badly wounded, shot by one of his own guards as he dismounted. The assailant had been instantly seized and burnt alive. Mirza was full of indignation at the attack.

'They say it was ordered by the *feringhi* in Peshawar – an assassination. If this is so, there will be revenge. If our Sirdar dies,' he said, drawing a finger across his throat in a cutting motion, 'you will all die too.'

Alice, like the others, remained in a state of acute distress as the days dragged on without further news of Akbar. Their fate hung in the balance. What on earth was happening to John too? Alice was frantic with worry. The spectre of Akbar's attacker being peremptorily murdered, all because of a whiff of suspicion that the British might have ordered the attack, left Alice in a torment as to what had happened to John.

Colin seemed to guess her fears for he tried to allay them. 'If Akbar lives, John will be safe,' he told her quietly. 'The Sirdar trusts him – and if the rumours that Sale is getting the better of him are true then Akbar will need John more than ever to broker a truce.'

But by the end of the month there was still no news about Akbar's fate.

'We would have heard if he was dead,' said Shelton. 'The fact that we remain alive means that he does too. That can only be good news.'

Each day brought a different rumour: a huge British force had been cut to pieces in the Khyber Pass coming to help Sale and thousands had been killed; Akbar was victorious or Akbar was dead; their horses were to be sent to replenish those Akbar had lost in battle. The most alarming rumour of all was that the captives were to be sent further away into Kafiristan – a shadowy country known to be fiercely hostile to any strangers and from which they would probably never return.

On Easter Sunday, they tried to rally each other's spirits with singing and prayers. Colin found some wild narcissi growing in the fort's ditch and presented one to each of the women. Alice clung to hers like a talisman; it was surely a sign of hope? But that night the sunset was lurid and a clap of thunder made everyone run into the centre of the courtyard, fearing another earthquake had struck. Instead, heavy rain drummed through the night.

April came with mounting tension. They heard how Afghan women – wives and relations of Mohammed Shah and his extended family – were being moved out of the valley to safety. Wounded Afghans, fresh from battle, were brought in daily. Colin managed to extract more news from the guards. There had been a great battle on the plain outside Jalalabad, which the British had won. There was consternation among the tribesmen that their vaunted leader, Mohammed Shah, had been killed.

The prisoners' elation was short-lived. The death – if true – of Akbar's father-in-law could only be bad for those held captive at his fort.

This, more than anything, worried Colin. Alice overheard a whispered exchange with Sandy.

'If their chief has died at British hands, they will take their revenge on us.'

'And we're utterly defenceless, thanks to Buckley's rash letter,' Sandy fumed.

Alice watched the guards for signs that they were plotting action. The Afghans gathered in groups and talked in hushed whispers, but was it more than usual? The next day the guard was increased; an extra thirteen men were placed around the fort. They spent the day polishing their weapons and making bullets. Mirza ordered the horses to be shod.

'Perhaps we are going to be moved after all?' said Jamieson.

'Or they're preparing the horses for themselves,' countered Shelton.

At midday, they were told the devastating news. One of the guards had heard they were all to be executed at sunset. He took no pleasure in telling them.

'You are in the hands of Allah,' he said, his eyes full of sadness as he watched the children jumping over stones in an improvised game.

Frances had hysterics. 'Why?' she bawled. 'What have we done to deserve this?'

No one could answer her. All they could do was to wait and pray that it wouldn't happen. Alice took herself off to a tumbledown corner and wrote a letter to John on a blank page torn out of a book sent up by Sale when Sultan Jan had been in charge. She thought of all the endearments she wanted to say to him and the list of regrets that tugged at her heart – their misunderstandings and missed opportunities. In the end, she wrote what was of most importance.

My dearest heart,

You know how deeply I love you – have always loved you from the moment I saw you. I was meant to save your life that night because we were meant to be together forever, you and I. If I am never to see you again then I will die knowing that you loved me too and that will bring me the greatest comfort in my final hours. Darling John, if you should survive this terrible ordeal and I do not, can I beg of you one final act of kindness? Will you do everything in your power to find and save my Lotty? It is the one pain that I cannot bear – to think of her in the world without her mother to love and protect her. Keep her safe. Is it too much to ask that you give her into the care of your people on Skye who have been so kind and loving to you? I would much rather that than my beloved child be sent to the Buckleys, who do not know her and have no interest in her.

May God protect you, my dearest love. I will continue to adore you until I take my last breath on this earth.

Adieu,

Your loving Alice.

Alice folded the letter, wrote John's name on it and tucked it into her tunic next to the Spanish coin that she always kept on her person. She felt a sense of calm descend on her as she watched the sun dip below the western peaks. Somewhere in that direction was John – and possibly Lotty. Her aching heart was soothed by the thought that John might find her daughter and that they would be of comfort to each other in the years to come. John would love her daughter far more than Vernon would ever be capable of doing.

A shout of alarm from Jamieson jolted her from her reverie.

'Afghan troops are coming! Lots of them.'

The prisoners gathered together in the courtyard, holding onto each other for courage. Some of the children were crying. Their parents both soothed and scolded them, their nerves at breaking point. Others began to pray out loud. Someone started whistling to keep up his spirits.

There was noise in the gateway, shouting and someone firing off a musket. A wail went up from the terrified British. Short moments later, tribesmen spilled into the square, brandishing guns. Mohammed Shah pushed through the excited throng and stood before them.

Alice's first thought was relief that the man was alive. Perhaps he could be appealed to for mercy? He advanced towards Shelton and held out his hand. The baffled general hesitated and then shook the offered hand. Mohammed Shah moved about shaking the hands of other officers: Sandy, Pottinger, Colin and Jamieson. Was this some final gesture of respect before he executed them all? Alice felt faint with the waiting.

Then the chief spread out his hands and invited them all to sit down. He squatted down on a blanket spread out for him by one of his henchmen and watched his captors struggle to sit comfortably on the ground.

'In the morning you shall be leaving Budeeabad,' he said, addressing his comments to Colin in Pashto.

'Leaving?' Colin queried.

The chief nodded. 'You are no longer safe here.'

'Where are we being taken to?' asked Colin.

'That is to be decided by the Sirdar.'

'So the Sirdar lives?'

'Luckily for you, yes.'

'What is he saying?' broke in Shelton.

Colin told him. Cries of relief went around. Mohammed Shah got to his feet in one swift movement.

'You must be ready to go at first light,' he said, 'and travel without your baggage. I am short of horses and cannot supply mules to carry your things. Your possessions will be kept safe and given to you later.'

He summoned one of his guards. Taking a sword from him, he walked over to Dinah and, with a touch to his heart with one hand, he handed her the sword with the other.

'The Sirdar wishes to return this to you.' With a slight nod at an astonished Dinah, he turned and left.

At the sight of it, the young woman clutched the sword to her breast and burst into tears.

With the chief gone, Colin explained about their personal belongings; there was indignation at having to leave their few valuables behind. The most distressed was the hapless Lady MacNaughten, who wept all night over the abandoning of her many beautiful shawls and chest of jewellery.

But Alice felt only a wave of gratitude that they were being spared and were finally leaving their crumbling mountain prison. That night she lay restless, impatient for the day ahead and yet anxious at not knowing where they were being taken next. For comfort, she touched the love letter to John that lay next to her heart, warmed by her skin. Her hopes soared to think she was being given another chance to live and find her daughter.

Chapter 38

A fort near Kabul, late July 1842

The wailing of Dinah's newborn baby filled the stifling room and competed with the feverish babbling of the ill in the hot night. The sound of a baby's cry cut at Alice's sore heart, reminding her of the happy days of Lotty's babyhood in Simla. Would that she had never left the safety of that paradise!

'Another female captive,' was Florentia's jaded response to the arrival of her granddaughter Julia two days before.

'She's beautiful,' Alice had said tearfully, having helped at the birth, 'and Julia is such a pretty name.'

Dinah had been grateful but exhaustion had soon overcome her and she was finding feeding her demanding baby difficult. They were all weakened by meagre rations and sickness, and dispirited by this captivity, which seemed without end. Despite rumours that General Pollock's army was in Jalalabad they seemed no nearer to being rescued.

'Can't you do anything to stop her crying?' Frances fretted. 'It's making my head pound, don't you know?'

Alice expected Florentia to jump to her daughter's defence but all she did was let out a pained sigh. Both Frances and Florentia were debilitated by the summer fever that was sweeping through the fort. Mrs Trevor and one of her children were also suffering – and a wet nurse had been found among the servants to feed the new Trevor infant also born since they had arrived at Noor Fort two months ago.

Colin was fighting with delirium in an adjoining room and Vernon too was ill. Alice thought her husband was liverish rather than feverish – his skin was a yellow hue – and his old leg wound was once more giving him pain and sleepless nights. That at least was his excuse for drinking most of the wine that was sent in to the prisoners from their old friend Zemaun in Kabul.

Alice thought bleakly how they were back within sight of the city and the destroyed cantonment that they had left in the depths of winter. Now it was so hot and the mosquitoes so maddening that she almost hankered after the snow and bitter winds of Budeeabad.

She got up and went to the window, where the shutters had been thrown open to try to catch a wisp of night breeze. Alice gazed out at the garden below – the one good thing about the fly-ridden fort was its garden of fruit trees – and beyond to the murmur of the river where occasionally they were allowed to wash themselves. She bowed her head under a familiar weight of despair. What had it all been for?

After two months of being marched among the barren hills – which had proved too much for dear, ailing Elphinstone, who had died en route – their hopes of being taken to Jalalabad and exchanged for Akbar's family had been finally crushed. They were back near Kabul at the mercy of different factions among the warring Afghans. Arriving at Noor they had been told of the murder of Shah Shuja and the proclamation of Shuja's son Futteh Jung as amir.

But the servants brought news of infighting between the chiefs in Kabul and Akbar's increasingly desperate attempts to hold them together in alliance. The rumours about what would happen to the prisoners swept about them like a poisonous miasma. Zemaun wanted them sent to Jalalabad and used in negotiations with the British army. The Ghilzais declared they would kill all the hostages if anyone attempted to move them. Akbar alternately promised them leniency and then threatened them with banishment to Bokhara or Turkestan.

Even Colin and Vernon had been demoralised by this; word had leaked out that the sadistic ruler of Bokhara had incarcerated two British envoys in a vermin-infested dungeon for months. No one knew if they were still alive. Lately the news had become even more alarming; to save the British forces still in Jalalabad and Kandahar, the troops were pulling out of these garrison towns and heading back to India.

'They can't do that,' Emily had cried. 'They wouldn't leave us to our fate, would they, Sandy?'

But Sandy had stopped placating Emily with false words of hope and would only shrug. It was left to a gaunt-faced Colin to try to reassure her.

'We won't be left here – it would be a stain on the honour of the British Army. We know that Pollock has already arrived in Afghanistan with fresh troops – he's not going to stop and turn tail now. Take heart from that, Mrs Ayton. We are not forgotten.'

But, later, Alice had overheard the men talking anxiously about the matter.

'Even if Pollock intends to fight his way back to Kabul,' said Sandy, 'we might be moved out of reach long before he gets here.'

'Or have our throats cut,' said Vernon.

'Don't let the ladies hear you say that, Major,' Colin had said impatiently.

'Well, if I was Pollock I wouldn't risk coming back for a handful of women and sick officers. The wives should never have been allowed to come in the first place – utter madness.'

Sandy had sighed. 'What's done is done.'

'Well, their being here has been the cause of all our problems. Our army wiped out and our country humiliated,' Vernon had said bitterly.

Colin had snorted with derision. 'I don't remember you complaining about the wives when they saved you from the retreat and certain death.'

'At least I didn't run away and hide in a cave like you did,' Vernon had retaliated.

'For pity's sake!' Sandy had cried. 'What good does your arguing do? It doesn't help us here or bring our missing children back.'

Alice had slipped away not wanting to hear any more, her heart leaden at the mention of their stolen children. The hardest trial of all to bear was the not knowing what had happened to Lotty. Her daughter's third birthday had come and gone, yet Alice did not know if the girl lived. As far as anyone knew, John was still alive and at Akbar's command but no further news had come through about the children abducted by the Ghilzais or the rumour that a fair child had been seen among the Afridis. All through the long, broiling, fearful summer Alice and the Aytons waited for news of Alexander or Lotty but none came.

August arrived; half the prisoners were delirious with fever. Gita fell ill and Alice nursed her as best she could in the searing heat, trying to reassure Gita's anxious sons. Colin recovered but Jamieson succumbed. His sudden death was a blow to morale. If a robust young officer like Jamieson could be carried off by fever in the space of two sunrises, then no one was safe.

The evening after he was buried, Alice went to sit under a nearby mulberry tree and mourn the young officer whom she had first met on that fateful trip into Kabul nearly two years ago. The dusty sunset was punctuated with gunfire coming from the city. Alice had no idea who was in charge or who was fighting whom. She felt utterly powerless. One by one, the people she loved were being taken from her. She curled up under the tree, pulled her shawl over her head and wept.

Shouts at the gateway woke her. Alice must have fallen asleep under the tree for dawn was breaking over the fort walls. She sat up, stiff and aching from the hard ground. She could hear a commotion. Her stomach clenched in fear. Was this a raid? Perhaps the chiefs who had threatened to kill them were finally coming to do so. She stumbled back inside. Joining other prisoners on the veranda, she peered down at the inner courtyard as the gates were being pulled open and a dozen blanketed men trudged through.

'I see scarlet jackets,' Dinah cried out.

'They're British,' Sandy gasped.

'Is that Lieutenant Sinclair?' Emily asked, seizing Alice's arm.

Alice strained to see in the shadowed courtyard, her heart thumping. The men were being jostled forward by armed Afghans. They appeared to be prisoners too.

'I'm not sure . . .'

Then the tallest of the men, shrouded in a bulky blanket, looked up and she recognised John's rugged face. She stifled a cry of joy.

'He's holding a child!' Dinah squealed. 'Look!'

Alice strained to see. The bulky blanket was indeed a child bundled up, with just a fair head of hair showing. Alice screamed and headed for the stairs, clattering down them as fast as her shaking legs could manage. The others followed, shouting out to the new arrivals. Alice raced barefoot into the courtyard, arms outstretched and making for John in the mêlée of men, mules and guards.

She saw the look of relief on his face as he caught sight of her.

'Alice!' he rasped.

'Lotty!' she cried. 'You've found her!'

The joy on his face vanished. As she reached him and pulled away the blanket she realised her mistake. A thin, wide-eyed boy looked at her, startled. She stared at him in confusion, not recognising him.

'It's Alexander,' said John, his face full of pity.

Alice stood frozen to the spot. She had been so sure it was Lotty. Behind her she heard Emily scream. Moments later, Alexander was being enveloped by his parents, smothered in loving arms and welcomed with kisses and tears of relief.

It was John who steered Alice aside into the shadows and put his arm about her shoulders. She turned into his hold and stifled a sob.

'I'm sorry,' John murmured into her hair. 'I'd hoped it would be Lotty too.'

She pulled away. 'But you said you'd found a fair-haired child among the Afridis. I got your message. It's what's been keeping me from giving up all these terrible months.'

'I'm sorry for raising your hopes but it was Alexander who they had rescued.'

'So where is my Lotty?' Alice wailed. She was shaking from head to foot with shock and disappointment.

'I don't know.'

'You must have heard something,' Alice said. 'All this time with Akbar and the Afghans – you must have picked up rumours. Can't you tell me *anything*?' She saw the hesitation in his face. 'You know something don't you? Tell me! I don't care how bad it is – nothing is worse than this purgatory of not knowing.'

At Alice's raised voice, others were turning to watch. She didn't care. She had to know what it was that John knew. He looked at her with such compassion in his green eyes that she wanted to break down in tears. But if she started to weep she might never stop.

'Tell me,' she ordered, digging her nails into her palms.

John nodded. 'It's fairly certain the Ghilzais had her for a while,' he said. 'I discovered she had been taken to Kabul.'

Alice's heart leapt. 'Is she there now?'

John shook his head. 'Zemaun has been looking for her – and my Kazilbashi friend, Khan Shereen Khan – but they think she has been passed on.'

'Passed on?' Alice felt sick. 'What do you mean?'

John swallowed. 'Sold on.'

Alice's throat filled with bile. The other women began to gather around her, patting and stroking her arms in comfort. But she had to know everything. She gripped her arms in front of her and asked, 'Sold to whom?'

'They don't know for sure.'

'But they have an idea?' Alice pressed him. 'Don't spare me the truth, Lieutenant Sinclair.' She could feel her teeth chattering as if the air was cold.

'There is talk of slave-traders having been in the city,' John said with reluctance. 'Many Hindus have been rounded up and taken too.'

'Taken where?' It was Sandy who asked.

'To the markets in Turkestan.'

A groan went up from the huddle around Alice.

'But that is just the rumour,' John said hastily. 'They can't be sure.'

'But that's what you believe, isn't it?' Alice said, feeling faint.

'I believe she is still alive,' John said, trying to instil courage with his look.

Alice turned from him and pushed away from the others. She went to the Aytons and put out a hand to touch Alexander's matted hair. Sandy held the boy tightly in his arms.

'Dear Zander,' she whispered, 'I'm so happy to see you.'

The boy gazed back with a dazed look, quite overwhelmed by it all. Emily put an arm around Alice and pulled her into her hold. Alice bowed her head and wept into her friend's shoulder.

The days that followed were tense ones for the hostages. The new arrivals brought word of the lawlessness in Kabul. Shops had been shut up and the women of the royal household had been sent out of the citadel for safekeeping in outlying forts. John told of how the Kazilbashi chiefs had retreated into the Kohistan not wanting to get embroiled in the latest battle for power. Akbar had failed to broker a truce with the British forces in Jalalabad and was furious at their refusal to withdraw to India. Instead, the British army was on the move up the passes towards Kabul.

But John soon dashed raised hopes.

'Akbar is in no mood to treat us well,' said John grimly. 'He is threatening to send us all to Bamian and sell us to the chiefs in the north in retaliation. He's back in Kabul to rally another army against the British. He no longer wants to broker a deal with Sale or Pollock. That's why I'm not wanted as translator.'

'So you're just a common prisoner like the rest of us, eh?' jibed Vernon.

'It would seem so,' John replied evenly, not rising to the baiting.

Alice couldn't bear to be near her husband. He had shown no emotion at the news that their daughter was probably in the hand of slavers and could end up in Bokhara in the household of the despot who tormented his British captives. All he could do was complain about how ill he felt and how she spent too much time fussing over her native servant rather than him. He had grown even more demanding and fretful since John's arrival so Alice kept out of John's way for the sake of peace with her fractious husband.

She could see the anger in John's face and his clenched fists when Vernon spoke to her rudely but there was no point in provoking an argument. The prisoners had been thrown together for so long that Alice knew how the slightest bad word or jealous comment could lead to friction. It was best just to ignore Vernon's carping. She could feel John's frustration at not being able to talk privately or snatch a moment alone together but Alice's heart had been shattered since hearing about Lotty's fate. Nothing John could say would be able to console her now.

The weather broke. Vivid lightning lit the night sky, followed by booming thunder and torrential rain that turned the courtyards to mud. Two days later, their gaolers came to tell them that they were to be moved. Ponies were brought in and Dr Campbell, who had arrived with the Kabul hostages, was ordered to declare who was fit to travel on a mountainous journey.

This provoked a panicked response from the sick and feverish. Several of the women, including Mrs Trevor, were ruled too ill to travel. Florentia though had rallied and was determined to stay with Dinah and baby Julia come what may. Campbell tried to get as many as possible on the list not to be moved as the word was that the prisoners were being taken to Bamian and then to Turkestan. A vengeful Akbar wanted the hostages beyond the border of Afghanistan where the British dared not go. Everyone knew that those forced to go were unlikely ever to return.

Emily surprised Alice with her stoical acceptance of their fate. Since Alexander's return, her friend had regained some of her former optimism.

'As long as I have Sandy and my boys with me,' Emily said, 'I can face anything.'

But Vernon insisted he was in no condition to march. Alice was speechless with disgust at her husband's successful pleading to be allowed to remain with the sick. He showed none of the loyalty he'd professed on the retreat from Kabul when he'd demanded that the husbands stay with their wives and children to protect them. But John couldn't hold back his contempt. He strode past Alice into the fetid room where Vernon was lying on a *charpoy*, smoking.

'Show some guts, Buckley!' John challenged. 'The women and children need all the men who can be mustered to guard them through the Hindu Kush.'

Vernon glared at John with bloodshot eyes. 'You don't fool me, Sinclair. I know you're itching to have an excuse to run off with my wife. Well, you're welcome to her. She's soiled goods in my eyes since you've had her.'

'You bastard, Buckley!' John sprang at him, knocking the water-pipe from his grasp. Vernon cried out. John hauled him off the low bed and landed a blow to his jaw. Colin and Sandy rushed in and pulled John off a dazed Vernon.

'You saw that!' Vernon panted. 'He attacked his superior officer. I'll see you hanged, you Scotch savage!'

As Colin manhandled a seething John out of the room, Sandy helped Vernon back onto the string bed.

'You're my witness, Ayton,' Vernon said, visibly shaken.

Sandy's look was full of disdain. 'I saw you fall on the floor, Buckley. That's all. Besides, Sinclair is probably going to a worse fate – and so is your wife. You'd do best to save your breath and say something of comfort to Alice before you're parted.'

Sandy stalked from the room, throwing Alice a pitying look as she stood in the doorway. She waited for her husband to apologise for the vile words he had said about her; surely even Vernon would be contrite in the face of them being parted, perhaps forever?

Instead Vernon went on the defensive. 'You put Sinclair up to that, didn't you? You wanted to see a sick and defenceless man being beaten by that brigand.'

'Don't be absurd, Vernon.'

'I know you can't wait to be with him. But your duty is to me. I'm your husband and master, not the Scotchman. I demand that you stay here and nurse me. Campbell can be persuaded.'

Alice nearly choked with indignation. 'You can stay if you like but the journey ahead holds no fear for me. I relish it,' she said, her eyes blazing. 'And not because of John Sinclair. If they are taking us to Turkestan then I have a chance of seeing Lotty again. Wild horses couldn't keep me from going.'

'Don't be ridiculous, woman! You won't find her. She's most probably dead. Sinclair is just trying to keep your hopes alive with his lurid tales about slavers so that you will go with him and be his whore.'

'Only a man with the mind of a cesspit would think such a thing,' Alice hissed. 'You obviously care nothing for our daughter but at least Sinclair's words give me hope. And hope is all I have.'

298

Unable to bear his presence a moment longer, she hurried from the room.

* * *

The prisoners were told they would travel by night to avoid the heat of the day. At moonrise on the twenty-fifth of August, there were many emotional farewells with the sick and wounded who were staying behind in the care of Dr Campbell. Yet Vernon tried to browbeat Alice till the last moment.

'You'll regret abandoning me,' he accused her, 'when you hear of my death through fever.'

'Goodbye, Vernon,' was all she could manage to say. Alice did not know if her pounding heart was from fear of the journey ahead or relief that she was finally being parted from the man who had bullied and denigrated her for so long.

The train of camels and ponies carrying the forty able-bodied hostages set out from Noor Fort under armed guard. Detouring widely to avoid Kabul, they crossed the Loghur River and headed for the Paghman Hills.

Ever since John's arrival with Alexander, Alice had felt numb to her core. Even Gita's recovery hadn't lifted her spirits as it should have done – or John's presence around the fort.

She had yearned for him for so long and yet her feelings were now cauterised. Her heart felt as hard as flint and she no longer believed that people were ultimately good. How could they be when they allowed a three-year-old girl to be snatched from her mother and sold to the highest bidder? All the suffering and bloodshed, the carnage of the retreat and the months of imprisonment were for nothing. They were pawns in the imperious games of bloodthirsty men – the men who sat in distant Calcutta and London as well as the murderous men who held them captive.

In Alice's corrosive thoughts, John was somehow tainted too. She couldn't help blaming him for the cruel disappointment of not bringing Lotty to her. She knew it was unfair and illogical but she couldn't help the bitterness that was eating into her heart with each new day.

At least they were on the move and away from the infernal heat of the fort and from Vernon. She could breathe again in the night air under a brittle star-laden sky. To move was all she could concentrate on and it felt good to be back in the saddle. With each step across the rocky plain she might be travelling nearer to her missing daughter. She held on fiercely to the thought and kept her eyes focused on the mountains ahead.

Chapter 39

For two nights they travelled across the hot plain and into the foothills, setting off at midnight each night. The caravan of camels and ponies covered about two miles every hour, jolting their passengers, many of whom were still weak from the summer fever.

John made it his business to be courteous to the guards and friendly to their leader, General Saleh Mohammed. The general – a warrior from the Khyber Pass region – approved of John's kinship with the Afridis and allowed him to carry his Uncle Azlan's hunting knife to help them procure food along the way. John also hoped that his bonds with the Kazilbashi families could be of help to the captives as they travelled through the Hindu Kush.

He was hurt by the way Alice had rebuffed him since his arrival in captivity but his heart ached for her in her constant worry over Lotty. At least she was away from the malignant control of her vile husband, he thought with grim satisfaction. Whatever happened, he would do what he could to protect Alice and stay with her till the last.

As they moved further into the hills, and after the muddy red waters of the Kabul river, John found himself once again relishing the clearer air and the sight of poplar trees lining sweet rushing streams. The armed guards commandeered supplies from passing camel trains to feed their entourage and they camped in what shade they could find during the daytime.

A further two days into the Hindu Kush, the band of captives arrived at Istalif – meaning lush orchards – the fort of John's Kazilbashi in-laws. Aziz came out to greet them, but his delight at seeing John turned to consternation to discover his brother-in-law was a hostage and not a guard.

'This cannot be allowed,' Aziz declared. 'We will pay to have you released.'

'My dear Aziz,' John said, an arm about the tall youth, 'you would have to buy freedom for us all. I shall not desert my comrades and friends.'

Deeply perturbed, Aziz ordered food to be brought out to the hostages – naan bread with apricot paste, pilaf, roast fowl and fish, grapes and pears – which they ate by the side of a chuckling river in the shade of willows.

That night, they did not travel on but camped in the Kazilbashis' orchard and Aziz entertained General Saleh Mohammed and John along with senior officers Pottinger, Shelton and Lawrence. John made sure that the Afghan general was well fed and also that Aziz provided victuals for the onward journey to make life easier for their chief captor. From talking with Saleh Mohammed, John knew that the general was uneasy about his role of transporting the British towards Bamian and beyond. He particularly found it distasteful that he was in charge of delivering women and children into the hands of hostile tribesmen – possibly slave-dealers. The general was a soldier of fortune who had fought alongside British cavalry in the early days before rallying to Dost Mohammed's cause. He said it had been the abusive language of the non-commissioned officers that had made him switch sides.

That night, John raised the issue of the missing Lotty in front of the general, asking Aziz if they had seen any traders passing through with a fair-haired British child.

Aziz shook his head. 'But there have been many armed bands travelling through the mountains in recent months,' he said, 'so it is not impossible the girl might have come this way.'

General Saleh Mohammed grew indignant. 'No true Afghan would do such a thing! She must have fallen into the hands of Uzbek or Turkic traders. They would sell their own grandmothers for a handful of rupees.'

'Then, sir, will you help us track down the missing girl?' John asked.

'When we reach Bamian I will send out my scouts,' the general declared. 'If she still lives, I shall rescue her myself!'

* * *

Alice woke to the sound of men's subdued voices beyond her makeshift tent under the apple trees and sat up. What surprised her was the soft laughter. What did any of them have to be cheerful about?

Getting up, she stepped beyond the cloth wall and peered into the moonlight. Two men, one turbaned and the other bareheaded, were lying on their stomachs by the edge of the river where the water collected into a deep pool.

They were reaching into the water. With a sudden pang, Alice realised that it was John with the young Kazilbashi, Aziz, who had laid on a feast for them that evening. Sandy had said the handsome slim-faced young man was John's brother-in-law.

With a suppressed cry of triumph, Aziz hauled out a fish from the pool and threw it onto the ground beside him. Alice saw the flash of silvery scales as the fish gasped and flapped. John clapped him on the shoulder and said something in a language Alice didn't know. The meaning though was obvious; John was praising Aziz. The affection in his voice made Alice's eyes sting with tears.

How could she have forgotten what John had suffered in losing his wife and baby son? Being with Aziz must be a comfort to him – and a painful reminder. But John was not eaten up with bitter hatred. He was doing all he could to keep the hostages safe. Sandy had spoken of how John was going out of his way to cultivate friendship with their captor, Saleh Mohammed.

'Sinclair could be a free man by now,' Sandy had said, 'but he's choosing to stay with us.'

Alice had pondered this. Why would John not take the chance of staying with his dead wife's tribe if he could? Yet the thought pricked her. For the first time in a month she felt the stirrings of some emotion deep inside. She didn't want John to leave them. Watching him now with Aziz she felt a sudden pressure on her chest. She gasped for breath. John turned. 'Who's there?' he asked.

'Alice,' she whispered.

Swiftly he was on his feet and holding out a hand. 'Can't you sleep either?'

She shook her head. John steered her to the riverbank and introduced her to Aziz. The men had a quickfire conversation. Aziz put his hand on his heart and said something to her.

John interpreted. 'He's sorry to hear about your missing daughter. They will keep watch for her should she pass this way.'

Alice's vision blurred. 'You've told him . . . ?'

301

'Yes,' said John. 'He knows about Lotty.'

At the mention of her beloved daughter's name, Alice felt the pressure lift from her chest. She let out an agonised sob. At once, John pulled her into his hold. All the misery and grief of the past months since Lotty had been carried off poured out of Alice in uncontrollable weeping. She had all but given up on ever seeing her daughter again, beginning to believe Vernon's words that she was probably dead. Yet John had not given up. He had told others to look out for Lotty. This young Kazilbashi man was prepared to search for the girl too – and maybe there were others like him.

How wrong she had been to dismiss all Afghans as thieves and murderers. That was what Englishmen like Vernon wanted her to believe. It was so much easier to hate, but so very destructive for the spirit. Alice cried into John's shoulder until she was exhausted. He did not try to stop her but simply held her tight.

By the time she had stopped and looked up, Aziz had gone. She let John wipe her tears.

'Please forgive me for being so unkind to you,' she whispered.

'There is nothing to forgive,' he answered.

'But there is,' said Alice. 'I've done nothing but push you away since you rescued Alexander. I have been so wrapped up in my own misery that I haven't seen how hard it has been for you. You have risked your life all these months being Akbar's messenger and trying to keep us safe – and you're still doing it. You amaze me with your courage, John.'

'There is nothing amazing in what I do,' he said. 'I do it for you, my love.'

'Oh, John, I couldn't bear to lose you as well as Lotty.'

Tenderly he kissed her forehead. 'As long as there is breath in my body I will never leave you.'

Alice reached into the pocket of her tunic and, pulling out a small cloth pouch, pressed it into John's hand. 'There's a letter inside – I wrote it to you in Budeeabad when I thought we were going to be executed. It says all there is to say between us, my dearest John.'

She saw from his glittering green eyes the emotion he felt at her words. He pushed the pouch into his jacket. Then, lifting her chin, he bent and gently kissed her on the lips. It seemed a lifetime since they had last been able to embrace each other. Alice felt love flooding through her once again like warmth thawing her frozen feelings. It was painful to feel such emotion and yet John's touch gave her courage.

She wanted to stay with him but he steered her back towards the encampment as a sentry called out and fired a warning shot into the air.

302

Chapter 40

Bamian, Central Afghanistan, September 1842

The mountain paths grew more rugged and the next few days were a relentless grind up rocky defiles, over high passes and down steep gorges, only to repeat the precipitous climb all over again. From the top of the Kaloo Pass, Alice saw more barren hills rippling to the far horizon like the waves of a petrified sea. The only vegetation was a prickly furze that the animals fed on. The land seemed even more desolate and remote than any she had seen before, and her spirit wilted to think that this wilderness was to be their place of captivity. Was it possible that any British soldiers would ever venture this far to rescue a handful of their hapless countrymen and women? Surely they would now be left to their fate?

Only John's strong presence kept Alice's spirit from breaking. Just a tender look or an encouraging word in a snatched exchange was enough to lift her morale for the rest of the day. In turn she was able to bolster the flagging spirits of the other women and children. She shared the responsibility with Sandy of riding with Alexander. The boy had become nervous and needy compared to his former boisterous self. He would cling to his father and whine until Sandy lost patience. Alice would intervene and coax the boy onto her pony, distracting him with games of spotting birds and singing songs.

Finally, in early September, they arrived in the wild high valley of Bamian, peopled by Hazara tribes with broad sun-baked features quite unlike the Afghans Alice had met so far. Surprisingly, the mile-wide valley was a fertile oasis among the dun-coloured mountains. Fields of golden wheat and gardens of green peas and beans were intersected by glinting water channels under a vivid blue sky. Fat-tailed sheep grazed in the shade of rustling tamarisk and poplars.

Most extraordinary of all, carved out of the rock face that reared up like a protective wall on one side of the valley, were two mighty statues of Buddha. The cliffs around the giant carvings were pockmarked with caves.

'Centuries old,' Pottinger told them. 'They were the cells of Buddhist monks. The Buddhists are long gone, of course.'

'I wish I could sketch them,' Alice said in wonder.

John gave a soft chuckle. 'Well, I imagine our hosts will be happy to lay on some sightseeing trips while we're here.'

Alice smiled back.

'I don't see why you're both so cheerful,' said Emily. 'I think the rarefied air has gone to your heads.'

John grinned. 'I think you might be right.'

The look he gave Alice made her stomach knot in longing.

But their levity was short-lived. Word came back that the fortress on the hill would not accommodate them, so they made camp under its walls. Just as they had got the tents pitched and the children settled, the guards told them they were to be moved on to another fort. There was general complaining but they were marched on another mile, past a honeycomb of ruined cave-dwellings and towers, to a crude mud fort.

'We'll be able to protect you better here,' the fatigued Saleh Mohammed told them.

'Keep us imprisoned he means,' Florentia muttered in a defiant tone, despite her exhaustion.

The rooms they were given were little more than a series of cow byres – airless and dark – around a high-walled courtyard.

'You could write your name in the soot on the walls,' complained Florentia.

'If we could see to write,' joked Alice.

They spent a sleepless night, bitten by lice and kept awake by the scratchings of rats and scuttling of cockroaches. In the morning, after protests from the women, they were granted permission to pitch tents in the gateway.

For the next few days, the captives lived in a strange state of limbo. They were allowed out under guard to explore the Buddhist caves and were fed on refreshing curds from the many cows in the fort. But there was an air of tension hanging over them. Alice noticed John having intense conversations with Pottinger and Sandy. She sensed that their fate was in the balance. Any day now they would be moved on – but to where and how many of them? There was rumour that they might be split up.

She longed to be able to speak to John in confidence but there was never any chance of them being alone. The guards watched them closely, seeming ill-at-ease, and the women were kept separate from the men.

* * *

John's worst fears for the prisoners were coming true. Saleh Mohammed had orders to march them on to Khullum and hand them over to the Uzbek chief, Umeen Khan. He had called John into his tent to warn him.

'The Wallee of Khullum?' John asked, aghast. 'He's a slave-trader, for God's sake!'

'These are my orders from the Sirdar.' The general looked harrowed.

'The women and children are exhausted,' John said. 'They won't stand another march over the mountains. It will kill them.'

Something about the Afghan's expression made John's insides turn leaden. 'What else have you been ordered to do?' he asked.

The general hesitated. When he spoke, his voice was grim. 'Those who are not fit to travel are to be put to death.'

John was horrified. His dear friend Colin would be one of them. The artillery officer had been weakened by the journey and had succumbed to another bout of fever. He spent the days lying in a tent and had to be helped up to do his ablutions or to eat.

'You can't allow it,' John cried.

Saleh Mohammed held his look. 'Then tell me how I am to avoid it!'

Outside, John reeled from the news. It was the sign of a desperate man, that Akbar should have issued such a dire command. Perhaps the Sirdar was finally losing to the British and no longer had control of Kabul. But even if Pollock's army or Nott's force from Kandahar were gaining ground, they were too far away to be of any help to the prisoners in Bamian. By the time any troops arrived, the captives would either have been butchered or sold into slavery.

John balled his fists in anger. There must be something he could do to save the hostages. As he stood in the bright September sunshine he heard children's laughter down by the stream; Alexander was playing with some Hazara boys. The Aytons' son was beginning to lose his fear and enjoy life again. John was reminded of his boyhood days at Ramanish, running around with Donald and Duncan. Something must be done to save Alexander and the other innocents from a brutal death or a life of captivity.

Words that Aziz had said to him came back suddenly to John. His heart quickened. There might just be a way of preventing this terrible deed. Perhaps that was why the Afghan general had given him forewarning. John turned on his heels and went to find Pottinger.

* * *

Late that night, closeted in one of the dingy rooms in the fort, they sat cross-legged: John, Sandy, Pottinger and Lawrence on one side, Saleh Mohammed and his second-in-command on the other.

'A pension of one thousand rupees every month for life in exchange for our release,' Pottinger offered, 'and a bond written out to honour the payments – signed by all the officers here in the fort.'

It had been John's idea, prompted by Aziz's attempt to buy John's freedom from his captors. It gave the general a way out of having to either put them to death or into the hands of slave-dealers, options which the Afghan found abhorrent. It was a gamble – the general might send word at once to Akbar of their attempts at bribery – but John knew Saleh Mohammed was a reluctant gaoler. The general's first loyalty would always be to his tribe and not to any ruler of Afghanistan, so John was staking their lives on the military commander's self-interest and concerns for his kin.

'That is all very well for us,' said Saleh Mohammed, 'but even if we agree, we still cannot defend you from Akbar's allies. There is talk of Sultan Jan's men being in the area – and the Uzbeks will send a force if they get wind that the prisoners are not going to be delivered into their hands.'

'What do you need,' asked Pottinger, 'to guarantee our safety?'

'The co-operation of local chiefs here in Bamian,' he replied. 'At a price.'

John had briefed Pottinger that this was likely to be the general's strategy: provide tribute to the local Hazara chiefs and build an alliance around Saleh Mohammed's renegade force. John held his breath. Pottinger was handling the situation with a cool decisiveness; John had been right to take his plan to the political officer and not to the belligerent Shelton.

'Then let us arrange a payment of ten thousand rupees,' said Pottinger, 'for you to distribute as you see fit.'

'Twenty thousand,' countered the general.

Pottinger made a pretence of conferring with the other officers. But they had already agreed in advance that they would offer the Afghan whatever he demanded and worry about honouring the payment later.

'Twenty thousand,' Pottinger said with a nod, 'and a remission of the taxes imposed by the British.'

The general nodded in approval. 'But you must give me proof that you can honour such payments,' said Saleh Mohammed, 'otherwise the chiefs will not believe me.'

At this point, Pottinger produced a casket and opened it. Inside were all the jewels and mementoes that John had been able to gather up from the anxious women; brooches, hairpins, lockets, wedding rings and even bills of fare – any bits of paper that looked official and legal. From the men he had demanded pocket watches, chains, medals and brass buttons.

'These shall be yours until we are reunited with the British Army and can pay you in money,' promised Pottinger.

The general looked satisfied. 'Then we are in agreement,' he said, smiling for the first time.

'I shall have a document drawn up in the morning,' said Pottinger, 'and signed by all the officers.'

Saleh Mohammed grinned. 'And we shall rally our Hazara brothers to your cause.'

* * *

The next day, instead of being force-marched to Khullum, the British prisoners suddenly found themselves no longer under armed guard. The Afghan general had his banner hoisted from the fort tower – a fluttering crimson-edged, green-fringed flag of defiance – to alert the neighbouring forts. Word soon spread that a deal had been done to save the British captives and that their former captor was rallying fighters to defy Akbar. That very day, two Hazara chiefs – Kurrim Beg and Meer Hassun – came and pledged support for the general and the British. By the next day, several more chiefs had thrown in their lot with the rebel force.

'They all have an eye to the future,' said Pottinger. 'They must have word from the south that the British are advancing and that Akbar's days are numbered.'

Yet no one could be sure. There were still rumours of men loyal to Akbar being within striking distance of Bamian. John went to find Sandy to see about amassing supplies in case they had to withstand a siege.

'Let me come too,' said Alice. 'I can at least lead a mule or two.'

'It's still dangerous away from the fort,' warned Sandy. 'You shouldn't come, my dear.'

'Let her,' said John with a smile. 'Alice Brown will be more than a match for any warring Afghans.'

Alice gave a wry laugh. Sandy looked at them quizzically but made no further protest. With an armful of clothes and a bag of coins they had collected from their almost penniless compatriots, they went in search of grain, cooking oil, fruit and nuts to buy from the local farmers. A chief who lived in a fortified farmhouse next to the fort sat them down in the shade of his courtyard while his wife served them tea flavoured with salt and butter, and curds sprinkled with sultanas.

Alice felt lightheaded to be sitting with John and Sandy in this quiet oasis with nothing to disturb them except the pastoral sounds of a trickling stream and sheep bleating. She still couldn't believe that they were to be spared. How had Pottinger managed such a miracle? Sandy had told her it had been John's doing but John would take none of the credit.

The chief was offering them accommodation, John explained. 'He knows that the fort has few creature comforts,' he said with a wry smile, 'so he would like to offer some rooms here at the farmhouse around one of his courtyards.'

'How kind,' said Alice.

'I'm not sure Emily will be persuaded,' said Sandy. 'It may be short on comfort but she feels safer in the fort – and she can keep an eye on the boys there.'

'Well, tell him that I would like to stay here,' said Alice, 'and that I'm very grateful. I think Colin should be brought here too. It's cleaner and the air is better.'

'A splendid idea,' John agreed. 'If there's the slightest hint of trouble, we'll retreat to the fort.'

Later that day, Colin was brought to the farmhouse and laid on a *charpoy* by the open door of a courtyard room where he could catch the breeze. The chief sent for a local physician to treat him with poultices and some strange-smelling concoction. Florentia elected to come down from the fort too, bringing Dinah, baby Julia and her *ayah*. Alice brought Gita and the boys. As she had hoped, John moved into Colin's room across the courtyard, next to three other officers.

At night they sat around on palliasses eating under the stars, the men smoking and chatting with the chief. Although the women of the household stayed hidden in an inner courtyard, the British women were welcomed to dine with the men. Alice was acutely aware of how often John glanced across at her. Her heart began a steady thudding at the desire she felt rising inside her. She knew from his look that he felt the same.

In the middle of the night, when the moon had dipped and when everyone had gone to their beds, a sleepless Alice padded out into the courtyard. A hound lay sleeping across the entrance to the house. The mulberry trees that lined the courtyard threw the edges into inky shadow. She breathed in the sweet smell of the trees and felt the cooling night breeze caress her skin.

'Alice.' John's deep voice was like a vibration through her. She turned towards it. He was a dark figure in the deep shadow beneath one of the trees, standing waiting for her. He held out his hand. Alice moved silently towards him and placed her trembling hand in his. John pulled her into the blackness. For a moment they stood there holding each other, looking into each other's eyes. Despite the darkness, Alice could see the gleam in his. It made her sick with wanting. She put a hand to his face and, leaning up on tiptoes, brushed his lips with hers.

'My darling,' she whispered.

She could feel the tension in him. He was wondering what her coming to him meant. Alice took John's hand and placed it inside her loose tunic, pressing it to her breast. Under his hold her heart banged furiously.

'Make love to me, please,' she urged him.

John bent and kissed her eagerly. Without pausing, he drew her down onto the blanket that he had spread under the tree as his bed. She had known he would be out sleeping in the open air. They kissed each other as they lay down, their hands exploring beneath their clothing. Alice pulled off his shirt; she wanted to feel his skin, his hair, his sweat on her. She had not touched his body since she had nursed and bathed him through his fever at the lighthouse so many years ago. His was now the hard muscled body of a soldier, yet he was as tender and gentle as the young man she had first fallen in love with.

John covered her in delicious kisses; she had to smother her gasps of delight as he touched her. Trying to keep silent while he pleasured her was sweet agony. She pulled at his hair and writhed in ecstasy as she wrapped her limbs around him. It was even more exquisite than she had imagined his lovemaking would be. If she was never to see another day, Alice would die knowing what true loving felt like. She knew she would never have any regrets about coming to him in the warmth of an Afghan night. She loved John completely, and he loved her.

Lying in his arms, John stroked her hair and murmured passionate words in her ear that sent desire pulsing through her again. They made love once more before she pulled on her tunic and pantaloons and slipped back across the courtyard.

The next day, Alice could hardly stop smiling. Each time she caught John's eye she saw the grin spread across his face. They were like conspirators relishing their secret. She wanted to shout to the world how much she adored him – desired every inch of him – but instead she helped Dinah cope with a colicky Julia, while she waited impatiently for night-time to come again.

That night, Alice fell asleep in John's arms after they had made love and it was only the sound of the call to prayer just before dawn that woke her and got her scrambling into her clothes. The sound of John's suppressed laughter had her smiling as she hurried back to her room.

The third night, their lovemaking was more languid. The night sky was shrouded in cloud and a mist had crept up from the river, cocooning them in a private world.

'Let's stay here forever,' whispered John, 'and live with the Hazaras. I shall hunt and you will go about with your sketching paper and draw charming pictures of their people.'

'And what about our friends?'

'They are welcome to stay too. Colin will and the Aytons. Would you like that?'

'I'd love that.' Alice smiled. 'And Dinah will have to stay. I'm growing very fond of Julia.'

'Then we will have our own children too,' murmured John. 'Start our own tribe.'

Alice had a sudden twist of grief for Lotty. Tears welled in her eyes. John was immediately contrite.

'I was just being foolish. I didn't mean to upset you. It's just I would like nothing more than to raise a family with you, my darling Alice.'

She turned and kissed his mouth. 'And I too.'

But it left her feeling sad and in the morning Alice felt the weight of reality pressing on her heart. Lotty was lost to her and someday soon she would have to return and face Vernon. This glimpse of paradise with John, playing at being man and wife, could never be more than that. Or could it? They had not spoken of what life might hold for them if they ever made it back to Kabul alive; their situation still seemed so precarious despite Saleh Mohammed's support.

Alice felt a new determination rising inside her, spurred on by knowing how much John loved her. She would never go back to living with Vernon. She did not care how much of a scandal leaving Vernon would create; Alice would do it. She would run off with John and never look back.

That day, startling news came from beyond the valley. There was insurrection in Kabul; the Kazilbashis had risen against Akbar and he had fled to the Ghilzais in the mountains near Kandahar. Pollock's army was halfway to Kabul and Nott's forces were almost there. And most thrilling of all was the report that a detachment of troops was being sent to the aid of the British hostages.

The excitement among the former captives rose to fever pitch. Pottinger and Shelton at once began making plans to march to meet the force.

'There's no point staying here any longer than necessary,' said Pottinger. 'There's still a chance that the Uzbeks will come down from Khullum to recapture us.'

'But won't we be in danger from Akbar's supporters if we leave the valley?' Alice asked.

'Yes,' agreed Sandy, 'it might be another trap – Akbar trying to lure us out of our safe eyrie.'

'Well, I think we should show more spirit than that,' said Florentia with impatience. 'Our men are on the way to save us. I think we should leave and make their job easier.'

Florentia and the senior officers prevailed. Alice could not hide her reluctance. Her few days of heaven were to be ended abruptly. That night would be her last chance to lie with John under the stars; tomorrow they would once again be on the march. Alice was impatient to be alone with him so that they could discuss their future plans. She knew he would help her stand up to Vernon and that gave her courage.

But John wasn't at supper that evening and, when she went looking for him in the dead of night, there was no sign of him or his rug under the mulberry tree.

'Alice.' A woman's voice startled her. She swung round to see Florentia standing in the courtyard draped in a blanket. 'Can't you sleep, my dear?'

'No,' said Alice, stepping guiltily away from John's tree.

The older woman sighed. 'Neither can I. I can't wait for us to be on the road again. I'm hoping it's my husband who is coming to our rescue. I imagine you do too? Separation is difficult, isn't it?'

Alice's heart thudded. She decided to be frank. She and Florentia had been through so much hardship together.

'I don't find it difficult,' Alice said quietly. 'It's been a relief not to have Vernon with me.'

'Ah,' Florentia said. 'I'm sorry to hear it.' Florentia stood looking up at the sky and then turned to give Alice a direct look. 'I'm aware that you and Captain Sinclair have grown close,' she said, nodding in the direction of the mulberry tree.

Alice flushed. 'Yes, we have. John and I have been in love since I was seventeen and he was a trainee cadet. If we hadn't been betrayed by my brother, we should have been married many years ago.'

'Oh my dear, that is sad,' said Florentia, putting out a hand to squeeze Alice's arm. 'I will say nothing of what I have seen between you and Captain Sinclair in Bamian – and I have sympathy for you, Alice. You have been through a great deal and can't be blamed for taking solace where you can find it. But when we get back to Kabul and our husbands, it will be a different matter. As wives we have responsibilities.'

Alice felt annoyance at her friend's blunt warning and pulled away. 'My husband,' she said with distaste, 'does he not have responsibilities?'

'Of course—'

'Well, he has broken all his vows to me long ago,' Alice hissed. 'He is an adulterer and a bully. He neither loves me nor shows me respect. He only married me for my wealth and now he has spent most of that. I have lived under his cruel rule for long enough and I shall not be going back to it.'

Florentia gaped at Alice. Alice thought she would rebuke her for her outburst. But she let go a weary sigh. 'I didn't know,' she said. 'I heard rumours of course about his philandering in Kabul and I can't condone the way he sometimes spoke to you in captivity – but I put that down to his illness and being under great strain. I never knew how unhappy he made you.' Florentia gave her a pitying look. 'You must do what you think is best. I wish you luck, dear girl.'

'Thank you,' Alice said, feeling a pang of gratitude. They said no more as they padded back to their rooms.

Chapter 41

By dawn, the former hostages were packing up their few possessions and making ready to leave. Alice was worried that there was still no sign of John.

'Perhaps he's gone on ahead with Saleh Mohammed,' suggested Sandy, 'to make sure the route is safe. I'm sure we'll meet up with him later in the day.'

The officers were buoyed up by the Afghan general's decision to issue them all with muskets to protect the group on the journey. They would meet their comrades on an equal footing and not as prisoners.

Alice's heart was heavy as they said goodbye to the pastoral people who had befriended and looked after them. The one thing that cheered her was that Colin was finally making a recovery from the fever that had bedevilled him all summer. He was thin and wan but insisted on riding a pony to allow Dinah a seat in his camel pannier where she could hold onto Julia.

Soon their caravan of camels and mules was wending its way out of the valley and back towards the Kaloo Pass. With each step of her mule, Alice was inching back towards Kabul and a confrontation with Vernon. She glanced back at the Bamian valley lying golden in the sunshine and fretted about John. Where was he? Why hadn't he told her he would be travelling separately? She would only be able to bear the future if she knew he would be there beside her. She doubted she could stand up to Vernon on her own.

At midday, they halted and took shelter under some huge rocks from the hot sun. Naan breads and fruit were passed around while Gita's sons helped fetch water from a nearby stream. They were told they would not linger long. Their Afghan escort was tense. Alice suspected they feared meeting Akbar's avenging troops on the road. Yet in the heat, Alice and the other women dozed.

Suddenly they were brought wide awake. The ground began to shake beneath them. Alice could see from the alarm on Emily's face that she thought the same thing: an earthquake.

But it soon became clear that the pounding noise was not an earth tremor but horses' hooves. The riders were yet to appear but from the hoof-beats they were riding rapidly from the Bamian direction. The women began to scramble to their feet and call for their children as the men picked up their muskets.

'Uzbeks?' Pottinger called up to the sentry who was keeping watch above.

'A dozen at the most,' the soldier called down.

'We can handle that,' Shelton said bullishly, loading his gun.

At once, Saleh Mohammed was ordering his men into defensive positions on the rocks above.

'Spread out in a line,' he commanded, 'and they will think there are more of us.'

The women and children were hurried behind the rocks. They crouched together, Alice holding tight to Alexander as Emily clung to a protesting, wriggling Walter. Heart pounding, Alice squeezed her eyes shut and prayed that they would not end their lives here on this barren mountainside, slaughtered like sheep.

A distant shot rang out in the clear air. There was shouting above. The Afghan soldiers were arguing with the British officers, their voices angry. Emily began to cry.

'Hold your fire!' Pottinger barked. 'The general's right – they're Hazaras.'

'It's Kurrim Beg,' Sandy cried.

'And bloody Sinclair!' Shelton shouted. 'What the devil . . . ?'

Alice pushed Alexander into his mother's hold and scrambled out from under the rocky overhang. A group of horsemen cantered towards them in a cloud of dust. It took her a moment to spot John among them, riding behind the Hazara chief, Kurrim Beg. Relief surged through her. What had delayed him?

Saleh Mohammed went out to greet them. It was only as they drew closer and slowed their pace that Alice saw John was holding something in front of him. Her breath froze in her chest. She hurried forward, ignoring Shelton's protest for her to stay back.

She could see John looking about, searching for her. Their eyes met and he grinned in triumph. He bent his head and spoke to the child in his arms – a child with golden hair who grasped onto the horse's mane.

'Lotty?' Alice gasped, her legs almost giving way.

John was swinging out of the saddle, and lifting the girl with him. Alice stumbled towards them. 'Lotty!'

The girl saw her. Instantly, her eyes widened. She threw out her arms to her mother.

'Mummy!'

The sound of her daughter's voice was like the sweetest music she had ever heard.

'My darling!' Alice held out her arms, tears springing to her eyes.

John carried the girl towards her and placed her carefully into Alice's hold. Lotty buried her head in her mother's neck. Alice hugged her tight, still in disbelief. She kissed her fiercely and stroked her tangled hair.

Around her, Alice's friends began to clap. Sandy raised three cheers for them.

'Hip, hip, hooray!'

Alice was laughing and crying and squeezing her daughter to make sure she was real. Lotty seemed suddenly overwhelmed by the attention and hid her face in her mother's shoulder. Alice's gaze met John's.

'How did you . . . ?'

'Saleh Mohammed heard a rumour,' said John. 'Kurrim Beg sent men to recce the village on the border where she was being held. Last night we went to fetch her. I didn't want to raise your hopes in case it wasn't her.'

Alice knew that it could not have been that simple. These men had risked their lives to save her daughter.

'I can never thank you enough,' Alice said tearfully. '*All* of you.' She looked around and smiled at the Afghan general and the Hazara chief.

Suddenly Alexander appeared at Alice's side. He tugged at her arm.

'Hello, Lotty,' he said, grinning up at his old playmate.

At the sound of his voice, the girl lifted her head from Alice's shoulder and looked down at him. She stared at him in puzzlement.

'It's Alexander,' Alice said. 'You remember him, don't you?'

Abruptly Lotty smiled, that dimpled smile that Alice thought she would never see again. Emotion caught in Alice's throat.

'Zander,' Lotty said.

Alice kissed her in delight. 'Yes, Zander!'

The children giggled at each other. Joy lifted Alice's heart. The miracle she had prayed for these past nine months had come to pass.

* * *

They did not linger. The Hazaras also carried alarming news that scores of horsemen from Khullum were in pursuit of the escaping British. They pressed on at once, Lotty riding in front of Alice. She knew now what Emily had experienced since Alexander's return; she didn't want to let Lotty out of her sight for a second.

The girl seemed remarkably unaffected by her ordeal; Alice shuddered to think what it might have involved and it was probable that she would never know. But Lotty seemed content to sit in the saddle and look around her, pointing and saying things in a jumble of English and words Alice didn't recognise. Perhaps there were those among her kidnappers who had been kind to the girl. Alice prayed that that was the case. She silently vowed that nothing would ever part her from her precious daughter again. She would spend the rest of her life making amends to Lotty and letting her know how much she loved her.

The armed caravan pressed on until after dark. If they got beyond the Kaloo Pass there was less likelihood of the Uzbeks pursuing them. The danger then would come from tribesmen loyal to Akbar.

They camped out just below the pass, not bothering to erect tents but lying on the stony ground in case they had to flee. The night air was chilly and Alice bedded down with Lotty tucked into the same blanket. Despite the anxiety that gripped the travellers, Alice revelled at the feel of the girl's warmth, the beating of her heart and the smell of her soft skin. Her hair smelt of smoke and hay.

In the moonlight she watched John sitting on the ground sharing a water-pipe with the Afghan guard. With his beard and native clothing, he could be mistaken for one of them. Most of the British officers had taken to wearing loose Afghan clothes and had let their beards and hair grow. What would their fellow officers make of them? Alice wondered in amusement. She gazed at John's broad shoulders and handsome profile. Her heart overflowed with gratitude. She had everything she wanted right here on this windy Afghan mountainside; her beloved daughter and the love of her life. Longing for John stirred inside and kept her sleepless. Soon – God willing – they would be able to start their new life together.

* * *

A messenger appeared in the dawn light. He brought news from the British camp. Help was a day's march away. Sir Campbell Shakespear, military advisor to General Pollock, was on his way with a force of six hundred Kazilbashi cavalry to protect them.

313

The camp was roused. If they could get over the pass and to the next fort, eleven miles away, they would be in less danger from attack. Sultan Jan's troops – regrouping in the Hindu Kush – were planning a reprisal.

They struck camp and moved on with renewed urgency. The Kaloo Pass at fourteen thousand feet left them breathless and labouring in the morning sun but they decided not to rest or stop to eat until they got down to the fort. By afternoon, sitting exhausted in the shade of the fort walls they were overjoyed at the sight of Campbell Shakespear arriving with a troop of Afghan horsemen.

John and Pottinger went ahead to greet them – John saluting his fellow Kazilbashis – and the pair rode in with Campbell Shakespear. The new arrival was soon surrounded by excited women and officers wanting to hear all his news.

Pollock's army, having fought its way up the Khoord-Kabul Pass, had defeated Akbar's Ghilzai force and reached Kabul three days ago. The British ensign was flying over the Balla Hissar. General Nott had reached the plain of Kabul several days earlier.

'Then why did he not send troops to free us?' Pottinger asked.

Pollock's advisor looked embarrassed. 'He decided not to risk his men.'

'Not to risk his men?' Florentia cried indignantly. 'So he leaves it to Afghans to save us? What sort of commander is he?'

'Some of his officers protested that they wanted to be sent but he told them no. That's why I volunteered to come at once,' said Shakespear, 'and General Pollock agreed. I've asked that a brigade be sent as soon as possible to protect us through the Kohistan and hold the passes on the way back to Kabul. In the meantime, I can lend you some of my horses so you can make quicker progress.'

* * *

For the following two days, the former prisoners and their Afghan escort pressed on through the mountains, bivouacking at night and relying on the generosity of local Kazilbashis for sustenance. When they arrived once more at Istalif, Aziz laid on another feast. Hearing that Alice's daughter had been found and reunited with her mother, Aziz had sweetmeats brought out for all the children and a special cake for Lotty. The girl seemed bemused by the fuss but ate the cake with relish. Alice was thankful to see that her daughter's appetite and health – apart from lice in her hair – had not suffered in captivity.

Two days later, the convoy of former captives was out of the mountains and crossing the plain. In the heat of midday, the vanguard of officers who had been scouting ahead came cantering back with news. A cloud of dust on the horizon was a column of British troops moving towards them.

Within the hour, they were surrounded by cheering men of the 13th Light Infantry led by Sir Robert Sale.

Dinah was the first to fall into her father's arms, weeping with relief. Then the hardened commander was embracing his wife and being introduced to his new granddaughter.

Alice could not prevent tears of emotion pouring down her cheeks at the sight of Florentia being reunited with her husband and his obvious delight at finding his family unharmed. How they deserved their happiness after these terrible months of separation and danger!

They arrived at Sale's camp to the sound of a royal salute being fired from the guns of an artillery mountain-train and all the officers rushed out to welcome and congratulate the rescued. That night, they bivouacked under the trees. Alice overheard some of the officers talking about her; they were wondering why her husband had not come to meet her. She felt humiliation that they should pity her but was almost faint with relief that Vernon had not come. By all accounts he had dramatically recovered from illness and was now attached to Nott's camp since being freed from the fort at Noor. She felt a rising panic at the thought of having to face him again.

John appeared at the edge of the awning and nodded for her to join him. Settling down Lotty in her blanket to sleep, Alice asked Emily to keep an eye on the girl for a few minutes. In the dark, she followed John behind a tree.

'What do we do next?' Alice asked him.

'I'm to report to Pollock when we arrive at the main camp tomorrow,' John said.

'Why so soon?' Alice asked in dismay.

'Sale says that Pollock is worried about trouble in Kabul – thinks that Nott is encouraging acts of revenge and looting,' John told her. 'Some of Nott's own officers are complaining that he's torching villages and turning a blind eye to attacks on local women.'

Alice gave an impatient sigh. 'Hasn't there been enough savagery? Are we to act no better?'

'That's what Pollock thinks,' said John. 'He wants a response in proportion to the deeds done. He's ordering that the Char Chouk, where MacNaughten's body was hung, be demolished. But not for every Johnny soldier to be allowed to run amok. He'll want me in Kabul to make sure that our Kazilbashi allies are protected. And I want to see that Rajban and his family are safe – I left them in the care of Khan Shereen Khan.'

Alice tried to smother her fear. 'I'd hoped you could be with me to face Vernon.'

'I did too,' John said, frowning in concern. 'Stay with the Aytons until I can be with you. From what I can gather, Buckley's been at Nott's camp since the captives at Noor were freed last week. Make sure you stay at Pollock's camp in the meantime.' He gripped her hands in his, willing her to have courage. 'We *will* be together,' John promised. 'You, me and Lotty. That is what you still want, isn't it?'

'Of course it is,' said Alice, 'more than anything.'

Quickly he pulled her to him and kissed her hard on the lips.

'This nightmare will soon be over,' he said, 'and we can begin our life together – just as we should have done long ago.'

Alice could hardly bear to let go of his hold. Reluctantly, she did so. They exchanged loving smiles and then she hurried back to Lotty.

* * *

The following day, they marched past a strangely quiet Kabul. There was no sound of commerce or bustle, just a brooding, ominous silence, as if the city were holding its breath.

In contrast to this was the reception of the freed captives at Pollock's camp on the slopes of the Siah Sung hills opposite Kabul. They were greeted by a twenty-one-gun salute and fêted like heroes and heroines returning from beyond the grave.

Alice and Lotty shared a tent with the Aytons. Surrounded by large numbers of well-armed troops with plentiful supplies, Alice went to sleep that night feeling that her daughter was safer than at any point on their hazardous journey. But the next day she could find no sign of John, and Sandy confirmed her fears that he had been sent to Kabul to help keep order for the beleaguered Amir Fateh Jung against remnants of Akbar's supporters.

Abruptly and without warning, five days later, Vernon appeared in the camp. Alice and Emily were resting from the midday heat when he marched into their tent. Struggling to her feet, Emily greeted him nervously and quickly left them alone. Alice could hardly breathe for the rapid hammering of her heart; just the sight of him made her chest tight with fear. He looked much healthier than when she had last seen him – fuller faced and walking with a swagger – and she imagined how he was enjoying being a soldier again. She wondered if he had been indulging in any of the orgy of revenge that Nott's men were rumoured to be carrying out.

'My dear, you look terrible,' he said with a look of dismay, making no attempt to touch her. 'Your complexion is quite ruined and I hardly recognised you in your outlandish clothes. I thought I'd walked into some native quarter.'

'It's all we have,' said Alice huskily, her mouth dry. How typical of Vernon to make a disparaging comment instead of welcoming his wife back safely. Yet his lack of sympathy gave her courage; if he thought so little of her, he would let her go without a fight.

'Well, we'll have to change that,' said Vernon. 'I'll order one of the *durzis* at Nott's camp to make you up something suitable as soon as you're settled there.'

'Nott's camp?'

'Of course,' said Vernon. 'We can't expect the Aytons to keep you – it must be very cramped here.'

'I'd rather stay here – and Emily and Sandy don't mind—'

'But I do.' His look was sharp. 'It looks like I can't take care of my own family. Now where is my daughter?'

'Sleeping,' said Alice, moving protectively towards Lotty, who was lying on a mattress next to Alice's.

Vernon stared down at the girl. She was pink-cheeked and her damp blonde curls were stuck to her temples. Her mouth was slightly parted in slumber. Alice wondered if Vernon felt the same hard tug of possessiveness that she did.

Suddenly Lotty's eyes fluttered open. They widened at the sight of the tall man looming over her. Alice reached out, fearing the girl might scream. But Vernon was quicker. He scooped up the child into his arms and planted a kiss on her forehead.

316

'My darling Charlotte!' His voice sounded hoarse. 'How your papa has missed you!'

'Papa?' Lotty echoed in bemusement.

'Yes, my little princess. Papa has come to keep you safe. Your naughty mother let the bad men take you but that is never going to happen again, is it? Papa is going to take very good care of you.'

'Vernon, don't say such things,' Alice protested.

He shot her a dismissive look. 'But it's true, isn't it? You can't be trusted on your own to keep our cherished daughter safe.'

Alice felt wounded. 'If you cherished her so much, why didn't you make any attempt to go after her and save her? You let others do that.'

His look turned icy. 'Oh, I've heard how Sinclair is taking credit for rescuing Charlotte – he and his heathen friends.'

'He risked his life for Lotty,' Alice hissed, her anger igniting.

'And I wonder why?' snapped Vernon. 'No doubt you paid him generously with your favours.'

Alice flinched.

'I thought as much,' Vernon sneered. 'But I'll not have you whoring under my nose in the British camp with that man. You'll keep your distance.'

Alice summoned all her courage. 'John and I love each other – we always have done. When this nightmare is over and we're back in India, I intend on leaving you.'

She thought she saw a flicker of surprise cross his face but it was soon replaced by his habitual sneer towards her.

'I don't think so,' he said.

'I want us to live separate lives,' Alice said with determination. 'You don't love me, Vernon, and I don't think you ever have. You certainly don't treat me with the kindness and respect that a husband should. I know now that you only married me for my money.'

He gave a mirthless laugh. 'What a pathetic romantic you are, Alice. Marriage has nothing to do with love. It is only ever a contract over wealth and siring the next generation.'

'Then you will have to go looking elsewhere for both of those. You have spent most of my fortune already – and I will not be forced into your bed again.'

'You better be careful what threats you make,' he said, his voice steely, 'unless you want to lose Charlotte for good.'

Alice's insides went cold. 'What do you mean by that?'

Vernon clutched the girl tighter and faced Alice with a look of loathing. 'If you run off with Sinclair you will forfeit all right to her as a mother.'

'Don't say that.' Alice felt faint. 'Lotty needs me.'

'What Charlotte needs is my protection,' he said. 'You have shown yourself incapable of giving it. First you risk her life by bringing her to this god-forsaken place and then you allow barbarous tribesmen to steal her away.'

'You know I couldn't have stopped that!' Alice cried.

'My daughter will never be put in such peril again. She's a Buckley, and from now on she will be treated as such – not dressed up like some native urchin and exposed to your loose morals. So don't think for one moment I would allow you to take her from me and let Sinclair step into my shoes as her father.'

'You've never shown the slightest interest in Lotty,' Alice accused him. 'You rejected her for being a girl and made it quite plain you wanted nothing to do with her. This is all about punishing me for loving John, isn't it? But if you deny Lotty her mother, then she is the one who will suffer.'

'The choice is yours, Alice. If you love the girl as much as you say, then you'll stay with her – and with me. Because I promise you this: if you leave me, you will never set eyes on her again.'

Alice stepped towards Lotty and held out her arms. She could see the girl's chin trembling; she was confused and upset by their arguing.

'Please, Vernon, give her to me.'

But he held her firm. Lotty began to whimper. 'You must promise first to come with me and not make a fuss,' he bargained.

Alice was appalled at his threats; she knew that he wasn't bluffing. In that moment she realised that Vernon would do anything to thwart her and John being together – to make them both suffer – and he knew that the only way of getting her co-operation was to deny her a life with her precious daughter. Even if John had been there to defend her, he could have done nothing to protect Lotty. The girl was the possession of Vernon and the Buckleys. If she left her husband, Alice knew that she would have no legal right to take Lotty. What a pipe-dream it had been, thinking that Vernon would care so little for the girl that he would be happy to see the back of them both. This was about Buckley pride – and revenge against John.

After the trauma of Lotty's kidnapping, Alice knew she could not bear to be separated from her daughter ever again; her life would not be worth living. The truth hit her like a blow to the stomach. She would do *anything* to keep her child – even stay with Vernon – and her hateful husband knew it was her one weakness.

Alice swallowed her disgust. 'I promise to come with you to Nott's camp,' she said. 'Now give her to me.'

'Walk out in front of me and say goodbye to your friends,' Vernon ordered, 'and then you will have her.'

Eyes smarting with tears of anger and humiliation, Alice turned and did as she was told.

Emily tried to protest at Alice's going. 'Wouldn't it be better to keep the children together, Major Buckley? Alexander and Lotty are such friends.'

'It won't be for long, Mrs Ayton,' Vernon said with a reassuring smile. 'But you can understand how I want to have my daughter with me after all this time of separation.'

'But, Alice . . . ?' Emily gave her a worried look.

'My wife is in complete agreement with me,' said Vernon. 'Aren't you, my dear?' He gave Alice a warning look.

Alice swallowed down words of rebellion. All she wanted was to have Lotty safe in her arms again.

'Yes,' said Alice. She tried to convey to Emily with her expression that she was going under duress but her friend just looked baffled.

Alice bade Gita collect up their few possessions and then she was following Vernon out of the camp.

Chapter 42

General Nott's Camp, outside Kabul, October 1842

Cut off from her friends and any attempt to get a message to John, Alice submitted to Vernon's wishes. She and Lotty were fitted with new petticoats, dresses and shoes. Alice found them painful and restrictive in comparison with the loose comfortable Afghan clothing and was thankful that the worst of the summer heat was over. Her only defiance was to carry John's Spanish coin in her pocket and touch it frequently as a talisman of hope.

It was early October and to her relief Vernon was largely away on forays with his new cavalry unit, putting down the last resistance of Akbar's forces. The short, brutal acts of retaliation soon had Akbar's supporters in retreat.

Vernon came back with spoils – jewellery and silks – for which he expected her to be grateful. Alice refused to even touch them, knowing how they must have come from the wives and families of plundered chiefs. She slipped a necklace to Gita – Alice had insisted that Lotty's *ayah* and sons come with her from Pollock's camp – and told her faithful servant to keep it to sell if she was ever in need.

'That murdering Ghilzai savage, Abdullah, is dead,' Vernon told Alice with glee. 'They say his widow has taken up the resistance. As if we British are going to be cowed by some young wench in a veil!'

Alice knew that Vernon relished the death of this chief above all others, for he was the brother of Vernon's murdered mistress, Raiza. Perhaps her husband had feared that Abdullah might come seeking his revenge for Vernon seducing his sister and dishonouring their tribe. Now, with the warrior chief slain, Vernon could sleep more easily.

Alice suspected that Vernon forced himself on the women he robbed. It sickened her to the core to think that he might do so but he had not ordered her into his bed as she had feared. He let her sleep with Lotty – guarded as they were day and night – and showed no interest in her sexually. Alice wondered if the thought of her and John being lovers had revolted Vernon as much as his philandering had her. She just prayed that his disgust of her continued.

'All that needs to happen now,' said Vernon, 'is to reduce Kabul to ashes and then we can all go home with our heads held high.'

'But Pollock doesn't want that to happen,' said Alice.

He shot her a look. 'How would you know?'

Alice looked away. She must learn not to say what came into her head. She would bide her time, allowing Vernon to think she was cowed by him. Once they were gone from Afghanistan, she would think of ways of making her and Lotty's situation better.

'Anyway, it's no concern of yours,' said Vernon with a dismissive wave of the hand. 'Tomorrow, they are going to blow up the Great Bazaar and then we'll have some sport.'

Alice's insides clenched. As far as she knew, John was still in Kabul trying to keep the peace and prevent his Kazilbashi friends from being attacked by either hostile chiefs or overzealous British troops. Word had it that Fateh Jung's brother, Shahpoor, was going to be placed on the throne with British backing, as the young prince had moderately more support in Kabul than his elder brother.

The following afternoon Alice heard the explosion. She was allowed to leave the tent to witness the destruction of the city's famous bazaar. As a column of black smoke spiralled into the autumnal blue sky and settled over the citadel like a storm cloud, she thought back to her visit there with the Aytons and kind Captain Jamieson. How very long ago that seemed now; there had been so much devastation and heartbreak since.

Vernon left with a party of horsemen to join in the spectacle. Alice thought in despair how her future with John was now further out of her grasp than ever.

Abruptly, the very next day, the order was given for the British withdrawal from Afghanistan. Nott's troops were to march at the same time as Pollock's. Alice heard the disgruntled remarks of some of the soldiers; they weren't to be trusted to be left a moment longer after the main army decamped. The stories of pillage and burnings from troops under Nott's command were now becoming well-aired.

Alice was amazed at how quickly the camp was dismantled and the baggage trains loaded. There was none of the chaos and fear that had marked the retreat of the previous winter. Yet she watched in horror as the camp-followers (many of them refugees from a burning Kabul) were driven out of the camp.

'What are they doing to those people?' Alice asked in distress.

'We can't be expected to take them with us,' said Vernon. 'Look what happened the last time – the bloody natives put all our lives at risk.'

'But where are they expected to go?' Alice demanded.

Vernon shrugged and went off to issue more orders.

Two days later, Alice and Lotty were bundled into a camel pannier in a heavily guarded section of the train as the march got underway. Pollock's camp, along with her friends, were far ahead in the vanguard of the column.

Passing Kabul, they could hear the roar of cannon from the Balla Hissar saluting the newly installed amir. Alice craned for a view. Was John still on duty in the city or had he left along with Pollock's men? Perhaps they would have a chance to meet up on the march to Jalalabad. But to what purpose?

Alice dreaded the moment that John and Vernon would come face-to-face. She feared John might do something foolish should Vernon goad him. She had murderous dreams of revenge in which her husband died in a duel, yet that would bring only further heartbreak. She would not allow John to go to the gallows on her behalf, however much she longed to be free of Vernon.

At night Lotty was tearful and wet herself. Alice knew how the memories of last year's horrors and abduction were being rekindled in her daughter's young mind the further they progressed through the high mountain passes. Even the piles of bleached bones of Elphinstone's slaughtered army could still be seen at the side of the dusty tracks. Alice retched at the sight.

There were a few nightly skirmishes on the baggage train in the rear but no organised resistance. The army marched quickly and if animals went lame they were shot and their loads set on fire so as to lessen the opportunity for plunder.

By the time they reached Jalalabad, Pollock's army had already left ahead of them for the Khyber Pass and Peshawar. Alice's hopes of meeting up with the

Aytons and the Sales were dashed. They halted long enough for the retreating British to destroy the defences of their former garrison and then, as November came, press on after the advance guard.

The tribes of the Khyber gave greater harassment as the army travelled through the desolate pass but again the attacks were at night and their sole purpose appeared to be plundering of the cattle train, as no guns were ever taken. The merciless, organised resistance to the British that the combined tribes had shown less than a year ago had crumbled.

Perhaps they were just glad to see the British go, Alice thought, her nerves still on edge as they finally left Afghanistan and came within sight of Peshawar. She had expected to feel euphoric at their long-yearned-for escape – but she felt anything but free.

The burden of being shackled to Vernon weighed on her spirit. Did she still have the will inside to fight him? She could feel the energy to be rebellious leeching out of her as they were jostled and harried out of the fierce mountainous kingdom. All she could concentrate on was keeping Lotty with her.

Ever since they had been back under Vernon's rule, the girl had grown increasingly timid and babyish. She had reverted to sucking her thumb, wetting herself and bursting into tears at any sudden noise or shouting. She clung to Alice most of the time – and to her battered rag doll that her *ayah* had managed to hold onto all this time. Vernon was easily irritated by Lotty's crying and tantrums and blamed Alice for mollycoddling the girl.

Alice did all she could to comfort and reassure her daughter, even though her own spirits were battered and her vision of their future together seemed so bleak. Somehow, she had to rally her defiance of Vernon. She would not allow him to extinguish the flame of her daughter's spirit too. She wanted Lotty to grow up as a happy and independent-minded girl with a thirst for life, just as she herself had on Black Harbour Island.

Alice knew it would be a battle of wills with Vernon, and one she would have to fight alone and without depending on John. This was her daughter's future that she had to protect and the thought gave her renewed determination to stand up to Vernon. As they drew near to Peshawar and the Punjab, Alice vowed that she would not allow herself and Lotty to be so cut off again from their friends.

* * *

Yet Vernon seemed intent on thwarting her attempts to link up with the Aytons. In the chaos of the desert garrison town of Peshawar, swelled by thousands of extra troops, Vernon found them temporary accommodation away from the camps and her friends. In the city *caravanserai*, he rented a couple of rooms that could be securely guarded. He was in high spirits. Word had come through from Simla and the new Governor General, Ellenborough, of a slew of awards and promotions for the veterans of the Afghan war.

It was as if the foolhardy invasion and disastrous first retreat had never been. Sale, Pollock and Nott were to be made Knights Grand Cross of the Order of the Bath. Alice thought fondly of her friend Florentia and how pleased she would be for her husband. Impatience rekindled in her to see the Sales and the Aytons again. If they were to be in Peshawar for a few days, she would seek them out no matter what Vernon said. How she yearned for news of John too.

'I'm to be promoted to lieutenant colonel,' crowed Vernon, 'and about damn time. I've killed enough of the barbarians to warrant a knighthood but I suppose that will have to wait. I'd like to see the look on the old man's face when he hears of my heroics.'

But he lost no time in telling her that John was to receive no glory.

'Ellenborough thinks nothing to the political officers,' Vernon sneered. 'He quite rightly says they're the ones to blame for the mess – throwing good money after bad and cosying up to the Afghans. What Sinclair did was tantamount to going over to the enemy – he and Akbar were thick as thieves. They say the likes of he and Pottinger might go before courts martial.'

'That would be most unfair!' Alice cried. 'If it hadn't been for them, we prisoners would be dead by now. You owe them your life as much as anyone.'

Vernon snapped, 'That's nonsense! Good plain soldiering and courage kept me alive.' He gave her a malicious look. 'But you needn't worry on Sinclair's behalf. I've heard he's resigning his commission – probably his way of avoiding the disgrace of a public humiliation. Running away. He's always been good at that, hasn't he, my dear?'

Alice had to leave the room before she betrayed her anger and hurt at his words. John would surely know by now that she had returned to Vernon. She had resigned herself that when it came to choosing between John and Lotty, she had chosen Lotty. But if John was leaving the Company for good, she might never have the chance of seeing him again, never be able to explain her decision. The thought left her desolate.

Two days went by but, to Alice's frustration, Vernon kept her confined to their quarters, saying the town was too full of thieves and murderers and that Lotty wouldn't be safe. He, on the other hand, was in buoyant mood. He boasted about his new promotion leading to an invitation to a celebratory banquet. General Avitabile, a French mercenary with the Sikhs and known for his generous entertainment, was hosting a feast in his comfortable palace for some of the officers.

While Gita bathed Lotty in the enclosed courtyard, Alice watched Vernon making ready to go out. Now was the time to take advantage of his high spirits.

'I'd like to arrange to see Emily,' Alice said, steeling herself for Vernon's displeasure. 'Lotty is missing Alexander and it would cheer her up no end. I thought we could spend the evening together while you men are out.'

'You're not going anywhere,' said Vernon. 'It's not the sort of dinner and entertainment that Ayton is likely to be at. But, if he is, I'll send a message on your behalf.'

Alice didn't trust him. She was sure that he had been withholding messages from her friends. Vernon had denied it but Alice could not believe that Emily would not have tried to communicate during these past weeks of separation.

'We can send Bali with a message to see if Sandy is staying at home,' suggested Alice. 'Then Lotty and I will be well protected.' She tried to keep the sarcasm out of her voice.

Vernon gave her a look of irritation.

'What is the point? Charlotte is going to have to get used to not having Alexander as a playmate.'

'Why?' Alice asked, tensing. 'We'll all be going back to Simla or Calcutta sooner or later – once all the planned victory parades and showing off in front of the Governor General in Ferozepur are over.'

Vernon paused in brushing his hair. The scented oil he used to slick his hair into place was making her nauseous. From the look of disdain on his face she could tell that her flippancy over the proposed triumphal homecoming angered him.

'I wasn't going to say anything until we were back in Calcutta but you might as well know. I've decided to send Charlotte back to England.'

Alice looked at him stunned. 'Back to England?'

'Yes, so my parents can make sure she is brought up like an English gentlewoman. She's been subject to too many bad influences out here – she's even picked up the language. God knows what the little blighter is saying half the time.'

Alice was completely taken aback. 'Do I have no say in what happens to our daughter?' she said indignantly.

'I've decided, my dear, that my mama and papa will make a far better job of raising Charlotte than you can – you lack the necessary breeding – but we'll take her back together.' Vernon carried on grooming his hair. 'I'll be due some leave after the victory festivities. Once we're back at Buckley Hall we'll see whether you are to be trusted to stay with my daughter or return with me to India.' He turned and gave her a warning look.

'Trusted?' Alice spluttered.

'Yes,' said Vernon. 'If you prove yourself a biddable wife for once and don't cause me any further embarrassment like you have over Sinclair, I will let you remain at Buckley Hall and stay with Charlotte.'

Alice felt her anger ignite. After all she had been through and the way he had forced her to be subservient to him, he would still threaten her with separation from Lotty!

'I refuse to let you bully me like this,' Alice protested. 'You have no right to take my daughter from me and give her away to your parents. You've never had one good word to say about your mother and father and yet you'd gladly hand over your own daughter to them so she can be frightened and chastised like you were?'

'How dare you speak about my parents like that!' Vernon slammed down his brushes. 'They were disciplinarians – and I was a better man for it.'

'Well, I won't let them frighten my daughter,' Alice retorted. 'I grew up in a loving household, no matter how lowly, and that's what I want for Lotty. You don't care what happens to her, do you? Six weeks living with her again and you can't bear to have her near you. You're sending her away to England just so you don't have to bother being a father to her!'

Vernon lunged at Alice and gripped her hair. She froze in shock at the contact. He had hardly touched her since coercing her back to live with him.

'No, I don't care about the girl!' he snarled. 'It's a boy I want. Give me a son and I'll let you be! It's my right as your husband.'

Alice saw the hatred in his contorted features but she would not be cowe
had taken his threats and cowardly bullying for long enough.

'You can keep me locked up like a slave,' she hissed, 'but I will never be you
If you force yourself on me, Vernon, the child won't be yours either – it'll b
John's. I'm already carrying his baby.'

His eyes widened in disbelief. 'Liar!' he shouted.

'It's the truth,' Alice said in defiance. 'So what are you going to do now? Beat
me till I'm senseless? There's nothing you can do to me that you haven't already
done – and I still won't be yours. And if you harm a hair on Lotty's head, I swear
I will stick a knife in you myself!'

For a moment, Vernon seemed so shocked by her outburst that he lessened his
grip.

'You whore!' he bellowed. With all his force, he shoved her violently away.

Alice lost her balance and fell against the side of his clothing chest, banging
her hip. As the pain shot through her, she braced herself for the next blow. But
at that moment, Gita's eldest son Adeep, appeared in the doorway.

'Buckley Sahib, your *doolie* is ready.'

Vernon hesitated. Alice could see how he itched to punish her. Instead, he gave
her a furious look.

'I'll deal with you later,' he threatened. 'You'll not stop my enjoyment tonight.
Avitabile is laying on the best dancing girls in the province. I'll take my pleasure
where I can be guaranteed a willing woman. I can't imagine what Sinclair sees
in you – or what I ever did.'

With that, he stalked from the room, leaving Alice shaking with relief. She
knew that Adeep had intervened to save her from a hiding and she felt a wave of
gratitude to the brave young servant. She struggled to her feet, her hip throbbing.

What had induced her to tell Vernon that she was pregnant? She had only just
suspected it herself. It had been a wisp of a thought floating in her mind for the
past couple of weeks but she knew that the growing sensitivity to smell and the
metallic taste in her mouth meant only one thing. John and she had conceived a
child on one of those few passionate and loving nights under the stars and
mulberry trees in the remote Bamian courtyard. The thought thrilled her but
made her fearful for the baby that quickened inside her.

As Alice limped out to the courtyard to find Lotty, she wondered if Adeep or
Bali would be brave enough to take a message for her and try to find John.
Whatever his plans, he had a right to know about their child.

Gita gave her a concerned look; her eyes were so full of compassion that Alice
felt suddenly close to tears. She knew Gita must have heard the argument with
Vernon.

'I'm all right,' Alice said with a trembling smile, sitting down on a stool. Lotty
scrambled into her lap. She held onto the girl, burying her face in Lotty's soft
hair and gulping back tears.

It struck Alice how she had been wrong to think that staying with Vernon was
the only way to keep her daughter protected and the two of them together. She
saw now how neither of them would ever feel safe while they remained under
Vernon's control.

not wait in fear for Vernon to return. That's what he wanted – to
 ith terrible thoughts of what he might do to her. She would go now
 ns and throw herself at their mercy to take in her and Lotty – and
 s. From there, they would know how to get a message to John.
 ourage, she said to Gita, 'Please can you fetch Bali. I have an
 ...'

 ayah gave her a steady look and shook her head. 'Sorry, Memsahib; the
 ooy is already taking a message.'

Alice felt a wave of panic rising inside. She must act tonight. 'When he comes
back, will you send him in to me at once? Or Adeep, if he returns sooner.'

Gita nodded. Alice shivered as the chill of the early November evening
descended and hurried inside with Lotty.

Chapter 43

Alice had thought sleep would be impossible but she must have dozed ͻ Suddenly she was being roused by a commotion at the gate. A man was shoutinͺ and the *sepoy* guards were protesting. Alice sat up at once, her stomach lurching to think a drunken Vernon might be returning. Then she realised the voices were arguing in Hindustani, a language that Vernon had never properly grasped.

Alice scrambled to her feet and, leaving a sleeping Lotty on the mattress next to her, hurried barefoot to the door.

A tall turbaned Afghan was pushing his way past the guards. Then, under his cloak, she saw a flash of red uniform.

'John?' she gasped.

He strode across the courtyard towards her. Alice felt her knees buckle at the sight of his concerned face. He caught her and held her firm.

'Alice! I've just arrived from Jalalabad. Emily told me Vernon's been keeping you locked up. Why didn't you send for me?'

Alice began to shake with distress and relief. 'I c-couldn't. He wouldn't let me send messages.'

She saw his jaw clench. 'That bastard!'

'He made me choose,' Alice said tearfully. 'Said I would never see Lotty again if I ran off with you. I couldn't let him do that.'

John pulled her into his arms. 'Of course you couldn't. And he's not going to threaten you anymore. I'm taking you and Lotty away from here and Buckley is not going to stop me.'

'But Vernon said you were giving up and leaving – resigning your commission. I thought I was never going to see you again.'

'That was Buckley spreading tittle-tattle. I've been cut off in Kabul for weeks, helping Prince Shahpoor and the moderate chiefs. But the situation there is hopeless. It's a matter of time before Dost Mohammed returns and reclaims the throne with Akbar at his side. The whole campaign has been for nothing. Khan Shereen Khan begged me to leave and take Rajban and his family back to India before there is further bloodshed.'

Alice gulped. 'I can't believe you're here.'

'I went straight to seek out the Aytons as soon as I arrived, thinking I would find you there. Emily told me Sandy's at Avitabile's banquet. No doubt that's where Buckley is too?'

Alice nodded. 'We had a terrible row before he left. I told him I would never submit to him no matter what he did to me. And I told him something about us that made him furious with me.'

John held her look. 'What did you say?'

'That I'm with child – your child.'

'My child?' There was wonder in his voice.

Alice nodded. Her eyes stung with tears of emotion at the look of love in John's face. He hugged her close and kissed her forehead.

'Oh my darling, you brave one! I love you so very much. I can't bear to think how you have had to put up with Buckley's indignities these past weeks. If I'd known, I'd have come from Kabul and rescued you.'

ıst have made matters worse,' said Alice. 'While we were still in
\ere was no chance of escape. But now it's different. I won't stay
ıent longer. All I want is for me and Lotty to be with you.'
\,' John said fervently. 'I'm not leaving here without you.'
ared. She felt brave again. 'How did you know where I was?'
...ıe at the Aytons',' said John. 'Gita sent him. She must have been
.. about you.'
'Dear Gita!' Alice gasped.

'Come on,' John urged, 'we must go. Gita and the boys can gather up a few
things. I'll carry Lotty.'

Alice returned inside with John. Lotty was curled up asleep with her thumb
half in her mouth. Tenderly, John bent down and picked up the girl. Lotty
murmured in her sleep but settled at once into his strong hold. Minutes later, they
were ready to leave.

Approaching the gate, Alice tensed. What if the guards tried to stop them? John
called out something in his native Gaelic and an answering call came back.
Stepping through the gateway, Alice saw Colin and Rajban standing armed and
waiting. Colin smiled in encouragement.

'We're going to MacRae's quarters,' John told her. 'It'll take Buckley a while
after he's sobered up to work out where you've gone. But he'll have to get past
us Highlanders first.'

Alice's stomach lurched at the thought of how maddened Vernon would be to
find her gone and how full of vengeance. If only they could leave Peshawar at
once. But John was still a Company officer and fleeing now would be treated as
desertion. She had felt guilty and responsible for his previous disobedience to
the Company when he had absconded to Ladakh. She would not be the cause of
ending his career for good.

She pulled her pashmina shawl around her shoulders – the material was almost
threadbare, but it was made from the wool that John had sent her and she would
never part with it. It was like a comforting hug giving her courage.

* * *

Alice and Lotty spent the rest of the night bedded down with Gita and her family
in a cramped upstairs room in a flat-roofed house occupied by some of the
artillery officers. They were all fellow Scots, Colin told her, and not about to
betray her whereabouts to Vernon. A couple of them remembered her husband's
arrogance towards them at Addiscombe.

She was woken by the call to prayer just before dawn. Alice sat up, her insides
clenching. Was Vernon home yet? Was he already sending out a search party for
her? Glancing through the gloom, she saw the glow of a cheroot. John was
standing in the doorway, on guard. He sensed her watching and turned towards
her. Even in the half-dark she could see he was smiling. A warm glow spread
through her.

She got to her feet and went to him, picking her way over Adeep and Bali, who
slept wrapped in their blankets.

'What happens today?' Alice whispered, slipping her arms about his waist.

He stubbed out his cigarette and pulled her into his hold, kissing the top of her head. 'You stay here. It won't be for long,' John promised. 'Colin says Pollock wants to press on quickly through the Punjab. We'll go in the advance party. Once we're across the Sutlej we can make for the hill states around Simla with Rajban – or wherever you want.'

Alice smiled at him tenderly. 'I don't mind. I'll go anywhere as long as it's with you and Lotty. Somewhere safe from . . .'

She couldn't even bear to say Vernon's name in case it somehow conjured him up. They stood together watching the dawn grow pink over the dark walls of the city. People, still huddled in blankets, were beginning to stir in the bazaar below. The smell of dung fires filled the sharp air. Alice could feel the tension grow tight across her forehead at the thought of Vernon out there, sore-headed and belligerent, seeking her.

John seemed to guess her worries. 'He will never touch you again,' he murmured into her ear. 'I promise you that.'

Just then, something soft brushed at her legs. Alice glanced down to see a sleepy-headed Lotty standing in front of them both.

'Lieutenant John?' she asked, gazing up at the tall man holding onto her mother.

John immediately crouched down and grinned at the girl. 'That's me. How are you and Gita-dolly? Did she sleep well?'

Lotty clutched the ragged remains of her cherished doll to her chest. She had not been parted from it since her reunion with Alice. The girl nodded.

'Good,' said John. 'Now perhaps she'd like some breakfast?'

Lotty whispered to the doll, then nodded at John. 'She'd like chapatti and curds with honey.'

John grinned. 'Then that's exactly what she shall have.'

Alice put a tender hand on Lotty's head and smiled at John. 'You know I love you so very much, don't you?' she said softly.

The smile John returned made her heart glow with warmth.

* * *

Alice could hardly bear to see John go.

'I'll knock hard twice when I return so that you know it's me,' he told her. With a swift kiss on the lips he left her. She and Gita bolted the door behind him. Alice listened to him clattering down the outside steps and calling to Colin, and then they were gone.

All day, Alice tried to distract herself from fearful thoughts about Vernon by playing with Lotty. Once or twice, she crept onto the covered-in veranda and peered through the latticework at the street below, half-expecting to see her husband causing a scene. There was plenty of hustle and bustle and the sight of soldiers in uniform made her heart race with alarm but not one of them was Vernon.

What if he had found John and the two of them had had a terrible fight? What if John was injured or worse? The waiting and not knowing were torture.

329

When the double knock came, Alice jumped in fright. She exchanged worried glances with Gita but John called through the door.

'Alice, open up. It's me – you've nothing to fear.'

The women scrabbled to unbar the door. John stood in the doorway, his tall frame almost blocking out the light. With his face in shadow, Alice couldn't see his expression but she sensed a tension in his broad shoulders.

'What is it?' Alice gasped. 'Has he hurt you?'

John shook his head. 'Gita, keep Lotty with you for a few minutes, please,' he told the *ayah*.

Then, taking Alice by the hand, he pulled her towards the outside steps that led up the side of the house. She squinted in the sudden harsh light after the gloom inside.

'What is it?' Alice asked. 'Something has happened, hasn't it?'

John held her look. 'Buckley's dead.'

Alice gaped at him in incomprehension. 'Vernon's dead?'

John nodded, his look grim. Even as the first wave of relief passed through her, Alice had a terrible foreboding.

'Did – did you . . . ?'

John gripped her. 'No, Alice. He was found murdered at Avitabile's a couple of hours ago but I had nothing to do with it.'

'Oh my God! Murdered?'

'Sandy's been looking for you to tell you.'

'I don't understand. A couple of hours ago? He's been there all this time? Who would have done such a thing?' Something in his look made Alice think he knew. 'Tell me. Please, John, you must!'

'The servants were told not to disturb him this morning. He'd taken one of the dancing girls to bed with him in the early hours.'

Alice blanched. 'Are you telling me that a *nautch* girl killed him?'

John shook his head. 'I don't think that's who she was.' He hesitated.

'Go on,' said Alice. 'Nothing you say can shock me now.'

'Buckley was found with his throat cut and his eyes put out,' John said. 'It was a very personal kind of revenge.'

Alice shuddered at the barbarity of her husband's killing.

'What woman could possibly . . . ?' Alice felt faint.

'A hunting knife was found beside the body. Sandy showed it to me – I've seen it before. It belonged to Abdullah, the Ghilzai chief.'

'Raiza's brother?'

John nodded.

'But he's dead,' said Alice. 'Vernon was jubilant about it. He said Abdullah's widow had taken up the fight . . .'

Suddenly her heart jolted. She stared at John.

'Exactly,' he said. 'I think Abdullah's widow has got her revenge. Whether she posed as a *nautch* girl or lured Buckley there with one, we'll never know. But I think she left the knife there to show that Abdullah's family honour was avenged.'

Alice reeled from the news. She would weep no tears over Vernon but she would not have wished such a violent end to his life.

330

'They will cover up that it was murder,' John said. 'An army surgeon will say that his heart stopped. A scandal like this could set off further revenge killings and Avitabile doesn't want that laid at his door – and neither does Pollock. He wants his men out of here and back into British India as soon as possible.'

Alice looked out over the sun-baked rooftops, the harsh light mellowing as the sun began to edge behind the stark western mountain range. Vernon was dead. The leaden feeling she had carried for so long in her chest was easing. She need never fear him again.

She turned to John and looked into his concerned face.

'I'm free of him,' she murmured. 'I'm *free*.'

John cupped his hands around her face. 'My darling Alice.'

'There is nothing to come between us now,' Alice said, feeling emotion welling up inside.

He kissed her tenderly and suddenly she convulsed in weeping. Tears of relief – of pain and shock too but overwhelmingly of relief – coursed down her cheeks.

John held her in strong loving arms and stroked her hair until she began to calm down.

'Tonight we begin our life together,' he promised. 'The life we should have started years ago. But it's never too late. We love each other and that's all that matters now. I will always protect you and Lotty.'

'And our baby,' Alice said with a tender smile.

'And the baby,' John echoed, his green eyes lighting with joy.

She looked into his handsome face, thrilling at his passionate expression.

'Oh, John,' she said, feeling the tears coming again, 'you've had my heart ever since we first met. Now that we're together at last, we must never let each other go. Promise me that.'

He kissed her fiercely to banish any lingering doubt. When they broke apart, John's look was intense. 'Until my dying day, Alice, I swear to you I will never leave you.'

Alice thought her heart would burst with euphoria at his words. They stood, arms around each other, and gazed out over the eastern town towards the sunset and the west.

'Some day,' said Alice, 'I'd like you to take me to Ramanish. I think Lotty would like it. Perhaps our child should be born there?'

She saw the emotion in John's face at her suggestion. His voice was raw with feeling when he answered.

'I'd like nothing more, my darling one.'

They fell silent as they watched the sun disappear and the bright evening stars begin to glint overhead. Alice knew they needed no more words to say what was in their hearts. They were as one – and from now on they always would be.

amir	king, ruler
ayah	nurse or nanny
bhisti	water-carrier
caravanserai	desert inn with courtyard
chaprassy	messenger
charpoy	string bed on wooden frame
dak	post or mail
deodar	Indian cedar
doolie	shoulder-borne carriage on poles
durzi	tailor
feringhi	foreigner (derogatory)
ghat	stepped riverside dock/landing
jampan	Sedan chair
jelabies	sticky sweets
jezail	muzzle-loading long-arm gun
mali	gardener
nautch	dance/dancing
Pashm*	soft underfur of Himalayan goats
sepoy	Indian soldier
sirdar	person of high rank
syce	groom
zenana	women's quarter
*pashmina is wool made from pashm	

The idea for this novel was inspired by my MacLeod ancestor, Lieutenant Donald MacLeod of the Honourable East India Company, who left his home on the Isle of Skye in the 1760s for a soldier's life in India. My great-great-great-great-grandfather Donald died on a passage back to Britain, of wounds sustained in battle, and never saw Skye again. Although the novel is set a generation later, my hero is from Skye and seeks his fortune in the East India Company army.

The early life of my Northumbrian heroine, Alice, is inspired by the heroics of Grace Darling, a lighthouse keeper's daughter who became a nineteenth-century celebrity for successfully helping to rescue passengers from the shipwrecked *Forfarshire* off the Northumberland coast.

The later part of the novel – the invasion of Afghanistan and the subsequent horrors of the retreat and captivity of the women – is based on fact. Many of the background characters are historical people: the Sales, MacNaughtens, various senior officers, Mrs Trevor and her children, as well as most of the Afghan leaders such as Shah Shuja, Dost Mohammed and Akbar. The sources for the historical detail include first-hand accounts from Lady Sale and one of the captured political officers, Captain Colin Mackenzie.

The main characters are, however, completely fictitious.

Acknowledgements

As well as a nod to my MacLeod ancestor, Lieutenant Donald MacLeod – and to his Skye family who nurtured him – I'd like to thank some of the currently living. Husband Graeme has entered enthusiastically into the research, reading aloud to me over many cups of coffee and tea as I've delved into the early-nineteenth-century world of lighthouses, illicit whisky distilling, the Grand Trigonometrical Survey of India and Himalayan explorers. Thanks for the excellent coffee! Also many thanks to my eagle-eyed proofreader Janey Floyd.

Janet MacLeod Trotter is the author of numerous bestselling and acclaimed novels, including *The Hungry Hills*, which was nominated for the Sunday Times Young Writer of the Year Award, and *The Tea Planter's Daughter*, which was nominated for the Romantic Novelists' Association Novel of the Year Award. *In The Far Pashmina Mountains* was shortlisted for the RNA Historical Novel of the Year. Janet's novels have been translated into eleven different languages. Much informed by her own experiences, MacLeod Trotter was raised in the north-east of England by Scottish parents and travelled in India as a young woman. She recently discovered diaries and letters belonging to her grandparents, who married in Lahore and lived and worked in the Punjab for nearly thirty years, which served as her inspiration for the India Tea Series. She now divides her time between Edinburgh and the Isle of Skye. Find out more about the author and her novels at www.janetmacleodtrotter.com

Printed in Great Britain
by Amazon

32243332R10190